A DEEPER BLUE

JOHN RINGO

A DEEPER BLUE

This is a work of fiction. All the characters and events portrayed in this book are fictional, and any resemblance to real people or incidents is purely coincidental. This book has no connection to reality. Any attempt by the reader to replicate any scene in this series is to be taken at the reader's own risk. For that matter, most of the actions of the main character are illegal under US and international law as well as most of the stricter religions in the world. There is no Valley of the Keldara. Heck, there is no Kildar. And the idea of some Scots and Vikings getting together to raid the Byzantine Empire is beyond ludicrous. The islands described in a previous book do not exist. Entire regions described in these books do not exist. Any attempt to learn anything from these books is disrecommended by the author, the publisher and the author's mother who wishes to state that he was a very nice boy and she doesn't know what went wrong.

Copyright © 2007 by John Ringo

A Baen Book

Baen Publishing Enterprises
P.O. Box 1403
Riverdale, NY 10471
www.baen.com

ISBN 10: 1-4165-5550-1
ISBN 13: 978-1-4165-5550-6

Cover art by Kurt Miller

First Baen paperback printing, June 2008

Library of Congress Control Number: 2007009071

Distributed by Simon & Schuster
1230 Avenue of the Americas
New York, NY 10020

Pages by Joy Freeman (www.pagesbyjoy.com)
Printed in the United States of America
10 9 8 7 6 5 4 3 2 1

"Before I brief you in, I just tell you something about the Kildar," Greznya said. "He has recently lost someone. Someone important to him."

"Is that why he was going to sit out this mission?" Britney asked.

"Yes," the Keldara replied. "And then Adams, who has known him for many years, and Sergeant Vanner who, I think, is something like a son to him, they were both very injured. He feels much guilt for this. And for the other, too. You know the thing Nietsche said about the abyss?"

"Yes," Britney replied.

"The Kildar exists on the edge of the abyss," Greznya said. "But for as long as he has looked at it, has dabbled at its edges and stuck his foot in, he has never entered the abyss. Or at least not that he could not swim out. Now he is in the abyss. He is being sucked down by it. He is drowning in it. If he becomes the abyss, well . . . We have had Kildars who ate their meals surrounded by dead bodies, for the pleasure of the company. We will, as you say, adapt and overcome. But I'm not sure the world will."

"What does this have to do with me?" Britney asked.

"If you can draw him back from the abyss," Greznya said, "that would be a very good thing. For us, yes, but for many other people. You remind him of . . . good times, I think."

"I don't," Britney said, setting down her cup, then reconsidering. That was exactly what Mike had said: "*Good times.*"

What kind of a crazy man considered holding off a battalion of commandoes and getting shot very near to death as "Good times?"

For the poor bastards, male and female, guarding the thugs in Guantanamo, stuck in paradise doing pretty close to the world's crappiest job. This one's for you, folks.

And, as always:

For Captain Tamara Long, USAF

Born: 12 May 1979

Died: 23 March 2003, Afghanistan

You fly with the angels now.

Acknowledgments

As usual I'd like to thank RingTAB, the Ringo Technical Advisory Board, for help on keeping the technical details of this book somewhat close to accurate. In addition I'd like to thank William Ringo, former Army chemical weapons instructor and current FEMA contract safety officer for help with both chemical weapons details and safety response.

Last, but certainly not least, I'd like to thank my daughters, Jenny and Lindy, for helping Daddy research details of South Florida culture, and Miriam, for her usual able support.

No more will my green sea go turn a deeper blue
I could not foresee this thing happening to you.
If I look hard enough into the setting sun
My love will laugh with me before the morning comes.

—Rolling Stones
"Paint it Black"

PROLOGUE

The freighter rolled eastward on easy swells, but nothing was easy about the task.

It might have helped if some of the crew were handling the winch, but they were all below under strict orders to forget anything unusual had occurred. And even stricter orders to keep quiet if they did remember. The crew wouldn't talk, though. They were all good Islamics and supported the jihad. What was more, they knew that if any word of this event got out, their families as well as themselves would pay the penalty.

So Ibrahim had to keep an eye on it all. He had carefully instructed the fedayeen on the plan, but nothing beat experience. And he was the only one with experience. He'd shipped out on boats just like this in his youth, escaping the hell of the Karachi slums. And over time he had worked his way up to bosun, the senior deck worker of a ship. It was then he came to the attention of the Movement.

The Movement often needed cargo shifted around and it had ships aplenty. What it did not have was enough trustworthy people who knew the ins and outs of how to move cargo . . . covertly. Oh, there were many such but there were never enough. Guns, rockets and ammunition, women and drugs to pay for the weapons, people, there were so many things the Movement needed . . . moved.

This mission, though, was so complicated Ibrahim could only hope *any* of it went right. But he only had to ensure this one small part. And that was difficult enough.

The offshore speed boat he was lowering touched the waves and Ibrahim slowed the winch. The massive boat, nearly fifteen meters long, was big and tough but it wouldn't take it well if the waves slapping the ship's side overwhelmed it or it slammed into the freighter's hull.

Hiding the damned things had been bad enough. If Ibrahim had had his way the boats would have been locally purchased; there were many such in the area. It would have been a joke straight from Allah to buy them from the American government. The Americans often seized such boats running drugs in this area and just as often sold them back to the drug runners at auction.

Instead, these had been purchased in Europe, shipped in one of the many freighters owned by the Movement to Africa, transferred to another and transferred again to Ibrahim's ship, carefully secured out of sight in the hold. The transfer had been effected in West Africa in a port notorious for its lax customs. If anyone had noticed the midnight transfer no word had come to the Movement.

Now it was Ibrahim's job to get the damned thing

into the water without it smashing against the side of the moving ship or being swamped by a wave.

It was down and he waved to the men on the boat to unhook. They had better get that one right; if one of them slipped over the side they were likely to be crushed between the two vessels. And even if they were not, the ship was not going to stop. Once this boat was in the water it could pick up anyone overboard. Until then, though . . .

The fedayeen, though, did the job right. Allah knows, Ibrahim had been careful enough in his instructions. First the young man, a Yemeni with some small boat experience, started the engine and unhooked the rear connection. Very important. If he'd unhooked the front, the boat would have spun in place and probably swamped or been pulled under the ship. Starting the engine was only good sense before casting off. Only when it was free did he make his way forward, carefully crawling over the broad, flat expanse of the front surface, and unhook the front connection. They were both fast connections with lanyards to release them. The front connection was under massive tension and sprung back with a twanging sound, striking the side of the ship hard enough Ibrahim knew he'd need to check it before the next boat was released.

It took nearly an hour before the five boats were in the water, following the ship in a long string; then came the last, and strangest, part.

A crew of fedayeen had been working on one of the surface containers, a standard shipping container carried on the deck. The fedayeen had fitted the container with a set of pontoons and a cable. The cable was attached to a massive steel plate.

The steel plate had to be suspended over the side, first, then the container swung out.

Ibrahim couldn't handle both of the winches for this one. The commander of the mission was on the main crane, holding up the container, while Ibrahim handled a smaller crane that lifted the plate. With both of them swung over the side, the ship was listing by nearly seven degrees, but it wouldn't stay that way long.

Ibrahim released the connections on the steel plate and it splashed into the water, the cable attached to the bottom of the container spinning out furiously. A bare moment later the container splashed into the briny deeps, floated for a moment on the surface, supported by its pontoons, then was snatched under like a fishing bobber. All that was left was a trail of bubbles.

"You have done well, Ibrahim," the commander of the fedayeen contingent said as the bosun climbed out of the seat of the winch.

The fedayeen commander was strange. He wore the proper dress and prayed five times a day as the Prophet decreed. But his eyes were gray, unusual in a believer, and sometimes he seemed more European than Middle Eastern for all his dark skin and hair. Little things you'd only notice on a long voyage, but telling.

"Thank you, Haj," Ibrahim replied, breathing in relief. "Go with God."

"And you as well," the man said, drawing a pistol. "Go with God."

Kurt Schwenke watched the body tumble over the side, slid the silenced pistol into the rear waistband of his pants, then walked to where a ladder dangled over the side. As he climbed down, one of the boats came alongside. It was tough getting from a moving ship to a small boat but Kurt had no particular problems. He kicked outwards and landed on one of the seats of the boat, then settled into place.

"Do we have it?" he asked.

"Souhi has it on sonar," Sayid Al-Yemani replied, powering up and turning, the boat splashing up and over the waves then crashing down in a shower of spray. "Allah's beard! I am still having problems with these, Haji. Sorry."

"Not a problem," Kurt, AKA Sabah Arif, replied, wiping at his face. "You will have much time to learn."

The boat turned away from the waves and powered up more, jumping over them now so that Kurt had to put on the safety belts. It was only about a quarter mile, though, to the place where the container had gone over the side.

"There," the driver said, powering down and pointing to the sonar screen. "It went deep, though. Now it is on its way up."

Kurt nodded and watched the sonar contact rising. The water in the area was nearly two thousand feet deep, so the massive plate had a ways to descend. The coil of cable on the container was supposed to play out evenly, never letting the container get too deep, until the plate hit bottom.

The container was hanging, now, between about seventy-five meters and a hundred. Deep. Possibly too deep. But even as he watched, the numbers began to drop. Sixty meters. Fifty. It leveled off at twenty and stayed there, steady.

"Are you ready, Kahf?" Kurt said, looking over his shoulder.

The Egyptian already was pulling his SCUBA rig out of the racks. A former dive instructor at the resort in Sharm Al Sheik on the tip of the Sinai peninsula, he was experienced in both conventional and "technical" diving. The rig he was using for this was a simple SCUBA apparatus, one steel 80-cubic-foot tank, two-stage SCUBAPRO regulator, the only difference from beginner-quality equipment being that it was a NITROX setup, which used extra oxygen in the mix to extend down time.

Kahf just held up a thumb and forefinger in an "Okay" signal and kept getting it on. In a few seconds he was ready to dive.

He tucked his regulator in his mouth and slid over the side into the warm waters, grabbing a rope on his way. Using the rope, he trailed behind the boat, searching the waters and occasionally using his body to plane downwards. After a moment he surfaced again and held up another "Okay" signal, then let go.

"He's spotted it," Kurt said. "Hold this position."

Kurt was surprised to see that he could pick up the diver on the sonar. The sonar system tagged him as a fish, admittedly, but he could still follow his progress on the three-D imager as the "fish" made his way down to the container.

The "fish" hovered around the container for a moment, then came back up.

"It's all good," Kahf said, pulling himself out of the water onto the dive platform at the rear of the boat. "I got the doors open. That was harder than we expected but they're open."

"Right," Kurt said, waving at another boat and making motions for them to dive.

This time the diver was carrying more gear. Double air tanks, a third dangling in front of him, and float bags were the big part of it. As Sayid pulled away, the second boat came over the container and as soon as it was there the pre-rigged diver hit the water. It was a bit of a wait but Kurt was patient. After a moment, though, two lift bags popped to the surface. Kurt watched as the boat came alongside the bags and the driver and a third man pulled a blue barrel over the side, carefully. The barrel was rolled out of sight just as another bobbed to the surface.

The process was repeated three times, a total of four of the barrels, and then Kurt gestured for the boats to assemble.

"I repeat," Kurt yelled. "Only one boat at a time. That is very important. Follow your bearings. You all know where to pick up your routes. Souhi goes first. The rest of you will wait." He stopped and then grinned. "By the way, welcome to the sunny Bahamas!"

"What are we doing about this?" the President asked.

"It's tough," the FBI director replied. "We don't want people panicking. But we've upped the terrorism alert level and we're flooding the South Florida area with agents. They've been told they're looking for a major shipment of something that's going to look like drugs but is terrorism related."

"We're clamping down on port checks," the head of Customs and Border Protection added after a glance from his boss, the secretary of Homeland Security. "All my people are on overtime for the foreseeable future and we're checking both pre-checked containers and uncleared. But even with the extra manpower we can't check them all, Mr. President. We're up from our normal, low, percentage but short of mostly closing the ports down . . ."

"National Guard is helping with the search," the Chairman of the Joint Chiefs said. "And I'm pulling in all the teams. We're not going to get caught forward like we were the last time. If it's something that Delta or Rangers can operate on, they're going to be ready to shoot."

"Shaking all the trees," the director of National Intelligence added. "NSA is on high alert and I've sent out a classified memo for any information, barring what we already have, on the shipment."

"Same here," the Defense Intelligence Agency director added. "And we're trying to squeeze anything we can from recent detainees. But I don't think there's much there other than what we got from Al-Kariya and his computer. Once Kariya broke, he broke hard. We've pretty much got everything he knew. Short of picking up someone high-level who is aware of the op, I think we're about done there."

"Where is the ship?"

"Should be just about to Miami," Homeland Security said. "We're low-keying it."

"But they were supposed to be 'transferred' before reaching port, right?" the President asked.

"Yes, sir," the DDIA said. "We picked the ship up late. It was definitely off the sea-lanes. The transfer possibly occurred somewhere north of the Bahamas."

"The Navy's looking for it," the CJCS added.

"Mr. President," the secretary of Homeland Security said, "we're using every available resource."

"Not *every* resource," the President said, looking at the secretary of Defense. "Call Pierson. Now."

"Sir," the DNI said, rolling his eyes since the President wasn't looking, "you're *not* talking about . . ."

"Get me the Kildar."

The painting had been made by a renowned cover artist, an artist of the "old school" that still used acrylics to create massive paintings just to grace a book.

The subject was a Valkyrie but one far different than most. She had the blonde hair and busty build of one, but her hair was unbraided, long golden tresses floating in the breeze of her passage. And instead of the traditional overendowed "breastplate," she wore only a white dress, rich with seed pearls, cut daringly down the front to nearly the navel and short in front, high on the thigh. She was riding, sidesaddle, a white, winged horse and held in her right hand a blazing minigun, pointed at the ground. And she was smiling, a vicious smile of triumph and victory.

Her face was a vision, but only to Mike. Oh, she was pretty, even beautiful, but you could see a dozen like her in any American college, three or four as good looking among the Keldara and several who were, arguably, more beautiful. But none of that mattered to the man in the comfortable chair placed at perfect viewing distance from the painting.

Mike lifted the glass and considered the lips for the thousandth time. He had given the artist very precise instructions and even a photograph. And in almost every way the artist had caught Mike's vision, or surpassed it. That, and the secrecy with which the picture was made, was why he'd been paid a fee four times his normal. But if the artist had one flaw, it was in lips. He almost invariably used his wife as a model for his art, and she had a very definite Hapsburg lip. Oh, pretty, yes, but not right. Not for this painting. Everywhere else the image was perfection. A way to ensure that no matter what, Mike would never forget that face. But the lips were creeping in, erasing the image of them caressing his chest, his stomach . . .

He lifted the glass, realized it was mostly ice, and poured in more Elijah Craig. Hey, you couldn't fly on just one wing.

Or two. Or a dozen or a thousand. At this point, the bottles lined one wall of the small room.

"When the mound reaches the very sky," Mike said, not looking at the bottles.

There was a tap on the door and he pressed a solenoid, dropping a steel plate over the painting. Then he hit the release on the door.

"Come."

"Kildar," Mother Savina said diffidently. "There is a call from Colonel Pierson."

"You can tell Colonel Pierson to fuck off, with my compliments," Mike slurred. "And tell him to tell his boss the same thing."

"Yes, Kildar," Mother Savina said, closing the door.

Mike pressed the solenoid again, locked the door, and took another sip.

"When the mound reaches the sky. When the *mound* reaches the sky. When the mound reaches the *sky*. *That's* when I'll talk to fucking Pierson *or* his boss. When the mound reaches the sky."

CHAPTER ONE

"Anybody got a *fucking* clue?"

The meeting was unusual. The group had all met each other before, even had meetings together, but there was one person missing and that threw the whole balance out.

Nielson looked around at the faces, searching for an answer to his question.

All six of the Keldara Fathers were present as well as two of the Mothers.

The Keldara were an ancient race of mountain warriors, descendants of the Norse guards of the Byzantine emperors, the Varangians. Marooned by the flow of history as the empire receded, they had endured a series of conquerors over the years but always maintained their traditions. Forced, like the Ghurkas and the Kurds, to be farmers for survival, they had, nonetheless, kept up their warrior tradition. In part this was due to a quiet and subtle breeding program.

11

Over the years they had had many "lords" occupy the
caravanserai where the meeting was taking place. Some
of them were courtiers exiled from centers of power but
most had been foreign adventurers attached to whatever
empire "owned" the Keldara at the time. The courtiers
didn't tend to last. They died mysteriously of diseases
or sudden heart attacks or hunting accidents.

The other lords, the warriors, well, "a soldier that
won't fuck, won't fight." Those lords, naturally, wanted
to sample the beautiful Keldara girls. And they *were*
beautiful, so much so that people who met them
commented on it constantly. Most such lords assumed
the right as part of their position.

The Keldara had made that right their own, though,
sending only girls who were about to be married and
also in their period of maximum fertility. And they
had insisted, quietly, subtly, but very determinedly,
that the "lord" pay for his "rights" by presenting a
dowry to the young lady.

Called the "Rite of Kardane," over the centuries
it had been used to carefully breed to dozens of different races, but every bit of that genetics had been
from proven warriors. Those that weren't . . . Well,
so many accidents can befall a person.

Tartar eyes, a legacy of Genghiz's hordes, blond
and red hair from the Norse, black from the Turks
and Ottomans; the men were powerful and handsome,
fell beyond belief in battle; the women gorgeous and
fey and nearly as dangerous.

But they needed their lord, their Kildar. They
needed his genes, yes, but very nearly as good sat in
the room with them. What they needed, most, was
his leadership and the knowledge that each generation

had brought to the Keldara of the best, most modern, way to destroy his enemies. The Keldara had been axemen from the North, bow-men riders and armored knights in their time. They had swung swords and fired long jazeels. They lived on the cutting edge of the blade; whatever would kill the most enemies was fine by them.

Now they armed themselves with M4s and machine guns, MP-5s and sniper rifles. Their armor was Kevlar and composite.

None of it was any good without the Kildar, though.

"I could beat him up," Master Chief Charles Adams said.

The burly and bald-headed former SEAL had known the Kildar for years, since both were in BUDS together in the infamous Class 201. They'd been on the same team, briefly, then the Kildar had gone off to teach meats while Adams climbed the ladder of rank. Adams had next run into his old buddy in a stinking underground fortress in Syria, finding him shot to ribbons after holding off, with very little support, a Syrian commando battalion.

Later his "friend" had called him up and asked him to assemble a team and come train some weird group of mountain people in the country of Georgia.

Adams had been hanging out ever since. The Keldara were great people, the scenery was awesome, the living conditions, given that there were three hookers in-house, were great and the beer was fucking *awesome*.

He acted as the Kildar's field second and had been at his side for several hairy ops. But it wasn't the ops, directly, that had led to this fuck-up. Just one fucking casualty. You'd think a big guy could get over one fucking casualty, no matter how good a piece of ass it had been.

"I don't think that would help," Colonel David Nielson said dryly.

The colonel was a former infantry and civil affairs officer, Ranger tabbed, airborne qualified and once an instructor at the War College. The only professional officer in the group, he acted as the Kildar's chief of staff. Short, with black hair going gray and green eyes that worked remarkably well on the ladies, he was about ready to go for the master chief's suggestion.

"It'd help me," Adams argued. "I'm about sick of his pouting."

"The Kildar is soul damaged," Father Kulcyanov said wheezily. The oldest remaining Father, Kulcyanov was a veteran of WWII, in the Red Army. He'd been in every major campaign, to include Stalingrad, and had so many medals he kept them in a very large box. In addition, he acted as the Keldara's high priest. Given that that position *had* to be held by a warrior, it made sense. "It has happened before."

"I hate to say this, but I have to question this whole Rite thing," Captain Kacey Bathlick said. One of the pilots recently hired to support the Keldara, she knew she was the most junior member of the group, at least in experience. But not only had she proven her merits on the last mission, she wasn't the sort to just keep her mouth shut. And, hell, Gretchen had been *her* crew-chief. She was pissed about her getting blown away but she wasn't sitting crying in *her* fucking room! She'd just sent the Chechens who did it to meet Allah. Blasted the hell out of them, actually.

"I mean, I get the whole point and the history. But fraternization is *never* a good idea."

"That is, unfortunately, a point that is past," Anastasia Rakovich pointed out. The "house manager" for the Kildar, she was a former harem slave and harem manager hired to fulfill much the same role. She had more or less inserted herself into the position of "house manager" since the Keldara housekeeper, Mother Savina, was less than experienced in managing the household of a lord. Anastasia had been a junior manager from the time she was seventeen and the manager of an Uzbek sheik's household from the time she was twenty-one. Still only twenty-seven, she was model beautiful with long blonde hair and blue eyes, much like the late Gretchen Mahona. But while she regularly warmed the Kildar's bed, and he her back, given that she was a high-level sexual masochist, the Kildar had never been infatuated with her as he had become with Gretchen. "And, frankly, if he'd had more time with her the hurt might have been less. Or more, I don't know," she added with a sigh.

"The reason we originally gave for the Rite is, of course, no longer . . . effective," Mother Mahona said. "Which is well, since I don't think the Kildar is willing to continue with the Rite."

The previous mission had involved the sale of WMD by the Russian mob to Al Qaeda. The mob had the WMD, the Al Qaeda members had a very large quantity of portable currency and gems. Most of that had been captured and brought back, despite the battle. Mike had stated, bluntly, that dowries, now and for the foreseeable future, were covered.

Gretchen had not been her daughter by body but

held her name due to being of the extended "Family" of the Mahonas. Mother Mahona and Mother Silva, Gretchen's birth mother, were both at the meeting to see if they had any idea how to pull the Kildar out of his depression. Neither had come up with anything.

"I'd be more than willing to let him sit in there until his liver gave out," Nielson continued. "But the point is we've got a mission. Pierson is *really* exercised."

"What?" Patrick Vanner asked. The crew-cut and stocky former Marine, former NSA analyst and current electronic intel chief wasn't sure *what* to do about the Kildar. The problem was, well, he was the *Kildar*. He owned the damned place, he was a total free agent and he had more money than God. There wasn't any way to shake him out of his depression unless the guy did it himself. And that didn't look to be happening any time soon.

"WMD, inbound to the States," Nielson said. "That's all I've got right now."

"So we'd be operating in the States?" Adams asked. "They don't have *enough* people?"

"The Boss asked," Nielson said.

"Oh."

"But I suspect he asked for the Kildar, yes?" Father Kulcyanov said.

"Yeah, but what the hell," Adams replied. "Kildar, Keldara, big diff. So he sits this one out. I can lead the teams, Nielson does the mission planning. Heck, I can do most of that. We bring a couple of teams, keep the rest here for positional defense. Not that we need it much, given the condition of the Chechens."

The last mission had been "the world's most successful fuck-up." Due to "insufficient data," notably that a large and professional Chechen brigade was moving into the area, the Keldara had ended up in a pitched battle. It was there that Captain Bathlick and her "co" captain, Tamara Wilson, had won their spurs. It was also the reason Gretchen Mahona had been killed.

The battle had broken the back of the Chechens—their main local threat—when the Chechens assumed that four thousand fedayeen could easily wipe out a hundred "pagans." In that, they had been so very very wrong. The battle had left the cream of the Resistance's most elite force scattered for the ravens. Patrols had not picked up *any* sign of Chechen movement in their sector in the two months since the battle.

"The Keldara are not the Kildar," Father Kulcyanov said cautiously. "If you choose to take the Keldara, if the Kildar approves, we will not stand in your way. They will, undoubtedly, win glory and those that fall will be lifted to the Halls. But do not mistake the Keldara for the Kildar. *We* do not."

The Keldara had masked as Islamics and Christians over the years. They did not care what religion their masters wanted them to practice. But they had retained their true faith in the Old Gods of the Norse and traditions drawn from both Norse and Celts. Since the Kildar did not seem to care, they had, slowly, come "out of the closet" about their beliefs. One of those was that a person could not enter the Halls of Feasting, Valhalla, unless they had been proven in battle.

To Father Kulcyanov the last battle had been a mixed blessing. Far too many of the Keldara had entered the Halls, but for the first time in a generation Keldara *were* entering the Halls. The dun of the

Keldara, their massive burial mound that most people mistook for a gigantic glacial hill, had been added to. The Keldara had added to their glory and had found favor before the Father of All. He would see his fallen children, nieces and nephews, in the Halls. *His* place was assured by the slaughtered crews of German Tiger tanks and broken units of the Wehrmacht and SS.

He had warned the Kildar, whom he had seen falling into soul-death, not to lose the path of the warrior. For the Kildar's sake, who was warrior born, and for the Keldara. The Keldara were *nothing* without war.

But his words had, apparently, been insufficient.

"He's got a point," Vanner said. "Master Chief, you're a good shooter and the Keldara will follow. And Colonel, you're a good planner. And I can, as always, handle the intel and commo. But ain't none of us the Kildar."

"I've known Mike since he was a wet behind the ears BUDS recruit," Adams said. "Of course, so was I. But the point is, he's human. God *knows* he's human. *And* he's replaceable. Everybody is. We do the mission. Maybe we find the WMD, maybe we don't. But if the Boss calls, we do the damned mission. Period fucking dot."

"Okay," Nielson said, sighing. "You take the teams. I'll stay back here and handle the details. I can do that long range. Who do you want?"

"I'm going," Vanner said. "There's some tech I've wanted to pick up in the States for a while, anyway. And I'd rather be on site to handle tricky stuff. I'll take four of the girls."

Vanner's staff was mostly Keldara females, most of them under twenty. They had soaked up the details of communications and intelligence as if they'd been training in it from birth. Lately, Vanner had been picking up some pieces of intel that made him wonder if that wasn't truth. While the Keldara men were top-flight warriors and many of them smart as hell, the Keldara girls were so smart it was scary. And they were sneaky in ways he was just beginning to souse out.

"I'll take Oleg . . . shit," Adams said, pausing. The Keldara's top team leader had had his leg blown off by a mortar in the battle. He'd gotten a state-of-the-art prosthetic, but he still wasn't in top shape. And his Team was shaky without him. His other top choice, Team Sawn, had lost its leader in the battle and was still shaking down. Padrek, another he would have liked for their technical expertise, had been ravaged. About half of them were dead or still recovering.

"I'll take . . . Vil and Pavel. Daria? I could use somebody to handle the—"

"Details," Daria said, dimpling. The Ukrainian girl had been picked up on a mission, a kidnappee being held in a snuff house in Montenegro, while the teams were hunting for another girl. A trained but out-of-work secretary, she was still kicking herself for accepting the offer of "a good job in Europe." That was a well known ploy that slavers used to capture females. But the con, and that was the only way to put it, had been well laid. She had been awaiting death when the Keldara showed up. She'd been hired while still on the mission to handle the burgeoning administrative details of the Kildar and stayed around ever since. The pay was good, the living conditions excellent and it wasn't like she had to worry about slavers. "I'll put in a call to Chatham for a plane big enough to handle two teams and support staff. And I'll coordinate with the BCIS for entry of the teams and their equipment."

"I'll go as well," Dr. Tolegen Arensky said. "If you'll have me."

The Russian WMD specialist, short, round with balding black hair, was a recent addition to the team. He'd been picked up during the previous mission after having been forced to betray the Russians and smuggle out samples of weaponized smallpox. He'd stayed on because he was also a trained physician and, well, not particularly welcome in Russia at the moment.

"With it being WMD, hell yeah!" Adams said.

"Okay," Nielson said. "You go break it to the Kildar. When you get his okay, I'll call Pierson."

"We taking Katya?" Vanner asked. "And has anyone seen J?"

"Two very good questions," Nielson replied, smiling grimly. "You're not him, are you?"

"Katya!"

Martya Dzintas wasn't happy to be knocking on the girl's door. But the noise was disrupting class.

Martya was fifteen, a harem girl and proud of it. She had been raised on a small farm not far from the caravanserai and at fourteen she'd been sold by her parents to a group of Chechens. She didn't hold it against her parents; being "sent to town" was just one of those things. Not only did the Chechens have guns and a serious interest in buying the beautiful fourteen-year old, her parents needed the money.

She didn't want to be a whore, which was what the Chechens intended for her, but there wasn't much anyone could do about it. Except the Kildar. When the Chechens made the mistake of kidnapping one of the Keldara girls, the Kildar had responded with his usual understated manner.

After he had the girls in the van cleaned of the blood, though, he had a problem. None of the girls had homes to go back to. To their parents they were "no deposit, no return." Not only were they, presumably, no longer virgins, the farms in the area were too marginal to bring another mouth back to feed.

The Kildar had, therefore, brought them into his own household as concubines. But he had a very odd view of what to do with harem slaves. The first rule he'd laid down, damn him, was that the girls had to be sixteen before he'd bed them. It was, as he pointed out, younger than his culture would consider "okay" but given that twelve was considered marriageable in the area it was a good median. The second rule he'd laid down was that the girls had to *learn*. When they were old enough he intended them to move on, to go get a job, go to university, get a husband, have kids, have a "real life."

And he'd been careful and considerate in bedding them. Yes, he occasionally had an evening just to relieve his need, but most of the time the girls returned to the harem half unconscious with endorphins and ready to go back as soon as they recovered. The Kildar was as good in bed as he was in battle. None of the girls who had done so minded bedding him, not one bit.

And then there was the matter of status. This region was very backward and she'd come to understand that. It was not a normal place compared to the U.S. or Europe. But it was the culture she had been raised in. And in *that* culture, the Kildar had very high status. The Keldara, and the Kildar, were legends in the region long before the present Kildar arrived. It had been a long time since a true Kildar was in the valley, and the old people had bemoaned that. The new Kildar, furthermore, truly *had* brought back the good times. The Chechens no longer extorted "taxes" and burned farms when they didn't pay up. They no longer stole children. They no longer took the food and livestock. And the money the Kildar brought in—often through killing Islamics which to the mostly Orthodox believers in the area was a good thing—spread out. Things were looking up in the region.

Thus, Martya's status, even as a "harem slave," was far higher than it had been as the daughter of a penniless farmer, much less as a whore. She loved the Kildar for bringing her into his household, for feeding her febrile mind through learning, for giving her status even in her parents' eyes. And she was counting the days to her sixteenth birthday.

But at the moment, she had a problem. The noise from Katya's room was disrupting class. Especially the whooping.

Katya was the one thing in the Kildar's household Martya did not enjoy. The Russian whore was . . . evil. Mean didn't begin to describe it. She would do small, petty, things that she could get away with to hurt the other girls. And there was little they could do about it. The whore was being trained by the Kildar as an "insertion agent," a spy. And the Americans had given her special powers and, notably, poisoned fingernails. Even before she'd started training, all of the girls had feared her. Now they were terrified of her.

But she had changed after the last battle. She hardly put on anyone at all anymore and occasionally did nice things for them. She had fixed Nikki's broken CD player. She had helped Martya with her English lessons.

But the girls weren't willing to place too much faith in the unexplained change. Not with Katya.

So knocking on her door to ask her to turn down the stereo was the *last* thing that Martya wanted to do. But Tinata had insisted. Nobody was getting anything done.

The music cut off and the door was yanked open. The sight left Martya staring.

Katya was a very beautiful blonde, just medium height with bright blue eyes that could be cold as a shark or innocent as a virgin depending on her choice and mood. At the moment she was looking pissed, but not deadly. What had Martya's attention, though, was that she was wearing a two-piece bathing suit and the top was dangling from her hand, leaving her topless.

The girls, naturally, had often seen each other naked. But answering the door holding the top of your bathing suit was unusual. As was wearing one in the depths of the Georgian winter. It was below zero Celsius outside and blowing hard. A bathing suit didn't make much sense. Even with the heaters, the caravanserai was cold.

"Katya, please," Martya said. "We cannot study with all the noise."

"That's a problem," Katya admitted, lowering the suit. "Because *I'm* studying."

"What?" Martya said, then noticed that there was another woman in the room. She was older and dressed in Western clothes. Not very pretty even when she was younger, Martya was sure.

"*That* you don't need to know," Katya replied.

"Can you at least stop the whooping?" Martya asked. "That is what is getting us."

"No, I need to do the whooping," Katya said. "I won't be doing this much longer. I think."

"Okay," Martya said with a sigh. "Sorry to have bothered you."

"No problem," Katya said. "I just need to get back in character."

"Okay," Martya said as the door closed in her face. "What did *that* mean?"

"I have to wonder if this is really necessary," Katya said, waving the bathing suit back and forth. "And I'm *freezing*."

"You'd be surprised how cold it can get at Daytona Beach in spring," Jay replied, gesturing with his chin at the muted TV set. "Look at the nipples. Most of those girls are *quite* cold."

"Yeah?" Katya said, striking a pose. "Well, look at mine."

"I've seen them," Jay replied evenly. "If you're prepared to continue?"

"Why in the hell would I want to be on a 'Girls Gone Wild' video?" Katya asked.

"You don't," Jay replied. "Ever. Be assured of that. But you *do* need to learn to mimic the actions. Girls like that can get into virtually anywhere but a shield room, and you'd be surprised how many have made it *that* far. Playing the stupid, wild, partying slut is a very good cover. Among other things, if you have to avoid capture, slipping into that guise is a good way for a girl as good looking as you to disappear. Change your appearance slightly, go into a club and be the sluttiest slut there. Pick up one of the many guys who are hankering for you, take him home and stay *there* overnight. No hotel room, no traceable apartment. I can think of a thousand reasons to learn this particular cover. That *you* cannot troubles me."

"This padwan asks the Master's apology," Katya said, bowing with a smirk. "I see what you mean, though."

"Now, let us work on removing the top again," Jay said with a sigh. "I will admit that I'm enjoying the sight, I am heterosexual, but you are just not *doing* it right. If you'd only spent some time as a stripper it might help. With mental conditioning if nothing else. You have to feel the *need* to expose yourself and you so dislike the very thought that it is interfering."

"I've been naked in front of many men," Katya said, coldly. "And none of them have ever known I was not happy about it."

"I do," Jay said. "Any trained observer would see it in you. Most men, yes, are not so trained. But it is not those you need fear. If you are in a situation like this the most you need to worry about is a Rohypnol slipped in your drink or date-rape. Don't drink anything you don't see poured by the bartender for the former. Since you are intending to fulfill your side of an implied contract inherent in going home with a male from such a party, you need not fear the latter. You, in fact, need to let go of your *fear*. That is what is trapping you. You will not be the agent you could be until you stop fearing men."

"I don't fear men," Katya said. "I just want to kill them all."

"Are you refusing to accept my training?" Jay asked calmly.

"No," Katya replied. That was the one agreement between them. Katya would do whatever Jay told her in training and the only punishment was that, if she stopped learning, if she decided she knew more than he, he would simply stop training her.

Since Katya wanted to know it *all*, she was very careful to be on her best behavior with the master spy.

"Then do not challenge that statement," Jay said. "Especially since it's true. Are you unaware that you fear men or unwilling to admit it?"

"Unwilling to admit it," Katya said after a moment.

"You *cannot* carry that baggage and be who you should be," Jay said. "Almost all women fear men at some level. It is one part of their nature, one you should be aware of. Men are, by and large, bigger, stronger and more aggressive. Men go through life with a predator mindset, women with that of prey. But you, Katya, need never fear them again. You *are* the predator. What do you fear? Being beaten? You have survived beatings and more. Being raped? You have survived that. Dying? If it came to that, most men would have a hard time killing you unless they surprised you. As you know having killed a few who were trying to do that. You are not one of the girls in this video. You are not virtually defenseless before a stronger male. But you still fear."

"Yes," Katya admitted.

"But these women, these girls, these do not," Jay said, restarting the video. "Watch them carefully. They

are enjoying themselves. They have no fear of the
stares, of the shouts, of the attention. Oh, a few do.
That mousey girl on the left, brown hair and nipples.
She is afraid of the attention. Basically introverted,
I suspect, or just raised in a prudish environment.
Generally not a problem unless you're in a situation
like that. I have no clue why she is up there hav-
ing ice water dashed on her. A dare from friends?
A boyfriend who has psychological power over her?
Drink? But she fears. Could you be her? You would
have to wrap yourself around your fear, show it, use
it, let it blossom in your eyes? Could you do that?
And still be the predator you truly are?"

"No," Katya said.

"Then, again, you are not the person you *must* be,"
Jay said, stopping the video again. "When you can be
that girl, up there on stage in a wet T-shirt contest, on
TV no less, afraid of all the consequences, the men suddenly charging the stage, her parents seeing the video,
her friends back at college whispering behind her back,
guys figuring she's a slut and only after her body, then,
padwan, you will be on the road to perfection. But we
will concentrate on the blonde in the striped bathing
suit again. Now, in character . . . Whoop!"

"Mike, open the damned door," Adams said. The
damned wood was hurting his knuckles.

He stepped into the room and looked around.
He hadn't been up to Mike's sanctum before but it
was pretty cozy. A radiator kept it warm, it had nice
paneled walls, the chair looked comfortable. On the
other hand, it smelled. Stank, really. Booze—the
bottles were all over the place—and just the reek of

a person who hadn't washed enough holed up in a small room too long.

"I gotta ask," Adams said. "What's behind the steel plate? Everybody is dying to know. A black hole? A TV? What?"

"None of your God-damned business," Mike said.

Mike Harmon was thirty-seven years old, brown of hair and eye, medium height with a muscular build due to years as a SEAL instructor. An almost prescient talent for silent-kill had earned him the nickname "Ghost" while on the SEAL teams. After sixteen years as a SEAL, mostly an instructor in everything from "direct action" to HALO, he had found himself physically beaten and psychologically unsuitable to the Teams. So he'd gotten out and gone to college. It was a long road to being the Kildar, one with half the terrorists on earth searching for a guy code-named Ghost, but he'd made it every step of the way. The scars on his body, and in his heart, were proof.

"What do you want, Ass-boy?" Mike asked.

"Ass-boy yourself," Adams replied. "We've got a mission."

"I heard," Mike said. "We really don't need the money and I'm tired of laying it on the line over and over and over again. So . . . no."

"I want to go."

"Go."

"I want to take two teams."

Mike finally looked at him, then back at the wall.

"Whatever."

"Is that a 'yes,' O Kildar?" Adams asked angrily.

"Just try not to fuck up too much," Mike said. "Now get out."

"Christ, I really *should* beat the crap out of you," Adams said.

"Do you really think you could?" Mike asked, his teeth grinding.

"In your current condition?" Adams said. "Hell, yeah. Let me tell you something, *Kildar*. I had a talk with your team chief after you quit. I wanted to know how such a God-damned good operator could have had his ass fucking fired by a chief I knew had his head on his shoulders. And do you want to know what he said? It had dick all to do with the AD, by the way."

"I could give a fuck less," Mike said. "Now would you get the fuck out?"

"He said you weren't hard-core enough," Adams replied. "Simple as that. You'd gotten soft playing big boy instructor with the meats. You thought it was all a big game, that you could just wave a fucking stress card and get a point for effort. He called you a fucking crybaby. When I pulled you out of that fucking bunker, I couldn't figure what the fuck he was talking about. But he saw it when I didn't. You're a fucking *crybaby*. So you lost a piece of ass. Ass is *cheap*, buddy. You got a dozen pieces here in the house. There's more in the Keldara and they're all willing and you know it. So get off your fucking *ass*!"

"You done?" Mike asked calmly.

"Yeah," Adams said, sighing.

"Go do the mission," Mike said. "Collect a bonus. Then stay in the fucking States. I don't want to see your face again after that door shuts."

"You're fucking firing me?" Adams said, incredulous. "Well then, fuck you, I'll just *leave*."

"Big mission," Mike pointed out. "American civilians might die. You might stop that. And do you really want the Keldara wandering around the U.S. alone?"

"Fuck," Adams said. "You know just where the buttons are, don't you?"

"You weren't hired for your brains," Mike replied. "By the same token, you should know when you're out of your depth on something. And you just proved you don't. So I don't want you around."

"What the fuck does *that* mean?" Adams asked.

"You've been married, what? Six times? Which means that you're the perfect SEAL, more balls than brains and no fucking heart at all. It's just a piece of ass. Big fucking deal. Which meant you had no clue what you were just saying. No fucking clue at all. Since you don't even have the introspection to realize *that*, please leave this room and get the fuck out of my life. Go do the mission and then just . . . leave."

"I should have left you to die in that damned bunker," Adams said, hitting the door control.

"I wish you had," Mike whispered after the door was closed. Then he raised the plate. . . .

CHAPTER TWO

Adams stepped off the plane and breathed deep. Humid as hell and about seventy degrees. Ah, Florida winter.

Homestead Air Force Base was located just south of the city of Miami near the town of Homestead, Florida. The base had once housed a variety of bombers from Strategic Air Command, back in the days when "pad alert" had teeth. But the end of the Cold War had caused various reevaluations of the base, especially given the pressures from the burgeoning Miami area.

However, its strategic location—it was the only base that really had a lock on the Caribbean—had kept it at minimal status. Demoted to an "Air Force Reserve Base" it, nonetheless, maintained a squadron of "reserve" F-16s as an antiterror Combat Air Patrol over the Miami area as well as supported the antidrug planes that patrolled the region.

The old girl was getting a little weary, but hanging in there.

"Mr. Adams?" the officer waiting for them asked,

holding out a hand. "I'm Lieutenant Mike Himes, sir. I'm your liaison officer."

"Pleased to meet you, Lieutenant," Adams said. The officer was tall and almost skeletally thin, maybe weighing one-fifty if he was soaking wet. A shock of red hair was apparent under the beret. Adams had learned to read Army doo-dads over the years, though, and the LT was wearing a CIB and a combat patch from the Third ID.

"I've arranged billeting for your personnel on base," the LT continued, waving to the terminal building.

"I think we've got a hotel set up," Adams said. "Sorry about that. The usual clusterfuck. But we'll need someplace to store our gear."

"About that . . . yes," the LT said. "We've got a meeting just about to start you probably should attend. The joint headquarters for the action teams is here on base. You'll be able to meet all the movers if you know what I mean, sir. And there are some issues to resolve."

"Ain't there always," Adams said with a sigh. "I swear that's why the colonel stayed behind; he didn't want to sit in the meetings."

"Possibly, sir," the LT said. "I've got escorts for your personnel and a truck is on the way to pick up their gear. We'll arrange transport to town. If you could follow me?"

"Hello, my old friend," Kurt said in perfect German. It was, after all, his native language.

He was sitting in an open air bar in Bimini, listening to some really awful rap music. But the view was spectacular since some Canadian girls were down on vacation and seemed to quite enjoy the caterwauling.

"Hello," the man on the phone said. "I thought you should know that your friends are arriving today."

"Is that so?" Kurt said. "Then I think we should make plans to receive them well, don't you think?"

"Arrangements have already been made," the man said. "I was just informing you. They will be well taken care of."

"Wonderful," Kurt said, hanging up the phone. "Just perfect."

The meeting room featured a long table with seats at it and along the walls behind. Most of the seats were filled when Adams arrived.

"This way, sir," Himes whispered, leading Adams to one of the chairs, then taking the one behind him.

"Who are you?" the guy next to Adams asked, leaning over. He was a heavy-set guy wearing a FEMA jacket. In fact, most of the people in the room, males and females, wore jackets denoting their agencies. Maybe he should have Mike make up jackets for the Keldara so people would know who they were. No, fuck Mike. After this one he was gone.

"I'm not sure I get to tell you that," Adams said.

"Or you'd have to kill me?" the man joked.

Adams turned and just stared.

"Been there, done that."

"Oookay," the man said, turning back to the table.

"This meeting is in order."

The man at the head of the table was a Navy admiral. Adams vaguely recognized him but he wasn't a SEAL admiral, not that there were many of those. Flyboy, if Adams recalled.

"We need to start by signing the standard form,"

the admiral said, unsealing the briefing document in front of him with a letter opener.

Adams looked at the folder, puzzled, for a moment then pulled out his Spyderco folding knife and slit open the top. Inside was another envelope with a form on the front. He perused it for a moment, shrugged, then signed the bottom.

"Collect them," the admiral said when everyone had finished signing the forms. It was apparent that some of them had taken the time to read the fine print. Slowly.

His aide circled the room, picking up the forms, then took them back to the admiral. The admiral then proceeded to read each of them.

"CBP," the admiral said, looking over at the representative from Customs and Border Protection. "You have an objection to Clause Two?"

Adams had long before learned the technique of sleeping at the drop of a hat. He wasn't sure how long it was before someone poked him the back.

"Mr. . . . Adams?" the admiral said.

"Sir?" the master chief replied, sitting up.

"You're heading the . . . Georgian contingent?" the admiral asked. "I see that you have clearance for this briefing but I'm not sure what your part in all of this is."

"We're just here to help out, sir," Adams said. "We have both a team of intel specialists and a team of shooters. If you localize anything, we can take it down. Guaranteed."

"Excuse me?" the FBI rep said, leaning over to look down the table. "What did you just say?"

"I think it was pretty obvious," Adams replied. "I mean, why else did we fly all this way?"

"We have two tac teams, highly *trained* tac teams I might add, standing by," the FBI rep said. "If anything needs to be 'taken down' it will be *licensed* officers of the United States government."

"Fine," Adams said, pulling out a cigar. He wasn't much of a smoker, but there were times . . . "Then I'll just sit here and nap."

"There is no smoking in this room," the admiral snapped.

"Admiral, you wanna check where *my* authority comes from?" the master chief replied, lighting up. "Because I could give a rat's ass if this is a non-smoking area. Or what anyone in this room cares about it."

The aide leaned forward and whispered in the admiral's ear at which point the officer nodded.

"Sorry, Mr. Adams," the admiral said. "Smoke your cigar by all means. In fact, smoke a dog turd if you so wish."

"Those things will kill you, you know," the FEMA rep said. But he wasn't waving the smoke away, which was something.

"I've got the life expectancy of a gnat anyway," Adams said, tapping an ash into the water glass in front of him.

"They're not that great for me, either," the FEMA rep pointed out.

"Yeah, well, I don't really care about your life expectancy much, either," Adams said. "And it would go up a bit if you'd lay off the fatty foods, Heart Attack Boy."

"Gentlemen and ladies, open your briefing documents, please," the admiral said. "The situation is this. We have highly credible intelligence that Al Qaeda is moving a shipment of VX gas into the United States."

"Fuck," Adams whispered.

"You didn't know?" the FEMA rep asked. He didn't seem too put out over the "Heart Attack Boy" thing.

"All I got was that it was WMD," Adams whispered back.

"VX, as most of you know, is a binary nerve agent," the admiral said, reading off notes. "That means that it has two chemicals that are combined to make VX in the field. In systems such as artillery shells they get combined after they're fired but the materials can be combined up to a week before use and still retain full potency. Each of the chemicals is dangerous by itself, defined as Class Four Hazardous Material. However, when combined they are lethal in very small doses. It's referred to as odorless and tasteless. What that actually *means* is that if you taste it or smell it you're already dead.

"VX, like all nerve agents, works by interfering with neurotransmission. I'm sure I'm covering old ground for most of you but the first sign of exposure is involuntary muscle movement, dizziness and nausea followed by convulsions, respiration failure and death. What it does not do, despite the movie about the stuff, is bubble your skin off. Twist you up like a dying bug? That it does.

"The best method of insertion is via the eyes followed by inhalation, especially through the sinuses, and then skin contact. The material is not a gas at normal temperatures so it is normally distributed as droplets. One droplet, smaller than a drop from an eyedropper, on the skin is lethal. For that matter, it only takes a few picograms in the eyes. That's smaller than you can see.

"There is a cargo container of VX believed to be bound for the South Florida area," the admiral continued. "Insertion method is unknown at this time. We have located and seized the suspect ship but it was empty of all such cargo. The crew has admitted, under questioning, that it veered from the sea-lanes and that there were others aboard who left sometime during that change of course. The numbers are unclear. The ship is a tramp freighter owned by shell companies probably connected to Al Qaeda. That is where we're at."

Adams actually managed to stay awake through most of the meeting. He wished he hadn't, but what the hell. And the situation was definitely under control. Definitely. The FBI had two thousand agents in place or on the way. The Coast Guard was redeploying. The CIA was "hot on the trail." The FBI was "developing leads." Customs and Border Protection had the ports "locked down solid." FEMA was "fully prepared," courtesy of the guy in the seat next to him. The Coast Guard was "all over the situation." Hell, the Navy had a "solid lock on all action items."

"And what do the Georgians have for us?" the admiral asked after about an hour of ritual chest-beating.

"Dick all," Adams said. He'd finished off the cigar long before and was wondering when the damned meeting would end so he could get a beer and wash the taste out. "Oh, we do have a top-flight intel team that doesn't give a rat's ass how it collects the intel. And one of the best WMD experts on the face of the earth. And a group of shooters who could probably wipe your Fibbies in about two seconds. And a record of doing this sort of shit and succeeding. Other than that? Not much."

"If you violate privacy there's no way we can get a conviction," the FBI rep pointed out, angrily.

"These guys are all going to Guantanamo, anyway," Adams said. "Who cares? You do, that's who. So you're going to go around 'developing leads' right up until you hit that constitutional protection thing. Then give it to us."

"Chief Adams," the FBI rep said diplomatically. "This is the United States. There are laws. While I'm sure you're very good at what you do, if you do any of those things, federal and local law enforcement would be forced to detain you pending charges."

"Fine, fine," Adams said, holding up his hands. "In that case, got nothin'. We done? I need a beer."

"I think we're done," the admiral said. "Could I speak to you, Mr. Adams?"

"I need a beer, too," the FEMA rep said, getting up and taking the documents he could exit with. "But good luck. My job is just to clean up the mess. This is too much mess to want to think about."

"I'll do what I can," Adams said. "Hey. You want some *real* beer?"

"Sure," the FEMA rep said, frowning.

"Get with the LT and we'll arrange a meet," Adams said, standing up. "Don't worry, you'll like it."

He made his way through the crowd to the admiral, who was talking to the CIA rep. Another guy wearing a DEA jacket was apparently part of the pitch.

"They're not used to smuggling into the U.S.," the

CIA guy was saying. "It's almost sure to be containers. We'll probably catch those with the sniffers, but I think the main angle of attack is on the shipping company. They are going to have transferred to another ship."

"So what do you need?" the admiral asked.

"More support," the DEA guy replied. "Especially from the FBI. They're trying to find the inside groups. Let's stop it before it gets here. Seriously, South Florida used to be a smuggler's haven but we've got it locked down pretty tight these days. I don't think they're coming in here. I think the ship was a feint; they're probably going through Mexico. The ship probably transferred on an out-island or at sea and *another* ship is carrying it to Mexico. And to crunch the numbers, run down those leads, we need to get the FBI to quit dicking around with opening doors all over Miami. The guys they're talking to my guys already *know*. They do drugs, not VX. Hell, they're ruining a dozen cases and stepping all over us!"

"I'll talk to the FBI," the admiral said. "But you guys are the outside. So get outside. If it's not coming in here, find out where it *is* coming in. You should be arranging that right now, not moaning to me. So go do it."

The two left, leaving Adams alone with the admiral and his aide.

"Master Chief," the admiral said, sitting down and waving to a seat.

"I wasn't sure if the admiral remembered me, sir," Adams said, taking the seat.

"I didn't," the admiral said. "I finally read the briefing document. But there are problems."

"Aren't there always," Adams said.

"I don't particularly like the way the FBI rep phrased it, but he was on point," the admiral said. "This is the U.S. We have laws. And, face it, we *own* the waters around this area. So I'm not sure what you're here for."

"I'm not sure, either, sir," Adams said. "But we're here. Turn us loose."

"And that's the other problem," the officer said, sighing. "Your intel group. I suppose you want to go around tapping phones and listening for intercepts and trailing suspects. The FBI can do all of that and I would suspect better. And they'll do it legally. Slowly, unfortunately. The fastest I've ever personally heard of one of them getting Title III clearance was seven days. And that can only be used for drug cases. FISA . . . longer. However, what you would be doing is illegal. As would be the case if you fire a weapon in anything other than self-defense. Now, given your pull, you could probably escape justice. If we could keep it off the news. You see where this is going?"

"We sit on our hands?" Adams asked angrily. "You want us to just sit on our hands?"

"I'll try to find something for you to do, legally," the admiral said. "But right now I'm not sure what."

"Yes, sir," Adams said, taking a deep breath.

"And Master Chief?"

"Yes, sir?"

"If you fuck me over on this I will put *your* ass in Guantanamo and throw away the key."

CHAPTER THREE

"Hey, Master Chief," Vanner said as Adams strode into the suite. "What you get at the meeting?"

"Dick all," Adams said, walking over to the fridge. He was followed by Lieutenant Himes who was looking around the room with interest. "You got anything?"

"Sort of," Vanner said. "I arranged for an intel dump, but it's not complete. Our clearances are 'under review.' It's a bunch, though. The girls are sorting it at the moment. I looked at the analysis and, frankly, it's shitty. These guys either don't keep up with the players or are incompetent as hell. I did pick up one item that's sort of funny, in a way."

"What?" Adams asked. "I could use some funny. LT, you want a beer?"

"Sounds great," Lieutenant Himes said, taking off his BDU top.

"The original data on this came from Al-Kariya," Vanner said, grinning. "Well, him and his laptop."

"Al who?" Adams asked, pulling out two ceramic

bottles and opening the wax tops expertly. He handed
one of them to Himes and flopped into one of the chairs.

"That Al Qaeda money guy we picked up in Chech-
nya," Vanner said. "The one we rolled into the bird
all wrapped up like a Christmas turkey."

"Wait," Himes said, holding up the beer bottle.
"You're the guys who were in that battle with the Chechens, right? Jesus, that *sniper* shot. Everybody's sure that
came from some guy bellied down closer. I've been
running that vid over and over again looking for him."

"Nope," Adams said. "Lasko. The guy's pure magic
with a rifle. Damn near three klicks. Yeah, that's us."

"Damn," Himes said, sitting back and taking a sip.
He pulled the bottle back from his lips and held it
up with a stunned expression. "DAMN. What the hell
is this stuff? It tastes *sort* of like Mountain Tiger but
it's . . . Fuck, it's *better!*"

"It *is* Mountain Tiger," Vanner said, chuckling. "It's
just that the stuff we sell in the U.S. is our crap. The
Keldara bitch unmercifully when that's all they get to
drink. So whenever possible, we bring the pure quill.
And that's . . ." He looked at the casting on the bottle
and shrugged. "Hell, that's Mother Kulcyanov's brew.
It's not a patch on Mother Lenka's."

"I think I'm gonna like this detail," Himes said,
grinning. "And I begin to understand why they're such
good shooters if this is what they're protecting. But . . ."
He stopped speaking when the side door of the suite
opened and a fucking *vision* walked in the room.

"What'cha got, Grez?" Vanner asked as the intel
girl walked over with a document.

"Do you Americans even *use* face-matching software?" Greznya asked angrily.

"Probably not," Adams said, burping. "Be accused of racial profiling or something."

"Zaman Al-Sabad," Greznya said, dropping the picture on the desk. "He is an Al-Qaeda member who specializes in shipping. He arrived on a flight from Mexico this afternoon under a false name, Farhad Nejat. There's a picture, though, from the customs' security cameras."

"Lots of people," Himes said, frowning. "Lots of faces. It would take forever to do facial matches on them all."

"Not if you do a visual sort for Islamic looks," Greznya said scathingly. "That only turned up about two hundred. We hit this one on the first pass. He's not even *disguised*! He's on your own terrorism watch list for the All Father's sake!"

"Racial profiling," Himes said. "That, right there, would get the data thrown out of court. Even if it didn't, the defense attorney would use it and if you got the right jury it would get the guy acquitted."

"Americans are so *stupid*?" Greznya asked, confused. "Every major terrorist attack on your people has been by Islamic males between the ages of seventeen and twenty-five. Paying particular attention to such people simply makes *sense*. When a person that looks Islamic comes through the Keldara region you can be sure that we take a closer look. What is that thing about if it walks like a duck?"

"Welcome to the land of the free," Adams said sourly. "You've watched CNN, surely. Liberals aren't going to admit that until the Islamics have cut off their balls and put them all under jizya."

"No wonder the President called us," Greznya

said, shaking her head. "He is not even covering his trail. There is a record of him, under his false name, reserving a hotel room here in Miami."

"The who?" Himes asked.

"Well, now, ain't that interesting," Adams said, ignoring the question. "Daria found us an out-of-the-way warehouse, yet?"

"Not yet," Vanner said. "But we can lay in some collection on his room, put in a trail."

"Yeah, but can we do a quiet snatch?" Adams asked.

"Where's the hotel?" Vanner asked.

"It's something called a Best Western," Greznya said. "Just south of here near the junction of your turnpike and a road called U.S. 1. I have a map. The layout is for exterior rooms. He has a room on the ground floor towards the back."

"Uh," Himes said, holding up his hand.

"You got a problem with any of this, LT, you just take your beer and go to the other room," Adams said.

"Actually," Himes said, "I was hoping I could go along. I haven't done an entry in a few months but I figure it's like riding a bicycle. . . ."

The Best Western was just north of the long stretch of marsh that separated the keys from the Florida mainland. Near the turn-off for Everglades National Park and convenient to the Keys, it was often packed on weekends.

At four o'clock in the morning on a Wednesday, the parking lot was nearly deserted. There was a large moving truck parked towards the back and a few tourist cars.

Vanner had elected to not even lay in a physical bug; they could get plenty of take from a laser mike. The laser bounced off the window of the room and reflected in tune with sound waves. By reading the vibration of the window, everything said in the room could be monitored. He'd put in a connection to the hotel phones as well and with Al-Sabat's voice print, which they already had, they could filter for all the other calls out of the hotel. They'd also pinpointed his satellite phone.

The target had left twice, once to go to a local convenience store and the second time to the nearby Golden Corral for dinner. He had participated in a number of conversations, including some to overseas numbers, during the evening, up until one AM when his light finally went off. Most of them, with the exception of a call to his mother, had dealt with moving, buying and selling various goods. All of them could have been codes but, if so, Sabat would soon be explaining that.

"You two stay back and take security," Adams repeated as the Ford Expedition started. "I don't know why you talked me into this."

"Because you like my stunning good looks," Vanner said, grinning. He was, for once, all suited up, MP-5, balaclava and all. You could see his grin right through the mask.

"Because I've done this sort of thing before," Himes added.

"I've got plenty of shooters," Adams said. "You just do the door, then swing back."

"Got it," Himes said, cocking the shotgun.

The Expedition pulled to a stop and he unassed, charging the door. He could hear the assault team stacking up behind him so he pointed the shotgun at the lock and pulled the trigger.

The round was a breaching round, a standard twelve-gauge shotgun shell but with a projectile that was a frangible powdered metal slug that would destroy the lock but not over penetrate or result in dangerous fragments to the shooter. The round worked as advertised, destroying the lock and permitting Himes to open the door with one swift kick.

He rolled to the side, pointed outwards, and cocked the shotgun, ejecting the spent breacher and load a livie, then he took a knee.

There was a sound of brief struggle inside and he turned to the side.

"Never done this before?" he asked the intel specialist.

"Not for real," Vanner replied. "I . . ." His eyes flew wide as the doors of the moving van rolled up and a similarly armed and armored group started to pile out.

"FREEZE! POLICE!" the leader of the tac team yelled. "Drop your weapons and get down. NOW!"

"Wait, we're with—" Vanner said, puzzled by something about the man's words, just as the first round cracked into his chest.

At the sound of the shouting, Adams turned to the door and saw the tac team running across the parking lot. He also saw them shoot Vanner and Himes, which was all he needed. Fucking cops don't just shoot people down who have their hands up. Besides, most cops, even in Miami, don't have accents.

He took a position alongside the door, not that it gave any sort of cover, and began returning fire, taking two of the tac team down with two shots. Suddenly, the three Keldara shooters were by his side and it turned into a general melee.

Adams rolled through the door, taking cover behind some tourist's Taurus, then popped up, getting two more.

The tac team was taking cover around the cars as well so he took it to them, running to the rear of the Taurus and spotting another. Tango down.

The Keldara had spread out from the room as well and they swept right.

But neither group had noticed one of the shooters huddled alongside a minivan. The man stood up, aimed his AR-15 and fired five rounds at the master chief.

Adams felt the hit, like a punch in his side, and spun sideways, firing one-handed into the tac team member.

The man flew back, a 5.56mm hole in the center of his browridge.

"Master Chief," Vil said, running over to where Adams was slumped against the Taurus.

"We need to unass," Adams gasped. He was hit pretty bad but he was still functional. He'd been hit before. Not this bad, but he could still function. "Go to the air field we landed at. Get into the cars and go. Don't speed."

"Vanner is hit badly," Arvidas said. "I think Lieutenant Himes is dead."

"Fuck," Adams said. "We got to *go*."

"Fuck."

Nielson rubbed his forehead angrily.

"Did they at least get Sabat?"

"According to the colonel I spoke to they are sure it's not Sabat at all," Vil said miserably. "Sabat is reported to have been at an office in Yemen for the last week.

And we recovered documents from the room. They are . . . I guess you would call it a script. And he had a modifier so that his voice was similar."

"It was a trap," Nielson said.

"Yes," Vil replied. "We are at the airbase in the town of Homestead. All of us. We have been given quarters and are . . . we are told not to leave. The master sergeant is at the hospital here, Sergeant Vanner is in another in Miami.

"Colonel, the man said one other thing. I think that this attack was supposed to get the Kildar."

"Yeah, well, I'll let him think about that one," Nielson said. "In about two minutes."

"What *now*?" Mike yelled.

"Open the door."

Nielson strode in, his face twitching, and stood in front of Mike, arms crossed.

"Open the God-damned plate," Nielson said.

"If that's all you've got, get the hell out."

"Open the GOD-DAMNED PLATE YOU WHINY ASSED BITCH! Is that good enough for you?"

"Fuck you," Mike snarled. "Fuck you, fuck Adams, fuck you all!"

"Just open the plate, Mike," Nielson said, calmly. "Then I'll tell you why I'm asking."

Mike looked at him for a moment, then hit the solenoid, raising the plate.

Nielson spun in place and considered the painting for a long time.

"It's good."

"Yeah, it is. Cost enough."

"The lips are all wrong, though."

"Yes, they are."

"The team liaison is dead. Vanner is critical. Adams is shot up."

Nielson spun in place again, arms still crossed.

"How?" Mike asked hoarsely.

"A trap," Nielson replied. "One meant to catch you."

Mike stood up very slowly and walked to the painting. He touched the shoulder of the girl, lightly, then turned.

"Call Chief D'Allaird. You know the Dragon?"

"Yeah, I know the Dragon."

"Paint it black."

CHAPTER
FOUR

"The good news is that if it's coming in on anything other than a freighter, we've got some time."

Admiral Ryan had to admit that was true. The storm wasn't a tropical storm or hurricane; those came later in the year. But it was a late winter cold front that had damned near the same effects. The wind howled, the rain poured, lightning flashed and there were small boat advisories all up and down the coast.

"Some good news for a change," Ryan said, leaning against the wall of the room.

If only that damned SEAL had told them! They would have cross-checked Sabat's movements and figured out it couldn't be him. If they'd picked up the data these Keldara characters had, it would have been an obvious ruse.

On the other hand, he'd looked at the data they were given and knew it wasn't all on their shoulders. Sabat was clearly shown on everyone *else's* data as being in Yemen. The Keldara weren't given the full update. Which had been pointed out to him, in very small words, by the Chairman of the Joint Chiefs. He wasn't sure why DC thought these guys walked on water, but . . .

Then there was the third point. The guy posing as Sabat *had* waltzed straight through every system designed to detect people just like him. And the Keldara had turned him up in less than three hours. Turned him up while their chief was in a meeting and snatched the supposed terrorist, successfully, despite being attacked from behind in a planned assault.

The Keldara hadn't fucked up, he had. As the Chairman was *also* good enough to point out. He'd chosen to give them the filtered database. But was he just supposed to hand over *everything* to these damned people?

"Sir, can I ask something?" the DEA rep asked.

"Sure."

"Why are you standing here?"

"I was told to expect a high-level delegate," the admiral said. "I was told that he'd be arriving by this door. And flying in."

"No planes," the DEA rep continued, looking out the door of the terminal. "The big guys can barely get out of Miami-Dade. No helos. Not for a couple of days."

The words had barely gotten out of his mouth when the sound of rotors could be heard through the storm.

"What the fuck is that?"

There was music, too. A slow beat and a man singing.

"Warren Zevon, I believe," the admiral said, shaking

his head as a black Hind dropped out of the storm. "The Envoy."

The Hind didn't bother with the marked helo-pad, instead dropping by the terminal with bare clearance for the rotors. As a piece of driving on a clear day it would have been impressive. With the storm it was amazing.

As a fork of lightning rippled the horizon, the door of the bird slid open and a man in casual clothes, slacks, polo shirt, nice shoes, got out in the driving rain. If he noticed that it was pouring, it was not apparent. He was medium height with a heavy build and brown hair that flowed onto his forehead in the storm. He strode through the downpour, not bothering to duck the rotors, straight up to the door.

"You Ryan?" the man said.

"Admiral Ryan, yes," the admiral said, straightening up. "And you are?"

"You can call me the Kildar," the man said, turning to the DEA rep, his head tracking like a turret. "Who are you?"

"Bob Johnson," the DEA rep said, sticking out his hand. "What kind of a name is Kildar?"

"The kind that will cut your fucking hand off if you don't pull it back," Mike said, tracking back to the admiral. "I read the report on this clusterfuck on the bird over. If you fuck with me I will have you chipping paint the next morning. In Diego Garcia. Are we clear?"

"Clear," the admiral said, his jaw flexing.

"You are going to open Harmony and every other base you've got, fully," Mike continued. "But my top intel guy is in a coma in the hospital so I need an intel spec familiar with your systems and DEA's and

FBI's and every other fucking acronym. I need her by tomorrow. Somebody who is not PC and doesn't give a fuck what happens to terrorists. Tell her to take a plane to Nassau, send her data to me, pic, name, the whole deal. This time *don't* leave anything out. I'll take over from there."

"Her?" Ryan asked, raising his eyebrows.

"All my intel people but one are women," Mike said. "The one is in the hospital. I'm not going to explain to some cockhound know-it-all to sit the fuck down. Her. Tomorrow. In Nassau." He spun on his heel and headed back out into the storm.

"Where are you going?" the DEA rep asked sharply. "The command center is *here*."

"I'm going where you dick-brains can't fuck *my* op up," Mike said, pausing but not turning around. "*Your* job from here on out is to give *me* intel. *I'll* take it from there."

Mike walked in the hospital room and shook his head.

"You grow 'em up, you let 'em wear shoes . . ."

"Hey, Boss," Adams said, wincing. "I'm good. Get these canker merchants to let me go." He was wheezing as he said it.

"You've got GSWs to the upper chest," Mike pointed out. "That's not something you just up and walk away from. Not even you, Master Chief."

"You see Vanner?" Adams said, looking away.

"Yeah," Mike said. "Still in ICU. Doc says he's probably going to make it. But he's unconscious, still. Not a coma they tell me, just sleeping. I told the doc I could wake him up if he wanted me to.

They didn't think it was very funny. But I need him back at work."

"I can work," Adams said, flexing his jaw. "If you still want me."

"I was stressed," Mike said, walking over and sitting on the bed. "I'd like to have you back. You okay with coming back?"

"I'm good," the master chief said, looking away. "Sorry about what I said."

"Not an issue," Mike replied. "I'd heard the crybaby line before, by the way. From the team chief. Right before I told him to shove it up his ass. But I've had a long time to think about it, too . . ."

"I was wrong to say it," Adams said. "Whatever you are, you're not a crybaby."

"Wrong," Mike said. "From his perspective, from yours, I *am*. Want to hear the rest?"

"This crybaby time?" Adams said. "Because I could cry a fucking bucket. I really fucked up."

"No, you didn't," Mike said. "I did. I sent you out on something that I *knew* was over your head. That's my fuck-up, Chuck. And that's what this is about. You got your thinking cap on, Master Chief?"

"Go," Adams said.

"What's a crybaby?" Mike asked. "I never shed a tear on the teams. Never whined. Never quit. But there was something different about me. I didn't fit in. It came across to the team chief as soft and in a way it is. You're always asking how come I can make the girls happy. That's part of it, too. You starting to get a feeling, here?"

"When you were talking about stalking," Adams said, nodding. "Something about feeling the other guy."

"It's called empathy," Mike said. "But it's more than

that. It's a . . . *feel* for a situation. I don't know if the alarm bells would have gone off on that op or not, but they have from time to time. You remember how I was so heavy on ammo for the raid on the last op?"

"Too much for what we were doing," Adams said, nodding. "Especially since we had to hump it all in."

"I knew that it was going to go to hell," Mike said. "Not how bad, but I knew it was going to go to hell. It's a sense, not just when things are right in front of me but broader. It's one of the reasons I can command well, too. I can sense the needs of the guys, sometimes before they even know they're there. But having that sense . . . it makes me soft. Soft like an M & M. Crunchy on the outside with a softy candy inside. Not much breaks that shell, but . . ."

"When it breaks," Adams said.

"Yep," Mike said, standing up and heading to the door. "One difference. When it breaks, then reforms, well, there's a good side and a bad side. Good side is, there ain't much crybaby there, now. Bad side . . . there ain't much of anything at all."

Lieutenant Britney Harder watched, fascinated, as the Lynx helo dropped towards the broad deck of the yacht.

The entire transfer had been interesting. First she'd received a call to report to the SOCOM commander. Not his office, the general. There she'd been handed tickets and told to wear civilian clothes. She was going to Nassau and that was all the general either knew or was going to tell her.

At first she'd been pissed. There was a major op going down right next door in Miami. She'd only caught pieces of it, it wasn't in her compartment, but it was big. Sooner or later she was going to get in. And she knew the op involved fucking muj. Britney seriously wanted a piece of anything that hurt Islamic terrorists. She had scores to settle.

But she hadn't been drawn in and, honestly, she probably wouldn't be. She'd drawn the South American shop, the Narc Shop as they put it. There was a low probability that she'd have a chance to do anything about the fucking muj. So flying to the Bahamas wasn't all bad.

When she'd arrived at the airport, though, she hadn't known where to go. When a man walked up and looked her up and down she'd assumed he was just more obvious than normal.

Britney Harder was 5'5" tall with long, curly, blonde hair, a deeply cleft chin and a gorgeous if underendowed figure. She also had an issue with guys just examining her at close range. She'd gotten over having issues with guys, period, but she still didn't care for jerks who couldn't keep their eyes in their heads.

"Can I help you?" she'd snapped.

"Lieutenant Harder?" the man had said. Accent. Balkans or Russian. Slavic derivation, anyway.

"Yes."

"Come."

He'd led her out to the Lynx, opened the door politely, then climbed in behind.

The pilots were females, Americans from what she'd caught of the accent, and they were *good*. The cold front that had pushed through Florida was breaking up over the southern Bahamas but Nassau still caught a piece of it. The skies were gray and the wind was whipping but if either pilot cared it wasn't apparent.

The ride had been rough but Britney kept her light breakfast. She'd once been one of those kids who could throw up in a second if it meant avoiding school. And it helped during her brief bulimic period in high school. But once upon a time she'd seen some things, done some things, that made throwing up thereafter pretty much pointless.

The pilots again showed how good they were by putting the Lynx down on the deck of the moored yacht in what could be called a gale as if it was perfect calm.

"Out," the man said, opening the door.

She was only carrying two bags and as she unassed the bird a man came over and took the larger one.

"It will be in your room," the man said. He was wearing a pair of white pants, a black belt and a tight shirt with a tiger embroidered on the upper left chest. Good looking, too. Damned good looking. So was the guy who'd picked her up for that matter.

"Thank you," Britney said, holding on to her purse and backpack.

"This way," her escort said, waving to a door, hatch, whatever, in the side of the yacht.

The yacht was big enough that it had a *hangar* for the helo. But men weren't rolling it in; they were tying it down instead. Given the conditions she was surprised. Maybe it was going somewhere soon. Maybe there was already something in the hangar. Data item.

The interior corridor was paneled in light wood with tasteful paintings gracing it and the floor covered in plush carpeting. Given that the yacht looked to be about a hundred and fifty feet long, it had

to run . . . whooo. High. She wasn't sure what she'd
stepped into but it was gonna be strange.

The man led her down a rather confusing maze to
a door and then knocked lightly.

A voice inside said something in what sounded
like Russian. Not Russian, but the word was similar,
a simple: "Come."

The room was huge, two levels and with a massive
glass window that looked out over Nassau harbor. The
view was mostly of whitecaps but it was still pretty.

A man was seated at a desk, his feet up, reading
glasses perched on his nose, reading a document with
a TS cover sheet. If he cared that he was doing that
in front of a plate glass window it wasn't apparent
but it made Britney's skin crawl.

The guy was medium height, pretty muscular build.
He worked out. Brown hair. The face . . . was vaguely
familiar. She could swear she'd met him somewhere.

Mike gestured with his chin for Vil to leave and
looked at the girl, taking off his much-hated reading
glasses.

"Lieutenant Harder?" he asked. "Good to meet
you. You can call me . . ."

"Ghost . . ." the girl said, her face frozen. "Oh my
God . . . *GHOST?*"

"Jesus *Christ*," Mike snapped, his feet hitting the
ground. "Lock it up, Lieutenant! Where in the fuck
did you . . ." Mike froze himself, his eyes flying wide.
"*Bambi?*"

"Oh. My. God," Bambi said, walking over to him.
She came around the desk and touched his face.
"Ghost. You're alive."

"Yeah," Mike said, grinning ruefully. "I'm alive."

"I see you spent the reward money well," Britney said, perching on the edge of the desk.

"Oh, that wouldn't cover this baby for more than a few weeks," Mike said. "I've . . . Well, that mission was sort of start-up capital. My God. Miss Liberal of the Month joined the *Army*?"

"What's that line about a conservative is a liberal who's been raped?" Britney said, shrugging. "Yeah. I joined the Army. I wanted in Delta. I heard they had a few women. I was told it was invitation only and if I wanted in I needed to just work my butt off. People would hear. If I was good enough . . ."

"Fuckers should have taken you in a walk," Mike said. "You've got balls the size of the Statue of Liberty. I never properly expressed that. Sorry. It was only you and Babe and Thumper that volunteered. Even Amy was drafted."

"She's in the Corps," Britney said. "Amy that is. And you expressed it well enough. Towards the end."

"Yeah," Mike said. "I sort of . . . caught up with a few of the girls. You know, after. But . . ."

"They didn't talk," Britney said, nodding. "Good. OPSEC is important. I changed schools. Too many memories," she added, her eyes dark.

"Memories," Mike said, frowning and looking at the wall where there was a painting covered with a cloth. "Yeah. I got those."

"I bet," Britney said, touching his face again. "Ghost. Damn. I never . . ."

"Keep the name down," Mike said. "My current name is Michael Jenkins. You can call me Kildar."

CHAPTER
FIVE

"That's a hell of a story."

Britney was sipping a glass of white wine after turning down the offer of a beer. Mike was working on a glass of tea.

"And most of it pretty highly classified," Britney added.

"Oh, hell, you know the big part," Mike said. "And I left a few details out."

"Including what I'm doing here," Britney said. "What you're doing here."

"You're here because my field second and my intel chief got shot up in an ambush aimed at me," Mike replied. "So I needed somebody familiar with the intel flow we're getting."

"Why weren't you there?" Britney asked, frowning. "I'd have expected you to go right in charging."

"I might have," Mike admitted. "But I had decided to . . . sit this one out."

"Again, not what I'd expect," Britney said. "Not from Mr. 'No, you can't be Flower.'"

"I'd forgotten that," Mike said, a nostalgic smile on his face. "Good times."

"Says you," Britney said, shuddering. "I still have nightmares about being put on that table. Why?"

"You don't give up, do you?"

"And who taught me that?"

"Long story."

"You just told me a long story," the intel specialist said. "And clearly some of the details you left out were important."

"Not anymore," Mike stated, flatly. "I'll introduce you to my intel chief, well, assistant chief. She's female, speaks excellent English. I'll get you briefed in on the mission, then you can get to work trying to find some nuggets."

"And if I do?" Britney asked.

"Then I get to do *my* job."

Britney's new guide was a pretty, no *beautiful*, brunette, tall and leggy but with a nice bust. Also slightly pregnant. That was obvious because she was wearing tight blue shorts and a tight, sleeveless T-shirt with a tiger logo on the back and "Mountain Tigers" on the front. Above the logo, just under the collar, was the name "Stella." In one of the corridors the two were confronted by a massive blond guy dressed pretty much the same way. Handsome as hell. Hell, everyone she'd seen was physical perfection. This guy wasn't *quite* perfect in that he was missing one leg from above the knee down. He was wearing shorts so it was pretty obvious. He'd apparently been walking the corridor for exercise and stood to the side as the two came down the passageway.

Britney could feel his eyes on her as they passed. The guy was a fucking mountain. It was nervous making. She wasn't sure if he was checking her out but she felt more like he was judging her. On what she wasn't sure.

"Who was that?" she whispered when they'd turned the corner.

"Oleg," the girl replied in accented English. "Team commander."

"Still?" Britney asked. "With the leg?"

"It is a very good prosthetic," the girl said. "German. It has some sort of spring in the knee. He says that it makes him run better than before. He intends to be in full form by the time we have a mission."

"How'd he lose it?"

"Last mission. It was very bad. A mortar landed near his position. His leg was . . . What is right English word? Mangled? Yes, I think mangled is right. Had to cut it off so he could keep fighting."

"Keep *fighting*?" Britney asked, incredulous.

"He was team commander," the girl said, pausing and looking at Britney quizzically. "He had to lead, yes? Could not lead with the pain of the leg. So Dmitri cut it off for him. They were in fighting positions, he didn't have to walk, run. Only fight and lead, yes? So . . . cut it off. Now he has new leg."

"Go *Oleg*," Britney muttered. And she'd thought *Delta* was hardcore. No wonder Gho . . . *Mike* fit right in.

The intel room was in the bowels of the ship and Britney could smell it had been freshly painted. From the look, it was in copper shield paint. Expensive but nearly as good as a full Faraday cage for a shield room.

The room was filled with computers and women. Like her guide, they were all very good looking and dressed in the same uniform. The effect was sort of overwhelming. Britney was used to being the prettiest girl in an intel shop. This was hell.

"This is the new liaison," the girl said in English.

One of the girls said something in that other language. Britney got enough to catch "last longer." It was close enough to Russian. Maybe Georgian, Mike had said that he lived in Georgia and that these were his . . . retainers. Strange term to use for your troops.

"I'm Greznya," one of the girls said, coming over and shaking her hand. "Welcome to Chaos Central."

"It always is," Britney said.

"I'm Stella, by the way," her guide said, then said something to Greznya. Something about the Kildar, meaning Mike.

"Interesting," Greznya said, looking her up and down curiously. "She looks like a Kildar girl, yes?"

"If you mean one of his former girlfriends," Britney said in Russian. "I'm not."

"You knew him, though," Greznya said, still in Russian. "Before."

"Yes," Harder replied. "And that is about all I can say on the subject."

"Come, sit," Greznya said, showing her to a chair. "Would you care for some tea?"

"An in-brief would be preferred," the lieutenant said. "Gh . . . The Kildar didn't even tell me what the mission is."

"I won't ask what the other name was," Greznya said, politely. "But before I brief you in, I must tell you something."

"I stepped through a looking glass and this is all a dream?" Britney said, taking a cup of tea from one of the girls.

"No, Alice," Greznya replied. "It is something about the Kildar. He has recently lost someone. Someone important to him."

"Is that why he was going to sit out this mission?" Britney asked.

"Yes," the Keldara replied. "And then Adams, who has known him for many years, and Sergeant Vanner who, I think, is something like a son to him, they were both very injured. He feels much guilt for this. And for the other, too. You know the thing Nietzsche said about the abyss?"

"Yes," Britney replied. She was having a hard time with disjunction. Yesterday she'd been perusing reports on Colombian drug smugglers. This afternoon she was sipping tea in an intel shop in the bowels of a multimillion dollar yacht and discussing Nietzsche.

"The Kildar exists on the edge of the abyss," Greznya said. "But for as long as he has looked at it, has dabbled at its edges and stuck his foot in, he has never entered the abyss. Or at least not that he could not swim out. Now he is in the abyss. He is being sucked down by it. He is drowning in it. If he becomes the abyss, well . . . We have had Kildars who ate their meals surrounded by dead bodies, for the pleasure of the company. We will, as you say, adapt and overcome. But I'm not sure the world will."

"What does this have to do with me?" Britney asked.

"If you can draw him back from the abyss," Greznya said, "that would be a very good thing. For us, yes, but for many other people. You remind him of . . . good times, I think."

"I don't," Britney said, setting down her cup, then reconsidering. That was exactly what Mike had said: "*Good times.*" What kind of a crazy man considered holding off a battalion of commandoes and getting shot very near to death as "Good times."

The sort that wouldn't stop until he tracked fifty girls down and freed them. The sort that had kicked her ass into overdrive when she thought she was about packed in. And she could tell what Greznya meant. The man upstairs had been more alive *dying* than he was now. She'd held his hand, then, dragged his heavy-ass body to cover, listened to him whisper that damned song. "This is my sacrifice . . ." he had muttered, almost joyous. Much more alive, then, with blood pouring out of him in scarlet rivers and still giving her instructions, his breath sucking in and out through holes in his lungs.

"I'll see what I can do," Britney said. "But I only met him once and that at . . . a very bad time in my life. But I owe him . . . everything. I'll see what I can do."

"Good," Greznya said, patting her thigh. "Good. And now, we will brief you in, yes? And you can try to help us with this idiotic database you Americans use."

"God, not *another* harem girl."

Britney looked up at the two women entering the salon and frowned. The two were dissimilar in looks except for being brunette. The shorter one was stocky, with almost a power-lifter's look and had a gleam in her eye that spelled trouble with a capital T. The taller was more slender as well, not exactly willowy but lighter looking. She also had a milder expression.

They were wearing flightsuits and carrying helmets. Ergo they were probably the pilots of the helo.

"I'm *not* a harem girl. Whatever that means."

"Dummy, that's the intel puke we picked up," the taller one said. "Sorry, term of art," she continued, walking over to Britney and holding out her hand. "Captain Tamara Wilson, late of the U.S. Marines. Currently . . . well . . . They put the handle *Valkyrie* on me. I usually handle dust-off and supply."

"Lieutenant Britney Harder," Britney said, standing up and closing the cover on the folder.

"How much harder?" the shorter one said. "Captain Kacey Bathlick."

"Do you?" Britney asked, smiling thinly. She'd put up with her last name all her life, after all. The jokes never made sense until she lost her virginity, but she'd heard them long before.

"Point for point," Wilson said, grinning. "You turn up anything, yet?"

"On what?" Britney asked.

"Ah, I think we need to do some more briefing," Bathlick said, pulling out a water and sitting down across from her. "This is the way the Keldara manage information. They don't talk to *anybody* outside the team. Inside the team, there are zero secrets. So do they have a line on the VX, yet?"

"No," Britney said. "Nada. Zip. Diddly. And since I'm a professional 'intel puke' I have to point out that while they may not *talk*, this room is not what I'd call *secure*. But thanks for asking. Now I've got a question."

"Shoot," Wilson said, sitting down with a diet coke in her hand.

"What's eating Mike?"

"You're on first name basis already?" Bathlick asked. "I called him Kildar for a couple of *weeks* before I remembered he'd told me his name."

"We've met before," Britney said. "Where is . . . not an item of discussion. Even in a secure room. Ever."

"Okay," Wilson said, nodding. "Interesting. But to answer your question . . . Jeeze, where to start."

"The Rite," Kacey said, taking a gulp of water. "Which is one fucked up thing in my opinion. And I'm all for people screwing."

"What right?" Britney asked. "A right to what?"

"Rite, R-I-T-E as in religion," Wilson replied. "The Keldara have some really weird customs—"

"Really weird," Bathlick interjected. "Really *really* weird. Like having parties on top of their graveyards . . ."

"It's a very ancient and . . . unusual culture," Tamara said, shooting a glance at her friend. "Do you know what the right of droit du seigneur is?"

"The . . ." Britney paused then her eyes widened. "Oh. Not *really*?"

"Really," Tamara continued. "The Keldara, though, have sort of made it their own. The girls who are getting married get . . . presented to the Kildar, first. Keep in mind that they are getting married to his *team* members. He then gifts them with a dowry which, I understand, was the reason they first gave for it. Mike wasn't really thrilled with the idea. Okay, virgins, sure, great. But not the fiancées of his team members."

"I got it," Britney said, unconvinced. "But he just couldn't *help* himself, right?"

"The pressure all came from the Keldara," Bathlick said flatly. "Tell her the rest."

"For the Keldara it's a breeding program," Tamara continued. "The Kildars have always been warriors for centuries. If they weren't, apparently they were . . . taken care of. Quietly. So they've been breeding for warriors for generations."

"And it's worked," Kacey said. "They're about as dangerous as the tiger that's their totem. More. I swear the *kids* are like little sharks."

"But the point is that the Kildar gets first crack," Wilson said. "And . . . Have you met Stella yet?"

"Yes?" Britney replied.

"You might have noticed that she's a bit pregnant," Tamara said. "Her husband is the guy who guided you from the airport, Vil, one of the team leaders by the way. The child is the Kildar's."

"They make sure they're right at ovulation when they put him to stud," Kacey said, cackling.

"That's . . ."

"Weird," Tamara said, nodding. "But that's the Keldara. And it's apparently worked. Even the women . . ."

"The women took on a Chechen force of about their own number during the last battle," Bathlick said. "They slaughtered them, the Chechens then being in prepared defenses. Keldara girls took five dead, about fifteen wounded. And just slaughtered the fedayeen. About a hundred. No quarter. Mostly chopped them up with axes. Then they got out shovels and filled in the trench. That's the *women*."

"The men took on about forty times their number and did much the same," Tamara said. "But we were talking about the Rite of Kardane. That's what the Keldara call it. Anyway, sometimes things . . . go wrong."

"Might have gone right," Kacey said, looking at her water. "Sometimes I wish this was beer."

"The Kildar participated in the Rite with a young lady named . . . Gretchen Mahona," Tamara said, swallowing and closing her eyes for a moment. "She was our crew-chief."

"Didn't have a fucking clue how," Kacey added. "But God she was willing. And good. Damn she was good." She took a drink of water and tossed the bottle across the room, dropping the bottle in the trash for three points.

"And unfortunately, the Kildar . . ."

"Fell in love," Britney said, connecting the rather obvious dots. "And Gretchen . . ."

"Got blown all over the inside of the bird by a 12.7," Kacey said. "Nothing we could do. We were loaded to overweight with wounded and had to . . . Fuck."

"We had to fly right through the fire," Tamara said. "Three bunkers, interlocked. We were moving about as fast as a person could run. Very high altitude, we were only making it on ground effect as it was. She was engaging the bunkers with the mini . . ."

"And she got blown away," Kacey said, jerking to her feet and pulling out another bottle of water. "Literally. Made a hell of a mess."

"The Kildar has not taken this loss well," Tamara said delicately.

"He went on a two-month bender," Kacey said bluntly. "Up until yesterday, no, two days before, he was nose deep in a bottle. I'm surprised he was able to recover so fast."

"Mike's . . . got a thing for women," Britney said.

"Oh really?" Kacey asked. "Do tell? He's only got a

harem of teenaged girls and a harem manager that's one hell of a fox. I *think* we were luck of the draw, but . . ."

"That . . . wasn't what I meant," Britney said. "I shouldn't have said that much. But . . . Yeah, I can see that hitting him pretty hard."

"He's only here because of Adams and Vanner getting hit," Tamara continued. "And he feels guilty about that as well."

"Might have a point," Kacey said. "I'm not sure that would have gotten him. He's got the *touch*. I've got it for flying but he's got it for . . . shit like this."

"I've heard," Britney said. "We did a little catching up."

"You keep dropping these *hints*," Kacey said. "He wouldn't 'catch up' with just anybody. Catch up about what? As far as anybody in the Valley knows he just appeared fully formed! Give, girl!"

"I can't," Britney said. "Let's just say that he saved my life and leave it at that, okay?"

"So you gonna save his?" Kacey asked.

"I'd be open to suggestions how," Britney admitted.

"Screw him," Kacey said.

"You think that will fix things?" Britney asked, blushing. "I mean, as you mentioned he has . . . Did you say a harem?"

"Screw him and then get him to open up," Kacey said, ignoring the question. "He won't fucking *talk* about it! He's gone all macho on everybody. Big boy that doesn't need to talk. He's fine. He just needs a drink or two. Or a hundred. He needs to get it off his chest. He won't talk to Anastasia, he won't talk to the harem, which is what it's *there* for, he won't talk to even his oldest friends. Maybe he'll talk to you."

"Methinks my overly testosteroned friend has a point," Tamara said.

"I'll . . . consider it," Britney said. "Just that. I . . . don't have sex with anyone much these days."

"Some issues there, too," Kacey said. "Bad boyfriend?"

"Oh . . . worse than that," Britney said with a sigh. "And not something I can discuss. I have a counselor. I work with it. But it's . . . Heck, most people I *could* probably talk about it . . ."

"Hints and hints and hints," Kacey said. "Thank God I'm not an intel puke; it'd be an itch I couldn't scratch. Me, I don't give a fuck. If you can get the Kildar back in shape, more power. If you can't, at least find me a target."

"I thought you were the driver," Britney said, smiling thinly. "The targets are for the guys with guns."

"You haven't seen our *other* bird. By the way, *my* handle is Dragon."

"No, I haven't," Britney said, distantly. "You did say 'harem,' right? I'm sure you said harem. . . ."

Greznya *was* an intel puke. And she was a good one. She, too, had the "touch," that special feel for a situation. And hers was ringing bells about the new intel specialist. She had spent a long time with the Kildar but had not been briefed. She knew him from before. She had something for him, something like the Keldara did. She was bonded. But she had said she was not a former girlfriend and she had that look. Whatever had happened it had not been a romantic relationship.

The yacht was rented but it was top-of-the-line and had massive satellite connectivity, including to the internet. The Keldara were tapped into every available database on earth and at the caravanserai Sergeant Vanner, All Father let him live, had built a gigantic server system capable of crunching data as fast as most supercomputers. They also had access to remote data systems, buying time on servers all over the world for anything their in-house system could not manage.

So she ran the name Britney Harder into the query and then on a hunch threw in possible connection words of "terrorism," "terrorist," and the various synonyms the Western press preferred such as "militant."

The system was highly intuitive and used advanced algorithms similar to those used by Google to get likely hits. The response was almost instantaneous and came from, of all things, Lexis/Nexus, the database for the international press.

Greznya found the girl's name, then went back to the beginning of the article. Then she pulled up other articles about the same event. There were thousands of such; it had been a world-wide event even if the Keldara were unaware of it. But "most read" often did mean the best information and most of it was repetitive. She sorted for some publications she knew were capable of actual in-depth reporting and nodded to herself.

Finally she was done and wiped the search. The search had been sent through two different intermediate routers so she was comfortable that it would not have been traced even if anyone was looking for them. A college student researching "recent events" would have done much the same as she.

On the other hand she now knew that people *were* looking for them. At least, they were looking for the

Kildar. And she knew that they had a *true* Kildar, warrior born, if it wasn't evident already. And that if anyone could bring him back, it would be the blonde lieutenant, a girl that would be considered moderately pretty among the Keldara even if she was a "ten" for most cultures.

But how, exactly . . .

CHAPTER
SIX

"WOOO-HOO!" Katya hooted, taking a swig from the bottle of tequila.

She wasn't the only girl on the yacht but she was, without question, the center of attention. Which had the other six girls somewhat pissed. And she was definitely the center of attention for the target.

The gathering could not be called a party simply because it was more or less continuous. Juan Gonzales was well-known as a center for partying, even in the fun-loving Bahamas. Wherever he went, his boat was filled with casual "company," most of the company young, good-looking females.

But except for during spring-break—when things got wild enough to make any of the various "party" shows would it be possible to smuggle a video camera on-board—the girls were rarely so . . . exuberant.

"I'm glad you're enjoying yourself," Juan said, raising a glass towards the new girl.

"I LOVE the Bahamas!" Katya shouted, taking another swig.

Jay had given her a drug that counteracted the effect of alcohol but she hardly needed it. She wasn't taking nearly as big slugs as it appeared for one thing. For another, she had a fairly high tolerance for alcohol. Despite that, she'd taken one of the pills, which were tucked in a special pouch under her left arm, before she came back on deck.

There were more devices secreted around her body. Under her right armpit there had been four bugs, newest generation "brilliant" monitoring devices. The bugs recorded conversation, screening for background noise and nonconversational sounds, then, when their memory was full, dumped a short directional squeal towards a central receiver.

One of the bugs, and the central recorder, Katya had placed in the bathroom. It was amazing what people, especially females, would talk about in the bathroom. And she'd wanted to get rid of the receiver as soon as possible. While it would normally require a body cavity search to find it, Juan might just be into backdoor.

The bug, which looked like a small wad of chewing gum, went under the sink. There was enough detritus under there it was clear that it was rarely, if ever, cleaned. The receiver went inside the holding tank of the toilet. It looked fairly natural there even if anyone bothered to lift the lid.

But she still had three more to plant, not to mention anything she could pick up.

Getting the data out, though, that was another problem. She could leave the boat freely, small dinghies regularly ran back and forth to the nearby town, but she couldn't off-load any of the data loaded in her head as she was used to. However, Jay had given her a number of drop points if she had anything to report. "The old-fashioned way" as he put it.

Juan Gonzales was a known cocaine trafficker. Convicting him, ah, that was the rub. As was getting anyone to extradite him given that the few witnesses willing to testify against him had all ended up dead. And he had very advanced measures to prevent exactly what Katya was, in fact, doing. While Juan was fully immersed in the partying, the several "security" men in the area were carefully watching most of the guests. Most. They had clearly been well-trained to ignore the girls. Otherwise one could be used as a distraction, right?

The one guy that had Katya nervous was the security chief. Michael Ritter was an Australian, a medium-height blond guy with a hearty laugh and long wavy hair. Pretty good looking if you ignored the broken nose that had been inadequately set. An Australian SAS veteran, he now did "international security contracting." He'd been hired by Gonzales after a serious attack that had nearly captured the drug trafficker while in transit in Colombia. It still wasn't clear if the attack had been by the Colombian government, American special forces or competitors.

Gonzales had escaped but only barely. And his bodyguards had performed less than ably. He'd come to the conclusion that he needed a professional, versed in all the modern methods of security and countermeasures and Ritter was highly recommended. Despite being formerly on the side of Light in most people's eyes, he had worked in enough shady places it was clear he'd gone over to the Dark side. What the heck, with rare exceptions the money was much better.

The rest of the security, though, were Colombians. They'd been spiffed up and given new shoes but they were still boys right out of the jungle. Big and probably capable in a firefight but they weren't expert watchers. Ritter had the eyes. He saw everything and he saw through many things. He was the one to convince.

"So where are you from?" Gonzales said, waving for the girl to sit in his lap.

"North Carolina," Katya said, dropping lightly into the lap and then giving a little wiggle. "I go to ASU, you know? And I just figured why hang around for winter quarter? There's hardly anything going on. So I caught a bus down to Miami and a guy gave me a ride over here on his boat. But it wasn't *nothing* like this! This is just *fine*."

She was aware that the southern accent needed some work but she'd watched all the episodes of Dukes of Hazzard she could stand.

"I'm glad you like it," Gonzales said, grinning. "I keep it just for ladies like you."

"Well, thankee," Katya said. "But you know the *one* thing here that's wrong?"

"What?" Gonzales said, furrowing his brow. "Simply ask and it shall be yours."

"*You're* not having any fun!" Katya said, squeezing her tits together and pouring some of the tequila into the skin-lined cup. "*Body shots!*"

Gonzales grinned and leaned forward, sucking the raw tequila out of the crevice.

"WHOO-HOO!" Katya hooted, pouring in another shot.

This *was* a lot better than getting beat up.

▲   ▲   ▲

Lilia frowned at the beeping. There were so many systems in the room and one of them was always beeping. But she couldn't figure out which one it was *this* time.

She spun back and forth in her station chair, looking for the source then, when it wasn't apparent, started hunting around the compartment.

"What?" Greznya said. She was compiling a report on known smuggling methods. Most of them related to drug smuggling, but people quite often tried the same methods without realizing they were reinventing the wheel.

"You hear that?" Lilia asked, turning her head from side to side.

"No," Greznya said, looking around. But Lilia was a top voice analyst for a reason; she had phenomenal ears.

Lilia finally tracked the sound to a case, one of the many they'd used to bring the gear over. It was third down in a stack. After she'd gotten to it she popped the latches and looked at the laptop sized device. A blue light was flashing on the edge and every few seconds it let out a "beep."

"Low battery?" Lilia asked, lifting the box out of the foam cocoon. The fact that she'd been able to detect the beeping through the foam was testament to her hearing.

"No," Greznya said, coming over and taking it from her. "You weren't on the Balkans op."

"That's Katya's box," Julia said from across the room. "What the hell is it doing?"

"I don't know," Greznya said, sliding a USB cable between the box and her computer. She brought up the communications software, then punched in her security code. Immediately, the data screen started to scroll.

"The reason it was beeping was that its memory was getting full," Greznya said.

"We dumped it after the last mission," Julia pointed out.

"Yes, but it's been receiving for the last two days."

"Katya's here?" Mike asked.

"Yes, sir," Greznya replied. "She is currently a guest of a man with a boat not far from us. Close enough that we've been getting her take for the last two days. We didn't know that. Sorry."

"Who?" Mike said, frowning.

"Juan Gonzales," Greznya said, sliding over a folder. "Suspected cocaine smuggler. Known for all practical purposes, but nobody will arrest him due to lack of evidence."

"Interesting," Mike said.

"We've been worried about drug smugglers hooking up with Al Qaeda for a while," Britney said. "One of the reasons we've got the Narc Shop. But if he's actually working with them, well, that's a first."

"And one that we're going to discourage," Mike said. "Very directly. We know anything about his methods?"

"Various," Greznya said. "Sometimes he'll send shipments hidden in containers. Some have been caught, others . . . presumably not. He's used planes in the past. A current method involves fast boats. They come in from offshore and drop bundles off. They've been caught with the bundles but Coast Guard and DEA have never figured out how they make rendezvous. And they don't know where the cocaine comes from. The boats don't have the range to make it all the way from Colombia."

"Lots of islands around," Mike said. "Famously. Lots of ways to transfer it, too. But transferring in closer . . . They probably rendezvous with boats offshore."

"Won't work," Britney said, walking across the office. "Greznya asked me to sit in on this one."

"Lieutenant Harder has experience in this area," Greznya said.

"I thought you were Army?" Mike said.

"South American desk of SOCOM," Britney replied, sitting down and crossing her legs. "We do a lot of counter drug ops. I spend more time in the DEA database than in Harmony."

"So why won't rendezvousing offshore work?" Mike asked, leaning back.

"You said you'd lived down here," Britney said. "You've seen those big balloons they have a couple of places in the keys and such?"

"Yeah," Mike said. "They're radar balloons, I know that. But one boat . . . There are *a lot* of boats around here, Britney."

"Sure are," Britney said. "The daily take is over forty *thousand* tracks including all flights. But the tracks are all dumped to a supercomputer, continuously, that has pattern recognition software. If a boat that heads inshore to the U.S. waters meets a boat that is from outside territorial waters or just coming out of Bimini or the Cut or whatever, that incoming boat is tagged. And the Coast Guard, nine times out of ten, does a 'safety inspection.' Boats running down the coast, outside territorial waters, have a lower tag rate. They could be going anywhere. Boats going out and coming in, lower still. Fishermen go out and come in every day, thousands and thousands of them. No way you can stop them all."

"So what's going on?" Mike asked. "Any theories?"

"Sure, lots," Britney said. "Some of Gonzales' boats have been stopped and found to contain illicit substances. Those are seized. There's some of his and a bunch more of other cartels' sitting in the Hollywood boat yard awaiting auction. Others were empty. They might have already gotten rid of their cargo; they might have just been testing the system. The Colombians do that, too. It's a real cat and mouse game. If you want the number one theory, they're dumping them, somewhere, and then other people pick them up."

"Run a boat out," Mike said, musingly. "Do a dive. Hey, it's in the middle of nowhere, but maybe the guy found a new reef to spearfish . . ."

"Exactly," Britney said.

"Hard as hell to figure out," Mike said. "Even with the radar and supercomputer. Boats have got to cross tracks all the damned time. If you're smart you drop a small buoy and the diver on the spot. The diver goes down, does his thing, comes back up, signals the boat. The current has *already* carried him away from the track. The boat comes back, picks him up, moves on. There's a bunch of problems, though."

"There are?" Britney asked, raising an eyebrow.

"They're going to need to follow a general track," Mike said, still looking at the ceiling. "So they're going to have to have orders on what track to follow. And they're going to need to know approximately where to drop on the track. Last, they're going to have to tell somebody where, exactly, they dropped. And *that* information is going to have to be passed to whoever is fishing the shit out of the water. That's bi-directional information flow. And you're not going to be able to do much of it via straight transfer. That is, if somebody picks up a phone and says 'The cookies are at x coordinates,' eventually somebody is going to pick that up in an intercept. Then your shit gets fished up by a sheriff's dive team."

"Congratulations," Britney said, chuckling. "You figured out what it took DEA about six months to do. They're looking for the information exchange method and trying to write an update for the coding but they're having a hard time."

"Yes, I think I understand," Greznya said, her eyes distant. "Yes, that would be *very* hard coding. And you would have many *many* false positives."

"Because boats turn like that all the *time*," Mike said. "You get a hit on the sonar. You see a school of tuna and go chase it. Your divers are doing a drift dive. Hell, you lose your damned hat! The weak point is the information transfer. There's some part of that that will tell us where the motherlode is."

He sat back and looked at the ceiling for a moment.

"Any way we can get intel on suspect tracks?" Mike asked, picking up his tea without looking and taking a sip. "Especially ones coming in from north of the Bahamas?"

"The data stream we're on has them all the time," Britney said, frowning. "Why?"

"We need some equipment and I think it's training time," Mike said. "I'll consider the conundrum of

Katya at another time. In the meantime . . . Greznya, get me . . . Vil and the pilots. Britney, want to take a trip to the Keys?"

"New girl," Ritter said, sitting down next to the computer console.

"Pretty," Suarez said. "But aren't they all?"

Enrico Suarez was a graduate of the University of California, San Diego. He'd gotten a bachelors in computer programming, then gone to Stanford for his masters. However, as much as he could have made in Silicon Valley, he knew he could make more working for the cartels. A few friends had gotten him introduced to other friends until he found someone who was willing to meet his, very high, price.

The nice thing about working for the cartels was that they didn't care exactly how you got information, they just wanted to make sure they had it and nobody had theirs.

Suarez did various jobs for Gonzales, but one of them was "vetting" the various visitors that came on his boat. Frankly, it was easy.

He keyed in the name Alicia Patterson and let the computer search. Quickly enough it came back with the information that Alicia Patterson was a sophomore at Appalachian State University in Boone, North Carolina. Her home address was listed in Highlands, North Carolina. She was listed as a former student at Highlands High School. Her grades at Highlands had been much better than those at ASU. She was not attending this quarter but was shown as permitted for qualified admission the next; she was right on the edge of academic suspension. There were four photos.

One was a very old security photo from a company that maintained a database for parents who were afraid their children might be kidnapped. The second was from her driver's license. She had had three speeding tickets in the last year and was right on the edge of suspension for that, too. The third was from her ASU student identity card. The fourth was a very old and grainy photo of her in a local newspaper database. She was one of six winners of her elementary school spelling bee.

"That her?" Suarez said, smirking.

"That's her," Ritter said, nodding.

"Her grades are taking a nose-dive," Suarez said. "Did she say how she got down here?"

"Something about a bus," Ritter said. "I guess she boat-bunnied from there."

"Bet she doesn't go back," Suarez said. "*Fins* and all that. Small town girl. Hits college, gets into partying. Takes off . . . Boat-bunny material par excellence."

"Good," Ritter said, standing up. "I felt it was convenient her showing up right now."

"She's for real," Suarez said. "No question. It all checks."

"Ali's Bargain Palace!"

Jay listened to the scratchy connection for a moment, then nodded.

"Yes, Hamid! I need the T-shirts very much! I must have by Tuesday! Yes. Good. In'shallah!"

He turned back to the two tourists from Dubuque who were looking over the selection of cheap T-shirts and even cheaper, if very overpriced, souvenirs.

"All very good, mon!" Jay said in an Arabic imitation

of an islands accent. "Very good. You look good in this one," he said, pulling down a shirt with a large shark surfacing and handing it to the very large woman.

Katya was in, they'd checked her CV and apparently hadn't had any questions since the hacks had only gone to that point and then stopped. If they'd had any questions they would have searched deeper. Finding Robert's trojans in the NC DOT database, the ASU student database and the Highlands Courier would have been hard, but the search would have been obvious.

Robert was expensive but, like Jay, a patriot and *very* good. The NSA had been idiots to let him go over one little unauthorized hack. Especially since the take had proven him right.

God *damn* the Clinton administration.

"Very good!" Ali Hamedi said as the couple walked away. The Midwesterners looked as if they didn't care much for Islamics.

Good for them. Neither did "Ali Hamedi."

"What is this place?" Britney asked as the white Lynx settled onto the helipad.

"Islamorada Harbor," Mike said, nostalgically. Things had been . . . simpler once upon a time.

The harbor was tucked inland about a quarter mile from the water, the only access a half natural, half man-made cut. For Mike, it was one definition of home.

"Thanks, Kacey," Mike said over the intercom. "You good on the way home?"

"We'll have to tank again," Kacey replied. They'd had to stop in Bimini as it was. "And again on the way back. No externals on *this* bird. But we're good."

Mike waved and climbed out of the helicopter, followed by Britney. The weather was still cool so they were both wearing windbreakers and jeans. Mike's had a snarling tiger face on the breast pocket and the name "Kildar" embroidered on the back over a much larger embroidered tiger.

So somebody was after him. That was just fine by Mike. Next time let them shoot the right target.

He made his way to the marina's offices, sniffing the air. It was a good day to go fishing; the recently passed cold front would bring the fish up a treat. And it was perfect sailfish conditions. Unfortunately, he just didn't have the fucking time.

He opened up the door to the grimy interior and grinned. "Hey, Sol."

"Mike!" the man said, standing up and coming around the corner. He shook Mike's hand, then gave him a bear hug. "Man, where you been?"

"You wouldn't believe me if I told you," Mike said.

"You disappear and then some DEA guys bring your boat back," Shatalin said, shaking his head. Sol Shatalin was a short-coupled, barrel-chested man, a former Navy bosun who had a part interest in the marina. The money was a guy in Michigan who'd made his fortune in bio-tech, then settled back to enjoy it. Part of that was buying a marina, partially because they were pretty good moneymakers but more so that he had an in on the Florida boat and fishing trade.

Sol ran the place, working his ass off most of the time but loving every minute of it. However, he'd worried about his friend, the former SEAL who had disappeared.

"Christ, they actually used *DEA*?" Mike said, shaking his head. "Great."

"Oh, they didn't wear the jacket or anything," Sol said. "But after you've been down here for a while you know. They were dressed like gang-bangers, you know? But they were . . . too straight. And bangers wouldn't be returning your boat; they'd be selling it."

"Captain Don's been running it, though?" Mike asked.

"Yeah," Sol said, shrugging. "Keeps it in good shape."

"Don's a good man," Mike said. "But I'm here about the *Late*."

"Tied up on D-43," Sol said. "Don's used that for a few charters, too. I've made sure it's up. Just put in a new fuel injection system, bottom's recently painted. You got the bill."

"I'm sure," Mike said, smiling. "I spend most of my time lately signing checks."

"Hey, where were you for that nuke that went off?" Sol asked. "You remember, about a week or so after you left? And where'd those two chicks with you go?"

"Uh, they caught a ride home," Mike said. "You know boat bunnies. And I was . . . Hell, Abacos I think. Yeah. Abacos. That day. I got the news a few days later in Nassau."

"Okay," Sol said, nodding slowly. "Just asking. 'Cause, you know the newsies. They get everything wrong. There was one news report said that the FAST that was supposed to have been the ones that found it got there . . . too late. That it was actually a one-man operation, a CIA agent. And the fucking terrorists were using cigarettes. Then, well, there's this cigarette turns up, two more DEA guys, by the way, say that it belongs to my old SEAL buddy. And guess what its name is? *Too Late*."

"Coincidences are hell, aren't they?" Mike said. "But unfortunately, we've got a date to make."

"We?" Sol asked, looking out the window. "Another hottie. You go, dude."

"Britney," Mike said, walking outside. "This is Sol Shatalin. Great guy. Sol, Britney Harder."

Shatalin didn't comment on the name, he just nodded.

"Army?" he asked.

"I was," Britney said, shrugging. "Just got out. Shows, huh?"

"Right, pull the other one," Shatalin said, shaking his head. "MP or intel?"

"Intel," Britney said, frowning.

Mike shrugged. "Sol's got an eye."

"Sollie's got eyes, Sollie's got ears, Sollie ain't got a mouth," Shatalin said, smiling. "I think Sollie's even got a current TS, for that matter. Not that I give a shit down here. People want to run drugs, that's their business."

"A lot of people *die* because of those drugs," Britney said, her face tight. "Not just cops and gang-bangers and innocents on the streets, here, but innocents in Colombia and Venezuela and all over South America. And American troops I might add."

"Then legalize them," Sol said, shrugging. "We've got enough problems as it is. In case you've got your nose stuck too far into the drug trade . . . *Ensign*."

"Army, Sol, Army," Mike chided.

"Sorry. Lieutenant," Sol said. "I thought you didn't give a rat about drugs, either, Mike. Shame on you."

"Inside," Mike said, gesturing with his chin.

"Okay, Sol, what do you hear?" Mike said. "Because, you're right, I don't. War on Drugs is stupid. Prohibition proved that. But this isn't drugs. So . . . What do you hear?"

Sol went behind the counter and picked up the stub of a stogie and lit it slowly.

"What is it?" Sol asked when the foul thing was finally smoking up the room.

"That's not for dissemination," Britney snapped.

"Fuck you, LT," Sol said, looking at Mike.

"Sol, first, Britney's not a meat," Mike said. "Yeah, she's an LT. A cherry LT. But I knew her . . . *Way* back, Sollie, way back. I covered her back, she covered mine. So treat her with respect. And the answer is more fucking WMD. What type is *not* for dissemination. And, yeah, the Andros job? That was a one-man operation. Want to see the fucking spare assholes?"

The scars from bullet marks make a puckered spot on the skin. They look very much like a small anus.

"You sure about this?" Sol asked through the cloud of smoke.

"Very," Mike said. "We don't know how it's coming in. But we're *very* sure."

"New boats," Sol said. "Up in Tavernier Creek. Two of them. Scarabs. The kicker is . . . Well, usually when you see Middle Eastern types with those, it's a Saudi prince or something. They've got a captain, in other words. What the fuck do most Ay-rabs know about fishing? These are a few guys staying at the Hampton Inn. Bought the boats from Hanson's up in Largo. Cash. They only go out at night. Say that they like sword-fishing. Never have much luck, though. Like . . . none."

"What's a Scarab?" Britney asked. "Sorry."

"Big two- or three-engine fast fishing boat." Mike shook his head. "You don't use a Scarab for night sword-fishing. They're run and gun boats. They rock like a son of a bitch, there's no amenities . . . If you've got that kind of money you get a yacht like mine. If you don't . . . Hell, you get an *older* one or a supply boat. Something with a stand-up head, a galley, bunks."

"Tell me something I don't know," Sol said, setting down the stogie. "And that's all I've got. And you didn't hear it from me."

"Never," Mike said. "But thanks. I guess I better go get the *Late*. See you 'round, Sol."

"You too," Sol said, pulling out a set of keys and handing them to Mike. "And keep your head down. You SEALs never learned the Navy rule about firefights."

Britney followed Mike down through the docks until they got to the boat, then shook her head.

"How long has this just been sitting here?" she asked.

The *Too Late* was a recent model Cigarette. Although "Cigarette" had become so generic that, like Kleenex, it was used as a general term, it was also a brand. And in the case of the *Too Late* it was actually a Cigarette as opposed to one of the company's many competitors. At only thirty-two feet long it was smaller than some of the newer speed boats but it was still a monster. Painted black and silver, it looked as if it was straining away from the dock, ready to *run*.

Most high-performance vehicles had their origins in smuggling: NASCAR was derived from bootleggers, and WWII PT boats were built by a company that had supplied booze smugglers during Prohibition. Cigarette boats were no exception. In the late 1940s the taxes on cigarettes, the things people smoked, were so extreme in Europe that it made it economically feasible to smuggle them. Fast boats crossed the Mediterranean from Algeria and Malta, dropping cigarette loads mostly on the Italian and French coast. Later, similar boats were used for the increasingly popular sport of offshore racing. But their origins remained in a moderate sized cabin forward. Originally designed for small, valuable cargo, in most modern boats it had been converted into underway quarters ranging from spartan to, in the case of Fountain high-speed boats, almost ridiculously luxurious.

"It hasn't *just* been sitting," Mike said, stepping off the dock onto the gunnel, then taking off his shoes. "A friend charters it sometimes. Shoes off when you board."

"Why?" Britney asked, but she took her running shoes off, holding them in her hands as she boarded.

"They track up the deck," Mike said, pointing to the spotless white interior. "Don Jackson's a captain down here. Used to be in the tobacco trade, still dabbles in it. He's got two or three boats himself but he also knows all the local captains. A lot of good guys don't have the money for a boat. So he sort of brokers a group of them with guys who don't use their boats all the time. Like, for example, me. He manages the upkeep, sets up charters and banks the money. Some of it goes to keeping up the boat. I think I'm actually in the hole on the deal, but you'd have to ask my accountant. Hell, I *could* be making money."

Mike got the lines untied, the door to the front cabin unlocked and started the Cigarette, backing it out of the slot and turning to make his way out of the maze of the harbor. His previous slots, C-19 and C-20, had been right by the turning pool that led to the cut. D-43 was *way* back.

He had lost some of his skills but he kept the first rule of close-approach navigation in mind; there is no such thing as *too* slow.

Once out in the turning pool he started turning on electronics. There was no other traffic to worry about so he could handle the distraction. There was quite a bit of it. Don had upgraded the GPS and autopilot with a new, fully integrated system that put all the sensors, GPS, radar, three-D depthfinder, even satellite weather on a single display. The old one had been pretty good so Mike was looking forward to trying out this one.

Three-D depthfinder, trim tabs, oil and fuel pressure: Mike ran through the whole checklist. He had to stop to make the turns out of the cut and watch for other traffic. There were far too many assholes in the Keys with boats bigger than either their dicks or brains. He'd nearly been run down several times by cigs similar to his going like a bat out of hell down narrow cuts, barely making the turns and swinging wide as they did. Bigger boats than dicks or brains.

He was trying to figure out the new GPS, which was cool as shit but also complicated as a motherfucker, when he cleared the cut. He kept the speed down until he hit the edge of the no-wake zone, then cranked it up a tad, getting up on plane and swinging into the channel that led out past the reef.

"This is nice," Britney yelled, shucking her windbreaker. The shout was more necessary for the engine noise than the wind; this version of Cigarette's line had a large windscreen and a nice profile that spread that away from the front seats. In fact, it was a tad warm even with the slight chill; with no wind the area was heating up from the bright sun.

Mike pulled his off and opened up a dry box.

"In there," Mike said. "We might need them later."

Once they cleared the first reef Mike punched coordinates to the autonav and dug deeper into the GPS. The two systems were connected but as long as he didn't give commands he was fine checking it out. Finally, he found some of Don's waypoints and tracks. He picked out a better one for crossing the outer reef and then found some for the Bahamas. Don had been taking his little baby far. But, hell, the Bahamas were better fishing and less than an hour away in the Cig.

"Can this thing go all the way back to Nassau?" Britney asked.

"On one tank," Mike said. "It's got extended range tanks. We may tank along the way, just to be safe." He thought about that and shook his head. "Big fast boats have more range than this one, but they're gonna *have* to tank somewhere. I mean, if they're running down from north of the Bahamas to here, dropping something, then . . . I doubt they're going to run right back. Too obvious. They'll swing around, maybe through the Cut. They've got to tank and they've got to drop off their waypoints. They've got to pick up their next track, probably, as well."

"So . . . where?" Britney asked. "And should we be talking about this?"

"Well, the boat hasn't been swept," Mike said. "And my name is affiliated with it." He paused. "Hell, there could be a bomb on board for all I know."

"That's a *great* thing to say right now!" Britney snapped.

"Unlikely," Mike added. "Sol's pretty good in case you hadn't noticed. But, yeah, we should be able to talk fine. There's no way to remote listen on one of these things short of a bug; too much secondaries. Not the engine and stuff; that can be screened out. But the wind going by? That makes it impossible. Anyway, they've got to tank."

Mike pulled up the GPS map, which was on a screen the size of a medium laptop, and pulled up an overview of the Bahamas.

"You've got the north Bahamas up here," Mike said, pointing. "Grand Island. That's where Freeport is. Then you've got this big area of open water, the Providence Channel. But here's the kicker."

"Most of the stuff comes in through the Keys," Britney said, nodding. "Which is south of Providence Channel."

"Right," Mike said, zooming in. "So, we're making one hell of a lot of assumptions, but . . . They have to run south of Bimini. If they're picking up north of the Grands and Abacos, they're going to have to use the Cut. It's the only way across the Banks. Really fucking narrow at the entrance, but easy enough for a speed boat. But . . ."

"Where do they tank?" Britney said. "I've been over this before."

"DEA?" Mike asked.

"Yep," Britney said. "They asked the same questions. Took a month, but they asked them. I figure some of the agents were going as fast as you, but the stuff only gets distributed once somebody high enough is willing to put it out. Otherwise, if it turns out to be stupid, they get egg on their face."

"I can give a shit about egg," Mike said, pointing to the Cut. "What's their answer?"

"Different situation," Britney said. "The boats are going the opposite direction. They're coming up from the south, they're not sure where they're getting the drugs as I said, then swinging into Providence and tanking in Nassau or one of the harbors in the Andros area. Then south again. They get in the islands and disappear as a hard track. Then they appear again. DEA is sniffing around for their drop points. They figure that the drugs and the waypoints never cross paths, too."

"Yeah," Mike said. "The tracks might, but not the waypoints."

They crossed over the outer reef and the waves started to chop up, the big rollers from offshore peaking into near breakers as they crossed the reef. Mike gestured at Britney's seatbelt pointedly.

"You're going to want to put that on," he said, reaching down and sliding the four-point restraint on. It was much like a military helicopter's straps so Britney had no problems.

Then he kicked it.

The boat rose nose up for a moment, then settled back down, hit the first wave and went momentarily airborne, the engine screaming. Mike didn't bother to throttle down, though, since when it hit it stayed mostly down, jumping from wave-crest to wave-crest in a continuous series, the props rarely leaving the water.

"Where were we?" he yelled over the engine noise.

"Tracks and waypoints," Britney yelled back.

Mike keyed in the opening to the Bahamas Banks Cut and leaned back in his seat. The motion was much like the FAST boats he'd ridden in as a SEAL but the seats were *much* more comfortable. And he wasn't wearing a hundred pounds of gear. The day was clear and the sun was warm. He'd made sure they both put on sunblock before they even boarded the helo so they were good. He checked the estimated time. Fifty-three minutes to the next waypoint. Not too shabby.

"They're going to need another tank point," Mike said, bringing up the measuring system. He created an imaginary track, running a notional boat through the Cut, then having them refuel at Crossing Rocks. He ran them back around the Grand Islands then down the Florida Straits and shook his head. "They have a bunch of range, but not *that* much."

"So where?" Britney asked.

Mike fiddled with the system, checking ranges from various fuel points.

"Nothing," Mike said. "Unless they're tanking at Bimini just before their speed run."

"No way in hell," Britney said. "Bimini's DEA central. One boat and crew, once, maybe. Over and over? It's a *small* harbor. And they'd have the materials already onboard. All it takes is the most cursory customs check."

"Yeah," Mike said, nodding. "That's the kicker. Once they've picked up or are even *near* their pickup, they're not going to hit land to tank. Unrep."

"Okay, that one's got me," Britney admitted. "What is . . ."

"Underway replenishment," Mike said. "They're tanking from *somebody* at sea. Probably a bigger ship to the north of the Grands. That's if we're not *totally* off base."

"But you don't think we are," Britney said.

"No, I don't," Mike replied. "And I don't think they're tanking in the Abacos. Or picking up their tracks, either."

"Where then?" Britney said.

"Nassau," Mike replied. "It's not that far out of their way. There's range for them to stop there then make a speed run up to the tanker up north. From there they go to pick up the materials. Then they do another speed run down south, drop the materials, come back through the Cut and head back down to Nassau."

"Why Nassau?"

"Katya's there," Mike said. "And if she's there, Jay's not far away."

"Who's Jay?"

"Who knows?" Mike said, grinning. "He's a freelance humint guy I hired. A spy in other words. Former CIA, got riffed during the Clinton administration. Very good. He's been training Katya. If he's sniffing around Gonzales, he has a reason. And Nassau's big. Offshore speed boats come and go all the time. There are lots of ways to do a drop there that would just disappear in the noise. You can't say the same about the Abacos; those towns are all tiny. They could be picking them up at a rendezvous at sea but even then. No, Nassau makes too much sense. Maybe *too* much sense but that's what my gut is telling me."

"Is that why you chose it?" Britney asked.

"No," Mike admitted. "I chose it because it was central in the Bahamas and there was a really fucking big yacht for rent. I needed a really fucking big yacht."

"Why?" Britney asked, chuckling.

"Because I've got nearly two hundred people packed in it belowdecks," Mike said. "Getting them all there, quietly, was hell. They flew in through Miami, then out to every damned airport in the Bahamas. Most of them came in through Nassau but others came in through everywhere from Andros to Freeport. Then we went out where we were reasonably out of sight and the Lynx went out to pick them up. That, by the way, was while I was getting established. Getting their gear in place is even harder. Most of it isn't here, yet."

"That was a big movement," Britney said, her eyes wide.

"Yep," Mike said. "And we did it in less than twenty hours from the go word. I've got good people."

"Like Gretchen?" Britney asked.

Mike hit the throttle and dropped the boat to a sudden stop, water splashing up over the bow as it slammed into a wave.

"Who the fuck told you about Gretchen?" Mike snarled.

"Friends of yours," Britney said. "People who care about you."

"If they care about me, they need to get their God-damned nose out of my private business," Mike snapped. "*Jesus*, I'm sick of this. I live under a fuck-ing *microscope*."

"For living under a microscope, you don't talk about things much," Britney said. "Not important things."

"I talk about important things all the time," Mike replied, starting the boat back up. But he kept the speed down to idle. "Stopping a shipment of VX is very God-damned important."

"Yeah, but not about things that hurt you," Britney said. "Big boys don't cry, do they?"

"You'd be surprised," Mike said, his jaw flexing. "And who the hell am I going to talk to about it? Anastasia? Adams? Nielson? One of the damned harem girls?"

"The commander can't show his weakness," Britney said, nodding. "But from what I heard, he showed his ass instead."

"Yes, he did," Mike admitted. "But he's over it, thank you."

"Bullshit," Britney snapped. "I'm not 'over' Syria. I live with it every damned night. It's not as bad as it was, but it's still pretty damned bad. Not the bodies, not scavenging the ammo, not turning the fuckers over to pull the grenades off their belts. No, I just sit in that damned chair and one of them comes over, key in hand. I'm next."

"I can believe it," Mike said, looking over at her.

"I've had hours and hours of counseling," Britney said, undoing the straps and turning on the seat. "I took your advice. Now take mine. Talk. Now. Here. Talk to me, Bambi. Start at the beginning. Go to the end. Don't leave anything out."

Mike undid his own straps and went below. The ice machine was working and the small bar was, per his orders, stocked. He pulled out an untouched bottle of Elijah Craig, filled two glasses with ice and went back up on deck.

"Here," he said, pouring two drinks and handing Britney one.

"I'm not a straight whiskey drinker," Britney said.

"I quit drinking alone three days ago," Mike said, raising his glass. "Salut."

"Blood in your eye," Britney said, sipping the whiskey. "This is good. Smooth."

"Yes, it is," Mike said, taking a large gulp. "I've got twenty-three empty bottles to prove how smooth." He looked at the glass, then sighed. "Gretchen."

It took a while, about half the bottle.

"I wasn't there," Mike finished. He'd refilled his glass with ice twice and now the second reload was about gone. "I didn't see it. I couldn't do anything about it. But I had to look under the God-damned sheet. I had to see her one more time. She'd been cut in fucking half. Her spine was sticking out. Ribs. I remember thinking 'that's a spleen, right?'" He closed his eyes, his jaw working, and shook his head.

"She was just a Kardane girl," Mike said, grimacing, his eyes tight. "Just another duty of the fucking Kildar. Be a good stud. Do the mares and go on." He lowered his head and his body shook. "And then she was just fucking *gone*. I'm never going to see her again!"

Britney took the man in her arms and laid his head on her breast, stroking the back of his head as he cried.

"I mean she was going to marry Kiril," Mike said, sobbing. "I *knew* I couldn't have her. She wasn't mine.

She never would be. But she'd be around, you know? I'd *see* her. And then *Kiril* gets wasted. It was all *my* fault! All of it . . ."

"Shhhh," Britney said. "You couldn't have done anything. . . ."

"Bullshit," Mike said, sitting up and turning away. "I was the fucking commander. I'm the God-damned Kildar! It is, de facto, my responsibility. And, what's worse, I *knew* the mission was fucked from the word go. I *knew* we were screwed. We had so many stupid fucking conditions put on us there was no *way* we were just going to ghost out. I should have thrown a shit fit when the Georgians refused us helo support. Let Markov take the fucking casualties! They're fucking mercenaries, that's what they're *there* for! And then the fucking Russians! Oh, did you hear about that *BASTARD*, Chechnik?"

"No," Britney said to the clearly enraged former SEAL.

"They knew," Mike said, snarling. "I can't prove it but they *had* to fucking know. If it had just been Bukara, well, that would have been one thing. We could have smoked him then smoked the defenses in the pass, somehow. Do what the girls did and bring up the mortars. Something. But *Sadim*? He was their fucking varsity! Nielson *told* the Russians we were picking up signals that looked like a moving unit. The Russians are *masters* of humint. There was no *fucking* way that they couldn't know Sadim was moving! That he was moving into the sector where the op was going down. Nielson and the girls had the intel way in advance, but they didn't know who was moving. They didn't know it was a fucking *brigade*. They

didn't know it was Sadim! *That* was what fucked us.
If I *ever* see Chechnik again, the motherfucker, I'm
going to sit him on a short stake and eat my lunch
in front of him! And fucking Vladimir had better
watch out, too."

"I don't get it," Britney said, blanching at the very
direct threat to the president of Russia. "Why didn't
they tell you?"

"Because then I'd have aborted the op," Mike said,
his face hard. "We had *ghosted* into deepest darkest
Injun country. The intel was building when we were
still in movement, we hadn't launched the op. We
could've aborted and ghosted *out*. But that meant
somebody else would have had to stop the . . . package.
And we had a deal. I did the mission, I didn't tell
the U.S. what the package was. If ANV or Delta did
an op in, say, Azerbaijan, then the U.S. would know
what the deal was. They'd know what the Russians had
really lost. They wanted me to stop the transfer even
if it meant hanging us out to dry. Maybe *especially* if
it meant I got smoked. Dead men tell no tales. The
motherfuckers."

"What was the package?" Britney asked. "Shit, that's
well above my clearance. . . . Forget I asked."

"It's okay," Mike said, taking another sip. "I'm not
going to tell you anyway. Funny. They go and royally
butt-fuck us and I'm still holding up my end of the
fucking deal. Go figure."

"You're a good man," Britney said. "And I think I
really don't want to know."

"I'm a very *bad* man," Mike said. "I will tell you
this, though. Feel free to pass it on to anyone you can
who has National Security Counsel clearance. Please

fucking feel free to pass it on. The Russians told the U.S. it was nukes. Three of them. That was what I was getting paid to recover. Three nukes."

"That's serious enough," Britney said, her eyes wide.

"Nothing compared to the real package," Mike said, his jaw working. "The real package was Armageddon on a fucking platter. But here's the kicker. I told the fucking Russians if I was going to keep their secret I wanted the deal sweetened. Four nukes. Five mil apiece was the vig. Twenty if I recovered all three. Hell, I turn up with four, that's another five, minimum, right? Enough to keep my mouth shut."

"Yes," Britney said, shaking her head. "That must have been an interesting negotiation."

"If I'd known they were going to fuck me as hard as they did, I'd have either told them to piss up a rope or told them *ten*," Mike said. "Then I'd have sent them back, VPP. But here's the real kicker. Guess how many I gave the U.S.?"

"Huh?" Britney said then her eyes widened. "Oh . . . shit."

"Three," Mike confirmed. "Hey, that was all they were expecting."

"You have a nuclear *weapon* in your possession?" Britney said carefully.

"Yep," Mike said. "About ten kilotons. In the basement of my castle. Partially disassembled I might add, thanks to the WMD expert I picked up on the same op. Something about retaining the quality of the tritium. But it can be assembled in about three minutes. And one of these days, *oh* let that day be soon, I'm going to take it and shove it up Vladimir's *ass*, then blow the son-of-a-bitch."

"I *so* didn't want to know any of this," Britney said, shaking her head. "I'm not even sure who I can tell."

"I can put you on the phone to the President if you'd like," Mike said, putting the boat back up on plane. "And you'd be surprised the shit you don't want to know about what's in the basement of my castle. Belts."

"We were talking about Gretchen," Britney said, strapping in.

"Yeah, we were," Mike said, powering up. "And now we're not. Thanks, though. I appreciate it."

"We're not done," Britney said as the boat started hopping waves again.

"No, we're not," Mike admitted. "And, yeah, we'll talk again. But it was a good start." He tossed the remains of his drink over the side and looked over at her. "Think you can survive making it down to the cabin and getting me a Coke?"

"Can I ask you one thing first," Britney said, undoing the straps while bracing herself.

"What?"

"What *is* the Navy's first rule about a fire fight?"

"Send the Marines."

CHAPTER
SEVEN

"Who now?" Jason O'Connor asked. "The Marines?"

O'Connor was the desk manager of the Hollywood Florida Central Governmental Surplus Repository. Run by the Marshals Service, it was the place where everything the United States government seized in its ongoing war on drugs was dumped for eventual resale. Stuff seized by the IRS, despite the "Central Government" part, was sold through another agency.

The law under which the government seized most materials was incredibly archaic, going back to the middle ages. Effectively, the condition of forfeiture meant that when a crime was committed involving a device, vehicle or even home, that device, vehicle or home was considered an accomplice in the crime. And being an inanimate object, it had none of the "rights" of an individual. It was assumed to be guilty.

Thus when a person was pulled over and drugs were found in his car, the person would be arraigned, have hearings and in some cases eventually be tried if there was sufficient evidence and if the DA was feeling lucky.

The poor car had no such rights. Oh, if the owner contested it was given a trial, but no peers! And if the owner didn't contest, usually because they were guilty as hell, the poor thing was sent directly to the Hollywood Florida Central Governmental Surplus Repository where it languished behind chain-link fence and barbed wire until some individual bought it at auction and freed it from durance vile.

Quite often that person was a friend or relation of the original drug dealer, who then transferred the title back. This was especially common with boats, some of which had been "incarcerated" four or five times for the exact same offense, the definition of recidivist. Alas, there was no three strikes law for boats.

Jason was having a bad day. Apparently, every government service in the nation was descending on South Florida for reasons he didn't know and, frankly, couldn't care less about. And they all wanted vehicles. Since the HCGSR had lots of vehicles, of every shape, model and description, and since the U.S. government already owned them, it was a natural source. Cars had been rolling off the lot all day. Not only did every one mean more paperwork, he *knew* they were going to be returned in poor to awful condition. Virtually unsellable. Cops *never* took care of their cars. Fibbies were the worst. No, *DEA* was the worst; what DEA did to a car shouldn't happen to a junkyard dog.

But this guy wasn't BU or DEA. No suit in the first case, no jeans and dreadlocks in the latter. He *might* be BATF. Some of the BATF guys had that military look. And *those* cars . . . Jesus.

"*What?*" Jason snapped.

"You have five offshore power boats," the man said in strongly accented English. He handed over a distribution form. "The Kildar wishes them."

"And what the *fuck* is a Kildar?" Jason asked, sitting on his stool and looking at the form. All the blanks were filled in but none of them made sense. He'd never seen the authorization code and the security code was . . . He turned to his computer and made his way through the menus, hunting up the code list. The authorization code was through SOCOM, which he'd sort of guessed. He'd seen one like it before. But the security code . . . The issuing office was listed as "Need-To-Know." Fucking black ops. It was a valid code but it just pissed him off. The five boats were the best thing he had in the yard. They were going up for auction, one at a time, over the next month and were going to mean *real* money to the U.S. government. Money that was going to buy new gear for cops for one thing. The *fuck* if he was just going to let them disappear into a black ops hole. Fuck *them*. He had authority to deny requisitions and he was God damned well going to use it.

And the guy was just too fucking pretty. He looked like a fucking movie star. That was what really tipped the scales. It just pissed the overworked, in his opinion, desk manager off.

"No," Jason said, handing back the form.

"This is the proper paperwork, yes?" the man asked, blinking.

"That is the proper paperwork," Jason replied. "But I've got authority to deny those. So . . . No. Goodbye."

▲   ▲   ▲

Vil considered the little man for a moment. He was puzzled. He was fully aware that most people outside of Georgia did not know who the Kildar was. That, in fact, the Kildar would prefer to keep it that way.

But he also knew, because the Kildar had told him, that the authorization was at a very high level. He should, by rights, have been terribly obsequious, perhaps not even asking for a bribe. The Kildar had told him the man would not ask for a bribe and that Vil should not offer, that that would cause problems. But there *were* problems.

"I would like to make a call," Vil said, pulling out a cell phone.

"Fine," Jason said. "Call whoever you'd like. The answer is still no."

The guy was still looking confused. He had a weird accent, maybe German or something. Maybe he would have understood "*Nyet*" or "*Non*" or whatever. Let him call whoever he wanted. SOCOM might think it was hot shit but it pulled *no* weight with the U.S. Marshals Service!

"Pierson."

"Colonel Pierson, this is Vil Mahona. I am one of the Kildar's—"

The guy was talking Russian so Pierson responded in the same language.

"Team leaders," Pierson said. "You're on an open line, Vil."

"Yes, sir. I apologize for that. Sir, I am having a difficulty. I have been tasked to obtain five vessels for the

Kildar's use from a facility in the town of Hollywood, Florida. You are familiar with this facility, yes?"

"I am familiar, no," Pierson said, smiling. "But I can figure it out. Go on."

"The desk manager has refused my request," Vil said. "The Kildar has assured me that I have proper paperwork and the man even admitted that to me. But he still refuses. I am wondering if I should offer him bribe?"

"No," Pierson said definitely. "Don't. Don't ever offer an American official, police or soldier a bribe. That's like . . . That's like saying a Keldara is a coward. Let me speak to him."

Now the guy was babbling in a foreign language. What the fuck were foreigners doing asking for *his* boats?

The guy finally stopped and held out his phone.

"This is colonel," the man said. "He is wishing to speak to you."

"I've got a *billion* other things to be doing," O'Connor said, but he took the phone. "*What?*"

"It's customary to state your name when you answer a phone," whoever was on the line snapped. "I just want to get this straight. You were presented with a requisition. Was all the information you normally require present?"

"Yeah," O'Connor said. "But I don't know who this fucker is, I don't know who you are and I've got authority to deny and I'm invoking it. So you can go revolve on your little stool as far as I care, *Colonel*."

"You're Marshals Service, right?"

"Yeah. We're not fucking Army, we're not fucking Marines, and we're not *your* God-damned boat dealer."

"Just checking," the man said. "Give the phone back."

"Vil," Pierson said. "Where are you?"

"The Hollywood Florida Central Governmental Surplus Repository," Vil said, reading it off the form.

"Just as a matter of interest, what are the authorization code and security code on the form?"

Vil read them off and got a read back.

"The security level on that is *Ultra Blue*?" Pierson said. "For real?"

"Yes, sir," Vil replied.

"And he kicked it back?" Pierson snapped. "Is he fucking insane?"

"You come to my understanding of the situation," Vil said, sighing in relief. "I feared it was me or that I did not understand."

"Oh, I *so* have some calls to make."

"You still here?" Jason asked.

"I am, sir," Vil said, closing the phone. "I shall be for a time, yes."

"Then wait outside," O'Connor said, gesturing with his chin. "I've got paperwork to do."

"Yes, I will," Vil said, picking up the form.

"We are getting the boats?" Sergejus Shaynav asked.

"There is a problem," Vil said. "I have presented it to Colonel Pierson. If it is not to be resolved, he will call us back."

"I have never driven a boat," Viatcheslav Devlich said, nervously. "I can barely swim."

"We are the Keldara," Vil said. "McKenzie has told

me the words to the Song of Remembrance talk of the days when we were feared warriors in boats. The Vikings, yes? We'll figure it out. How hard can it be?"

"How long do we wait?" Viatcheslav asked.

"Until dark," Vil said. "Then we call the Kildar for further instructions."

However, it was barely thirty minutes until a government sedan pulled into the yard and a tall man wearing a Marshals Service windbreaker got out. Unlike the man in the office, the newcomer was wearing a gun and badge on his belt although he was in civilian clothes.

"Which one's Vil?" the man asked, walking up to the group.

"I am," Vil replied.

"Gimme a minute," the man said with a sigh.

Jason sat up and tried to look busy as the regional supervisor walked in the room.

"Sir, it's good to see you!"

"No, it's not," the RS said. "Pack up your personal stuff and go home. You're on unpaid administrative leave pending termination."

"What?" Jason said, his face going gray. He felt like he was going to faint. He *was* going to faint.

"You are too fucking stupid for words, do you know that?" the RS said, angrily. "Did you look up that guy's security classification? I won't even get *into* the authorization."

"Yes, sir," O'Connor said, suddenly realizing how truly he had screwed up. "But it was listed as Need-To-Know."

"Well, keep in mind that if you whisper this in your

next job, you've got a one way ticket to Marion, Illinois," the RS said angrily. "But an Ultra Blue security classification can *only* be issued by the National Security Council. And since you're too *stupid* to probably know what that is, let me make it clear. They were authorized to draw on your equipment by either the President, the Vice President, the national security advisor or the secretary of Defense. The *good* news is that it only got up to the level of the commandant who called *me*. So the President has not heard about our little *fuckup*. But *I've* now got to explain to the commandant why I had a shit for brains like *you* working this desk."

"All Father," Vil whispered, looking at the boats.

Each of them was different. Two had two hulls, the others just one. But all were in a series of wild colors and just looked *fast*. He suddenly knew how Captain Bathlick must feel when she looked at the Dragon. But the captain, he reminded himself, was a highly trained professional. He had no clue how to even *start* one of these.

"We got one Fountain, a Nordic, a Cigarette, a Drone and a Hustler," the regional supervisor said. He didn't know who these guys were, but they had White House clearance so he was going to handle them with kid gloves. "You've driven one before, right?"

"No," Vil said, shaking his head. "But we are to pick up instructors on the way. We must get them from here to there, though."

"*Ever* driven a boat before?" the RS asked cautiously.

"Never," Vil replied. "I grow up in mountains."

"O-kay," the RS said. "In that case, take it *slow*. There's no such thing as too slow. They're all gassed, but I can't guarantee performance. We sell these things as is. They all worked when they got here and none of them have been tied up long."

"We will be careful," Vil said. "I can assure that."

The RS gave each of the two-man teams a short class in how to handle the boats, then helped them untie and get pulled out. Two of them collided, briefly and lightly, getting pulled out. Then he made sure the gate was open as the line of boats slowly motored out towards the intercoastal waterway.

He wasn't sure where they were going but he hoped that nobody got in their way.

"We will go very slow," Vil said. He'd donned the standard team headset as had the other drivers. "Very very *slow*."

"Where are we going?" Clarn Ferani asked.

"A bar," Vil said.

Randy Holterman sat at the Caribbean Sports Bar and Grill and considered whether he was making one fucking huge mistake.

The former PO had been a FAST boat driver with the Norfolk Underwater Support Group up until about a year before. The reality was that while FAST was the shit, the guys they were supposed to support, SEALs and very rarely Delta, hardly ever used them anymore. Most of the ops that Norfolk supported were in Europe and Africa. And nobody had used a FAST in operations in a couple of years.

So when his reenlistment date came up he got out and turned his car south for Florida.

His rep as a former FAST driver had gotten him

a gig as a mate on a dive boat which gave him time to get his civilian captain's license. The combination had him doing gigs as a part-time captain, filling in for guys who had been around for a while. He'd figured out the deal; you worked your way up in the local community, you learned the fishing waters and eventually made enough to get a boat. Maybe you got picked up by some guy with money who had the sense to know he needed a captain. You networked. You built customers. In the meantime, you got a lot of water time, which was the name of the game.

Randy was an easy-going guy and he got along with the customers so he was doing well there. But he was a long way from his own boat. Not a good one. He wanted either a good solid yacht or a fast fisher. And that was serious money. You had to show you had a business before you could get the financing on one. Randy figured five years.

Then he got a call.

"Captain Randy. The fish are here, where are you?"

"Randall Holterman?" the woman had asked. Foreign accent, Slavic probably.

"That's me," he said, trying to figure out which payment he was behind on.

"Mr. Holterman, my employer would like to retain your services for up to two weeks. Are you available?"

"I don't know," Randy said, thinking about his schedule. He had *lots* of things going on over the next two weeks; you stayed busy or you got poor quick. But nothing he couldn't slide to somebody else if the money was right. "That would depend upon the nature of the job and the price. If he wants to go fishing for a couple of weeks . . ."

"That is not the nature of the job," the woman had said. "He has some employees who need training in handling small boats. Fast boats."

Randy's alarm bells started ringing hard at that. There was only one group in South Florida that had multiple fast boats and people that needed to learn how to use them. Racing teams, well, they didn't need trainers. And nobody had multiple boats *and* needed a trainer except druggies. Randy didn't really give a shit about the running, but he also didn't want to end up with a Colombian necktie, also known as having your throat cut and your tongue dragged out of the hole to hang down in front.

"Not interested," he said.

"I suspect you think we are drug runners," the girl had said. "Very far from the case, Petty Officer. We obtained your name from your service record, not from 'the street' as you would say. The vig, as my employer would put it, is twenty thousand dollars. It can be in cash if you so desire. Oh, and at the completion of our stay here, one of the boats is yours."

"What kind of boats?" Randy asked.

"I do not know," the girl said. "I am only told they are very fast 'cigarette' type boats."

"Jesus," Randy said. Anything along the lines would set her "employer" back a hundred and fifty, two hundred big ones. The pay was peanuts compared to getting a boat like that as a fucking *tip*. "You're *sure* you're not drug runners?"

"Quite," the girl said, chuckling. "We are in, as you say, the *other* war."

Randy frowned at that and then nodded.

"Which side?" he asked. There *had* to be a catch.

"The side of the angels, Petty Officer," the girl said placatingly. "Truly, we need your expertise. Are you in?"

I'm going to regret this.

"I'm in."

So here he was, eating a cheeseburger and nursing an overpriced but *really* fucking good Mountain Tiger beer while watching the sun slowly sinking towards the yard arm. Two o'clock in other words. Whatever you could say about the gig, whoever these fuckers were, sitting on a dock, eating a burger, beer in hand, watching the intercoastal on a balmy day in a Florida winter, well, that weren't bad.

He didn't know who, exactly, he was meeting. Not even any names. No names at all, in fact. All he'd been told was that there would be five boats, "fast boats." Five turning up all at once, well, he'd be able to figure out who that was.

And sure enough, here they came, motoring along in a straggling line and *really* slow. Not even idling. Lug speed, that spot where a boat still wasn't planing but it was digging up one monster wake, nose pointed at the sky. It was just . . . *ugly*.

But, Oh, My, God, the *boats*! A couple of them were in rough shape, one was a Cig 36 circa '99 if he was right, and the Nordic had seen better days. But the lead was a practically *mint* fucking Fountain Lightning 42! He'd nearly fainted when he saw one at a show; the fucker *smoked*. Reggie Fountain made "the fastest, safest boats on the water." Just ask him. Not to mention some of the most luxurious. Forget two hundred bills, the Fountain was closer to three quarter mil and worth every penny. God, if only he got to *choose*. He didn't even care if it had the full racing pack. Fuck selling it, too.

He walked down the dock, beer in hand, then set it down as the drivers tried to dock. They acted like they'd never driven a boat before. No clue about sail area, no clue about dual engines. The guy driving the Hustler powered up when he should have backed and slammed, hard, into the pilings. Ouch. Jesus Christ, they were fucking *cherries*. *Real*, "What's a *throoottle*?" cherries. He could tell. Christ. Oh, this was *so* gonna suck.

"Vil, we suck," Clarn said as he rebounded off the pier. "I think I just broke my boat."

"We have to learn," Vil said. "Remember what the man said, there is no such thing as too slow." Vil was taking him at his word, barely creeping into the slot.

A bit of a crowd had come out of the bar. Fast boats were pretty common in the South Florida area, but five at once was somewhat unusual. As was a group with such bad boat handling skills driving them. Randy seriously didn't want to do the introductions with people wandering around looking at the boats. But that was how it was going to go.

The Fountain was driven by a tall, really handsome guy. Hell, all ten of the group were damned good looking. Randy wasn't a slouch, but these guys were drawing the girls for more than just the boats. The rest stayed in the boats as the guy clambered out. Randy had handled most of the line work with just a toss from the rear from the throttler.

The tall guy walked over and Randy held out his hand.

"Randy Holterman," Randy said.

"Petty Officer," the guy said. In Russian. Shit, somebody *had* been reading his service record. Randy had picked up the language thinking it might be useful. It had turned out to be about as useful as tits on a hog except for picking up the occasional Russian girl that hung around South Florida. "Lieutenant Vil Mahona, Georgian Mountain Infantry."

"Hello, Lieutenant," Randy said. "My Russian is poor now."

"It will come back to you," Vil replied. "Few will be able to understand us, yes? Oh, if asked, we are the Mountain Tiger Racing Team. I am team leader."

Randy bent down and held up the bottle.

"*This* Mountain Tiger?" he asked, wrinkling his brow.

"That Mountain Tiger, yes," Vil said. "We are here to learn to drive fast boat."

"Mountain Tiger *speed-boat* racing team," Randy said in English, shaking his head. "Is that anything like the Jamaican bobsled team?"

"I do not know," Vil answered in Russian. "I do not know what bobsled is. Jamaica . . . is an island in the Caribbean, yes?"

"Yes," Randy said, grinning and shaking his head.

"Well, let us talk," Vil said, turning and waving to the rest of the team. "I see they serve our swill here. Let us find out how bad it is after travel."

CHAPTER
EIGHT

"This is suck," Danes said in English, holding up the bottle. "Is shame upon our name. Is insult to Fera, Goddess of Beer. Is Mother Lenka knowing how bad this is?"

"Yes," Beso said, belching. "Have you not heard her cackling about it?"

"I have," Vil said, shaking his head. "Has been asking me to find reviews on internet. Have not seen her so happy since cutting up Chechens in pass. Is laughing so hard tears are coming out of eyes. Mother Lenka. Laughing." He took a swig and winced. "World is coming to end."

"Guys, this is good shit," Holterman said, taking a sip. He couldn't figure out what they were complaining about. Mountain Tiger was expensive as hell but it was the *shit*. It made the best German beer he'd ever had taste like Budweiser.

"It is swill," Vil said, in Russian. "Fit only for pigs. Our pigs would turn up their noses. When we get to

Bahamas, we will show you what *good* beer tastes like. But that is for later. We are needing to take boats to Nassau. You are coming with, yes?"

"Sure," Randy said. "They said I'd be traveling. I've got a bag. But there's a problem."

"Which is?" Vil asked.

"Well, there's about a thousand," Randy said, shaking his head. "You guys are obviously clueless about boats. Okay, it's my job to make you less clueless. But there's one of me and ten of you. There's five boats. I can only be in one place at a time. That's problem one. Problem two is that all those boats don't have the same range. I didn't look close but they all look stock. Some of them are going to have more gas than others. If you're planning on doing long runs, they're going to need extended range tanks. On the way over we can tank at Bimini. But if you're going to be doing distant running . . . you need more tankage."

"Where can we get those installed?" Vil asked.

"The problem is not *where*," Randy said, shaking his head. "The problem is *when*. The boat yards around here have a month or more backlog."

"Can we do it in the Bahamas?"

"Same problem," Randy said. "They're backed up, too."

"Where can we get this job done, quickly?" Vil asked, sighing. "Think outside the box, yes?"

"Any boat yard that has the parts and the time," Randy said, shrugging. "The parts . . . some of them could be custom manufactured by a boat yard. Others you could order from the manufacturer if they're in stock. But you need people that are capable of doing this stuff with boats. And they're scarce."

"Would your Navy have such?" Vil asked, cocking one eyebrow.

"Well, yeah, up at Little Creek they've got a mobile yard, but . . ." Randy paused and shook his head. "Don't tell me you guys can . . ."

"We will see when we get back to base," Vil said. "Next problem."

"Timing," Randy said, glancing at his watch. "I can't figure out whether you guys are more of a menace in the intercoastal or offshore, but if we're going offshore we need to clear the Bal Harbor cut. Now, you seem like fine people, but Bal Harbor any time but slack tide is a ball-buster. There are standing waves run twenty feet high. If you fuck up with one of these on those waves, you can do a somersault and pancake. You get me?"

"Turn upside down?" Vil said, frowning.

"Exactly," Randy said. "It's easier than it sounds. You have to keep your hand on the throttle, throttling up and back, anyway. You hit a wave, you jerk forward, you push the throttle forward, thing goes from a thousand RPMs to three thousand in an *instant*. You're all of a sudden looking at sky then water then *darkness*. So we need to hit the cut at slack tide. It's about twenty minutes from here if we hurry. Slack tide is in three hours. When slack hits, everybody who's been too terrified to do the cut comes barreling through. So you're going to have to be good enough in two hours and forty minutes to survive the traffic jam. Either that, or we're staying *here* overnight."

"We can do that if necessary but it is not preferred," Vil said. "So we must hurry. Any *other* problems?"

"Oh, loads," Randy said. "But one's really bugging me."

"What?" Vil asked, seriously.

"I got this sinking feeling that not *one* of you knows 'Margaritaville' by heart."

"How much is this one?" Souhi asked, picking up a Garmin GPS from the display.

The kiosk was in the Straw Market in Nassau, an outdoor market that mostly sold woven straw products that were "locally" produced even if many of them had "Made in China" stickers. However, besides the ubiquitous straw hats, donkeys, dolphins and every other conceivable shape, it also featured cheap T-shirt outlets, various souvenirs and, notably, a fair selection of boating gear. This particular shop specialized in navigation systems and had a pretty good selection of new and used on display.

"For you, two hundred," the Pakistani shopkeeper said. "Very good model. State of the art."

"Too much," Souhi said, setting it down. "How about another?"

"This one is less," the Pakistani said, shrugging and pulling out a cheaper model. "Not as nice. For you, since we are friends, one thirty."

"I have a trade," Souhi said, pulling out a similar model and setting it on the counter.

"You want my children to starve," the Pakistani said, picking it up and keying it on. He sorted through the menu, then shrugged, tossing it carelessly on the counter. "I give you twenty dollars in trade. It is old and worn." The device was practically brand new.

"Thirty," Souhi said, picking up the new GPS. "One hundred even."

"Done," the Pakistani replied.

Souhi counted out the money in twenties and handed it over.

"My children will go hungry," the Pakistani said, putting the cash in his box.

"But they will live to see wonderful things," Souhi said, pocketing the new GPS.

"This is wonderful," Katya said, looking around the stateroom.

The sun had set and the gathering had moved indoors. In Katya and Juan's case, *much* farther indoors to his bedroom.

Katya was sitting on the edge of the bed, wearing only a string bikini patterned in the American flag, bouncing up and down and, frankly, jiggling.

"*You* are wonderful," Juan said, somewhat thickly. He'd had quite a few body shots between tits and navel. Also a rather professional lap dance. "Do you know you look *just* like Britney Spears?"

"Before she shaved her head?" Katya asked, grinning. Damned right she knew she looked like the American tramp. She'd slid inserts into the pouches in her cheeks and done her makeup carefully. Juan's weakness for blondes, and that one in particular, was part of his dossier.

"When she was younger," Juan said, sitting down next to her. "You look very much like her." He leaned over and pulled her bikini down. "I have always wanted to be sucked by Britney Spears."

"Then you just make like I'm her, honey," Katya said, whipping off the top and standing up. "I'm your Britney tonight, baby!" She swung the top around and wiggled her hips. "You want Live in Las Vegas or Baby Hit Me?"

"I wish you had a school girl outfit," Juan said, panting as he dropped his pants. "Come here and suck me, you little slut. You know you want to."

"Oh, yeah, baby!" Katya said, dropping to her knees.

The guy was flaccid from being so drunk but she could take care of that. She was also pretty sure that he wouldn't notice the difference between one highly trained professional giving him a blow-job and the sort you usually got from college girls. On the other hand . . . Hey, that meant she *didn't* have to give him a good blow. Excellent.

The position, however, gave her a chance to slip one of the bugs under the bed. As she slowly and somewhat inexpertly fellated him, she slipped one out and placed it. That's two.

"Harder," Juan said, grabbing her hair and pushing. "Faster!"

She kept her suction down but sped up. He wasn't coming *this* way. She wanted him to keep her around, though, so she'd have to figure out *something*.

"My jaw's sore," she said, pulling back. "Lemme get on top."

She pushed him back on the bed and pulled off her bottom, then slid his still slightly flaccid member into place.

"Touch these," she said, bringing his hands up to her breasts as she pumped up and down. "You're fucking Britney now, babe!"

"Sing to me . . ." Juan panted. "I want it all . . ."

Katya started singing one of the vocalist's better

known songs, trying like hell to remember the words. One of the harem girls was a big fan but Katya didn't really care about music. She hummed through most of it. All she could really remember was the chorus because it pissed her off so badly. She'd been smacked around enough in her time.

"I want to fuck your ass off," Juan said, rolling her over. "Little slut!"

Then he hit her. Hard. A solid slap on the face. Katya hadn't been expecting it and it nearly broke her out of cover. Her first response was to sink her fingernails into him and start pumping the bastard full of poison. But that would truly fuck the mission. It took her a moment to figure out the response that some American college girl in the same situation would have. In the meantime, he'd backhanded her as well, cursing the singer all the time.

"Ow!" Katya said, raising her arms. If he'd been a pimp, if she was in her usual cover as a whore, she would have just taken it. But that was the wrong response for her current cover. "Wait! Stop!" she pleaded. Damn, why was she *always* getting *hit*?

"Little ass-shaking *bitch*!" Juan shouted, slapping at her again. "This is what you deserve!"

"Please stop!" Katya whined. She had to dig deep for that act. She hadn't begged since she was . . . She really didn't want to go there.

Finally he came and pulled out almost immediately.

"I like you," Juan said, pulling her up by her hair. "You're going to stick around."

"I just want to leave," Katya said. "Please . . ."

"Just try," the Colombian replied. "You're going to stick around. And you're going to make yourself up just the same way. You're going to be my Britney and I'm going to fuck your ass off. I'm going to fuck your *ass*. And you'd better learn to suck better, too. You'll go when I tell you to. You'll call your parents when I tell you to. And you'll tell them you're having a great time. Or you won't be going home. You got that?" He shoved her back onto the bed, releasing her hair. "Little party sluts like you, they get what they deserve."

"Please," Katya pleaded, tears in her eyes. The fucker was, some of them were real. It was the surprise. Now that she knew what was coming, she'd be able to handle it.

"Yeah, you go on begging," Juan said, pulling on his pants. "Just like that little bitch should beg."

After he'd left, Katya got up and shuffled to the bathroom of the suite, got a towel to control the drips and went back to the bed. She lay down on her side, still sniffling although tears were, finally, fake, and fumed.

This motherfucker was purely going to *die*. But first she was going to fuck him over. Big time. And before he died she'd make sure he knew it. *Just* before he died.

"Hello, Gloria, is Daria, how are you?"

Gloria Chatham shook her head. They'd just done a charter for the Kildar. Two big planes. Now Daria was calling again.

"Hello, Daria," Gloria said. "I'm fine. How are you?"

"Very well," Daria said. "I am in Bahamas. You know Bahamas?"

"I do," Gloria said. "I wish *I* was in the Bahamas."

"Well, perhaps you can get time off, come down with plane," Daria said. "Kildar is needing Gulfstream. Two weeks at minimum. May be longer. Two crews. You have?"

"I do," Gloria said. "Captain Hardesty is on another charter at the moment, but . . ."

"Perhaps send crew and half," Daria said. "Have Captain Hardesty come down later. We will pay plane fare and that. Have quarters ready. Nassau Airport, yes?"

"We can do that," Gloria said. "I'll send two crews and when John gets free he can come down and relieve one of the pilots."

"Very good," Daria said. "We pay for both ways, of course. Usual fees?"

"I don't know," Gloria said. "Are we going to get our plane back?"

"If you do not, Kildar will buy," Daria said, obviously grinning. "But, yes, you get plane back. Is not problem this time. Promise."

"I'll get the plane rolling within the hour," Gloria said. After she hung up the phone she raised her voice. "Thooomas!"

"Yes, dear?"

"Mr. Jenkins again," she called. "Needs a Gulfstream in Nassau. Wants John when he can catch up. Tickets paid both ways and so forth."

"Then send them first class," her husband called back, somewhat angrily. "I swear, that man . . . I don't think we should take *any* more charters from him!"

"The pilots love it and you know it," Gloria said, getting up and walking to the door of her husband's office. "James Bond and all that. Mister Super-Spy."

"The man's a menace," Thomas Chatham said. "One of these days we're going to lose a plane and a couple of pilots, mark my words."

"There's a reason you only hire fighter pilots, dear," Gloria pointed out. "And they do get so tired of ferrying Mister 'I made my money in stocks and bought a trophy wife' around. Besides, it's the Bahamas. I'd like to take off for the Bahamas myself."

"Who'd tend the shop?" Thomas asked, waving his hands around.

"Maria, dear," Gloria said. "Take one of the pilot slots. You're always saying you don't get enough stick time. And I could meet Daria. She seems like a lovely young lady."

"You just want to meet Mr. Super-Spy," Thomas said, grinning. "'My name is . . . Jenkins,'" he added, dropping his voice. "'Mike Jenkins.'"

"Actually, I think he's just called 'the Kildar,' now."

"This is the Cut," Mike said, gesturing around.

"It doesn't look like much," Britney said. She could see it was shallow water in every direction, but other than that it wasn't much to look at. There wasn't even an island to mark it. Hell, there wasn't even a buoy. "It's not marked?"

"The current moves it around all the time," Mike said. "The entrance, anyway. And the Bahamas government is not the greatest about channel markers, anyway."

"You think this is where they're going through?" Britney asked.

"If we're not totally off base," Mike replied. "And they're going to *have* to tank somewhere north, before they load; there's not many fueling facilities down here between Bimini and Nassau."

"Do *we* have enough fuel?" Britney asked.

"Plenty," Mike said. "Extended range tanks on this baby. It's one of the cigarettes the muj were using down in the Andros."

"You mentioned that one," Britney said. "And to Sol."

"He'd figured it out," Mike said.

"We need to call in his tip on those two suspects," Britney said. "Where were they?"

"Tavernier," Mike said. "Between Largo and Islamorada. Got the cheapest gas in the area if you know where to look. Okay, time's awastin'. Let's take the cut."

CHAPTER
NINE

"Bal Harbor Cut," Randy said, pointing at the entrance. The dark brown water rushing through the narrow, concrete-walled channel was humped up in head-high waves.

Bal Harbor Cut was one of the few openings in this section of the string of barrier islands that lined the Atlantic coast. About fifty yards wide, it was deep enough to take a major vessel, but too narrow. Not to mention the fixed bridge that crossed it. However, since it was the only way through to the ocean for miles, it was a busy place. Fishermen lined the fishing pier, a former bridge, that jutted out over it and a cluster of boats was gathered on the inshore side of the cut, where it opened out into the intercoastal waterway. The boats were mostly motoring in circles, occasionally dodging each other or backing and filling.

Randy had led the group of racers off to the south side of the entrance, grounded in shallow water. The tide was incoming so getting off shouldn't be hard and he'd rather have to recover one of the racers than have one of the meat drivers smash one into some guy's fishing boat. The boats had anchors out and he'd gathered all the guys on the Lightning.

"In about ten, fifteen minutes the waves will go down," Randy said. "Then everybody and their brother will go running through. Those guys will go gunning for the exit. There's going to be another group on the other side; they'll be running to enter. There's probably more people that are going to come running from around the corner. Arguably, boats like this could do the cut easy," he said, pointing as a big Donzi came in through the cut, pitching up and down on the waves. "But until you're a little more comfortable with the boats, I'd rather not."

He'd spent time with each of the boats, running the group through basic maneuvers and rules of the road. Most of it was common sense and, thank God, these Mountain Tiger guys seemed to have that in spades. They also were quick studies. Most of the minor mistakes they'd made so far was just stuff he hadn't had time to cover. And they only made the same mistake once.

The problem being, the sea was an unforgiving mistress and there were a million mistakes you could make that were fatal.

"While staying right, stay as close to the centerline as you can," Randy continued. "Avoid the rocks along the sides. Ignore the waves from the other boats, just take them head on. I'm going to wait until the beginnings of the outflow to start. Any questions?"

"Why is that water acting like a river?" Shanar Mahona asked after a moment. "Is the ocean, yes?"

"You guys don't know what tides are, do you?" Randy said, backing up and realizing he had a *long* way to go with these guys. "Oh, Jeeze. Okay, the moon pulls up a bulge of water as it circles the Earth. That means the water rises as it passes overhead. More or less. Sort of. Right now it's rising. In a bit it will stop at what's called high tide. Also called slack. There's slack low, when the moon is on the other side, and slack high. When it starts to flow out it's called ebb tide, the tide's 'running.' Coming in it's flood tide. Everybody with me so far?"

"Yes," Vil answered but the group generally nodded.

"Okay," Randy said, trying to think how to put the rest. "That back there," he said, pointing toward the intercoastal, "that's a sort of big . . . basin that's cut off from the ocean by islands. When the water starts rising it rises in the ocean easily, but there are only so many places, sort of like the necks on a bottle of beer, for it to get in. This is one of them. So it rushes in, really fast. The reason for the standing waves is too complicated to get into," he added, grinning. "But that's why it looks like a river."

"My boat is floating," Clarn said, pointing to the Hustler. "Because water is rising, yes?"

"Yes. Go over and start it up," Randy said. "Run it in a bit more and tighten up the anchor." The boats had been arranged practically touching but the Hustler and now the smaller Cigarette were both drifting out from the formation.

"Nice boats!"

The hail had come from a small dinghy with three teenaged girls in it. *Young* girls. Fourteen will get you twenty girls.

"Thanks," Randy called back as the Keldara clambered over the side.

"They yours?"

"My boss's," Randy said. "We're delivering them to him in the Bahamas."

"Can we go for a ride?" the driver of the boat asked. She was a cute little blonde, the other two being nearly as cute brunettes.

"You're *way* too young to be accepting rides from strange men in boats," Randy said. "I'd love to, but we've got to hit the cut and then head for Bimini. And I don't think your folks want you riding over to Bimini."

"Damn," the girl said. "Okay. Maybe another time."

"You got any questions?" Randy said as Vil pulled the boat forward. Genrich was up front, pulling in the anchor line and securing it. The one thing Randy hadn't had to teach these guys, thank God, were knots. Those they knew. Probably from climbing.

"A million," Vil admitted in Russian. "Not all of them about boats. Was that young lady serious?"

"Yeah," Randy said. "Stupid but serious."

"Very stupid," Vil said. "I will not speak to her morals, I know that the cultures are different. But . . . where I came from, until the coming of the Kildar, girls such as her were always escorted by men. Because of moral issues, yes, but also because they were often kidnapped and turned into whores."

"Plenty of girls get snatched in the U.S. every year," Randy said. "Boys too, but more girls. And they usually either disappear or end up as a rape/murder case. But . . . generally not by guys driving quarter-of-a-million-dollar boats. Oh, there are exceptions. A guy like that, identity unknown, is still the top suspect in a multiple rape murder over in Tampa. But mostly they're safe; they've got too much to lose to screw some fourteen-year-old. So she figured she'd get a ride in a fast boat, which is always fun, get dropped off and motor on her way. Hell, she's probably done it before. The waters around here are still safer on that score than about anywhere else in the world."

"Very confusing," Vil said. "I wish that the Kildar had assigned Sawn's team to this. I love the boats, don't get me wrong. I think we will do well. But it is all very confusing. Sawn is . . . was better at confusing."

"Was?" Randy asked.

"He . . . bought the farm you say," Vil replied. "In a battle about a month ago. And much of his team bought the farm or are recovering. Was very bad battle."

"Wait," Randy said, his eyes wide. "That sniper shot on TV?"

"Yes," Vil said, nodding. "Lasko. He is magic. *Black* magic. Nearly three kilometers. Impossible shot. Right through the X ring."

"Damn, that was your guys?" Randy said. "Bet you're glad *you* weren't there."

"I lost two men," Vil said. "More in hospital. Tuul is still home recovering. Clarn probably should be; he took a chest shot at nearly point-blank range. Two units of whole blood are the only reason he's here."

"Oh," Randy said. He'd kept up with the discussion of the battle on the boards. The questions about it were still raging. Nobody could believe that the group had survived the reported correlation of forces. Or that the sniper shot had been made at the range that it looked like on TV. That was damned near two miles. But here he was sitting next to one of the guys who had been in the battle. If Vil had questions, Randy had as many.

"Well, you're doing fine with the electronics," Randy said. Vil had figured out the complicated navigational system for a treat. He was still learning to read the markings, but the controls he had cold.

"These are not complicated," Vil said, sighing and gesturing at the console. "We work with satellite communications, battlefield computers, GPS, all of that very much. Water. These boats? The society? Father of All, they are complicated."

"Father of All?" Randy asked.

"Is our way of saying God," Vil replied. "The boats are starting to move."

"Yeah," Randy said, standing up. "Okay!" he yelled. "Weigh anchor!"

"How are we to weigh it?" Clarn yelled. "Where is the scale?"

"Oh, Jesus," Randy said, grabbing his hair.

"I'm getting a base," Mike said. "Not just the yacht. For one thing, the Keldara are hot bunking."

The run from the cut to Nassau had been fast. The passage had lower waves than the Florida Straits so he'd cranked the boat up to the maximum he felt he could run given fuel usage, which went *way* up at max speed. At ninety miles an hour, the run had gone quickly.

"We need some sort of confirmation on what's going on," Britney said. "If you get a base near Nassau and it's all happening down around Andros . . ."

"I'm not going *near* Andros," Mike said, chuckling. "My *pilots* won't go near Andros. Not on a bet. They, through a remarkable coincidence, are the pilots who were flying the FAST in when the nuke went up. Kacey still bitches about that. Only bird she's ever dumped."

"She's very . . . cocky," Britney said.

"Pilots usually are," Mike replied. "Good ones. But in her case it's justified. None of the Keldara saw her take out the bunkers that got— Well, anyway, there were some Rangers watching. Words like 'unbelievable' and 'awesome' were the minimum they used. Apparently she just went insane. You can . . . do incredible things when you're out of your mind."

"Seen it," Britney said, grinning.

"That wasn't as far as I've gone," Mike said. "The Keldara are still whispering about the Charge of the Kildar in the last battle. I don't really remember it. But even Adams was impressed and he's hard to impress. And then . . ."

"You collapsed," Britney said. "It happens. Post-combat reaction can be as bad as postpartum depression. As I said, lots of counseling. And, hell, that's why I got my bachelors in psych."

"Great," Mike said, shaking his head. "Just what I need. A shrink."

"Frankly, you probably do," Britney replied. "But I'm not going to analyze you. We'll talk, when you feel up to it."

"Nassau," Mike said, pointing at the island on the horizon. Boat traffic had definitely picked up and the Cigarette jumped over a series of waves from the wake of a freighter. "And that freighter could be the very one we're looking for."

"No," Britney said. "If they're already moving things in, it's not. The one we're looking for is somewhere up there," she added, pointing north.

"Sir, got a strange track," the radar tech said.

The deck officer for the CIC of the aircraft carrier *Ronald Reagan* walked over and looked at the screen.

"Whatcha got?"

"Freighter," the tech said. "Sierra forty-two. I only bring it up cause I saw it yesterday. And the day before. It's just cruising back and forth." She highlighted the track, then brought up a previous day's track. "Same general position. It's doing a long figure eight, just running back and forth."

The CIC officer didn't know why the carrier battle group, which normally was doing "power projection" somewhere in the Middle East, was stuck patrolling up and down the Florida coast. But he did know that they were told to report anything "suspicious" to higher.

"Could be a Lloyds Looper," the tech said, shrugging.

And that was the problem with it being "suspicious." It really wasn't. Freighters were a business, which meant that most of the time they should be going from point A to point B, preferably filled with cargo. But under certain circumstances, related to obscure insurance rules, circling around in the middle of nowhere made more financial sense. Six ships had been detected, shortly after the Iraq war kicked off, circling in the Indian Ocean. After debating it for a while, spec ops teams descended on them in the middle of the night. No illicit cargo was found in them. In fact *no* cargo was found in them. It turned out that for insurance reasons, it was more profitable for them to stay at sea, waiting for their next load, than to tie up along shore. Even burning as much diesel as they did.

The term had become "Lloyds Looper" even though Lloyds was no longer the only insurer of freighters in the world.

"Keep an eye on it," the deck officer said, shrugging. "If it stays there we'll drop the data in the net and put up a Viking to keep an eye on it. Good eye, PO."

"Thank you," the young lady said, smiling. Then she got back to work. All the "Atta-girls" in the world could be erased by one "Oh, shit."

"Oh, shit," Mike said when he looked at the invitation.

It was just after the rapid tropical dusk when he'd pulled up alongside the yacht. And the first person who confronted him was Anastasia with an open envelope in her hand.

The message was simple:

> *You are cordially invited to a small party onboard the* White Line. *Festivities begin at eight but feel free to turn up earlier. Casual dress. Up to seven invited.*

"That's Gonzales' boat," Mike said, blinking. He was sunburned and sore from being beaten around in a Cigarette all day. And now this.

"And it is nearly eight," Anastasia said. "But I would recommend a shower."

"If I'm going," Mike said. "This guy may be connected to the people that shot up Vanner and Adams.

And I need to be briefed in on what's been going on. And why *seven*?"

"I asked about that," Anastasia said, dimpling. "I met a very nice lady in the market, a local who sells baskets. She has much knowledge of the local customs and we'd chatted yesterday. So I dropped by after we got the message. The *White Line* is a noted party boat, yes? But only pretty ladies and the . . . better class are invited. And the better class . . . Well, they generally bring a guest, a partner, female or male, and a few . . . assistants."

"Oh," Mike said, nodding and chuckling. "I can bring up to five bodyguards."

"Yes," Anastasia said. "I would recommend Oleg, Shota . . ."

Either of the two could have been NFL linebackers.

"Telling me my job, are you?" Mike said. "Yes. Oleg and Shota. Tell Oleg I want him in shorts. Oleg, Shota . . . you, Britney and Greznya. Tell Greznya to get dressed, then head for my stateroom. Anything else?"

"Daria wishes to speak to you," she said.

"Tell her to come on in the bathroom," Mike said. "It's not like she's never seen me naked."

"Kildar?" Daria said, walking into the large bathroom.

The Kildar was in the shower, soaping his short hair.

"Hey, Daria, whatcha got?" Mike called.

"I have found a land base," Daria said, looking at her notes. "A villa on a private island in the Abacos. That is the area you wished, yes?"

"Yes," Mike said.

"It has fourteen bedrooms, a private landing strip capable of handling a small jet and underground refueling tanks," Daria said. "Also servants' quarters. Enough room for the Keldara to 'spread out.' I have contacted a company to ensure they are fully fueled for both diesel for the generators and aviation fuel for the boats. The same company is delivering food and other supplies. The shipping company's boat with the container has been diverted. I contacted Chatham Aviation and requested a Gulfstream and two crews."

"That wasn't on the list," Mike said, sounding puzzled.

"You are probably going to be flying back and forth from here to there," Daria pointed out. "A Gulfstream is faster than the Lynx."

"You're a gem, Daria," Mike said.

"The boat has been reprovisioned," she continued. "We have bunker fuel for a four-thousand mile run and sufficient provisions. I had a call from Vil regarding the boats he picked up, though."

"How's that going?" Mike asked.

"They are on their way," Daria responded. "They have had some problems, but they are on their way. However, all of the boats are not set up for long range operations . . ."

"They need tanks," Mike said, sighing and stepping out of the shower. He picked up one of the supplied towels, which was so thick it was almost a nuisance, and started drying off.

"Yes," Daria said, turning away politely. She had, in fact, seen him naked several times. But right now she didn't need the distraction. "I contacted a number of boat yards in the area and none of them could get free even when I suggested a large sum of money for a rush job. Apparently—"

"Nassau is awash in money," Mike said, nodding. "And do you have a fix?"

"Possibly," Daria said. "But it will require calling Colonel Pierson."

"Fix it," Mike said, shrugging. "Fast."

"I will do so," Daria said, making a note.

"Good girl," Mike said, pecking her on the cheek and wrapping the towel around his middle. "I'm sorry I'm not bringing you to the party. I can dump Britney if you wish."

"No," Daria said, shaking her head. "I have been in the lion's den. I do not wish to go back. Thank you. I will go take care of these issues."

"Okay," Mike said, striding out into the bedroom. "Thanks. Oh, hi Greznya."

"Hello, Kildar," Greznya said, blushing slightly.

"Hey," Mike said. "Stay there," he continued, walking into the closet and shutting the door. "Go."

"I have a list of the probable people that are being invited to the party," Greznya said. "Along with some background bio. Most of them are more or less legitimate businessmen or retirees. Mostly European but a few Americans. There are a few key members of the Bahamas government expected as well."

"Not surprising," Mike said. "I'll look it over before I head over. Go."

"I have had a brief conversation with Lieutenant Harder," Greznya said, her voice slightly raised. "If your surmise is correct we should be getting some data. There is a carrier battle group patrolling the Florida coast. Only on their south end, though, do they get into the area where the freighter would probably be located." She paused and looked at her notes. "We put the information about the two men into the law enforcement database that is being used for this mission. The current emphasis is on containers coming in. There is a note from CIA that that is the intended method of insertion."

"Love to know the means on it," Mike said, walking out fully dressed. "CIA usually can't find their ass with both hands." He paused and held his arms out. "What do you think?"

"What is that shirt?" Greznya asked, her eyes wide.

"It's a Hawaiian shirt," Mike said, looking down at the eye-searing monstrosity. It was mostly purple flowers with a red and yellow background. "It's all the rage."

"As you say, Kildar," Greznya said. "If I am going with you, I had better change." *And put in some contacts*, she thought. *Eye shielding ones*.

"Absolutely," Mike said. "Meet us at the poop deck in ten minutes."

"Why do they call it the poop deck?" Greznya asked, pausing.

"It's where the poop heads used to hang out."

Souhi was exhausted. He could barely think as he brought the cigarette up alongside the freighter.

The loop the boats were taking took nearly two days. Two days of constantly being banged around by waves, except the rare flat periods when they were interior channels. Run up from Nassau through the Abacos. Tank. Run up to the freighter, arriving under cover of darkness. Tank while riding alongside, not the easiest thing in the world. Pick up the cargo then run down the coast. Hope they had enough gas to make it to Nassau. If they were critically low on fuel they could stop at Nicoll's Town, but that was an easy way to get detected. In Nassau they were given one night's reprieve. Then they had to do it all over again.

The crew of the freighter lowered a fuel hose. Zakharia Al-Shemari, the third member of the team, grabbed the hose, then pulled off a small, sealed box and dropped it on the deck. Then he laboriously dragged the hose to the hungry maw of the fuel tanks.

Kahf, moving slowly, picked up the box, then sat back down, holding it in his lap.

Souhi kept the cigarette as close to the freighter as he dared as the tanks filled. He had to fight the wash from the freighter, which alternately threatened to push them so far out they lost the hose, then drag them in to crash into the side of the freighter. And this was *good* weather.

Finally, the tanking was done, the hose retracted and he could pull away. As the crew strapped down he turned opposite to the freighter's course and added power.

Kahf sat down next to him, still holding the precious box, and strapped in.

"I don't know how much longer I can do this," the fedayeen diver said, bouncing in time with the boat.

"Only three more runs," Souhi pointed out. "Where's the next drop?"

Technically, Souhi was the only one who was supposed to know the key operational details so Kahf looked at him quizzically, then opened the small box. Inside was a scrap of paper.

"Twenty-four, fifty by eighty, twenty-seven," Kahf said, then slipped the paper back into the box.

Souhi, still driving the boat, punched the coordinates into the GPS and then nodded.

"Off Largo," he said. "Closer this time by a bit. A long run, though. First, to the pick-up point."

The cigarette plunged across the big Atlantic rollers, headed east. . . .

CHAPTER
TEN

Mike pulled the Cigarette up to the landing platform and backed as he came alongside, reversing the starboard engine to bring the rear of the boat around.

The line handlers were much better trained than the Keldara, he had to admit. They scrambled aboard, picking up the mooring lines before any of Mike's party could do more than stand up, and had the boat secured in an instant. However, they didn't look Colombian. Indonesians at a guess.

Mike climbed out of the boat, showing his invitation to a big guy wearing an earbud.

"Mike Jenkins," the Kildar said. "Pleased to meet-cha. Nice boat."

"Yes, sir," the man said, nodding and gesturing to the ladder up to the yacht. "Welcome aboard the *White Line*."

"Am I supposed to salute?" Mike asked, as he walked up the stairway.

The rear deck of the yacht was about packed with

people already. Another man, much smaller and dressed in a white blazer, held his hand out for Mike's invitation, read it briefly, then nodded.

"Michael Jenkins and associates," the man boomed. He had a much more resonant voice than his appearance suggested. "Mountain Tiger Breweries."

"And bearing gifts," Mike said, gesturing to the crate that Shota was carrying. "The good stuff."

The man waggled a finger at one of the waiters and the crate was hurriedly shuffled off to the bar.

"Mr. Jenkins," Juan Gonzales said, walking over with his hand out. "A real pleasure to meet you. I've heard so much about you."

"The pleasure is all mine, Señor," Mike said, shaking his hand affably. "And if I could introduce my friends?"

"And lovely friends they are," Gonzales said, nodding.

"Britney Harder, Anastasia Rakovich, Greznya Mahona, Señor Juan Gonzales," Mike said. "Juan, meet Bambi, Anna and Grez."

"Please make yourselves at home," Gonzales said, shaking hands. "My boat is your boat. Mr. Jenkins, there are some people that I think you *must* meet."

"Glad to," Mike said, grabbing Lieutenant Harder's hand. "I think Bambi wants to meet them, too."

"Of course," the lieutenant said, smiling.

"Britney Harder," Suarez said, shaking his head. "Second Lieutenant, SOCOM G-2, South America section. She's one of their people for tracking people like, well, *us*."

"Unsure of herself but combat trained," Ritter said, nodding. "Look at the walk."

"I can see," Enrico said. "Anastasia Rakovich. Former harem girl of an Uzbek sheik. Jenkins' domestic manager. The other girl, the two guys, I got nothing on them."

"You don't need it for the guys," Ritter said, pointing to the monitor. "One of them was either in a bad wreck recently or, more likely, serious combat. Look at that prosthetic. But he doesn't seem slowed down by it. The other one . . . pure muscle."

"He's big enough, that's for sure," Suarez said. "The girl I've got nothing on, either."

"Have you penetrated their system?" Ritter asked.

"Not even close," the Mexican admitted. "Their encryption is a stone bitch, they've got firewalls from hell, some of them ones I've never *seen* before as if they're something custom made just for them. And they're paranoid; I've tried, twice, to do a serious attack and both times they nearly tracked me back even *though* I went through multiple systems. Hell, they tracked me through *satellites*. And about half of the boat's screened against electronic penetration. Unless we get somebody on the inside, forget it. I don't even know, for sure, what they've got in there. But the traffic level, both directions, is massive. And they've been running stuff through distributed servers a lot. I've gotten the data but without the encryption scheme it's just ones and zeros. Mostly zeroes."

"Mr. Michael Jenkins," Gonzales said, walking over to a man in Bahamas Constabulary uniform, "Colonel Horatio Montcrief, regional constabulary commander."

"Colonel," Mike said, shaking the man's hand. "It's a pleasure to see you again!"

"And you, Mr. Jenkins," the colonel said, grinning. "The last time was . . . in Andros wasn't it?"

"Bimini," Mike said, shaking his head. "The blonde and the redhead."

"Ah, yes, them," the colonel said. "Whatever happened to them?"

"Back at school I presume," Mike said, shrugging. "How is Deirdre?"

"Just fine, Mike," the colonel said. "Just fine. I understand you have minions, now."

"Friends," Mike said, shrugging. "Associates. Buddies. I could hardly call them minions. And if I could introduce Miss Harder?"

Britney's eyes were wide as she shook the constable's hand. For all the reports she'd read, the sight of a senior member of the constabulary sharing a friendly drink with a noted drug dealer was hard to take.

"Call me—"

"Bambi," Mike interjected. "She likes that."

"Bambi," she said, shooting Mike a glare.

"A pleasure to meet you, Miss Harder," the colonel said, grinning again.

"Sir," a waiter said, holding out a tray of champagne glasses.

"Dom Perignon '96," Gonzales said.

"Nah," Mike said, waving at the tray. "But could you get me some of the Mountain Tiger? Dom you can pick up in any liquor store by the case. I brought the pure quill, Mother Mahona's brew. *That* you can only get from the Kildar!"

The waiter shot a glance at Gonzales, then scurried

away with his tray at the expression on his boss's face.

"Nice boat," Mike said, looking around. "Bit smaller than mine, though, I think."

"Ah, but mine is owned, not rented," Gonzales pointed out.

"Point," Mike said, shrugging. "But, hey, I hardly get a chance to get down here anymore. I just brought the harem down for a vacation. Georgia's cold as a witch's tit in the winter."

The waiter had returned with four pilsner glasses filled with a rich brown beer.

"Ah," Mike said, picking one up and taking a sip. "Nectar of the Gods."

Gonzales picked up one of the beers, a frozen expression on his face, and took a sip. His face cleared instantly as he pulled the glass back to look at it.

"I take it back, Mr. Jenkins," Juan said, nodding. "I confess to having your Mountain Tiger beer one time and finding it . . . good. This is . . ."

"Amazing," Mike said. "And that's just Mother Mahona's. The boys have been trying the stuff we ship out for export and laughing their ass off. No comparison."

"This is very good," Colonel Montcrief said. "But I think . . . Did you say 'harem?'"

"Do not all rich men have a harem?" Juan asked, waving at the girls that were scattered through the crowd.

"Absolutely," Mike said, raising his glass. "But I'm a traditionalist. It started off as a bit of a joke, tell the truth. Some Chechen pimps thought they'd snatch a daughter of one of my . . . associates. Well, I mean, what would *that* have done for my reputation? So I had to explain to them that that was unwarranted. When we'd cleaned up the blood, I had seven teen-aged virgins on my hands that were no deposit, no return. A harem seemed like the natural thing to do at that point."

"Of course," Colonel Montcrief said, taking a sip of his beer. "I take it that the young ladies here in the Bahamas are . . ."

"My official wards by the grace of the Georgian government," Mike said. "Poor orphans that I took in out of the goodness of my own heart and feed and clothe by my own expense. I've got the paperwork if you'd care to see it?"

"Not at all," Montcrief said, smiling.

"The poor homeless waifs," Mike said, shaking his head and wiping a mustache of foam off his lip. "What could I do but take them in and . . . train them."

"Of course," Gonzales said, trying not to snarl.

"So *I* make the best beer in the world," Mike said. "What pays for *your* yacht, Juan?"

"Oh, buying and selling," Gonzales said. "A bit of manufacture."

"Mr. Gonzales is a drug dealer," Colonel Montcrief said, taking a sip of his beer. "And a very good one. Good enough that neither the government of the Bahamas nor the U.S. government have ever found enough information to prosecute."

"A base canard, I'm sure," Mike said, shaking his head. "You thought much the same of me once, Colonel, and I assured you you were wrong. I refuse to believe such of Mr. Gonzales. He's far too much the gentleman to be involved in anything like that."

"Well, I understand you do a bit more than make beer, Mr. Jenkins," Gonzales said, showing a bit of teeth. "Something about Amnesty International petitioning the International Criminal Court? Killing wounded or some such. A . . . base canard I'm also sure."

"Oh, hardly," Mike said. "Actually, I don't think most of them were actually dead when we buried them."

"So the ICC will be bringing charges," Gonzales said, shaking his head. "I am *so* sorry."

"Oh, hardly," Mike repeated. "No, no, rest assured on that stake. The ICC was presented the information and refused to even view the evidence."

"Why?" Montcrief asked, honestly curious.

"Probably something about the governments of Russia, China, Japan, Germany, England, France . . . Oh, it's a long list, telling them to mind their own business," Mike said, smiling thinly. "The ICC can only exist with international support. When they considered touching me they were disabused of their . . . notion of power."

"Why?" Montcrief asked.

"Well, they all like my beer, don't they," Mike said, taking another sip.

"So you consider yourself untouchable?" Gonzales said, his jaw working.

"Oh, no, I've frequently been touched," Mike said, pulling Bambi into his side. "Isn't that right, babe?"

"Oh, yes," Bambi said, giggling. "He gets touched all the time. Why, I once saw him touched by over a dozen—"

"That's enough, dear," Mike said, slapping her on the ass. "Why don't you go see if there's a dance floor?"

"Okay," Bambi said, giggling again. "I just *love* dancing!"

"I, too, have guests I must attend to," Juan said, setting down his half finished glass of beer. "If you'll excuse me?"

"Absolutely, Mein Host," Mike said, picking up the glass and topping off his own. "You go."

"That's a very dangerous enemy you just made," Montcrief said.

"Keep your friends close and your enemies closer, Colonel," Mike said. "By the way, your wife's name *is* Deirdre, right?"

"Yes."

"This is a very nice party," Anastasia said as she and Greznya approached the dance floor. Most of the dancers were women and most of those in their early twenties. Most of them had come with the men who were doing business of one sort or another on the rear deck; there were enough trophy brides on the dance floor to host their very own convention. "I used to love to go to the club in Samarkand."

"I've never done this sort of dancing," Greznya admitted. The two were speaking Keldara, which was close to Georgian but had not only a very different accent but various loan words that weren't in any database Greznya was aware of. Even if anyone was monitoring over the industrial "club" music, hard to do, it was unlikely they could do a full translation.

"WOOO-HOO!" one of the girls hooted, stumbling out of the crowd. She was obviously drunk off her ass already. Pretty with heavy makeup, she was close to the spitting image of Britney Spears. The large and impossible to cover bruise on her cheek, however, was off-putting. "This is a GREAT party!"

The girl had a bottle of tequila in her hand and handed it to Anastasia.

"I'm Alicia!" she said, happily. "Who're you?"

"Anna," Anastasia said, looking at the bottle in her hand blankly.

"You've got a funny accent," the girl said. "Russian?"

"Georgian," Greznya said.

"Nah, I *heard* a Georgia accent before," the girl said in a thick southern drawl. "Ain't like *yer's* a t'all!"

"Oh, Father of All," Julia muttered. "What *is* that girl playing at?"

"What?" Olga asked, coming over to look at the monitor. As always, it was jerking around as Katya's eyes moved, but they settled for a moment on Anastasia's face and then Greznya's. "Oh, that *is* bold."

"Katya," Julia said, tapping the transmitter. "We *know* you're there. But thanks."

"Drink up, girl," Katya said, gesturing at the bottle. "This ain't yer Russian *vodka*. That there's te-*queee*-la! That's a *pahty* drink!"

Greznya took the bottle from Anastasia's unresisting hand and took a swig. She felt a capsule drop into her mouth and tongued it over to the side, drinking as little of the raw spirits as she could.

"Wooo," she said, having a hard time with the hoot while holding the capsule in her cheek.

"Come on!" Katya said, taking the bottle back and taking a swig. "Let's *party*!"

▲   ▲   ▲

"What just happened?" Julia asked. The monitor had flickered so fast she hadn't been able to follow it.

Olga hit the replay and backed up, going frame by frame.

"There," she said. There was a very brief flash of something sliding down the neck of the bottle. Katya had been watching it, too.

"God, I hope their people didn't catch that," Julia said.

"Be hard," Olga replied. "They're watching a lot of people."

"Two of the females with Jenkins have hooked up with Alicia," Suarez said when Ritter walked back in the room.

"Can you filter for conversation?" Ritter asked.

"With *Alicia*?" Enrico said, chuckling. "It's mostly 'WOO-HOO' or 'PAR-TEE.' But, yeah, and I listened in. She's just learned that there's a country called Georgia as well as a state and isn't assimilating it well. That girl is just about dumb as dog shit."

"No pleas to be rescued?" Ritter asked. "How about transfers?"

"She doesn't have any pockets," the computer guy said, backing up the recordings and starting at the beginning. "The only thing that's been transferred is a bottle of tequila which is rapidly disappearing."

Ritter replayed the video and watched the American girl's hands. She hadn't touched anything but skin on the two girls. Nowhere near their clothes. Although she . . . He backed up and watched her interaction then grunted.

"What?" Suarez asked. "What did I miss?"

"That that little bitch is bi," Ritter said. "She's making moves on the blonde, Rakovich."

"I think this might make video of the week," Enrico said, leaning forward.

Anna was enjoying the dancing but not the company. The American girl was extremely loud and kept *touching* her.

Anastasia had played with her friends in the harem. Otryad was as regular as clockwork about his sex with the girls and, frankly, lousy. You had the choice of your own fingers or others' and she had even enjoyed it. But she was not naturally bisexual; she liked men, preferably men holding a whip.

The American girl, though, was clearly bi. And she'd settled on Anastasia as a play partner.

Anastasia had, also, virtually no experience with anyone trying to pick her up. She knew that was what was going on and wasn't sure how you said "No." Saying "No" wasn't anywhere in her training.

As the dance number stopped the drunken girl let out another hoot and grabbed her, sliding her hand onto her breast.

"You are *so* hot!" Alicia said, pulling her head down. "Gimme a kiss!"

"Please," Anastasia said, jerking back. "I don't . . . I'm not . . ."

"Oh, quit lying," Greznya snapped. "You know you are, you're just *shy*," she added, grabbing Katya. "I'm not, though. Forget the blonde, how about a redhead."

"Oh, yeah!" Alicia said, sliding into her arms.

The group let out a loud holler as the two women started kissing on the dance floor.

Naturally, quite a few of the men drifted over as the two started a hard make-out session, writhing with the new music.

"What's going on?" Mike asked as one of the men came back, shaking his head and grinning.

"Couple of girls going at it on the dance floor," the guy said. "And I mean 'get a room' going at it."

"This I gotta see," Mike said, walking over.

The crowd at the door was thick so he eventually just hopped up on a chair. Several of the men had.

When he saw what was going on, though, his mind froze. Anastasia was standing in the middle of the dance floor, hands on hips and looking more pissed than he'd ever seen her while Greznya was . . . Jesus was she making out with some chick that was a total blank to him.

Greznya. Making out. In public. With a *woman*. He got a hard-on just *thinking* about it, much less watching. They weren't just kissing, either, their hands were all over each other. And they'd started a cascade, a bunch of the girls, probably because nobody was watching *them*, had started doing the same thing.

As Mike watched, frozen, Britney strode across the floor, pushing dancers and other couples out of her way and walked up to Greznya, yanking her back.

Britney wasn't sure what was going on but she knew that it was *something*. Greznya simply wasn't the type to make out in public. Which meant she was doing something in regards to the mission.

And the toughest moment is always when you're trying to egress Injun country.

But she had an answer to that, too.

She walked over and yanked Greznya off the other girl then slapped her, hard. She didn't know if Greznya could fake taking a blow and wasn't going to try under the circumstances.

"You bitch!" she screamed. "You two-timing *bitch*!"

Greznya had nearly lost the message capsule but managed to catch it at the last moment. She ducked down, her face working and trying to summon up tears. They didn't come naturally to the Keldara.

"I'm sorry, Bambi . . ." she sniffled. "I'm sorry . . ."

"How *dare* you!" Katya screamed, grabbing the blonde by the hair. She'd seen her come in with the Kildar but didn't recognize her. From the accent she was a real American, probably the liaison officer. "Just because *you* can't keep her satisfied . . ."

If the make-out session had had everyone riveted, the two swearing women, tearing at each other's clothes and hair, had them cheering.

Mike jumped down off his chair and forced his way through the crowd, making it to the two before the bouncers. Shota was right behind him. Quite a few people trying to get a better look bounced off unnoticed.

"God *damn* it!" he bellowed, grabbing the by now half-naked Britney and pulling her away from the girl. She had the other girl by her long blonde hair but he managed to pry her fingers off, simultaneously shoving the stranger away. "Bambi, I am going to tan your *hide*! I swear I can't take you girls *anywhere*!"

"Oh, get your fucking hands off of me!" Britney swore, lunging at Katya. "I'm gonna tear that bleached hair out of your head, slut!"

"That's *enough*," Mike shouted, pushing her towards Shota, who got a grip on her upper arm that the lieutenant wasn't going to break in her wildest dreams. "Anna, Grez, come!"

"I'm very sorry about this," Mike said, as he passed Gonzales on the way to the door. "The girls were just having too much fun and it went to their heads. I apologize."

"Not a problem," Gonzales said, grinning. "It will be the talk of the harbor for at least a week."

The security had spotted that they were exiting and Mike's Cigarette was alongside before they'd made it to the ladder, Mike dragging Greznya and Anastasia by their upper arms.

"I am *so* going to tan your hides," Mike said. "And Anastasia! I'm surprised you let this happen!"

"I'm sorry, Kildar," Anastasia said, practically sobbing. "I don't know what happened . . ."

"We are going to have a serious spanking session when we get back, that I can assure you," Mike said, shoving the two girls into the boat. "One that you are *not* going to enjoy."

"Are you *sure?*" Ritter said, looking at the video. "Nothing was passed?"

"Not a thing," Suarez said, standing up, a flash stick in his hand. "Trust me. I reran that clip a dozen times. Maybe more. Zoomed in all over it. Now, if you'll excuse me, I'm going to my quarters. . . ."

▲   ▲   ▲

Mike jerked the two still-pouting girls out of the boat and dragged them up the stairs, Shota still dragging Britney and Oleg stumping along behind. He took them downstairs but instead of turning towards his bedroom, took them down to the intel shack. As soon as Oleg followed and shut the door, Britney dropped into a chair and started laughing so hard she choked.

"I don't know exactly *what* just went on," she said through the tears, "but I'm pretty sure it was a drop. Right?"

"Yeah," Greznya said, pulling the capsule out of her mouth. "Father of All, Lieutenant, you were *wonderful.*"

"That was Katya," Mike said, chuckling. "Damn. Even *I* didn't recognize her."

"We were dying over here," Olga said. "When the lieutenant called Greznya a two-timing bitch . . . Oh, *All* Father." She started laughing again, helplessly.

"How'd you recognize her?" Mike asked.

"I knew Katya was there and couldn't leave the boat," Greznya said, shrugging. "When an American girl came over and started woo-hooing I knew it had to be her. So I had a drink of tequila. She'd put a message capsule in it. I think she offered it to Anastasia first, knowing that Stasia would be too . . . refined to drink from the neck of the bottle."

"And making out?" Mike asked, raising an eyebrow.

"She was trying to *start* a fight," Greznya said, shrugging. "If Stasia had been more prepared for this sort of thing, *she* probably would have started the fight. As it was, the lieutenant did nicely."

"Yeah," Britney said. "But, damn, that girl can hit."

"She can do more than that," Mike said. "Be glad you're alive. What did we get?"

Julia had opened the capsule and extracted the note.

"Set of signals and pick up and drop points," she said. "Probably for Jay."

"So we can signal Jay that Katya can't get off the boat," Mike said, nodding. "Hopefully he's developed some data." He considered the situation, then nodded again.

"We're moving," Mike said. "Up towards the new base. Time to off-load some of the troops and get the base set up. Julia, you and . . . Lilia hang back. With a team of security. Take a hotel room and do a drop. Does anybody know if Jay has our codes?"

"We've got codes for him," Greznya said, rubbing her cheek. "By the way, Lieutenant, Katya's not the only one who can hit."

"Sorry about that," Britney said, grinning.

"Okay, make up a micro of everything Jay needs to know to date," Mike said. "Do the drop tomorrow. Take some gear with you but you're not going to be secure; Gonzales is definitely onto us. But do the drop and wait for a pickup. We'll be back in two days."

CHAPTER
ELEVEN

The run up to the Abacos was done overnight so when Mike woke up the next morning the yacht was docked at an island that was in the middle of nothing but green and blue seas.

The island was a remote outlier of the Abacos chain, the buildings originally part of a lighthouse, the tower to which remained. It had been bought in the early 1900s by a wealthy British shipping magnate and upgraded to the then standards of modern. Over the years it had passed through several hands, and several upgrades, and was currently owned by an American information-tech CEO. He wasn't stupid though. He only visited the island a few times a year. The rest of the time it was rented out to discerning clientele. The definition of "discerning" was anyone willing to spend a half a million dollars a week and plunk down a larger deposit against damage.

Mike was feeling worn out, though, so he more or less sat out the initial transfer as the Keldara were ferried to the island via the boats. The five new speed boats had turned up, after one hell of a long run, and Mike had Vil's team crash while others, including members of the yacht's crew, did the ferrying.

He was holding back Yosif's team and the rest of Vil's on the yacht for security. With the rest of the Keldara gone they were finally able to stretch out. The Keldara had been packed below like sardines. Even a hundred-and-fifty-foot yacht didn't have enough room for them all.

Yosif was coming back on one of the boats and as it approached the ship he said something to the driver, one of the yacht crew, who slowed the boat. Yosif, cautiously, slid over the side of the boat and began swimming towards the yacht. He didn't do it really well, what used to be called a California crawl, arms windmilling in a crawl but with his head out of the water. But he was clearly enjoying himself, given the grin on his face.

Mike watched him for a second, then frowned. He'd *never* seen the Keldara swim, didn't even know they knew how. But Yosif was doing pretty well. Not exactly Olympic quality, but he'd clearly been in the water before and wasn't afraid of it.

"Yosif," Mike said as the team leader came up the ladder, horking some water out of his ear. "I didn't know any of the Keldara could swim."

"Not many," Yosif admitted. "I enjoy it, though. There is a deep spot in the river, where the Karl stream joins. It is *cold* though. This water is . . ."

"Wonderful," Mike said, nodding. "I've been wanting to hit it, too. Anybody else on the teams swim?"

"Most of mine," Yosif said, shrugging ruefully. "It's not considered . . . important to the Keldara."

Mike blinked and considered that for a second. Every team had its specialty except Yosif's. They were just rounders; they could do patrol well enough, entry well enough, shoot well enough, but they didn't have a niche like, say, Pavel, whose team was the shit for anything involving altitude, be that air ops or mountain.

Mike, with some subtle prodding, had chosen the team leaders. But the teams had fallen out on their own in a process remarkably similar to the way that kids chose ball teams in school. The team leaders had tended to choose people that were like them. Oleg was a bull so his team was bulls. Vil was more subtle, his team was subtle. And so on. Yosif's, from Mike's perspective, had been the leftovers. But if they were, in fact, the strange ones who enjoyed swimming . . .

"Ever swim underwater?" Mike asked.

"Yes," Yosif said, cocking his head. "Do you?"

Mike snorted and then had to laugh out loud. He'd put a bathing suit on under his shorts so all he had to do was take them off along with his shirt. In about ten seconds he was over the side.

He hadn't hyperventilated and it had been a while since he did a breath-hold. But, Christ, he'd been a swimmer long before he joined the SEALs. All the breath-hold training he'd gotten had just added understanding and refinement. So he didn't have much trouble impressing a Keldara.

He followed the bottom, given that there were boats moving overhead, and headed for the shore about fifty meters away. It was a long damned swim for not having prepared and, he realized, being really out of shape for it. But he made it to the shallows and then popped up, standing up and taking long breaths. When he was sure he'd vented all the CO_2, he headed back.

The return was harder. His muscles had warmed up and were pumping CO_2 into his system at a higher rate. That was what caused the strangling "I have to breathe" sensation when doing a breath-hold, too much CO_2 not too little oxygen. The chemical sensor was actually a small bundle of special cells called peripheral chemoreceptors attached to the carotid arteries in the neck.

He let some of the breath out on the way back—getting some of the air out of his lungs reduced the need—then popped back up when he came to the landing platform.

"Kildar, are you well?" Yosif asked, running down the stairway.

"Fine," Mike said, taking more deep breaths to vent the air. "God, I'd forgotten how much *fun* that is."

"That was a *long* swim," Yosif said, his eyes wide.

"Yosif, I think that most of the Keldara have figured out I used to be a SEAL, right?" Mike asked. "You do know what SEALs do, right?"

"Oh," Yosif said, shaking his head. "I suppose worrying about you in the water is . . . silly."

"A bit," Mike said. "Yosif, you and your team are going to be doing some special training. And, unfortunately, I'm the only one around who can give it. So we'd better get started. But first I need to see Daria. We're going to need some gear."

▲　　　▲　　　▲

Kahf put his regulator in his mouth, sucked on it a couple of times to make sure his air was on, and rolled over the side of the moving boat.

The container had very dim strobes attached to it. In these waters, from the surface, they looked more like a school of phosphorescent jellyfish than a container moored seventy feet down.

Kahf had to fight some current on his way down. That was going to be a pain. The currents in the area, not far from the Gulf Stream, tended to swirl randomly. One day there'd be none, the next it could be high and from about any direction.

He made it to the container, though, breathing somewhat hard, and then paused. He slid a small device out of his buoyancy compensator and slid it down into the container on a lanyard. It stayed green. Good.

Swimming head-down he got to the first rank of remaining barrels. Bracing himself with a fin stuck between two of them and blowing out all the air in his BC, he pulled a mesh bag off his side and started pulling out items. First there was a long rope, which he dropped to settle against the barrels. Then he pulled out a nylon harness and clipped the bag back on his BC.

The harness went around one of the barrels and clipped together. It was a pain to get on but he had plenty of time. He was wearing double 105 cf tanks, over-pressured to 4000 PSI, and NITROX. The boat wouldn't be back for over two hours and he could stay at this depth for longer. Of course, he'd have to decompress, but the way things were set up that wouldn't be hard.

He uncoiled part of the rope and attached the barrel to an already tied-in loop knot. One down.

Working faster now, he fitted another barrel and another until he had four. Only then did he release the ties holding the pre-weighted barrels in place.

Now was when he was going to have to use up some air. First he tied down the rope with a quick release. Then he attached four large float bags to the rope and inflated them from a spare hose attachment on his regulator. His air supply dropped noticeably but he still had plenty. Last, he grabbed onto the ties that had held the barrels down, wrapped the rope around his body and released the tie.

The bags wanted to jump to the surface but that would be bad. Instead he belayed them up until the rope was taut. Then he undid it from his body, grabbed the barrels and went for a short ride.

The rope was fifty feet long. The top of the container was at seventy. He slid out of the opening, easily missing the side and popped up twenty feet. A glance at his dive computer indicated that was not an issue. The computer said he'd need to decompress at twenty feet and ten but he had loads of time. Then he checked the watch built into the computer. Loads, the boat wouldn't be back for over an hour.

He reinflated his BC and slid up the rope to the loop at twenty feet. Once there he adjusted his buoyancy, clipped himself in and lay back to enjoy the peace and quiet, bobbing lightly up and down due to the bags at the top. He'd have to be careful; he could very easily fall asleep. It wouldn't kill him, when the regulator slipped out he'd just get some seawater in his mouth and maybe lungs and cough a lot. But it would be a pain. And this was just *too* pleasant after being slammed around in that damned boat for two days.

"Okay, this is just too much fun," Mike said, sliding out of the water like, well, a seal. "I feel like I'm playing."

"You may," Yosif said, climbing out on the dock next to him and gasping for air. "I don't. I *thought* this was going to be fun . . ."

"Try doing it in twenty degrees," Mike said, referring to the temperature in Celsius. "This is the shit."

Yosif's team had been doing cross-overs, swimming one way, surfacing for a breath and then swimming back, for nearly an hour, and one by one they all managed to clamber onto the dock. And they were all gasping as if they'd just finished a marathon.

Cross-overs were deceptively exhausting. At first they were easy. This section of the harbor was barely wider than most pools and had concrete walls on both sides. Mike had shown them how to push off and you could coast most of the way on a push. And you weren't actually underwater all that long. But you were only allowed to come up for a fast breath and then you had to dunk back down and do it again. And again and again and again.

The muscles in the body quickly ran through their anaerobic energy stores, and those caused lactic acid generation anyway, then they had to switch to aerobic. Aerobic exercise released CO_2 as the body converted O_2 molecules into energy via ATP in the mitochondria. CO_2 caused the "desperate for a breath" reaction. And the short bobs were never enough to get rid of all the CO_2, much less get enough oxygen.

Doing it over and over again was debilitating in the extreme, worse than a fast run of the same time duration. The Keldara were only able to survive it because of two factors: they were all runners thanks to Mike's training, and they were from a high-altitude environment. They had grown up with about two thirds of what most people considered normal oxygen and their bodies had reacted by producing an abundance of red blood cells. Those were able to scavenge extra oxygen from their short breaths and carry more of the CO_2 to their lungs to be expelled.

And, of course, they were very hardcore and were not about to disappoint the Kildar.

Mike had managed to scrounge swim goggles for all of them from the well-appointed yacht and from the estate. Now they pushed them up or off, sprawling in the Caribbean sun.

"You guys are going to have to do better than this," Mike said, shaking his head. "I thought you were swimmers!"

"Kildar," Yosif said, finally getting his breath. "The pool we swim in is perhaps the size of a large bathtub. I have swum across the river on a bet. This is . . ."

"I know," Mike said, relenting. "But, seriously, if we have to do a water insert, you're the guys who are going to have to do it. I'm going to set up a lesson plan because I'm going to have to head back to Nassau." He paused and considered something then nodded. "The master chief is probably about done with his hospital time and, frankly, this would be a good place for him to convalesce. He can oversee it. He'd consider it refreshing. Just don't let him try to swim!"

"Yes, Kildar," Yosif said.

"You guys give it fifteen minutes," Mike said. "Then I want you to swim over to that point," he said, pointing across the vaguely curved island to a point about a quarter of a mile away. "Stay along the sides. Yosif, drag that rescue buoy," he added, pointing at the device that was hanging by the harbor. It was cigar shaped and had a harness that went across the chest. "If anybody can't make it, call the swim and swim in. Let them hold onto the buoy. I don't want anybody dying. But the guy who calls the swim . . . He gets to work with the women in the kitchen tonight."

"Yes, Kildar," Yosif said, grinning. "I don't think anyone will call the swim."

"Guys, if you're going down, call the damned swim," Mike said, looking at the team. "Yosif, Edvin," he added to the assistant team leader, "it's your job to make sure everybody makes it. On second thought, Edvin, you carry the buoy. Stay near the back. Don't drown yourself."

"Yes, Kildar," Edvin said.

"Work on the sidestroke I taught you," Mike said. "Pull, breathe, kick, glide, repeat. Every four or five strokes look up to make sure you are heading the right way, otherwise just follow the shoreline. We can easily add fins as soon as they get here. Stay with your swim buddy. Repeat after me: Stay with your swim buddy. If you don't, life will get interesting."

"Well, this is interesting."

"What?" David Levin said, looking up from his computer.

David had been a kid in New Jersey, planning on

working at the chemical plants around Trenton just like his dad, when he saw his first Jacques Cousteau show. One show was all it took.

His parents hadn't had the money to pay for the, back then, incredibly expensive sport of SCUBA diving. So when he'd turned eighteen he'd hitchhiked to Florida and found a dive shop that needed somebody to work in their back room for just enough to survive and, oh, yeah, they'd throw in dive lessons.

Twenty-seven years later he was the owner of Diver's Headquarters, one of the largest suppliers of dive gear in South Florida. With ten locations and a warehouse jammed with gear that was sold not only through brick and mortar stores but also on the internet, he was a "mover" in the international dive community. He had decades of experience in what did and did not work in sport diving and was frequently consulted by manufacturers when they had a new system, light, fin or suit they wanted to sell.

"It's an e-mail," Joe Barber replied. David had hired Joe when the kid came in the door trying to sell him some orange solvent cleaner. The kid was clearly underage and Dave suspected, and later confirmed, that he was a runaway. But the kid had been such a hard seller, Dave offered him a job on the spot. On the phone, and back then they got a lot of phone-in orders, there was no way anybody would know the kid was underage. And there were ways to make the paperwork disappear.

Once he hit eighteen, Joe had worked his way up fast, first as a top floor salesman, then a store manager, then back to the phones and now internet and finally to manager of the whole direct sales division. Dave had seen that gleam in the runaway and known he had a player on his hands. Dave had been married and divorced three times but nary a kid despite trying. Maybe it was the chemicals in Trenton. But he sort of had a son in Joe, who was, everybody knew, his heir apparent.

"Don't keep me guessing," Dave said.

"Lady in the Bahamas wants thirty sets of gear," Joe said, wonderingly. "Everything from fins to tanks. All top line. Zeagle regs and BCs, Pro wetsuits . . . Everything listed by model. She's asking if we can supply it overnight or even for delivery late today. They're willing to pay to charter a plane."

"Do we have the systems?" Dave asked.

"Not in the warehouse," Joe replied, tapping at keys. "We'd have to scrounge the stores. She wants thirty ZX Zeagle Flathead VI. We've got, total, twenty-seven."

"Get ten from Zeagle's warehouse," Dave said. "They're just up in Hialeah. Tell them we need them delivered today and don't fuck with us. Hell, get the entire shipment if you can. Tell the lady the plane will take off tomorrow before first light and be there at first light. Private strip, right?"

"Yep."

"Tell her there's going to be some extra costs with such a rush shipment," Dave added. "Figure out what it's going to cost us. Add fifteen percent. See if she geeks."

"Whatever the market will bear?" Joe said. "I'll add twenty."

"Good boy."

CHAPTER
TWELVE

"I should have charged you through the nose for this," Don said, gruffly, shaking Mike's hand. "Long time."

Don Jackson was a tall man, heavy of body with white hair, and skin that was bright red from the sun. He never seemed to really tan but he never seemed to really burn, either.

Besides running a charter business, and a tobacco distribution system and a few condos and rental boats— the guy was just a compulsive businessman—Don ran some special shipping interests. Oh, not smuggling, just niche shipping. Don ran landing craft.

Landing craft were, in general, a horrible way to ship cargo. They were capable of sailing in almost any sea but their engines drank fuel and they couldn't carry all that much compared to their fuel costs.

However, landing craft had one great benefit; they could take the cargo anywhere there was a beach and roll it right out.

Don's landing craft had done various jobs over the

years, generally for the very rich. You wanted a party for a hundred on an otherwise inaccessible tropical island? Don could roll off a container containing, literally, everything from soup to nuts. Bring your own cooks, though.

He'd participated in multiple movie shoots as well. Movie makers generally wanted somewhere "unspoiled" for shoots. Unspoiled just as often meant inaccessible. Don had developed a reputation among the guys who arranged things like that for being there on time, guaranteed. In the islands, that was pretty unusual. The Bahamas ran on "Bahamas Time," which was less precise than "In'shallah," which was orders of magnitude worse than "mañana." There was no time on earth less precise than "Bahamas Time."

Don didn't work on Bahamas Time. A New Yorker who had been south long enough that the accent was barely noticeable, he still ran on New York time. If he said he'd be there at ten AM you could set your watch by it.

"That's one heavy ass container, Mike," Don continued, as the mover, basically a small tracked bulldozer converted to pull containers, started pulling the containerized cargo off the landing craft's ramp and up the white sand beach. "And you know what?" he added. "When we checked in with Bimini customs, they looked at the manifest and just waved us through. It wasn't sealed or bonded but, you know, they just didn't seem to care. That's lax even by Bimini standards, Mike. I could have been carrying a container packed with coke for all they knew."

"Going the wrong way to be coke," Mike pointed out. "How you been?"

"The arthritis is starting to kill me," Don admitted.

"Too many fast women," Mike said, drawing a snort. Don had been married for damned near fifty years.

"So what's in the container?" Don asked.

"You don't want to know," Mike said. "You're not even asking about my associates."

The Keldara were scattered around the estate getting it in gear but many of them had stopped to see the arrival of the container. Even the boat class had stopped to watch it being rolled up the sand. If Mike were to put one word on their expressions, that word would be "avid."

"They look like a bunch of extras," Don said. "You doing movies these days?"

"Nope," Mike said. "Well, not often. I collect a few."

"Was talking to Sol after you up and disappeared," Don added. "Interesting coincidence you going and disappearing, then that nuke going up in Andros."

"I swear you guys are like a couple of old women," Mike said, shaking his head. "Next you'll be accusing me of being the guy who killed Osama."

"Well, let's see," Don said, rubbing his chin. "Osama gets killed in October. You show up in December in a brand new boat and immediately spend the next couple of months basically out of sight. And I've seen you with your shirt off, buddy."

"Dangerous ground, Don," Mike said seriously. "The guy who did that has every jihadist on the planet looking for him."

"Which is why I'd only mention it to an old friend," Don said. "But you were the one who brought it up. So what's in the container?"

"You really want to know, 'old friend'?"

▲   ▲   ▲

"Holy fucking Jesus," Don whispered.

The container had been rolled to a concrete pad in an interior courtyard, then the mover pulled away. The Keldara had immediately gathered around and on Mike's nod, opened it and started unloading.

Cases of ammunition. Rocket launchers. Body armor. Cases of Semtek plastique. Guns. More guns. Sniper rifles in cases. MP-5s and M4s and SPRs. M-60E4 machine guns capable of delivering 2500 rounds in three minutes of continuous fire.

Then the big stuff started coming off. Miniguns. Pallets of ammunition, multiple each. Fifty-seven-millimeter rocket launchers. A pallet of rockets. The container had been stuffed to the ceiling.

"I had all that on *my* boat?" Don said, his eyes wide. "Jesus Christ if customs had even *suspected* . . ."

"Why do you think they didn't open it, Don?" Mike asked. "The guys who were there when you arrived were hand-picked."

Don looked up at the sound of rotors and blanched as a black Hind helicopter flared out for a landing. It had come in at nearly water level and was out of sight from the launch. The pilot, a female, grinned at the sight of the rocket launchers, gave Mike a salute and started getting out of the cockpit.

"I so didn't want to know this," Don said.

"Yeah, but I figured you should," Mike said. "I'm going to need you to pick it up in a couple of weeks. Well, except for the ammo."

"And I'm supposed to just float this back to *Miami*?" Don said, shaking his head. "You think that the U.S. government isn't going to ask a *few* questions?"

"Who do you think arranged to pass it through Bahamanian customs?"

"How's it going?" Mike said, sitting down on the dock next to Randy.

"Pretty good, actually," Randy admitted. "These guys are soaking it up like a sponge and you can't beat sitting in the Bahamas sunshine."

"Mike Jenkins," Mike said, sticking out his hand. "We haven't met."

Mike had been very careful about that. Over time he'd dealt with a lot of FAST boat drivers on both coasts. Finding a combination of one who a.) was available and b.) he'd never met had been hard. And he'd had to do it on the plane over since it wasn't something he could delegate.

"Randy Holterman," Randy said, shaking Mike's hand and watching as the speed boat made a hard turn around a buoy. "You're the one they call the Kildar."

"That would be me," Mike said. The Nordic was headed back in, slowing and backing as it approached the pier, then backing one engine to swing around and pull in backwards. The Keldara at the helm, Sergejus Makanee, did the maneuver as if he'd been born on a boat.

"They're very good," Randy said.

"Yes, they are," Mike replied.

"I don't know that they can win any races . . ."

"Among other things, the boats need work, right?" Mike asked.

"And if you're going to be doing long runs," Randy said, "and I somehow suspect you are, they're going to need bigger tanks."

"That's being worked on."

▲   ▲   ▲

"Okay, this is a 'what the fuck' moment, sir."

Senior Chief Edward Marrow had been in the Navy seventeen years. As a young recruit, fresh out of machinist mate's A school, he had been transferred to the aircraft carrier *John F. Kennedy* sure in the knowledge that he'd be working on the massive engines, the arresting gear, all the parts that made a carrier work.

Instead, he'd been placed in the tiny unit that maintained the carrier's many small boats. It was a proverbial Siberia, the place where the more senior machinist mates who were unfit to work on "important" systems were shipped. But the unit was short a slot, he was a machinist's mate and thus he'd ended up there.

However, he'd quickly come to love it, despite the company. The boats were just *fun*. He'd become a specialist in making sure that small engines ran to the very top of their performance. He even extended his knowledge—despite superiors who barely knew which end of the wrench was which—to hull design, tankage and all the small bits that made a boat work. Whereas if he'd been in one of the bigger sections he'd have worked on just one small part of a complex system called a carrier, here he could do it all.

He'd reenlisted, made PO2 and eventually ended up on shore duty, doing the same thing with small boats at Norfolk Naval Base. There he had come to the attention of people who really *cared* about small boats, via a brief conversation in the Norfolk enlistedmen's bar. Shortly afterwards he was asked if he'd like a transfer. The unit was small and it only did small boats. And it still counted for sea duty. There might be some travel involved.

The NCOIC of the Little Creek shipyard had been fixing FAST boats, and various other small, fast, lethal vessels for the last twelve years. There wasn't a thing he didn't know about high-performance engines and how to coax every last bit of energy out of them. And he'd done some travel, oh, yeah. FAST boats were complex machines and where the FAST boats went, there went their maintenance crews. A shipping container and a dock was all they needed. And the shipping container was a type that would fit on an aircraft.

The Team didn't just work FASTs, either. They supported not just the FAST unit but every other spec ops group on the East Coast. Delta, for example, wanted a lower profile than FASTs. They tended to train and operate in cigarettes almost purely but Ed had ended up working on just about every civilian boat on the market. Hell, he'd flown out to Rota one time to fix a sailboat's engine for some guys who sure didn't *look* military. He wasn't as good with diesel but he could hum the tune and once he got to fumbling around in the guts of a machine he could generally make it purr.

But the travel orders on the latest job were pretty worrying. NCOIC, team of five technicians, one container with assorted materials, specifically long-range tanks. Civilian clothes only. No mention of rank. Commercial bird to Nassau. Transportation from there to be arranged by a contact to meet at airport.

"Agreed, Senior Chief," the lieutenant commander said. "Delta probably. Maybe some of the CIA operations guys. But, hey, it's the Bahamas. Get moving. They want you in the air in six hours."

▲   ▲   ▲

Allen Barksdale, a brown-haired, brown-eyed slightly overweight dentist from Cleveland on his first island adventure, sat down on one of the benches that lined Nassau Harbor and pulled out a package of Ritz crackers. He bit into one, then threw the remainder into the air.

Seagulls poured from everywhere, filling the air with their raucous cries. One swooped down ahead of the others, plucking the morsel out of the water and flying off. It was attacked by a dozen others but they banked away as another cracker flew through the air.

The man tossed two more crackers in the air, then slid his right hand down onto the seat to lean forward, watching the loathsome birds. He could feel the package. A handful of crackers and the birds were now swirling all around him. Another lean and the GPS was in hand, slid into the pocket. Another handful.

The dentist leaned back, setting the Ritz box down and pulling another package out of his pocket. He opened the container of Alka Seltzer and tossed one in the air. A seagull immediately caught it, midair, and quickly swallowed the small morsel. Kurt tracked it through the throng until the bird suddenly staggered in midair and then fell to the water, shrieking piteously for a moment then going still to lie, wings spread, on the surface of the bright green waters.

Kurt Schwenke grinned and stood up, wandering through the cloud of birds towards his hotel.

"I want to buy some candy, Ali!" the boy said, grinning, the white teeth standing out against his black skin.

"You are a thief, Robert," Ali said, waving him away.

"I want a candy bar," the boy said, holding out his hand. "I have money this time. Really!" The money was a small bill and some change. There was a suspicious bulge under the bill.

"Okay," Ali said, taking the money from the boy's hand and giving him a Snickers Bar. "But you must have the money, yes?" He handed back change. In fact he handed back more money than he'd been given.

"I will, Ali," the boy said, grinning as he bit the Snickers.

"Now get out of here you thief! I have *real* customers to attend to!"

"He could *kill* us for this," Katya moaned as Suarez stroked her belly.

"Ritter and Juan are both gone," Suarez said, dropping his pants. "The boat is nearly empty. And what is life without a little danger?"

It had taken Katya two days to arrange the assignation in the computer room. She wasn't sure if the bug would even be able to pierce the walls but it was worth a shot. Besides, at this point she'd bugged the main bathroom, the main salon and Juan's bedroom. This was the only place left worth dropping one of the transmitters.

She leaned back in the reclining computer chair, stretching her arms over her head and moaning as the Mexican went down on her. The bug slid under the console and stuck with barely a flick of the finger. It was away from Suarez's main station, just in case he was a nose picker. The little rotter probably was. He'd clearly been watching the video of her fight with that American bitch; God knows he'd mentioned it often enough.

"Oh, yeah, baby," she moaned, glancing at the computer. Stuck on the underside of the keyboard was a strip of tape with a long series of numbers and letters on it. She looked at it in astonishment for a moment then remembered to moan. "Oh! Oh!"

She looked at the numbers and letters, trying to burn them into her memory. Oh, hell, she didn't *need* to.

"Oh, my," Julia said, watching the take from Katya. "Would you look at *this*?"

"That *is* interesting," Lilia said, holding her finger up to her lips.

"The internet is a wonderful thing," Julia nodded. There was no way to ensure that the room was secure. The windows, alone, guaranteed that. The computer was, however, a secure console. Surrounded by a metal cage, nothing could be remotely detected from it. Words were something else.

"I didn't even know you could *do* that with a donkey," Lilia said, batting her eyes.

"I'm sure you've tried," Julia shot back, writing down what was obviously a password. She wasn't sure what they could do with it, but it was interesting.

The inshore waters of the Abacos chain are renowned among boaters. With strong offshore breezes from the Atlantic, but protected from the swells, they are perfect for sailing. By the same token, they are perfect for all sorts of boating and had, literally, thousands of miles of beaches and coves, a lover's paradise.

They also had thousands of rocks and shoals, which was today's lesson.

"Watch the water," Randy shouted, pointing to a disturbance up ahead and to the right. "You can see where the rocks are jutting up. Not always, but usually even if they're slightly submerged. And if you hit one going this speed . . ."

"Airborne," Vil shouted back, grinning. He knew the thrill of battle and the thrill of doing really well in a video game or the Ondah contest. None of them really matched the thrill of taking a fast boat and cranking it up to max power.

"Okay," Randy shouted. "There's a series of them up here. Wide spread. You figure them out."

Vil knew the instructor wasn't going to let him slam into one of the rocks. Among other things, they'd both probably be killed. But he still knew he had to get this right. He could see the first one, almost straight ahead. He banked left then saw another that way. To the right looked clearer but he wasn't sure he could turn back fast enough.

He realized that was the reason for the hours they had spent turning around the buoys back at the base. He knew, instinctively, that he didn't have the turn radius to make it back to the right but he could slalom through the two rocks successfully.

He continued the left turn for a moment then banked hard right, the boat skipping across the water, dangerously close to the second set of rocks, then banked back hard left to line up again.

Movement on the water like a shoal. No, a skein of fish jumped out of the water ahead of the fast-moving craft, some of them clearing the nose and slamming into the low windshields, splatting like overlarge bugs.

Vil ignored the distraction, continuing to weave. He'd learned that distractions were death. Learned the hard way.

The guy was doing good. Before he'd set up this test, Randy had carefully navigated the same course, years of experience filing away all the functional routes through the jutting reefs. Vil was taking the simplest, admittedly, but he was proving he could spot the rocks and shoals.

Rocks and shoals were the proverbial bane of the Navy. The very term was used for any sort of trouble and had been the nickname of the long defunct Navy Manual For Court-martial. If you got into trouble with your NCOIC, you'd hit "rocks and shoals." Same for wife or girlfriend. Actual rocks and shoals had ended more than one promising Navy career.

If the guys all passed this test they'd made it through the very basics. This was the easy stuff. Doing the same thing at night? That was another thing. Doing it at full speed would be suicidal, but even at any sort of high speed it would be tough. But they'd do the run tonight if everyone passed. Slowly.

Tomorrow, they'd be back on the ocean. Randy had kept their crossing slow and easy. But the Atlantic beckoned just beyond the nearby islands to the east. Let them face the monster at full speed. If they could cross the rollers as well as Vil was doing in the shallows, ah, then glasshoppah . . .

Randy looked up, briefly, as a shadow passed overhead. It was a small business jet. Nothing that had anything to do with him. He went back to making sure they both didn't die.

Mike watched as the golf carts pulled up to the main entrance of the estate. Besides the four pilots, there was a woman with them. Maybe in her fifties but looking younger. Brunette and busty although there had to be some modern medicine involved.

It was getting on towards evening and Mike was glad the plane had made it in. The strip had lights but there was no way to do traffic control. Day landings were *much* safer under those conditions. Especially since the strip was a bit short for a Gulfstream. Putting it down at the very beginning of the strip was more or less a necessity. Doing that at night was . . . tricky.

"Thomas Chatham," the first pilot said. Also older, perhaps older than the female, big and beefy with a florid expression but very sharp eyes. "Chatham Aviation."

"Pleasure to finally meet you," Mike said. "Mike Jenkins."

"The way it usually goes with customers as good as you is that *I* host," Chatham said, grinning. "But I thought I'd pop by. If that's okay."

"Not a problem," Mike said, as the lady walked up. "Lots of room."

"And my lady wife," Chatham said. "I believe you've spoken on the phone."

"Gloria?" Mike asked. "Glad to finally be able to put a face to the name."

"Same here," Gloria said, shaking his hand. "But the one I really would like to meet, sorry, is . . ."

"Daria's inside," Mike said, gesturing to the entrance. "Let's get out of the wind."

"Winds *were* a bit tricky coming in," Chatham said as they walked in the entrance. The main living quarters of the old lighthouse had been gutted more than once and were now the front entrance, a vast room filled with comfortable furniture and bric-a-brac, the back wall being mostly one large, heavily constructed, window.

"He's going to start doing the thing with the hands again," Gloria said, holding up both of hers palms down and twisting them back and forth. "The Zero was right on my tail—"

"It was a Mirage," Thomas said, smiling.

"You were in the Falklands," Mike said.

"Just before I got out," Chatham admitted. "Harriers, of course. Went to BOAC just before it went tits up. But even for as short as I'd been there, there was a nice severance package. I'd set a bit of money aside so I bought an airplane. Well, the bank and I bought it."

"And here you are on an estate in the Bahamas," Mike said, smiling. "What would you like?" he added, waving to the bar on one side of the room. "Daria's around here somewhere . . ."

Mike paused as Tinata, wearing only a purple and green string bikini, walked into the room.

"Tina, darling, could you ask Daria to step over here?" Mike said.

"Yes, Kildar," the busty redhead said, dimpling prettily. "And if you want to join us, some of us were going down to the beach."

"Love to," Mike said. "But if you could hold off

and get a couple of the girls in here for a bit, I'd appreciate it. Company."

"Of course, Kildar," the girl said, smiling. "We *love* company."

"Nice," Chatham said, whistling. "She looked—"

"Young," Mike said. "Just about seventeen, she thinks. I hope that doesn't shock you, Gloria."

"In fact, I am unsurprised," Gloria said with a wry smile. "Sorry."

"The story of why I have a harem of teenaged girls, some of whom are too young for even *me* to bed, is a long one," Mike said, stepping behind the bar. "And it will be shorter for some Mountain Tiger. Who's *not* on call?"

CHAPTER THIRTEEN

They'd never made it to the beach. Mike had ended up trading war stories, those he could, with Thomas Chatham. Britney had turned up and sat in on that one, occasionally passing on a story she'd picked up that wasn't classified. Daria, Anastasia and Gloria were in a colloquy in the corner, laughing rather frequently. The rest of the harem had swarmed into the room as soon as they heard there were visitors, the poor dears just didn't get out much, and were now surrounding the other three pilots, who were looking poleaxed.

Mike looked up as Oleg stumped into the room. He was wearing shorts and a T-shirt but he still smelled like cordite.

"Kildar," the team leader said in Keldara. "We've set up the shoot facility and we're knocking off for the rest of the day. Mother Savina asks when you want dinner and where?"

"In here," Mike said. "Ask her if buffet will work. Grab a shower and come join us along with the other

team leaders. Ask Greznya as well and tell her if
they've got the time a couple of the other girls. Oh,
and the pilots."

"Yes, Kildar," Oleg said.

"Hey, Oleg," Mike said, looking over the side of
the bar and pulling out a bottle from a bucket of
ice. "Have a Mother Lenka special. You look like
you could use it."

"Thank you, Kildar," Oleg said, grinning and breaking the seal on the bottle. "Miller Time, yes?"

"For some," Mike replied.

Vil looked at the things laid out in the steamer,
his expression extremely unsure.

"They're lobster tails," Randy said, picking up two
and putting them on his plate. "Grab a couple. I'll
show you how to eat them."

The party was in full swing as Vil settled on the
couch. One of the Kildar's girls was talking to one
of the pilots, her butt slid over to one side and he
had to crowd the arm of the couch to avoid it. It
reminded him that it had been a long time since he
had "been with" Stella. Days, in fact, since he'd even
seen her. His wife was carrying the Kildar's child.
He knew that and did not mind, quite the opposite.
But it had been . . . too many days since they last
were . . . together. The smoothly rounded butt, covered
in the barest of bikinis, reminded him rather force-
fully of that fact.

"Hot butter," Randy said, setting a bowl on the
coffee table. "You crack the underside and pull the
meat out."

Vil watched dubiously, then followed suit, aware

that it couldn't be any worse than combat rations. But when he tried the lobster, butter dripping down his chin, he found that it was really rather good. Very good. And after a full day of hard driving he realized he was ravenous.

Before he knew it the lobster tails, as well as the red potatoes he *did* recognize and the asparagus he'd at least seen before, were gone.

"Let me," the girl said; she'd sat up shortly before and now took the plate from him. She was one of the Kildar's younger girls, unbroached.

"Thank you . . . Martya," Vil said.

"Anything in particular?"

"More lobster if there's any left," Vil replied.

"Is that girl as young as I think?" Randy asked as the little brunette walked towards the buffet.

"Yes," Vil said. "Fifteen, I think."

"And these girls are . . . the Kildar's *harem?*"

"She is not yet . . ." Vil said then paused. "She is still virgin. The others . . . are not. For your culture they are young. For mine . . . Greznya," he said, gesturing to the intel chief who was talking with Gloria Chatham, "she is what you call 'old maid.'"

"She doesn't even look twenty," Randy said.

"Just turned," Vil replied. "She has much trouble with getting married. She was to be promised to a boy, Brone. He is killed in fall. We have dowry system, you know this?"

"Yes," Randy said, frowning. "I know what a dowry is, but, *really?*"

"Really," Vil said, shrugging. "It is our way. Anyway, when her match is killed, dowry is spent on another girl. Not enough dowry for her. And not many men she can marry. There are more women Keldara than men. No one knows why but is happen every generation, yes? She was . . . Greznya has always been good on farm. She learns numbers and writing very well. She works hard. Normally, she would have been . . . She would have left. But she stayed. Then the Kildar came. Needed people to help with . . . many things. She works for Kildar."

"Is she part of the harem?" Randy asked, confused.

"No," Vil said, chuckling. "Good that you ask *me* that question and not her. Not sure I can say what she does for Kildar."

"Got it," Randy said, shrugging. "Hey, I'm just the instructor."

Martya came over and sat down with two plates heaped with lobster tails.

"What are these?" she asked.

"Lobster," Randy said nervously. The girl should have been playing with dolls, not in a harem.

But he showed her how to eat lobster and that was okay.

"You are the man who is teaching the boats, yes?" Martya said, licking some butter off her fingers.

Okay, maybe *not* so okay.

"Yeah," Randy said, clearing his throat when it came out as a croak. "Yeah. I'm uh, teaching the guys how to drive."

"Can I ride in boat?" Martya asked. "They look very fun."

Randy had heard the question plenty of times, including from girls as young as this one. And he'd taken a few out, including quite a few that were significantly . . . okay, *not* much older. Because there was very little that could get a girl going as much as taking a ride in a boat that went *very* fast.

"Uhm, maybe later," he said. "We're doing an exercise tonight."

"Okay," Martya said, picking up the plates. "I hold you to that. You have to give me ride."

"Oh, I'd *love* to give you a ride," Randy muttered. "In about . . . three years. And assuming your Kildar doesn't mind."

"That one," Vil said, grinning, "the Kildar would mind. But that brunette over there . . ." he added, pointing . . .

"That brunette *what*?" Stella said, leaning over the back of the chair and blowing in his ear.

Vil leaned into his wife's head for a moment and just breathed.

"Can you believe it?" she asked, sliding over the couch and taking Martya's place. "We have a bedroom *all to ourselves*!"

"Really?" Vil said, grinning.

"Really," Stella replied. "Oh, the room is small and the bed smaller, but I don't think that will be an issue."

"Sorry, Randy," Vil said, looking at the instructor. "My wife, Stella. Stella, Randy Holterman."

"You're the man who's trying to kill my husband, yes?" Stella asked. She'd stretched across the length of the remaining couch, her feet up on the top, resting most of her weight on Vil.

"Trying to keep him alive," Randy said. "Pleasure to meet you, Mrs. Mahona."

"Mother Stella soon," Stella said, smiling and patting her tummy. "But not Mother Mahona for many years I think."

"Our clan names are complicated," Vil said, shrugging. "Mrs. Mahona is sort of correct and . . . sort of not."

"I'm figuring that out," Randy said. "I'm glad you guys are okay with first names."

Martya came back and pouted, looking at her seat.

"You can sit on Randy's lap," Vil said, gesturing.

"Okay," the fifteen-year-old said, plopping down and wiggling to get comfortable. Or for some reason.

"Oh, thanks *so* much, Vil," Randy said, grimacing.

"As I was saying," Vil continued, "about Illya . . ."

"What were you saying about Mopsy?" Martya asked, her eyes narrowing.

"I was just saying that if Randy was interested in a . . . companion for the evening," Vil said, grinning. "As he's assuredly going to need one after you're done with him, minx."

"Flopsy, Mopsy and Cottontail," Martya said, giggling. "I didn't understand it until I read the story."

"Shhhh," Stella said, her finger to her lips. "We don't speak of Cottontail."

"So how is she?" Vil asked.

"Getting screwed and beaten as usual," Stella said, sighing. "Doing very well, in other words."

"Jeeze," Mike said. "Greznya, Stella and Irina are here. Who's holding down the shop?"

"Olga," Daria said, leaning past him and pulling out another beer. "Greznya is going to go relieve her in a bit."

"What's the word on Vanner and Adams?" Mike asked.

"Vanner is out of ICU and under observation," Daria

said. "He's doing fine but still unconscious. Adams is ready to be released."

"That's your first run, then," Mike said, looking at Thomas. "Take . . . Daria and part of Oleg's team over to Miami and pick up my wayward second in command."

"He get arrested by the shore patrol?" Thomas asked, grinning.

"No, actually," Mike said. "He got shot up by either some Colombians or terrorists who were aiming for me."

"Shit," Chatham said. "Sorry."

"Not a problem," Mike said.

"That's something that Greznya wants to talk to you about," Britney interjected.

Mike looked at Chatham, then shrugged.

"Go."

"The answer is Colombians."

"Now that's damned interesting," Mike said. "Dash my eyes if it's not."

"You're hanging out with Brits too much," Britney said, rolling her eyes. "And there's more. Florida State Patrol pulled over two Colombian mules. Regular drug stop. But, lo and behold, what *did* they find?"

"A blue barrel?" Mike asked, raising an eyebrow.

"No," Britney said. "But close. Heroin. Very high quality. Damned near pure. And the mules were known associates of your friend."

"Oh, that explains so much," Mike said, looking at the far wall.

"Not to me," Chatham said, taking a sip of beer.

"No, it wouldn't," Mike said, still looking into the distance. "And, sorry, it must remain a mystery. Thomas, are any of your pilots current in, oh, something along the lines of the Beaver?"

"The amphib or land version?" Thomas said, winking. "Yes, as a matter of fact, *I* am. Know Beavers well, wet or dry."

"Daria, dear?" Mike said.

"Find a Beaver for rent," she said. "Somewhere in South Florida or the Bahamas. Can it wait until after the party?"

"Assuredly," Mike said, watching Vil and Randy get up to leave. "And we'll have to keep the party running long into the night, apparently."

"Can I ask one thing?" Daria asked.

"Sure."

"What *is* a Beaver?"

She seemed rather pissed when both the men snorted in unison.

"See the buoy?" Randy yelled.

"Yes," Vil shouted back. But he had to admit that seeing it was only half the problem.

Night vision goggles are wonderful things but they have one serious flaw; they give the user virtually no depth perception.

The trick to getting some idea of range is called "pointing." Effectively, the NVG user moves his or her head from side to side, getting a slight angle on the scene with each "point." The problem being that while that is hard to do in, say, a low-flying helicopter, it's much harder in a fast-moving boat. The motion of the boat throws the head around to such an extent that it's nearly impossible for the brain to process the images. Vil knew the technique; he'd sometimes practiced it in combat training on land. But he was finding it hard to manage even though there were virtually no waves.

He had to guess the point to make the turn and very nearly crashed into the buoy, swerving only at the last minute. And this wasn't even full speed.

"Don't worry about it," Randy yelled. "I don't know many FAST drivers that can manage real high speed at night. Not in tight quarters. It's more art than science. Swing it around and try again. . . ."

Two hours later the group of boats was gathered by the rock circuit.

"Okay," Randy said, calling across to the group. They'd turned their navigation lights off, which was a huge no-no, but they had to have time for their eyes to dark adapt. "We are *not* going to take this at high speeds. You're going to find it hard enough to do at *low* speeds. You'll each do it twice, low speed first then slightly faster. Vil?"

"Okay," Vil said, glaring at the view. Almost none of the clues that showed where rocks were by day were apparent at night. In the fuzzy image of the goggles he could barely see the ripples on the water's surface. But he engaged the power and started forward. Suddenly he realized the rock that had nearly gotten him the first time, the one that had been on the left side, was right in front of him. He was sure it was the same rock. He turned right, nearly clipping the rock, then back to the left only to have another one confront him. He couldn't see far enough ahead to figure out a route. He slowed down more, picking his way through the rocks.

"You're way off course is the problem," Randy said, pointing to the compass. "You're supposed to be going north. You're headed west."

"Shit," Vil said, spinning to the right, dodging a rock and then seeing what looked like open water ahead of him. Suddenly he felt a scrape on the bottom and the boat lurched to a stop.

"You're aground," Randy said. "That flat patch of water was a shoal."

"Father of All, this is *impossible*," Vil said, pulling off the NVGs. The green light from the goggles had partially blinded him but he rapidly got his night sight back. There was a quarter moon and it actually gave him better vision, for this, than the NVGs. "I can see better this way."

"Tonight," Randy said. "But not if there's no moon, which is the best time to do an op in one of these. And not if it's overcast. NVGs are the only way, then."

"Fine," Vil said, putting the goggles back on and settling them. "Try to back off?"

"Yep," Randy said. "Then do a pivot turn right. That will get you out of this mess. There's some deep water right behind you and to your right. Take that back south, pivot left when you see more open water that way and start over."

"Yes, sir," Vil said. It was going to be a *long* night.

Mike sat under the quarter moon, his feet dangling off the end of the dock, and watched the play of the light on the water. He was a little drunk, which bothered him. He remembered his recent drunk way too well. But he was on a mission. Getting drunk and maudlin would not be a good thing.

It was hard to avoid the latter, though, given the former. He'd always been a pretty maudlin drunk. And he couldn't help but think how much Gretchen would have enjoyed this. Of course, like most of the Keldara women she would probably still be back in Georgia. Well, Stella was here, but . . . Oh, crap. No, never mind. Yeah, Stella was not going to be door gunning. She was here for intel, not as a crew-chief. No dust-off Hind. That might be a problem. No, they could use Dragon. He belched.

His thoughts were disjointed. Flashing golden hair and pale skin. A Hind firing a Gatling gun right at him. Blue eyes clear as the stars. Tracers smoking in his chest. A ravaged body. He lay back and looked up at the sky. What did it matter? One little death. VX that could kill thousands. To the stars, what was the difference? We were all less than fleas on the back of a dog.

He closed his eyes and set the beer bottle down. To have just one day . . .

Vil was exhausted. It had been one long damned day.

So he was taking his time making his way into the harbor. He didn't want to ding the boat any more than he already had. He'd made it through the course the second time, faster, without getting actively lost and off-course. But right now he was wondering if he could find the dock.

So he was somewhat surprised when a figure sat up on said dock. He clutched at his chest, reaching for a weapon that wasn't there, then recognized the Kildar in his NVGs.

"Oh . . . crap," he muttered. "Why the *hell* did they leave him alone?"

"What?" Randy said, leaning down.

"The Kildar . . . is not well," Vil said. "I'll explain later."

Mike sat up and gasped shaking his head to clear the nightmare. He'd been dancing with Gretchen, slow dancing, but she'd suddenly only been a torso. Still talking, still smiling, her guts hanging down and she was so heavy . . . Stella and Vil danced by, elegantly, two rotting corpses, the whole room was filling with a heavy green fog and he was trying to get them out of the caravanserai but it was a ship, a merchant freighter, filling with VX . . . the Keldara dropping around him and he was the only one that survived, always the only one . . .

Mike stood up, beer bottle in hand and shivered in the wind. The temperature had really dropped and all he was wearing was shorts and a Hawaiian shirt. But he'd been cold before. He felt, sometimes, as if he'd never be warm again.

"Hey, Vil," he said cheerfully. "How'd it go?"

Vil recognized the tone. *Fuck*, he thought again. *Who was stupid enough to leave him* alone?

"Went pretty good," Randy said. "Pretty good. For their first few days, they're coming along great."

"Good, good," Mike said. "I know it's correct and traditional to clean gear after you use it, but why don't we take one night off. Scrub down in the morning?"

"Sure," Randy said. "Not a problem. Guys, see you here at dawn."

"I could do with a beer," Clarn admitted, stretching his back as he climbed out of the driver's seat. "Then, I think, bed."

"I think I may skip the beer," Vil admitted. "I have a room *almost* to myself somewhere in this place and I intend to find it. Are you coming up, Kildar?"

"Nah," Mike said. "It's a nice night, I think I'll just stay here."

Vil followed the other Keldara up to the estate wondering what to do.

Mike was afraid to fall asleep, now. He wondered that he'd done so earlier; one of the reasons for the two-month bender was the dreams. When he was drunk enough he didn't dream. The problem was, he wasn't drunk enough, yet.

He started to get up and saw a silhouette coming down the dock. Light dress, too light for this wind, and blonde hair. Britney.

"Hey," Mike said, jovially. "Enjoying the party?"

"It's winding down," Britney said. "You were missed."

"Ah, I wasn't in much of a partying mood," Mike said, setting the empty bottle on one of the pier posts.

"You were the life of the party for a while there," Britney said. "What happened?"

"I just wanted to come out and look at the water," Mike said turning back to the view. "I'd missed it. More than I realized. Don't you ever just look at the water?"

"Yes," Britney said, stepping up to stand in the shelter of his bulk. "And the stars. It was one of the things I thought about when I was in that damned bunker. That I'd never see the stars again."

"Flashbacks getting any better?" Mike asked.

"More like I've gotten better at handling them," Britney said. "I work in a shield room in the basement of the SOCOM building. They have to pump in sunlight. Trust me, I've gotten better at handling flashbacks. Including in the middle of meetings. You?"

"Not so good," Mike said. "Didn't think I'd ever have the problem. Some people don't. I never did. They suck."

"So do the nightmares," Britney said, shivering.

"Those too," Mike admitted. "We need to go in. You're freezing."

"You know what I'd rather do?" Britney asked.

"I am as ignorant as an apple," Mike said.

"Go for a ride in the *Too Late*," she said, gesturing at the boat.

"I thought you'd had all you wanted of Cigs?"

"There's not a ripple," she pointed out. "What I was tired of was being beaten to death in one."

"Okay," Mike said.

The keys were still in it; it wasn't like anyone was going to steal it. The Keldara had, without even asking, set up a perimeter patrol. Anybody trying to steal one of the boats was going to be facing a group of highly trained commandoes and some serious questions.

"Did you dream?" Britney asked as Mike slowly motored out of the harbor.

"Yeah," Mike admitted.

"Dream or nightmare?"

"That would be the latter."

"Yeah," Britney said. "There's things you can do about that, you know? It doesn't always work, but I've been doing it for a year and a half. It's called dream management. You teach yourself to control your dreams. Sounds impossible, but it's not."

"And when the guy's coming towards you with the key?" Mike asked. "What do you do?"

"Usually I can turn the dream off before that point," Britney admitted. "I change it to a meeting or something. When I can't, well, I have somebody come in and break things up. Guess who?"

"You're welcome," Mike said, gunning the boat as they passed the breakwater. The time was between the land breeze and the sea breeze, the stillest part of the night. There was barely a ripple on the water and the Cigarette seemed to float above the water.

"I've been through a lot of counseling," Britney shouted. "Some strange stuff, too. Stuff that actually works. There's this thing they do where you flick your eyeballs while you think about what's bothering you. I shit you not. And it actually helps. One of those weird brain chemistry things. The point is, Mike, you don't have to just fucking suffer."

On the way over Mike had never really opened the Cigarette up. Now, he glanced at his gauges, made sure everything was solid and opened the engine up full bore.

The difference between seventy miles an hour and a hundred does not seem that great. But in a boat arrowing a bare meter over the water, it is.

"Holy shit," Britney shouted, snatching at the grab points on the seat. The boat seemed to be a rocket headed into darkness. She knew there wasn't anything in the way, to the south of the island was open water, but if they hit so much as a piece of floating debris she was afraid the boat would go airborne.

They'd gotten far enough away from the island that they were hitting a light chop, ripples from Atlantic waves to the south. The boat started to leap like a gazelle over the waves, the extended props staying down below the water but the rest of the boat catching air and coasting through midair for bounds of twenty or thirty feet.

"If you're trying to frighten me, you're succeeding," Britney shouted.

Mike didn't answer, just leaned forward and touched a control on the dashboard. The boat turned slightly to the left, staying mostly down this time, barely kissing the waves as it screamed through the night. The moon had set and the only light source was the stars, glimmering off the surface, and yellow and green flashes of phosphorescent jellyfish, revealing their presence to predators while calling for a mate.

Another touch of the controls and it was straight again, jumping the light waves, the air filling the world with sound.

Suddenly, he pulled back on the throttles and hit the quick release on his straps.

"Lieutenant Britney Harder, I would very much like to screw you."

"I was wondering when you would ask," Britney said, pulling her sundress up over her head.

They made love under the stars, the boat rocking on the light waves, no words, no analysis, just a desperate coupling of two ravaged souls reaching for one moment of peace.

CHAPTER FOURTEEN

"Track 738," Greznya said, pointing to the screen.

The Kildar was looking . . . odd this morning. It would only be noticeable to someone who knew him well but it was clear to Greznya. He looked tired and the Kildar very rarely looked tired, no matter how long an op had gone on. Given that this one had been fairly easy so far, it was . . . strange.

"It came into range of the balloons from the north, somewhere north of Grand Island," she continued, tracing the track. "Very high speed run down to the waters off Key Largo. Then it turned and headed over to the Bahamas cut. It was lost from radar while in the cut."

"And it never slowed off Largo?" Mike asked, taking a sip of his coffee.

"No, Kildar," Greznya said. "But it matches the profile perfectly."

"So the boat is somewhere inside in the Bahamas," Mike said, frowning. "Along with a billion others."

"Yes, Kildar," Greznya said.

"Okay," Mike replied. "Let me think about this for a while."

Mike left the intel shack, yawning. Fucking *dreams*. Even screwing the ass off of Bambi hadn't helped. He wasn't sure it had helped her, either, but at least she understood where he was at.

He walked out the back door and looked at the water. The boats were gone. Randy was taking the Keldara out for offshore practice. They'd only get in about an hour on the rough before they'd have to come back due to fuel constraints. Which led his mind to . . .

The landing craft headed for the beach. It had come around the point from out of his view. Don was on the way with the Navy guys.

Mike walked down to the beach and waited as the boat approached, sipping his coffee. The techs would have had a miserable night. The LCT had some bunks, but the crossing would have been awful; the damned things rocked like nobody's business.

The problem being, he needed them to get started right away. Well, as soon as the boats got back. But it was going to take them at least that long to get set up.

When the ramp dropped, the first person off was a big blond guy with a civvie bag over one shoulder. He was looking around with interest but the techs behind him were clearly just glad to get back on land.

"You the NCOIC?" Mike said, walking up with his hand out.

"Yeah," the guy said, eyeing Mike warily but shaking his hand.

"Welcome to the Abacos Estate," Mike said. "The

boats are out training right now. They'll be back in an hour or so. I need the extended range tanks installed and the engines tuned by sundown. That a problem . . . Master Chief?"

"Senior," the guy said, his jaw flexing.

"Get my boats functional and it won't be for long," Mike said. "Any issues?"

"Parts," the senior chief said. "As in unavailability of."

"I'll hook you up with my logistics lady," Mike replied. "She'll see to anything you need. I'm headed over to the mainland in about an hour. You give her the list, I'll get anything you need and be back this afternoon. If you need more, well, the Gulfstream's just sitting there. If you need to go get it or send somebody to get it, that can be arranged, too. But I need those boats up. I'd prefer them by this evening since I've got an op going down that I need them for."

"Yes, sir," the chief said, looking pissed.

"What's this all about, the chief is thinking," Mike said, sipping his coffee. "Who the fuck is this guy giving me orders? Is he Delta or what? He's in civvies, his hair's a little long . . . Maybe he's ANV or whatever they're calling it this week. The answer, Chief, is that I'm a fucking merc. I'm a fucking merc who has been hired to do all the things that even ANV can't do in their wildest wet dreams. And I'm going to do those things and in doing so I'm going to stop American civilians from getting killed. You, Senior Chief, are going to help me in doing that by making sure my fucking boats are up by sunset. I don't care what you need, I don't give a rat's ass how much it costs. Because I've got a target I need to intercept to find out where Al Qaeda has dropped some nasty shit off the Florida coast. If I don't get them tonight, that means that nasty shit gets used on American civilians. Are we clear, Senior Chief?"

"Clear, sir," the senior chief said, nodding.

"So get your gear set up," Mike continued, taking another sip. "Chow's in the big house, as are quarters. Quarters are okay, chow's good; I'm a big believer in steak and lobster as motivators. And, speaking of motivators, there is good news."

"Yes, sir?" the senior chief said, suspiciously.

"The only beer on the island is Mountain Tiger," Mike replied, grinning. "And if you're a very good boy, I may let you sample the pure quill."

The Wal-Mart driver cursed under his breath when he saw the blue lights in his rearview. He'd been doing right at the speed limit so it had to be a random check.

He pulled over to the side, though, there being plenty of room on the side of the nearly deserted turnpike. On weekends and holidays the road would be packed, but on a weekday afternoon there wasn't much traffic.

Marshes stretched in every direction in the Big Empty between the burgeoning Miami area and the even faster growing sector around Orlando and Disney World. It was real old Florida, the Florida from back in the days when "I've got some dry land in Florida to sell you" was a scam. A kite swirled above on the light winds, searching for its morning meal.

Officer Jose Coqui, Florida Department of Commercial Vehicle Enforcement, got out of the driver's door, after checking to make sure it was clear, and made his way down the narrow strip between the road and the truck until he reached the driver's door.

"Hey, officer," the driver said. His window was already down and he had his manifest out. "I'm clean."

"I'm sure you are," Jose said, smiling. "Just checking."

"I weighed after I dropped my last load," the driver said. "It's in the manifest. Just running up to Orlando distribution center."

Jose looked at the documents and nodded. The driver had followed all the restrictions that the government had put on truckers to the letter, including a mandatory rest break the night before. Gone were the days of "pop me up, jack me up, flying down the highway." Truckers were only permitted to drive a specified number of hours a day. Violate it and they were liable to lose their commercial driver's license.

They could also lose their CDL for being overweight. The interstate highway system was primarily paid for by taxes on trucks and those taxes were based on the weight of their cargo and how far they ran between pick-up and drop-off. The weigh stations by the side of the highway, though, were being more and more replaced by a series of sensors that picked up data from the trucks about their load and destination automatically and random stops, such as this, which made sure that the truckers weren't cheating.

Jose's partner had already rolled the scale in front of the truck's rear tires and now waved.

"Could you pull forward a few feet?" Jose asked.

"Certainly," the trucker said. "But you'll see. I'm clean."

Wal-Mart trucks almost always were. The company was too big, and too professional, to fuck around with a few pounds of cargo here and there. As the controlling company of the truck, they'd get fined, too.

The trucker pulled forward until he was on the portable scale and stopped, looking in his rearview.

Jose walked back to the scale with the manifest and held it out.

"Twenty-two, five thirty," Jose said. "Running light."

"Really?" his partner said. "Try twenty-three and change."

"You sure?" Jose asked, looking at the readout.

The scale was a solid state model that used induction as opposed to the old "pressure" models. Sometimes they were off, but not by that much.

"I think we have ourselves a winner," his partner said, grinning. Robert O'Toole was new to the department and "keen." He loved finding truckers that were trying to skate the rules.

"Doesn't make sense," Jose said, shrugging. "But I'll go get him."

"Is there a problem?" the trucker asked when Jose walked back to his cab. He knew the drill. They should have rolled him off the scale after the check.

"You're overweight," Jose said. "Mind explaining why?"

"Honest to *God*, Officer," the trucker said, opening his door and climbing down. "I weighed just before my stop. I *can't* be overweight."

"Well, we got to check your cargo against the manifest," Jose said. "Open it up."

"God damn," the man said. "Nothing against you but . . ."

"I understand," Jose said. But he let the man go first.

The threesome, hugging the side of the truck, walked to the rear where the driver opened the doors. Sitting at the rear of the palletized cargo were two blue plastic fifty-five gallon drums.

"Mind explaining *that*?" O'Toole said, looking at the manifest. "Not a damned thing here about drums of liquid. Or *is* it liquid?"

"Calm down, Bob," Jose said, shaking his head.

"I didn't put those there," the driver said, his face ashen. "Honest to God!"

"You might not have." Jose sighed as O'Toole clambered into the truck. "It's a new way to run drugs. You do your mandated stop, a couple of smugglers slip this into the back. You have another stop in the interim, accomplices slip it out. It's *another* reason we do these stops. But, if it's illicit substances, I'm going to have to place you under arrest until you're cleared."

"Oh, fuck," the trucker moaned. "Is it going to go on my record?"

"Not if you're cleared," Jose said. "And you probably will be. But the whole thing's getting impounded until it gets cleared."

"Fuck, fuck, fuck," the trucker cursed.

O'Toole had managed to get one of the lids off and frowned down at the contents.

"It ain't cocaine," he said, leaning down. Then he flew back, his eyes wide and started gagging.

The officer fell to the floor of the truck, gasping and convulsing.

"JOSE!" he managed to gag. "What . . ."

Jose grabbed the officer and dragged him to the ground, over into the verge, then pulled his shoulder-mounted mike around.

"This is Unit 27," he shouted. "We have a hazardous materials incident at mile marker one seventy-eight, turnpike! I need HazMat and an ambulance. Now! Officer down!"

▲   ▲   ▲

"So they're inside," the President said, frowning.

"Yes, sir," the secretary of Homeland Security confirmed. "So far, Wal-Mart is agreeing to the cover story. Hazardous materials somehow were loaded on one of their trucks. The turnpike was shut down for about two hours but it's open again."

"We got those, but we don't know how many others have made it in," the FBI director said. "Florida has reopened all their weigh stations in South Florida. The cover story is an outbreak of Mediterranean Fruit Fly. All trucks are being searched. Even moving vans are being searched."

"But they got inside," the President said, angrily. "What are we paying all this money for if they can just slip through?"

"We don't know their methods, sir," the CBP director said, nervously. "If they brought in a container, they're apparently breaking it down somewhere in South Florida. We'll find it."

"And if they didn't?" the President asked.

"That is the top theory at the moment, Mr. President," the DNI said. "We're relatively certain they brought in the full container. Find that and we find the mother lode."

"I don't care if they brought it in by *balloon*," the President suddenly shouted. "FIND IT!"

"Yes, sir," Greznya said, handing over the headpiece. "The President."

"Hello, sir," Mike said, looking at the document on his lap. The track had come from north of Grand Island. That meant that there should be a refuel ship up there. But, if so, it was probably sitting outside the two hundred mile "economic zone" of the U.S. Very long damned run. On the other hand, the *Ronald Reagan* CVBG was up in that area. They should have seen *something* by now.

"Where are you?" the President asked. "I called the primary number and they transferred me."

"On the way to the hospital to see my two wounded men," Mike replied. "Don't worry, it's not interfering with the mission."

"That's open for debate," the President said. "Two barrels of VX were intercepted in Central Florida. The officer who found them only got a whiff of one of the binaries but he's in the hospital. Tell me you have some good news."

"I can't," Mike said. "What I have so far are hunches."

"Your hunches have been pretty good in the past."

"Okay, sir," Mike said, closing his eyes. "I have a hunch that the boats are picking up their cargo from a container that's floating somewhere north of Bahamas Grand Island. Probably underwater. That they then run down the coast of the Keys and drop it off. Another boat, probably two Scarab fast-fishers that we've lost track of, pick the stuff up. How were they moving it?"

"In the back of a Wal-Mart truck," the president said. "Apparently it was loaded into it while the driver was eating. But we're checking all the trucks now. They won't be able to do that again."

"You can move one of these in a big trunk," Mike pointed out. "Two or three in an SUV. You can't stop every vehicle."

"I'd already thought of that," the President admitted.

"And I'm getting tired of everyone telling me the situation is 'under control.' Thanks for not doing so."

"Under control is an overstatement if I've ever heard one," Mike said. "Where'd they stop it?"

"On the turnpike, just south of Orlando."

"Interesting," Mike replied. "But not getting us anywhere at the moment. I've got an op planned that may turn up something soon. But I'm going to need some political muscle."

"What do you need?"

"PO Johnson?" the CIC officer said, walking over to the radar tech with a message form in his hand.

"Yes, sir?"

"Your Lloyds Looper has generated some high-level interest," the officer said. "We're going to be putting a Viking up. When the Viking has to return they're putting up a P-3. The take from both is going to go to your screen and your screen only. You will then send the take to this address," the officer said, handing over the form. "You will not discuss any take from it with anyone else. Vanders will be briefed in on it but only Vanders. You may receive classified requests for retasking which you will then pass· on with the minimum possible discussion. The classification on all data is Ultra Purple under code name Thunder Child. No one onboard this ship, with the sole exception of you and Vanders, is cleared for data regarding Thunder Child. Are those orders clear?"

"Yes, sir," the tech said, her eyes wide.

"For anyone listening in," the officer said, raising his voice slightly, "there had better not be any ~~~estions about this. Not here, not in the mess, not in the bunks. Forget you ever heard it. Chief, lock this down."

"Yes, sir," the section NCOIC said. "It is locked." The crew might ignore such an order from the OIC, but they weren't about to cross the chief.

"Sir, can I ask one question?" the tech asked. "The codeword I get. But what is Ultra Purple? I don't recognize the security classification."

"The group with access is restricted," the officer said. "So even *I* don't know. But Ultra class refers to working groups with CJCS and higher clearance. However, CJCS is only at Ultra White. Purple is higher."

"Yes, sir," the PO said, turning back to her screen. On it a contact, labeled as a friendly Viking, was just taking off. Somebody wanted to see what the ship was doing and not only did they not want the ship to know about it, they didn't even want the *captain* to know about it. Hell, they didn't want the commander of the CVBG or FLTATL to know what was going on.

What was so special about one Lloyds Looper?

CHAPTER
FIFTEEN

"Hey there, man," Mike said as he walked in Vanner's room. "I am really upset with you."

"Why?" Vanner said, trying to sit up.

"I thought I told you to duck!"

The former Marine was looking wan and had lost weight. Mike had seen the look before, quite a few times in the mirror. Some time in the Bahamas sunshine and Mother Savina's cooking would do him good.

"I did," Vanner said, smiling in relief. "Right *after* they shot me."

"Doesn't do much good *then*," Mike pointed out.

"No, sir," Vanner replied. "But I've been thinking about those chicken plates a lot lately. There's a guy at Georgia Tech who came out with some better ones. They're expensive as hell, but . . ."

"But you suddenly realize that expense is relative?" Mike asked, grinning.

"Something like that, yeah."

"I'll look into it," Mike said. "In the meantime,

you're going to be cleared to be released in a couple more days. And I've got the perfect place for you to recuperate. Besides, the girls are getting all piney without their boyfriend around. Speaking of which," Mike said, opening the door.

Greznya came in and shook her head.

"Sergeant, you were supposed to *avoid* getting shot," the Keldara girl said, coming over to the bed and taking Vanner's hand. "I'm sure I told you that." There were tears in her eyes.

"I'm going to leave you kids alone," Mike said. "I suggest you both have a talk about . . . things. Grez, I need you back at the island, though, so be ready to leave in no more than thirty minutes. That's as long as they're going to let you hang out in here, anyway."

"Yes, Kildar," the girl said.

"What about all that stuff with not being alone with Keldara girls?" Vanner said weakly.

"I don't think that's operable anymore," Mike said, pausing in the doorway. "Not after Greznya was making out in public with another girl."

"Kildar!" the girl snapped as the door closed.

"What did I miss?" Vanner asked, chuckling. "Ow! That hurts!"

"Hey, man," Mike said, walking into Adams's room. "You are about to be officially discharged. There's a plane from Chatham waiting to whisk you away to a tropical island where you can continue to recuperate. Say 'Thank you, Mike.'"

"Right," Adams growled. "I'm fit as a fiddle. I can take on a platoon of Delta. Let me at 'em."

"I think that's troop or squad or something," Mike

said. "They've got that weird cavalry thing going. Seriously, you're scheduled to be released. We're in place. I've got an op going down tonight. But you're not on it and don't ask."

"Ain't gonna," Adams admitted. "Sitting in the sunshine is really all I'm up to at the moment. But I'll seriously be ready for *light* ops in a few days."

"I know," Mike said. "Which is why once you're up to speed, you're going to start training Yosif's team on swim-ops."

"Yosif?" Adams asked. "Swimming?"

"He's actually not too bad," Mike said. "For a guy who grew up in mountains. But I got to go finish the paperwork on getting you out of here. We'll talk on the bird."

Thomas Chatham looked at the Super Beaver and rubbed his chin.

"It's not really for rent," the salesman said. "I mean for a few hours, yeah. But if you need it for a week . . ."

"Possibly more," Thomas said. "How much to buy it?"

"Five five," the salesman said. "I mean, it's practically straight out of the upgrade. Cherry."

The basic airplane had been built in 1956 but Beavers were considered eternal. One of the best small bush planes ever made, most of the original run that had not crashed, and given the conditions under which they flew a lot had been destroyed over the years, were still in use. Recently, new engines and avionics had been developed for them that extended their range and improved their survivability. With the upgrades, the new class of Super Beaver might still be in the air when the original airframe was pushing the century mark.

This Beaver had been configured for amphibious operations, with pontoons that featured small wheels for strip landings. It would be perfect for use in the islands. Although with a Gulfstream and two helicopters, Thomas wasn't sure what the Kildar needed it for.

"I'll need to call my . . . supervisor," Chatham said. *He* didn't need a Super Beaver, that was for sure. "That was more than we were looking at. I'll get back with you. By the way, do you take cash?"

"I got the materials," Oleg said as Mike, pushing Adams in a wheelchair, approached the Gulfstream.

"Good," Mike said. "You ready to walk, yet, crybaby?"

"I'm *fine*," Adams said, standing up and then swaying. "God *damn*."

"I've got you," Oleg said, grabbing the master chief's arm. "I was the same way. It is not something to be ashamed of."

"I'm not ashamed," Adams said. "I'm *pissed*."

With Oleg's help he was loaded on the plane. Mike climbed onboard, followed by Greznya, who had clearly been weeping.

"You okay, Grez?" Adams asked, grimacing in pain as he settled in the seat.

"I am, in fact, very good, Master Chief," the girl said, then burst into tears again.

"Vanner finally popped the question," Mike said, grinning. "Hey, Grez, how you fixed for a dowry?"

"Thanks to you, Kildar, just fine," the girl said. "And I hate to say it, but the one condition that Patrick put on the marriage is that I *not* enter the Rite."

"Fine by me," Mike said. "I was wondering when he'd finally get off the stick. Damn, that boy can be slow sometimes. Besides, he's good genes, too. The Mothers should be well satisfied."

"Damn," Adams said. "Color me clueless."

"Like I said," Mike replied. "You weren't hired for your brains."

"Daria!" Mike yelled as soon as he was in the house.

"Here, Kildar," the girl said, walking into the main room.

"Where are we—"

"The boats have been surveyed," Daria said, almost simultaneously. "The senior chief says they are all in good working order but he is 'tuning' them. They have most of the materials they need to install the extended range tanks. He assures me they will have them installed by dusk. They are being painted as well. Some of the Keldara are assisting in that. Vil's team is considered 'marginally prepared' by Mr. Holterman. Mr. Chatham has found a plane meeting your requirements but it is unavailable for rental. They want a bit over a half million dollars for it."

"Buy it," Mike said, walking across the room towards the secure room that had been set up.

"The captain of the yacht says that he's ready to move when you are," Daria continued. "Gear has been moved to the yacht. The Hind is fueled and back onboard. Yosif's team is ready to board. To refuel the boats offshore the yacht will need to take on aviation gasoline in Nassau. It is available and the captain is aware of the necessity."

"Anything I'm missing?" Mike asked.

"Lunch," Daria said. "It's being laid on right now. I suggest you eat before you board the yacht, although there is food there as well."

"Thanks, Mother," Mike said. "I'll take that under advisement. It's a pretty long run."

"You should also sleep," Daria noted. "It's going to be a long night."

"I'll take that under advisement, too," Mike said, frowning.

He walked in the secure room and shook his head. Greznya had beaten him there and most of the girls were crying.

"This is what I get for setting up an intel shop of nothing but women," Mike said.

"Daria!" Irina said, ignoring him. "Sergeant Vanner has asked Greznya to marry him!"

"Oh, that is wonderful news!" Daria said, running over and hugging the girl.

"He is so weak," Greznya sniffled. "He is so tired."

"He'll be out here in a few days," Mike said. "You can feed him up. He'll get better. Trust me, I know."

"He knows," Britney said, nodding. "Boy, does he know."

"Quiet, you," Mike said. "I hate to break up the party, but do we have anything new?"

"It turns out the *Ronald Reagan* had already identified a probable contact," Irina said, wiping her eyes. "A freighter is tracking back and forth north of Grand Island. They have launched a plane to keep an eye on it."

"Excellent," Mike said. "Sort of."

"Sort of?" Irina asked. "I will not ask. We also

have gotten information from Jay." She handed Mike a form. "He believes he has a lead."

"Also very good," Mike said, nodding. "Anybody seen Dr. Arensky?"

"He is in an outbuilding," Daria said. "The other side from the harbor."

"I know it," Mike said. "Okay, Irina, who's on for tonight?"

"Myself and Creata," Irina said.

"Okay, be at the yacht in thirty minutes," Mike said, then paused at a frown from Daria. "Make that forty-five. And get some lunch."

Mike walked in the door of the small coral building and paused. Most of the interior was filled with plastic sheeting.

"Tolegen?" Mike called. He could see a shape through the plastic and assumed it was the doctor.

The interior was very cool and smelly. There was an acrid stench that was overlaid with various fruity odors. Mike didn't recognize any of them, but "cloves" came to mind.

"Ah, Kildar," the Russian scientist said, pushing aside some of the plastic. "Welcome to my laboratory." He said it the way any good mad scientist would: Lab-oooor-a-tory. Roll the Rs.

"Just can't keep from tinkering?" Mike asked.

"I have never had a chance to study some of the properties of tropical fauna," the Russian said. He had a Petri dish in one hand and a glass beaker filled with a yellowish substance in the other. "There are some very vile poisons to be found in tropical species. I wonder if you're ever going to go to the Australia area?"

"At this rate I'd put it as 'likely,'" Mike said, sitting on the edge of the room's desk. There was a small chemical lab set up on a table on the side. While it was incredibly, almost unbearably, neat, the desk was littered with papers. "Got a question for you: can you come up with something that will incapacitate a large number of people? I'd prefer not to kill them because I'm going to need to ask some questions. But just unconscious or very sick would do."

"Easily," Tolegen said, frowning. "But how large an area? If you're talking about a lot it would be logistically difficult."

"A small freighter," Mike said. "I'm not sure of the cubic footage. I can probably get that for you. But I'd like something that's pretty potent and portable. Getting it *onto* the freighter is going to be the bitch."

"That is harder," Arensky admitted. "Very high potency, but not killing. Sarin for that area . . . With a good distribution system, which a freighter has, you could do it with a tank the size of one of your SCUBA tanks. There is one substance, a Russian product, that will act as a hallucinogen. Would that do?"

"Probably," Mike said. "But I've got to be able to get something out of them."

"Oh, it is very fast acting but also very briefly effective," the Russian said. "The effects pass in no more than thirty minutes. Inhalant so if anyone realizes what is happening they need only put on a breathing apparatus. I'm going to need some chemicals that are not here. You will also need a container and a distribution system. I can make both from available materials but it will be the equivalent of two of your SCUBA tanks. In fact, that is *exactly* what it will be . . ." he added, looking distant.

"That's perfect," Mike said. "Get with Daria on what you need. I'm going to need it by tomorrow night."

"If I can get the materials rapidly," Tolegen said, nodding. "Yes, that will work. It is easy enough to make. If you know how," he added, grinning. "You don't want them killed?"

"No," Mike said, walking out. "I'll take care of that."

"Oh, hello Juan," Mike said.

He had been wandering the Straw Market, just poking around. Anastasia had wanted to take a look around and it was a good enough way to build the fact that he was, in fact, in town.

"Mr. Jenkins," the Colombian said, nodding back.

Gonzales was clearly taking some of "his" girls out shopping as well, Katya not being one of them. He also had four large, suited Colombians with him, earbuds in place and eyes scanning the crowd.

Mike had brought pretty much the entire harem, including Martya, all dressed in identical Mountain Tiger outfits. Anastasia was wearing a sundress. The group was being shadowed by seven of Oleg's team, with Oleg in the lead, suited up in shorts, T-shirts and Mountain Tiger jackets that poorly concealed their body armor and weapons. They were wearing Invisio Bone-Mics, the absolute state-of-the-art in interpersonal commo. They also, individually, out-massed any of the Colombians by at least twice.

The two groups eyed each other like competing wolf packs as their principals sparred.

"I see you decided to show back up," Gonzales said.

"Just went out to show the girls the out-islands," Mike said. "Getting covered in nude teenagers is a bit much for even Nassau."

"Of course," Gonzales said. Although the three boat-bunnies with him were pretty, the harem was orders of magnitude beyond any of the three.

"But, hey, girls like to shop, too," Mike said, shrugging. "I swear, even after you cover one of them in rubies, they want sapphires."

"Women are that way," Gonzales said. "They are always wanting more. It is a pity they cannot just be satisfied with what they have. But men are the same way, don't you think?"

"Some," Mike said. "Then again, some just want to make sure things stay the way they were."

"Change is inevitable," Gonzales said.

"Oh, absolutely," Mike said. "I mean, look at evolution. All those mutations occurring all the time. But you know what's neat about evolution?"

"What?" Gonzales said.

"Well, most of those mutations don't take," Mike said, removing his sunglasses and looking the Colombian in the eye. "You see, better species wipe them out because they thought that change was the way to go when it was just a short road to extinction. Only one out of a billion mutations succeed. Me, I'd tend to go for the conservative route."

"Some of us are more courageous," Gonzales said, his jaw working.

"There's a difference between courage and stupidity," Mike said, putting his sunglasses back on. "And most of those mutations only realize that after they're extinct."

CHAPTER
SIXTEEN

"Marathon, Marathon, Charlie Three One Five," the coast guard pilot said. "We have a suspicious fast mover, fifteen miles east of Largo. Has been hailed, refuses to heave to. Request fast vessel for intercept, over."

"Charlie Three One Five, Marathon," the base said. "Roger on fast mover. We have it and you. Negative on support. All fast boats outside support area."

"Fuck," the pilot muttered, looking over at his co. They'd just tanked before taking off and had another hour's fuel.

"Marathon, Marathon. Fast mover turning east towards Bahamas. Request pursuit."

"Roger, Charlie Three One Five," the headquarters said a minute later. "Pursue to PNR, over."

"Roger," the pilot said, banking the Lynx. "We got a hard lock?"

"Rog," the co said, looking at the Forward Looking Infrared readout. "I don't think he knows we're back here. He's headed for the Cut."

"Good," the pilot said. "It's nice and narrow in there. But I'm not sure we're going to get him with cargo. He's already headed home."

"Fuck cargo," the co said. "There's going to be residue. What's the status on Bahamas?"

"Marathon, Marathon," the pilot said tiredly. "Any chance of Bahamas intercept?"

Mike leaned out the door of the Hind, holding onto the fast-rope and watched the speeding Cigarette below.

He was trying to decide whether to stay in the helo or be in on the boat intercept. There were benefits and detractions with each. With the boat intercept, it was more likely he was going to get to kill someone. On the helo, on the other hand, he could control the intercept better.

"We got a track on this thing?" Mike asked.

"It's almost to the cut," Irina said, looking at her computer screen. "But I've got another track that looks as if it's following it. Air track."

"What the fuck?" Mike asked. He walked across the interior of the bird and squatted down, looking at the screen. The take from the balloon radar had been filtered to only vector on the track and items immediately around it. Sure enough, about four miles back there was a blue icon of an air track, following along neatly.

"Shit," Mike said, looking at the icon. "It's fucking 315."

"Excuse me, Kildar?"

"It's a Coastie, a Coast Guard helo," Mike replied. "They were the bane of my existence when I lived here.

Turned out they were under orders to keep an eye on me. I always wondered why they showed up every time I moved. And now they're chasing our track."

He thumbed his throat mike for internal.

"Dragon, we have a complication."

He was glad he'd stayed on the helo.

"Marathon, fast mover is in Bahamanian waters," 315's pilot said. "Continuing pursuit. Any data on Bahamanian intercept?"

"Negative, 315," the headquarters said unhappily. "All vessels out of area. You are cleared to continue pursuit into Bahamas territory."

"We're about bingo on fuel," the co-pilot pointed out. "I mean I know this is fun and all . . ."

"It's frustrating is what it is," the pilot said. "But we can tank in Bimini if we have to. They've got pretty good av-fuel."

"What the hell?" the co said. He was getting a feed from the radar balloon as well, a much more complicated one, and he now shook his head. "I got fast movers. Air and sea. Five sea, one air. Closing on the track."

"Marathon, Marathon," the pilot said, then unkeyed the mike. "What do I say? 'What the fuck, over?'"

"Dragon, close the helo," Mike said.

It was not long before Before-Morning-Nautical-Twilight, the "darkest before the dawn" and lowest ebb in the human system. Four AM in other words. With the moon down the ocean was pitch black, barely reflecting a welter of stars.

Kacey poured on the power, banking away from

the approaching terrorist boat so as not to blow the
op and swinging north to get behind him.

"Coast Guard 315, Coast Guard 315, this is Dragon
Flight, over," Mike said. They had full codes and
encryptions for everyone running in the area in the
U.S. government. And Vanner had been very complete
in his commo gear selection.

"What the fuck is Dragon Flight?" the pilot of
315 asked.

"How the fuck do I know?" the co said. "But they're
coming in on encryption nine."

"Dragon, Dragon, this is 315 . . ."

"315, you need to exit this AO. You are not cleared
for the operation that is ongoing. Over."

Mike unkeyed the throat mike and wondered what
response he'd get.

"Fuck," the pilot said, frowning. "Fucking black
ops bastards. That's *our* track."

"Yeah, but ain't shit we can do about it," the co
pointed out. The helo could outrun the cigarette boat,
but stopping it was another issue. If they were *stupid*
they could drop down in front of it. If they wanted
to get run over or shot to shit. The Coast Guard helo
had one pistol on board. The cigarette, assuming it
was a Colombian, was probably bristling.

"Dragon, Dragon," the pilot said. "Negative. Our
track. Let Bahamanian authorities handle it."

"Dumbass," Mike muttered then keyed the mike.
"No intercept vessels in area." He paused. "Trust me,

we made sure of that. We didn't figure Coasties would pursue *this* far. You have to be bingo and we're not going to retank you. Now Bank Off."

"Arrogant fuck," the pilot said. "Negative, Dragon. Our track."

"Stupid bastard," Mike muttered. "Okay, 315. Be aware that you are now placing yourself, by your own recognizance, in a high-level security op. Feel free to watch. You talk, you go to Marion. Do not pass go."

"Boss, maybe we shouldn't . . ." the co said nervously, then looked at the radar take. "The other helo . . ."

Had swung in behind and now blew past them like they were standing still. With dual miniguns and spare tanks mounted on the pylons, it was closing on the cigarette from behind at about twice the cig's speed. Dim silhouettes perched in the doors could be seen holding weapons. Sniper rifles.

"That's not one of *ours*," the co said, confused.

"No, that was a fucking Hind," the pilot replied. "Who in the *fuck* uses a *Hind*?"

"I thought they were pretty . . . piggy," the co said. "That don't look piggy."

"No, it doesn't," the pilot said, speeding the Lynx up to try to catch the barreling Hind. It was pointless; the normally sluggish Russian attack bird had clearly been upgraded; it was leaving the Coast Guard Lynx in its wash.

"This sucks."

▲   ▲   ▲

"Oorah!" Mike shouted at the team in the bird.

"AER KELDAR!" Pavel shouted back, giving him a thumb's up. He was leaning out, holding onto the other fast-rope. Perched in a harness in the door was Braon Kulcyanov, his team sniper.

Perched in the door next to Mike was Lasko Ferani, the Keldara's *top* sniper. Admittedly, this was a clap shot; Mike could have done it just as easily. But there was no reason to just keep Lasko around for the occasional Hail Mary when there were other missions he could do.

"Dragon, Dragon, slow down a bit," Adams said, watching the converging tracks. There were ways to do it by computer but that was too complicated. He'd watched this sort of thing enough to figure it out by eye and it was clear that Dragon was going to get to the cig before it should. "About ten knots."

"Hah!" the Lynx pilot said. "Now we're catching up!"

"Yeah," the co said. "But *why*?"

"There it is," Tammy said, tapping her FLIR read-out. Not that Kacey could see it since she was in a completely different compartment.

"Got it," Kacey said, dropping the helo slightly closer to the deck. Most cigarettes didn't have radar. But she didn't want one of the terrorists looking behind them.

That wasn't likely. Sayid Al-Yemani was exhausted as was his crew. All he could think was how much he was looking forward to a few hours' sleep in the hotel in Nassau. Farid and Abdul were both half asleep since it was the first calm water they'd hit since the Abacos, which was over twenty-four hours before. None of them were looking behind them.

"Dragon," Adams said, watching the converging vectors. "Bank left."

Mike held onto the rope as the bird banked, the water flashing by underneath, lit by the stars. He'd doffed his NVGs and now was trying to spot the cigarette by Mark One Eyeball. Soon enough it was easy; the boat was leaving a green phosphorescent wake that was distinctive.

He leaned down and tapped Lasko's shoulder, pointing towards the boat. But the old tracker had already acquired the target.

He stroked the trigger of the Barrett twice, sending a single round into each of the engines of the cigarette.

"Target is slowing," Mike said, thumbing his throat mike. "Converge."

"There," Beso said, pointing ahead. It was hard to tell how far away the boat was but it had to be close. Seeing much beyond five hundred meters with the NVGs was tough.

"Got it," Vil said, looking left and right. He could make out the shapes of the other converging boats. Everybody was well spread.

"Viking, Viking, Keldara Three."

"Go, Three."

"Converge . . . now."

▲   ▲   ▲

"Uh?" Farid said, his eyes flickering open as the boat slowed. "What . . . ?"

"The engine quit," Sayid snarled, turning around. Prophet's Beard, it was *smoking*! "Fire!" He snatched at the fire extinguisher and started making his way towards the rear just as the sound of helicopter blades penetrated his battered consciousness.

"NVGs OFF!" Mike shouted. "Dragon, spot NOW!"

Sayid was blinded by the sudden light, holding his arms up to shield his eyes. For a moment he couldn't think, then he reached for the portable GPS with the drop points on it. He had to fumble for the damned thing; he could barely see in all the light.

Vil banked the Cigarette alongside the boat and backed, hard, as Yosif's team started scrambling over to the other boat.

Sayid got his hand on the GPS and tossed it over the side just as the boat started filling with men in body armor and carrying weapons. He knew what else he had to do, drawing his pistol and triggering two rounds into the mounted GPS. Then he placed the barrel under his chin and fired a single round.

"Fuck," Mike muttered as the driver shot himself. He'd seen him toss *something* over the side as well. "Dragon, pull to the starboard side of the boat. Now!"

As the helo pulled across, nearly over Vil's Cigarette, Mike quickly dumped his body armor and attached vest. Then he dove out of the helicopter.

He could barely see without a mask, but there was plenty of light from the helo's spot. He could see an out-of-focus shape, descending rapidly, and he followed as fast as he could in his uniform and boots, frog-kicking and swirling with his arms. The damned thing was falling fast, though. Then it seemed to pause and he realized the depth here wasn't more than twenty feet. The GPS, a small dark shape, was clearly outlined on the white sand bottom. He grabbed it and headed back for the surface.

But his uniform was weighing him down. Getting back *up* was a hell of a lot harder than getting *down*. He put the GPS in his teeth and doffed his top, then pulled off his boots. *Now* he could swim.

Creata gripped the fast-rope and dropped through the air as the helo balanced over the terrorist cigarette boat. Creata wasn't normally a data stripper. Stella was the top expert at ripping out electronics in the middle of a firefight. Creata, whose small stature and gentle appearance had landed her with the nickname "Mouse," was a cracker. Not the electronic kind, the safe kind. She'd been trained to open one safe for the Balkans op and managed it with finesse despite having to kill a guard that her security had missed, much to their everlasting chagrin. Since then she'd been taking advanced classes in what the FBI referred to as "black bag" operations. Lock-picking, safe-cracking, quiet electronics insertion: those were Mouse's specialty.

But she could hum the tune of ripping out some electronics and there were only so many girls along on this venture. Needs must and all that.

The two surviving terrorists were being tossed across the gap to Clarn's Hustler as the dead body of the driver was being loaded into Vil's Cigarette. She landed on one of the seats, stumbling slightly, then sat down in the driver's seat. Taking a look at the configuration she rolled under the console and pulled out a power screwdriver. Four screws secured the console-mounted, shot-to-shit, GPS. She had the screws off in seven seconds and the GPS out in another ten. Not bad for a cracker.

She tossed it to Clarn, then jumped the gap to the Cigarette.

"Don't think we'll get much," she said, shrugging, as she buckled in.

"That's up to you guys," Clarn said as the rest of the team scrambled onboard. "Anything else?"

"Nothing we saw," Genrich said, setting his weapon into a deck-mounted rack. "We're clear."

"Then we're out of here," Clarn said, putting the Hustler into drive.

Vil turned, his MP-5 coming up to ready position as a hand came over the side of the Cigarette. He held his fire, though, since the mission was to capture as many of the terrorists as possible. He was glad when he saw the head of the Kildar come over the side, drop something on the floor, then slide up with a kick.

"Damn," Mike said, breathing hard. "I'm getting too old for this shit."

The fast boats pulled away as the light from the helo went out. The cigarette rocked on the waves for a few moments then went up in a flash of fire. In a second, all there was left to indicate that a small battle had happened here was a bit of gasoline burning on the surface. In seconds that was gone.

"They just blew it the fuck up," the co said, shaking his head. "That's a quarter of a million dollars just went sky-high."

"315, this is Dragon Flight, over."

"Go, Dragon."

"This mission is classified, codeword Thunder Child, security level Ultra Purple. Need to know is restricted to CJCS and above. Your participation will be reported to appropriate persons. No one in your chain of command below CJCS has need to know. Do you acknowledge, over?"

"Acknowledged, Dragon," the pilot said. "We're out of here."

"Roger, 315. Suggest next time you mind your own business."

CHAPTER
SEVENTEEN

"We have a portable GPS," Mike said, scrambling onto the helo. The boats and the helo had rendezvoused on a bit of sand—it couldn't be called an island—south of the intercept. The sand was half mud and Mike lost one of his socks. He hoped nobody found it; it was about the only sign that anything had happened in the area.

"I got the dash mount," Creata said, holding up the destroyed unit. "*I* can't get anything out of it."

"Somebody might," Mike said, shrugging. "And this might have something," he added, handing over the hand-held.

"If they're smart, they don't even turn it on until they get near the drops," Creata pointed out.

"True," Mike said. "Take a look."

Creata had tried to memorize all the GPS configurations she could but this one was easy. The Garmin GPS was similar to one that the teams had used before they got more advanced gear. She keyed it on and sorted through the menu, then grinned.

"There are four points on it," she said. "And a track. But, yeah, it starts about fifteen miles north of the first point. Nothing before then."

"Well, we've got those," Mike said. "That's something," he added, keying his throat mike.

"315, 315, this is Dragon, over."

"What the fuck does he want *now*?" the pilot snarled. "Go, Dragon!"

"Stand by to receive coordinates," Dragon said. "Probable WMD drop points."

"Oh, shit," the co said, blanching. "That wasn't a *drug* boat . . ."

"Roger, Dragon," the pilot said. "Your bird. And get off the line."

"My bird," the co said.

"Go, Dragon . . ."

Mike read off the coordinates then paused.

"315, what is your status?"

"We are bingo. Headed to Bimini for fuel."

"Roger. Vector to coordinates upon refueling. We are vectoring to that location at this time. Contact your higher upon refueling. They should have orders for you."

"Roger, Dragon," the pilot responded. "And, uh, sorry for jumping your shit, over."

"Acknowledged."

"Tammy, give me a direct link to the joint task force."

"JTF Six."

It was late but the admiral had been awake. He'd

been sleeping in catnaps for the last two days. He'd developed the ability years before and knew he could keep going, and keep functional, for another two, max.

"This is the Kildar. We have four probable WMD drop points. I'm sending the coordinates over on a secure link. I recommend we wait for a pick-up before we hit them. The boats picking up are probably Scarab fast fishers. I'm vectoring my team to stand-by positions but do not intend to engage. However, make sure you have fast boats this time. Note: the Scarabs probably have radar."

"Roger, Kildar," the admiral said, frowning. *Teach your grandmother to suck eggs, you arrogant prick.*

"The locations are near Largo. If you don't have fast assets in that area, call me back."

"Roger, Kildar," the admiral repeated. That was actually a point. There might *not* be fast assets in the area. "I'll call you back."

"Roger. Kildar, out."

"Vil, what's your fuel state?" Mike asked.

"I'm at sixty percent. Most of the other boats are in the same range. Clarn is at about forty-seven."

"Roger," Mike said, frowning and thinking. "Head for coordinates 52 East by 27 North at this time. If Clarn can't make it to tankage in a round-robin, have him break off and head to Bimini to fuel."

"Roger, Kildar."

"Dragon," Mike said, changing frequencies. "What's *your* fuel state?"

"I could practically fly to D.C.," Kacey said. "We're good."

"Right," Mike said, sitting down in one of the jump seats in the bird. "Lasko!" he shouted.

The shooter looked over his shoulder and tossed his head in acknowledgement.

"Close it!" Mike shouted, motioning him to close the door.

"Dragon," Mike said. "Head for Largo."

"You're *kidding*!" Admiral Ryan snapped.

"Sir, I'm sorry," the Coast Guard rep to the JTF said, shrugging. "We don't have all that many fast boats. We had two experimental ones, faster than just about anything out there, but we never got funding for more, or parts, and had to eventually scrap the one we had left after one crashed in a chase. DEA had some but they mostly wrecked them. The ones they've got left are up in the Palm Beach area or down by Key West. The ones in the Palm Beach area, if we can get them scrambled, will take a couple of hours to get there. The Marine Patrol has some and *all* their boats are as fast as a Scarab. I suggest we call them."

"Okay," the admiral said, sighing. "I need the FDLE rep, right now. But . . . I'm going to let someone else take point. Marine Patrol can help but they're to remain distant from the engagement. I have another call to make."

"Kildar," Creata said over the intercom. "Admiral Ryan."

Mike keyed his throat mike as Creata transferred the call.

"Go, Ryan."

"You were right," the admiral said sourly. "There

aren't any fast boats, not Cigarettes or equivalent, in the area."

"There's a reason I'm here, sir," Mike said. "Besides the fact that I'm trusted by higher and get the job done, I know the waters and the players. I was pretty sure that was the case. I may need some discreet tanking after the job is done."

"The base at Largo has avgas," the admiral said. "That good enough?"

"As long as we can get this done by dawn," Mike said, glancing at the sky. "Hell, I've got an alternative, even if we can't. We'll get it done, sir."

"Roger," Ryan said. "Marine Patrol is on standby to intercept if necessary."

"Hopefully not," Mike said as Creata gestured at him. "I'll get back with you in a bit, sir." He changed back to local. "What?"

"We have two winners," Creata said, pointing to her screen. "Two boats are approaching two different drop points. They're in about two hundred feet of water, by the way."

"Deep dive," Mike said, shrugging. "But you can do it on trimix. What's our time to intercept?"

"About an hour and a half," Creata said. "For the boats. Less for the helo, of course."

"No, we're going to need the boats," Mike said. "Keep an eye on those contacts."

"There," the technician said. "There are the two boats. They're heading for the coordinates."

"They won't stop," the admiral said, looking over his shoulder. "See if they slow down, but I bet they don't stop."

"That one . . . it's circling. Circling. Now it's leaving."

"Bet it heads to another drop point," the admiral said.

"Direct vector," the technician said, nodding.

"Tag that contact and zoom out," the admiral said. "Look over towards the Bahamas cut and look for some fast boats and maybe a helo."

"One helo approaching Bimini," the technician said. "Coast Guard 315. There . . ." he added, highlighting a group. "Four fast boats and a helo following headed west out of the cut. Looks like a fourth that might have been with the group heading north to Bimini." He paused, puzzled, and pulled up another control. "The helo does *not* have a transponder."

"Is there a way for me to cut out all the take on this to anyone but us?" the admiral asked.

"The control is the Joint Drug Task Force command, sir," the technician said uneasily. "But, yes, it can be done. But, sir, there are all sorts of ops that depend on this system. There are probably three or four drug ops going down right now using this take."

"I need everything related to these tracks filtered out," the admiral said. "The security on this op is at a very high level."

"Yes, sir," the tech said. "I know how that can be done, technically, but I'd need clearance codes from JDTF."

"I'll get them. And I might have to cut *you* out, as well. If not, you're going to go into a very restricted compartment."

"Okay," Mike said over the team circuit. "These guys probably have radar. So we're going to be detected on the way in. That means they're going to run. A

Scarab has a top speed around fifty knots. Top speed for our boats is closer to a hundred. The helo is faster. When we get in detection range, if they run, two of the boats will take off after one contact, the other two after the other. Lightning and the Drone to the south contact, Cig 36 and the Nordic to the north. The helo will vector to the south contact, wait until the boats are close, then take down the contact. Boats will close, secure gear and determine if there is WMD already aboard. If so, NO SHOOTING. You're not in MOPP gear. If there is any evidence that the WMD is active, do NOT board. The helo will then vector to the other chase. If the boats get inshore, continue to pursue. Do NOT let this stuff get onto land. If they get inshore, there may be Florida Law Enforcement in the area. You will not interact with Florida Law Enforcement. You will not speak to them and you will carry out your mission even if they attempt to interfere. Secure the personnel, transfer them to the helo and leave any WMD you find. FDLE and the JTF can clean that up."

"DTF is locked out for take," the technician said, punching in the last code. "For these tracks and these tracks only."

"Okay," the admiral said. "I have the board," he said, gesturing for the technician to stand up. "I'll call you back when you can have your board back."

"Sir, with all due respect," the technician said. "I'm not going to talk. I have a very high clearance. And I can do this job—sorry, sir—better than you can. I would, with respect, recommend that you let me stay."

The admiral considered that, then shrugged.

"Okay, lady, but if you so much as breathe a word of what is about to happen, you can plan on spending the rest of your life behind bars."

"Yes, sir," the tech said. "Clear, sir. But you might want to get a chair. This isn't going to go fast."

They were closing, but not fast. The boats had gone to the second drop point, circled around again, then headed back to the first.

"They're carrying two divers," Mike said. "They spot the contact, toss over a buoy and drop the diver. The diver goes down, finds the barrel, secures it and raises it with a float bag. Probably it has some sort of transponder so they can find him again since he's gonna float. They go back, pick up the first one then go pick up the second."

"Yes, sir," Creata said. "But they appear to have picked up one, now," she said, pointing to the screen. The boat had stopped, not by the first drop point but close. Now it was heading north again.

"Are there other boats in the area?" Mike asked.

Creata hit a control and brought up All Tracks.

"There's a boat northwest of the second drop point," she said, pointing. "It's not moving. Could it be a support boat?"

"Probably some guys out night fishing," Mike said. "If they see us intercept they'll probably assume it's FDLE or Coast Guard after drug dealers. When's sunrise?"

"One hour," Creata said.

"We are about to become somewhat unblack," Mike replied, frowning.

▲   ▲   ▲

"AER KELDAR!" Edvin shouted, grinning. The Lightning 42 was flying across the waves of the Florida Straits, leaping out of the water then slamming down. Edvin had a solid grip on the grab handles, but he was loving every second of the trip. "What is that song that the Kildar plays? About coming from the land of the ice and snow?"

"The Keldara were boat warriors once," Vil shouted back. "Now we are again!"

The Navy chief had, without being asked, installed racks for the guns. Which was fortunate because without those racks the weapons would have been battered to pieces. As it was, two of the team's radios were out. The ride was brutal but exhilarating.

"We're going to have to tank!" Vil noted, tapping his fuel state. "I think we are going to be seen!"

"That is for the Kildar to figure out! All we have to do is capture some fucking Islamics. Then find out what they know!"

Abdullah al-Egypti pulled the exhausted diver over the side and clapped him on the back.

"Good job, Farid," he said. "Time to head home."

"I used to enjoy diving," the former commercial diver said, pulling off the elaborate dive rig. "But this is getting to be a bit much."

"Well, we will have a break in—"

"Abdullah," Jamal said, pointing to the screen. "We have two boats approaching from the east. Fast. And a plane or a helicopter."

"Get that stowed," Abdullah said, running to his seat. "And for Allah's sake, secure the barrel!"

"We need to get it below," Farid shouted.

"No *time!*" Abdullah said, starting the engine and turning in-shore.

"There they go," Creata said.

"Alpha team," Mike said. "Target is rabbiting. Say again, target is rabbiting."

CHAPTER
EIGHTEEN

The sky was turning a deep blue overhead, a sure sign of the sun coming over the horizon, as Vil tried to coax everything he could out of the Fountain, trimming the engine up a tad more to reduce the amount of hull hitting the water. He was slowly leaving the Drone driven by Tuul in his wake. In fact, the Drone had dropped directly *into* the wake as a way to pick up just a bit of speed. In flat water the Drone was, perhaps, a tad faster than the Fountain. But in these heavy waves the bigger single-hull boat was *definitely* faster. The problem with running in a wake, Randy had told them, was that the bubbles from the lead boat, the "cavitation effect" reduced the power the trailing boat's propellers could convey. So despite the lighter waters the Drone was still falling behind.

"We're on them, Kildar," Vil said, touching his throat mike.

▲   ▲   ▲

"Alpha team, turn fifteen degrees west," Mike said. "Cut the corner."

Abdullah looked at his GPS. It was five miles to the outer reef. The Scarab would be faster once he got into the slightly calmer water. As it was, he was having to keep his speed down to prevent the barrel of VX breaking free. Farid had lashed it down in the corner but if it broke loose they'd *have* to stop and secure it again. Otherwise it was likely that the barrel would break open. And while Abdullah didn't mind being a martyr, he'd like to take at least a *few* infidels with him.

"Farid! How is the barrel?"

"Holding," Farid said. He was crouched by the barrel, tying in another knot. "So far!"

The boat driver looked at his radar next, then shook his head. The two boats pursuing him were cutting in from the south, not following him directly. They were going to try to cut him off. And they were *fast*. Allah's Teeth they were fast.

"I can see them," Dmitri said, reaching down to the deck and unstrapping his MP-5. "Team," Yosif's assistant team leader continued, thumbing his throat mike. "Lock and load. But unless forced, do *not* fire. Take a bullet if you have to. But whatever you do, *don't* shoot one of those damned barrels!"

"Dragon, move to take-down position," Mike said.

The helo sped up and Mike gestured to Lasko to open his door.

"Lasko," Mike said. "Two outboards. *Don't* hit the barrel."

"Of course not, Kildar," Lasko said, thumbing his mike. "Who do you take me for? Shota?"

Lasko leaned out the door of the Hind and lined up the port engine. He could see a man crouched by a blue barrel at the rear of the boat. The man looked up at him and made a gesture with his hand that was as ancient as any human culture, a thumb thrust up between index and middle finger.

Lasko couldn't care less. All he wanted to do was make the shot. He targeted the port engine and stroked the trigger. The boat almost immediately swung hard to port, then corrected back and began weaving.

That was okay, let it weave. He waited, then stroked the trigger again. Target.

Abdullah cursed as the second engine went out. "Fire back!" he shouted.

A man passed up an AK to one of the people on the boat and Lasko leaned back.

"Mannlicher!" he shouted, holding the Barrett behind him like the proverbial Great White Hunter switching from elephant gun to lion in the midst of a charge.

Mike grinned, handing him the 7mm while taking the Barrett. Then Lasko leaned out as rounds started to crack upwards.

He found the man with the AK and swung the barrel down as rounds flew past. One of his rounds cracked into the man's knee. The Kildar wanted them alive and it wasn't like taking someone down at two miles.

He continued to track around, taking down one target after another. The boat was rocking in the waves, still moving slowly to port and the targets weren't exactly standing still to be shot. Not to mention the movement of the helo.

So what?

Abdullah dropped, screaming and clutching his shattered knee. The sniper was *unreal*. He had fought the Americans in Afghanistan and even *they* could not have shot four men in four rounds in under four seconds through the damned *knees*! From a *helicopter*, no less.

He reached for the AK that Jamal had dropped and tried to raise it but even as he did it was snatched out of his hand, the breech destroyed by another round.

Farid crouched by the barrel in horror as the first of the boats came alongside. He was the only one who had, so far, not been shot. It could only be because they did not want to hit the barrel.

He didn't want them to hit it, either.

As men in battle armor and strange digi-cam uniforms jumped over the side of the boat, he raised his hands, slowly, and put them on top of his head.

They said Guantanamo was a nice place, three square halal meals and even some pretty female guards. . . .

"North contact," Mike said. "Close it, Lasko. Vil, head for the Largo Coast Guard station. Give the commander, and the commander only, the location of the WMD. Keep the driver. Find out anything you can fast. Turn the others over to the Coasties."

▲   ▲   ▲

"Hello," Dmitri said, sitting down by the man who had been on the deck by the driver's seat. "My name's Dmitri. What's yours?"

The man spat out a curse in Arabic and Dmitri shook his head.

"That's not very nice of you," he said, taking the butt of the MP-5 and slamming it into the man's bandaged knee. He waited for the screaming to die down, then smiled. "My cousin was just killed by some Islamic motherfuckers like you, so you'll excuse me if I don't give a shit about your opinion of me or my gods. Now, what is your name?"

"Abdullah," the man gasped. "Abdullah Al-Egypti."

"Well, Slave of God who is Egyptian," Dmitri said, "I'd like to know what you did with the other barrels."

"Go to . . . hell," Abdullah said.

"Wrong answer," Dmitri said, slamming the butt down again. More screaming. It was most distressing. There were boats moving around, now.

"We leave them," Abdullah said, panting in pain. "We have a drop point sent to us. We leave them behind stores. In woods. I have the next drop points," he said, gesturing with his chin at his pocket. "Please . . ."

Dmitri fished in the man's pocket and came up with a scrap of paper. It said "Behind Largo Seven-Eleven. Behind Pizzeria."

"Thank you," Dmitri said, smiling. "See how easy that was?" He thumbed his throat mike. "Vil, we still have the Kildar?"

"I can uplink," Vil said, hitting a switch on a dash-mounted satellite communicator. "Freq four."

"Kildar, Kildar," Dmitri said. "Alpha team. Intel update."

Admiral Ryan nodded as he took down the communication.

"Thank you, Kildar. I have a Coast Guard boat on the way to tow in the Scarab. You're sure the WMD is not active?"

"Positive. We're going to drop all these guys with the Coasties. Make sure that they know that they're not to talk to them or even listen to them. And my boats need to fuel."

"It's taken care of," Admiral Ryan said, nodding. "Your other contact . . ."

"Is nearly inshore," Mike said. "And the sun's up."

Jeff Hopkins looked up at the sky and sighed. It was going to be a good day to fish.

Jeff had been born and raised in the Keys. He'd never gone to college but he always found one thing or another to keep him from leaving the increasingly expensive area. He'd been a boat mate, a guide, worked construction. Presently he was selling boats at Key West Boat Sales in Key Largo.

The problem with that job was it was so damned *constant*. He rarely got a day off.

He'd managed one, finally, and was damned well going to get some fishing in. It was just about dawn, perfect fishing time.

He coasted his Mako 26 around the corner of Tavernier Creek, moving carefully. Idiots would come roaring down the cut and if you didn't watch out you'd get run over. He could do the run about six times as fast as he was currently going but not if some idiot swung wide on the corner.

He powered up on the straight, then slowed, slightly, as he approached the next turn. Lined with twenty-foot mangroves, Tavernier Creek snaked back and forth several times before opening out to the ocean. There was no way to see a boat or hear one coming over the sound of his own motors. So he was only half surprised to see a Scarab, going flat the fuck out, come screaming around the corner *way* over on his side.

The AK in one of the men's hands, though, was another thing. And so was the helo, some sort of strange aircraft with pylons on the side, that came over the mangroves at about ten feet off the tops.

He pulled the boat off to the side and powered down as the spray from the Scarab covered his front and the wind from the helo battered him.

"Fuckin' drug dealers," he snarled.

He started to power up when he heard *more* engines, going flat out. He put on just enough power to stay in the lee of the turn and was glad he did when a Cigarette, closely followed by a Nordic, came screaming by. He had to admit that they did a pretty good job, actually staying on *their* side of the damned channel despite doing damned near seventy.

"And there goes DEA," he muttered. The guys in the boat were wearing battle armor and balaclavas. "Figures." The helo must have been DEA, too.

He cut the engines for a second as the wash rocked the boat, listening. Nope, nobody else.

Fine. He could still get his fishing in.

▲   ▲   ▲

Lasko was just lining up the engine as the boat cleared the cut but it turned, hard, to the right, engines screaming. He started to line it up again, then lifted the Barrett as the boat suddenly went airborne. From his seat he could see that the water was only inches deep on that side; the boat had "run aground" but so hard and fast it went vertical instead of sticking.

"Oh, fuck no," Mike said as the Scarab launched fifteen feet into the air and rolled. It hit upside down in the shallows and the back of the boat broke. Fuel began spilling out, leaving a slick of rainbow on the green waters. "JTF, JTF, we have a HazMat situation, over!"

When Arvidas saw the upside-down Scarab he banked left and slowed, looking for the channel markers. It was pretty clear that the water to the right was shallow; he could see the flat water and line of small breakers that indicated a shoal. Clearly the terrorists had not been as well trained.

A boat was screaming in from the north, following a poorly marked channel that, when Arvidas checked, wasn't on the chart. It had a blue light going, though: local police.

"Marine Patrol vessel approaching Tavernier Creek, respond over," Mike said. "This is Dragon Flight, helo in service of the U.S. government in your vicinity. Respond, over."

"Dragon Flight, this is Marine Patrol Four-Eight."

"Marine Patrol Four-Eight, this is Dragon Six. Vessel you are approaching is a HazMat condition. Stand clear. Stand clear."

"Roger. Acknowledge HazMat."

▲   ▲   ▲

"Fuck," Officer Norman Funk said, pulling back on the power of the Mako 24. He'd just had a HazMat class a few months before and the one rule they were drilled on over and over was Stay Far Away. "Dragon," he continued. "What is the nature of the chemical?"

"Marine Four-Eight, that is restricted. Highly lethal, over."

"It's that shit they said would look like drugs but was a HazMat," his partner said. "The stuff those Commercial guys got hit with up on the turnpike. Terrorists?"

"Probably," Norm said. "Roger, Dragon, acknowledged."

"Marine Four-Eight, please secure area. Our boats are bingo on fuel."

"Roger," Norm said. "Area is secured. Marine Patrol Headquarters this is Marine Patrol Four-Eight."

"Four-Eight, Headquarters."

"We have a HazMat at west entrance to Tavernier Creek. Request immediate response," he continued, speeding up to run down a boat headed towards the wreck. "And we're going to need more boats to close the area."

"We were monitoring and had already been informed, Four-Eight. Three-Six and Two-Five headed to secure east entrance. Monroe County Two-One and One-Five en route to your location. County HazMat inbound to Tavernier Marina. Be advised, material is airborne and extremely toxic. Maintain three hundred yards separation, minimum. Stay upwind as much as possible. We are broadcasting that Tavernier Creek is closed for the foreseeable future."

The damned fishing boat, a Cape Horn 20-foot center console, was totally ignoring him, of course. He cut in front of them and hit a long blast on his horn and they *finally* stopped.

"What's up, officer?" the man driving shouted. He had a lady, probably wife, and kids onboard.

"We've got a hazardous materials situation here!" Norm shouted. "You need to back away from here. Fast!"

"We got another coming in from the north," his partner said.

"Back off and stop any boats coming this way!" Norm shouted. "Get over by the point!"

"Yes, sir!" the man said, powering up and turning hard to the south.

"Damn, this is getting out of control," Norm said as a boat came cruising through the channel from the east. The big yacht slowed when it saw the wreck and turned towards it. There was a Cigarette that way and they turned to intercept the yacht. Both of them, though, were way too close to the HazMat and downwind.

"I hope this is a false alarm..."

"You need to leave here!" Yosif said, waving to the yacht. "Go away!"

"That boat..." the woman leaning over the side of the yacht said, pointing.

"Is very bad place, ma'am," Yosif shouted back. "Go awa..." He froze as he suddenly felt a strong twitch hit his entire body. "Go..."

"GAS! GAS! GAS!" Sergei screamed, clawing for his mask as Yosif fell to the deck. He could feel the twitching, too. He managed to get his mask on and cleared, then ripped out an atropine injector and slammed it into the inside of his thigh.

The atropine injector, the brand name being Atro-Pen, looked a good bit like a small vibrator and nothing at all like a syringe. And despite what Hollywood might think, you didn't inject it into your chest. It was designed to be injected into the thigh. People basic trained in its use were instructed to inject it in their outer thigh. Experts in the field went straight for the inner thigh, which had more blood vessels and picked up the atropine faster, hopefully missing the femoral artery. It had a spring-loaded needle two centimeters long that first flew out like a spring-blade, penetrating cloth, skin and muscle then, in one massive pump, dumped two milligrams of atropine into the human system.

Atropine was not an antidote for nerve gas, though. All it did was counteract the effects. He followed it with his 2-Pam injector. 2-Pam chloride neutralized most of the major nerve gas chemicals.

The secondary effects of both chemicals, however, were severe.

The yacht had turned away and was now lumbering up to top speed and headed south. The woman wasn't appearing to suffer any effects but there were houses in the area. The gas would be drifting towards them.

"This is very ungood," Mike said as the crew of the Cigarette either dropped or started donning masks. He should have told them to do that immediately.

But, fuck, they didn't even have MOPP gear. Another fuck-up on his part. They should have done the whole fucking mission in MOPP.

"JTF, JTF, HazMat is active," Mike said with a sigh. "I have a team down." He looked out the door and blanched as a news helo approached from the north. "And we are *so* out of here."

"This is Maria Consuella with Miami Five Live," the woman said. She had headphones on and was looking out the door of a helicopter. *"We have a report that a major hazardous material spill has occurred near Tavernier Creek in the Keys as the result of what appears to be an antidrug operation . . ."*

"What a way to start the morning," the President said, shaking his head. Two cigarette boats were just speeding away to the east and there was a flash of a Hind helicopter, dropping down to treetop level and heading east as well. The camera, fortunately, did not track in on them but focused on the upside-down boat and the police boats that were gathering in the area.

"They stopped four barrels," the DCIA said, shrugging. "Give them that. But, yes, it's pretty public."

"We might as well go public, then," the President said, looking over at his chief of staff.

"The press release is prepared," the COS said, nodding.

"Call the networks," the President said. "Tell them we're requiring time under emergency broadcast regulations. Call all the cable groups, too. Tell them that we need *everything*."

▲   ▲   ▲

"Can you make base?" Mike asked.

"Plenty," Kacey said.

"Get high and head for base," Mike said. "Keep an eye out for planes. Try to keep completely out of sight. We're public enough as it is." He changed frequencies and sighed. "Vil, what's the status on Yosif's team?"

"Kildar," Vil said. "Yosif was hit hard. So were two more of the people on that boat. They are headed for the station. We are just arriving." They were pulling into the dock even as he spoke and a crowd of Coast Guardsmen were gathered watching the spec-ops team pull in.

"Tell the commander that we need to minimize this as much as possible."

"That . . . is going to be hard."

Coast Guard Captain Paul Howard looked at the gathering crowd and shook his head.

"Bosun!" he shouted. "I see a bunch of people that need to find something to do!"

"Everybody but the fuel crew, clear the area!" the senior NCO of the station bellowed. "I can *find* things for you to do if I have to!"

The fueling crews caught the tossed lines and tied up the Fountain and Drone, then started pulling out hoses. The fuel was pumped over from the helo supply point but it was identical to what the cigarettes used.

"Who's senior?" the base commander asked.

"I am," a balaclava-clad figure said in a thick accent. Eastern European by the sound of it. The guy jumped up to the dock and saluted. "Team Vil, sir."

"I've been instructed to keep this as quiet as possible," the captain said. "But that's going to be tough, given that it's broad daylight."

"Could not be avoided, sir," the man said. "We had to intercept the shipment."

"This the WMD we've been looking for?" the captain asked. "I was told to dispatch a boat to pick up a Scarab and beware of HazMat."

"Yes, sir. That was the boat we took down." His men were hoisting wounded, liberally strapped up with duct tape, onto the dock. "These gentlemen we turn over to your care. Also this," the battle-armored man said, handing over a scrap of paper, "is pick-up points for WMD. Should be giving to police. Maybe pick-up still happen. Maybe not."

The captain took the paper, then looked closely at the prisoners. All but one were wounded. And all the shots were through knees. "Been doing a little torture, have we?" he asked angrily.

"Only a bit," the man said, shrugging. "And only one of them. The shots were by a sniper to prevent them releasing the WMD."

"No fucking way," the bosun said, shaking his head. "You don't shoot like that in a boat!"

"Helicopter," the man corrected. "And we have a very good sniper, yes? We have wounded coming in as well. Poison gas. They must be taken to hospital."

"Crap," Howard said. "I'll get some medics in suits right away. How contaminated?"

"Is no such thing as little contamination, yes?" the man said. "My boat is fueled. I am leaving drivers. Please to wash down boats and turn over to drivers. Decon everyone but they come back on boats, those that are functional. Even if exposed. We have very good doctor take care of them."

"Will do," the captain said, shaking his head. "Bosun . . ."

"Decon crews," the bosun said, nodding. "Medics in suits. Air evac. Wash down the bird. And talk to *everybody* . . ."

"This incident did *not* happen."

CHAPTER NINETEEN

"I am here to discuss the incident that has recently occurred in South Florida," the President said, ignoring the lights from the cameras. "It has been reported that this was part of an antidrug operation. This is not, in fact, true. The incident was the result of an anti*terrorism* operation. The hazardous material released was VX nerve gas that terrorists were attempting to smuggle into the United States."

He paused at the muttering from the room. It was pretty clear that while it wasn't "confirmed" enough to have made the news, yet, the reporters had had the word it wasn't some sort of hazardous drugs.

"As was the material recovered from the Wal-Mart truck, yesterday. I would like to thank the Wal-Mart corporation for their cooperation in this matter. By allowing the report of it being regular hazardous materials to remain, thus staining their reputation, we were able to intercept this second shipment.

"The area around the release has been evacuated,

the majority of the material has been secured and the area is being decontaminated. No civilians were hurt by the release. I have been informed by experts on the scene that the release was very small and that once they are done there will be no threat to human activity in the area. It is expected that Tavernier Creek will be reopened sometime tomorrow. The Florida Bureau of Fish and Game has ordered a suspension of fishing in the area as a precautionary measure. However, given the small fish-kill, it is likely that there was very little contamination of the waters.

"This shipment is not the only one that we believe to be coming into the U.S. The entire U.S. government, as well as allied and friendly governments, has been actively attempting to prevent this terrorist operation from being successful. This was the reason for the increased terrorism alert and for the recent activity by law enforcement organizations in South Florida. During this operation, two more barrels were recovered without incident.

"I am asking the people of South Florida to keep an especially sharp look-out for suspicious activity and anyone who has any suspicion or knowledge of this terrorist operation to contact the FBI tip line or any local law enforcement agency. VX nerve gas is lethal in very small doses and a terrorist attack using VX could be more devastating than the attack on the Twin Towers. I will now, briefly, take questions."

The President pointedly ignored an old lady in the front row who was practically hopping up and down in her seat and pointed to the man sitting next to her.

"Thank you, Mr. President," the CBS reporter said, being first chosen. "The operation appeared to be by a special operations group. Was this an American Army unit, such as Delta, and would that violate the laws against posse comitatus?"

"First of all, we never discuss operational details," the President said, sighing. "You know that, Larry. Second, posse comitatus doesn't come into it. This is a direct attack by a foreign group on the U.S. and falls under the War Powers Act. I am free to use any force I have at my disposal to stop it, be they military or law enforcement."

"Mr. President," the second reporter asked. She was a leggy blonde from Fox and not technically the one who was supposed to be next in line by seniority but the President had learned to pick his reporters carefully. "There was a brief flash in the camera shot of what I am told is a Russian attack helicopter. My informant was unaware of any U.S. group that uses those helicopters, at least operationally. Could you comment?"

"Not at this time," the President said, pointing to the next reporter.

"Mr. President, some of the special operations unit appeared to have been struck by the hazardous material we now know to be VX," the reporter said. "Can you comment on *that*?"

The President paused and thought, then shrugged.

"Only in the abstract and there I'd be glad to," the President said. "What I'm going to say will seem callous to some people, but ninety-nine percent of the soldiers, Marines, airmen and sailors in the armed forces would agree. The duty of a soldier is to place himself between danger and the people he or she is sworn to protect. If you'll pay close attention to that video, you'll see that the boat deliberately drove between the wreck where the VX was possibly being released and the civilian yacht. They placed themselves, in fact, very much in harm's way. That was their job, their mission. And, yes, several were injured by the gas. By doing so, they saved the lives of the people on that yacht. Think about *that* the next time you're reporting on the actions of our soldiers. They *deliberately* placed themselves in a position where they could be exposed to nerve gas to save the lives of civilians they've never met. No further questions."

"Dude, you are sooo blown," Randy said as Mike walked into the house.

"No shit, Sherlock," Mike said.

"How bad are the guys hit?"

"Yosif's pretty bad," Mike replied, walking over to the bar and pulling out a bottle of Elijah Craig. He paused, then poured a small amount in a glass and tossed it back. "He's at Homestead and is going to stay there for a while. The rest of the guys barely got a brush. Shouldn't be any long-term damage. The stuff's not very good as a skin contactant in low densities and they were washing down even as they headed to the Coastie base."

"You still planning on doing an op tonight?" Randy asked.

"I dunno," Mike said. "Ask me in a couple of hours."

"Kildar," Greznya said, walking into the room. "Phone. The President."

"Shit," Mike said, looking at the bottle, his jaw working. "I got it." He turned away from the bottle and headed to the secure room.

▲   ▲   ▲

"First of all, sorry," Mike said when he had the headset on.

"It was bound to happen sooner or later," the President replied calmly. "And at least now people know. Good job on finding these."

"But now they know we know their methods," Mike said. "They could change and then we're up shit's creek, pardon me, sir. I need to find the mother lode. The only way to do that is to intercept one of their boats and get the driver to talk. The last boat we got, the one we got these coordinates from, the driver shot himself. We've got the GPS off the boat but he'd shot *that*, too. My people can't get anything off of it. The one guy I've got who could . . ."

"Is still in the hospital," the President said. "Mike, you don't have to go this entirely alone. Send us the GPS. I'll make sure that top people get to work on it."

"Yes, sir," Mike said. "I'll get with Admiral Ryan on getting it into U.S. hands."

"Where do you think it is?"

"North of Grand Isle, somewhere," Mike said. "Probably moored below water level. But there's no way to find it. If you got every damned sub we've got down there and Yankee searched, you couldn't find it. It's a needle in a haystack. We've got an op planned for tonight that might get us the location. That is if I can get my boats back fast enough. I hadn't planned on going to *Largo* last night."

"Understood," the President said. "I'll say it again, you did good. And if you need *anything* that will stop this stuff, *ask*."

"Yes, sir," Mike said, thinking hard. "I'll get with Admiral Ryan."

"I'll call him, personally, and ensure that he knows that whatever you need, you get it," the President said. "Getting those barrels is the first good news in this entire thing we've had."

"Yes, sir, Mr. President," Ryan said, his head down, rubbing his forehead. "I have to say that I agree. And I'd say that even if you weren't the President. Yes, sir. I will, sir. Thank you, sir. Goodbye."

He hung up the secure phone and looked at his aide. "Get me the Kildar."

"Kildar," Mike said when the call was transferred. He had a sandwich in one hand and a glass of tea in the other. He was chewing.

"This is Admiral Ryan. What do you need?"

"Hang on," Mike said, swallowing and taking a drink. "Sorry. Long night. Can any fast birds from the *Ronald Reagan* land on a thirty-five-hundred-foot runway? I've got a GPS that's all smashed up but it might still have something we can get from it. I've got an op going down tonight that, I hope, will tell us where the mother lode is. But if not, the GPS might."

"An F/A-18 can. *Barely*. If it's lightly loaded with fuel."

"I'll send you the coordinates of the airport," Mike said, taking a sip of tea. "Other than that, we're good. I'll get back with you if we find out anything on the op."

"Roger," the admiral said. "Good luck tonight."

"Kildar out."

▲   ▲   ▲

Mike woke up at the sound of high-performance aircraft engines overhead, opening his eyes in slits. The fighter passed overhead, twice, clearly checking out the *really* short runway.

Mike got up, wincing at the pain in his joints, and pulled on a bathing suit. Then he checked the time. Three hours' sleep; that would have to do.

He wandered out the door of his room, then down the hallway, scratching at his belly and yawning. The F/A-18 was headed back around and he walked out the side door to watch it come in.

The bird had every flap up, coming in at a steep angle of attack. It hit, hard, then stood on its brakes. The bird stopped about fifteen feet from the end of the runway but, what the hell, there was a slight coral rise there that would have probably stopped it before it went off the end of the runway. Of course, depending on how fast it was going it could have either bent the nosewheel into a U or jumped it into the ocean.

The jet shut down its engines and one of the Keldara walked up, opening up a step point and clambering up alongside the canopy. He handed over the shot-up GPS, then climbed down. Mission accomplished.

"Let's hope they get something," Daria said.

"I think we probably will tonight," Mike said, stretching out his back. He felt like he'd been beat to crap. "How's Yosif?"

"Conscious," Daria said. "Doctors are testing his reflexes and psych profile today. They say that, so far, there are no 'gross signs of degradation.'" She was clearly quoting and said the phrase in English.

"I need to talk to Chatham," Mike said, walking back towards the lounge. "Any idea where he is?"

"Down by the beach," Daria said. "Watching your harem have fun."

"And that's what it's all about," Mike said as jet engines spooled up to max power in the distance.

The F/A-18 pilot had no clue what he was carrying. The thing was in a box. It could have been a snake for all he knew.

But the mission was the shit. There were tankers stacked from here to Langley. His job was to bust ass, top speed, to Washington. "Make a record," the captain had said.

He piled on the power until the brakes were practically smoking, then released. It wasn't as good as a catapult launch, but he had more runway. Halfway down the runway he kicked in the afterburner. Keeping it on the ground, he nosed up at the last possible moment and damned near his stall speed. The bird, though, kept gathering speed as the wheels came up, then more as he closed the flaps. When he had enough velocity, he pointed it at the sky.

He was at three thousand feet when the left engine snuffed out. It sent the bird into an immediate flat spin with not damned much altitude.

He powered down on the right engine, fighting the spin, until a glance at the altimeter told him it just didn't fucking matter. Then he reached over his head, pulled down the grab bar and punched.

Mike looked up at the change in the engine noise and began cursing, luridly.

"Eject, eject, fucking *eject*!" Chatham said, walking up behind him.

"Fuck the pilot," Mike snarled. "That's my god-damned intel going into the sea!"

"Fuck the pilot, huh?" Chatham said angrily.

"Yeah," Mike replied. "Because the lives of maybe five million people just went . . ." The pilot ejected and his zero-altitude chair rocketed upwards to high enough for his chute to deploy, safely. But he was limp in the chute. " . . . into the drink . . ." he finished as the bird smashed into the water. "FUCK!"

He began sprinting for the dock but Randy was ahead of him, the Cigarette started to pull out and Mike leapt off the dock, landing in a sprawl in the back.

"Go!" he shouted, grabbing the handles of one of the backseats.

Randy hammered the throttles and the Cigarette practically leapt out of the water, then settled down, swinging around to the east as he cleared the break-water. The water there was shallow, but he'd spotted a deeper cut. Now to find out if it was deep enough.

The propellers scraped across the sand, picking up the rear of the boat, but it kept going, Randy power-ing back and forth until they were over the bar. The pilot was still in the air as the Cigarette gained power speeding towards his probable point of impact.

The waters to the east were deeper, slightly. The props hit another underwater obstruction and Mike winced.

"Try not to break my boat, okay?" Mike yelled.

"I'm trying," Randy said. "You ready?" The pilot had come down and his Mae West automatically inflated on impact.

"I'm good," Mike said as the Cigarette started to slow. "But swing wider on the way back, okay?"

"You've got a repair group," Randy pointed out.

"Yeah, and a doctor," Mike replied.

The Cigarette came alongside the pilot and Mike snagged him by the back of his harness, pulling him over the side. The guy had a ripped-up leg and a big smacked spot in his helmet. He was breathing, though.

"Go," Mike said, laying the pilot out on the deck. He'd have put a cervical collar on if he could. But wasn't much they could do until they made it back to the island.

"The pilot has a concussion," Dr. Arensky said. "No apparent gross damage to the cervical area but there's only so much I can do with the X-ray machine I have here. He needs to be evacuated."

"Kacey," Mike said. "Load him up and take him to the carrier."

"Okay," the pilot said. "I hate to ask this but am I going to get any crew rest at all?"

"Tammy can take the Hind out and drop him off if you'd prefer," Mike said. "You can do your Dragon thing tonight."

"The Hind's going to need some TLC, too," Kacey said. "But, yeah, Tammy can take him. Valkyrie and all that."

"Works," Mikes said. "Go get some rest. I need to go find Chatham."

"The pilot is unconscious but doesn't appear to have sustained any critical injuries," Mike said when he got down to the beach. He flopped in one of the chairs and grimaced. "My *op* just did, but not the pilot."

"I'm finally putting two and two together," Chatham said. "I actually did that when the news mentioned a Hind helicopter."

"So now you know why that bird going down was so fucking important," Mike said. "He had a GPS onboard that, while fucked up, might have led us to the source of the VX. He'd have had to use it to find it and even if the track was deleted, you can often get stuff off computers that just . . . lingers. Unfortunately, my top guy for doing that is in the hospital. I've got, I figure, one more shot at getting the intel. The op tonight. And it's going to be a very slim chance."

"I'm not sure we're going to make it on time," Vil said, shaking his head.

"And only two boats," Dmitri said. "But we will do the mission, yes?"

"I hope that the Kildar has an idea, because I'm clueless."

CHAPTER
TWENTY

"I am getting tired of this helicopter," Creata said.

"Be glad you're not with Vil," Mike said, shaking his head. "They've been going flat out in cigarette boats since yesterday."

"That would be worse, yes," Creata admitted. "I think I have the track. It's a fast mover, not ours, headed for the target freighter."

"I need a vector," Kacey said, dropping lower to the waves.

Creata fiddled with the controls for a moment, then nodded.

"Turn to nineteen degrees," she said, yawning. "Sorry. Range . . . one hundred kilometers."

Souhi was getting very tired of this round-robin. The brief rest in the hotel had done nothing but make him look forward *less* to this trip.

The sun was setting as they headed northwest towards the tanker. At least the weather was good.

And there were no other boats around. He'd heard about the other boat so he kept looking behind him. But, so far, nobody.

The radar tech on the *Ronald Reagan* was watching the activity with interest. Everyone on board had heard the news and the captain had added some additional items. And now everybody knew the reason they'd been steaming up and down the coast for the last week. But the tech suspected she was the only person onboard that was actually *doing* anything about it.

A P-3 radar craft was circling high over the area, sending its take back to the *Ronald Reagan* and not even looking at it itself, supposedly. She knew the crew was probably sneaking a peek.

And there was stuff to watch, now. A single track had exited the Abacos chain and was headed for the freighter. Another track had exited not long before but they turned east and were now doing a slow figure-eight. The tech did some calculations and determined that they would, probably, be below the horizon of the fast mover.

As she watched, two more tracks came into the area, surface fast movers, then a helo came up from the Abacos, flying not far off the water and *fast*. It was going faster than a Super Cobra. And no transponder. Interesting . . .

Mike opened the door and slid out, holding onto the rope secured to his STABO harness.

There had been two choices. Try to capture the ship and then take down the cigarette from it or take down the cig and take the *ship* from it. Taking down a ship is *hard*, especially in the initial assault. SEALs trained in it, extensively, but the Keldara had not. Mike was unsure about taking it down at all, but if they did it would *have* to be by surprise.

Which meant capturing the cigarette and, even more important, the driver. The driver, obviously, was going to be the only one who knew where the mother lode was.

He reached the end of the harness, hanging a mere fifteen feet under the helo and spinning like a top. Spreading his arms he stabilized, then held his right arm out.

Pavel was having more trouble but Mike could tell he was grinning behind his balaclava. Oh, hell, so was Mike. He was having a blast. But he wasn't going to let it interfere with the mission.

They linked hands as the helo banked, turning to come in behind the blacked-out cigarette.

Souhi had stopped looking behind him. There hadn't been anything by dark and it was unlikely that anyone could track in on him out here. There weren't any aircraft in the sky, nothing but these damned rollers. This was, in a way, the worst part of the trip with the waves coming in at an angle, a nasty quartering sea that sent the cigarette corkscrewing on each breaker.

The damned movement was a bitch. The targets were corkscrewing back and forth and the driver was seated. All that was really visible was his head and shoulders. Doing the shot was going to be a stone bitch. Which was why *he* was doing it.

"Keep going," Mike said, thumbing his mike with difficulty. "Get right *over* the son of a bitch."

There was a strange note to the engine. Like a whopping sound. But it was still running. Hopefully they would make the ship. There was a technician onboard just in case they had problems.

"Strike, NOW!" Mike shouted over his mike.

The helo sped up and Mike, still holding Pavel's hand for stabilization, slid across the boat, his feet barely over the heads of the startled muj in the back, and fired the taser downward into the shoulder and neck of the driver.

It was a tough shot. Forget the corkscrewing, he had to figure windage for a vessel going nearly seventy miles per hour and he was swaying in the STABO harness.

The taser plunked into place perfectly and the driver began spasming.

Which created its own problems. His hands fell away from the steering and the boat went into an out-of-control turn, nearly broaching in the waves.

The helo banked, throwing Mike and Pavel outwards. Due to the same effect that children use to play "Crack the Whip," they suddenly started pulling more Gs than Mike wanted to experience *ever* again.

"Fuck," Kacey snapped, seeing the boat go out from under her. "Lasko, where's it at?"

"Left, it went left," Lasko said. Then, as she was banking, he shouted again: "No, it's turning back right!"

"Where's the Kildar?" Kacey asked.

"Over it!"

Hoping against hope, Kacey dropped the helo down.

Mike felt the lurch downward and saw the boat coming *up* at him, fast. He let go of Pavel's hand and braced, expecting to slam into one of the many hard surfaces that were more or less vertical.

Instead his feet hit the deck, right between the driver's seat and the AD's, as the boat was jumping over a wave. He grabbed one of the chicken bars, hit the quick release of the STABO and lurched across the driver, his feet going airborne, to kill the throttles.

That fucking pilot was *magic*. He didn't pay her *nearly* enough.

The two muj in back were scrambling to their feet but his pistol came out faster than they could react.

"You can be martyrs if you'd like," Mike said as a dripping Pavel dropped onto the deck. "I really don't care."

The muj had been winched into the helo, Oleg's strike team had been brought up and Mike was now headed for the rendezvous, Dragon banking off to take up attack positions. The range on the freighter's radar, to waterline, was about thirty miles. They were still over fifty from the freighter so the intercept shouldn't have been visible.

"So far so good," Mike said. "Now comes the hard part."

"We will do it," Gregor Makanee said. Oleg had felt that, by rights, he should be one of the men on deck. But Mike had pointed out, persuasively, that none of the muj on the boat were over two meters, blond and weighed in at damned near a ton. The three darkest Keldara in his team had been chosen instead. Mike figured that the rendezvous was going to use minimum lights. The fun part is that they probably didn't stop. He wished Randy was driving. He was a SEAL with some time in a Cig. This was something for an expert.

"Yes, we will," Mike said loudly. "We always fucking do, don't we?" he added, so quietly he couldn't be heard.

The tech was *really* resenting the security restrictions on this take, now. Wow. They'd intercepted and presumably captured a cigarette doing damned near seventy. That had to have been fun. And now it was headed for the freighter. And the other cigs and the helo were hanging back, presumably out of range.

This was gonna be good. . . .

"So, they have the cigarette," the President said. Just because the CVBG commander couldn't watch didn't mean the President couldn't.

"And they're going to use it to assault the ship," the defense secretary said, nodding. "That's going to be fun."

"We could have sent SEALs," the President pointed out. "We've got two full teams sitting on their hands."

"Presumably the Kildar didn't want that. One suspects he wants the freighter crew. Alive."

Mike conned the boat in alongside the freighter and headed for where a group was gathered by the side.

He hadn't thought about it until the last moment, but he didn't actually know which side the guys used to fuel from. That, right there, could have blown it.

"You didn't radio!" the deck man yelled as Mike approached. "But we are ready."

Mike just waved, then pulled closer.

"Get ready," he said to Gregor.

The Keldara nodded and headed to the rear.

A hose was dropped over the side and Gregor grabbed it, then it slid over the side.

"Allah's Beard," he shouted in rather bad Arabic.

"Son of a goat!" the deck crew yelled, pulling the hose back up.

As the crew of the freighter were distracted dealing with the hose, Gregor and Valentin drew silenced pistols from under their loose shirts and fired upwards.

There were four targets. It was a rocking boat. They missed two shots but all four were down before any of them could cry out.

The assault team came pouring up from belowdecks, the lead holding a grapnel thrower. The grapnel punched upwards with a "thunk" sound from the thrower. When it caught on the gunnel, the rope was reeled in and a ladder went up. As soon as it connected to the grapnel, Oleg started clambering up. If the leg bothered him it wasn't apparent.

Mike waited for the first yell. There should be one any second. Then it would get tricky.

A rope came over the side and Gregor secured the front of the Cigarette to the boat. It was going to knock hell out of it but Mike killed the power and let it coast into the side of the freighter. Then he headed for the ladder.

As he climbed, Gregor slid under the console and pulled out a power screwdriver. If the women could do it, so could he. The boat was rocking up and down and banging into the side of the ship but he managed to pull three of the screws. The fourth, though, was stripped out.

He let out a curse and grabbed the thing, pulling and twisting until it came loose with a nasty cracking sound.

Shit. Maybe nobody would notice. No, there were bits of the guts pulled out. Damn.

Maybe they should have let one of the women do it.

Mike joined the team and looked around as Shota slid his body armor on and handed him his silenced M4. By rights *somebody* should have seen them.

"Okay," he whispered, pointing to the ladder to the bridge. "You know the drill."

Oleg led, clambering up the ladder as silently as possible, then ducking down at the rear of the bridge to take up position by the door. The rest of the team spread to either side.

Shota was last up, right behind Mike. He had a breaching charge in his hand and his favorite blast armor on. If he was encumbered by the massive stuff, it wasn't apparent.

"Wait," Mike said as Shota attached the charge. "There might be a better way."

"Are they done, yet?" Captain Faisal asked. He had his eyes fixed on the horizon.

"They haven't called," the first mate said. "They call when they are done with . . . whatever."

"Fueling," the captain said. "We both know it's fueling boats. Like that one that was caught in Florida, yes?"

"I know nothing," the mate said. "Absolutely *nothing*."

"Look and see if they are done, at least," the captain said. "Container Sixteen is working loose. I can see it from here. We need to get the crew up."

"We are not to look," the mate said.

"Then *I* will," the captain said as the back door to the bridge opened. He expected it to be one of the fedayeen that had been loaded onto his boat. Instead it was a man wearing a light white shirt under body armor. And he was pointing a gun.

"Hello," Mike said. "Pleased to meet you. Anyone who wishes to be a martyr, raise one hand. Anyone who doesn't, raise both."

Mike stood by the ventilator intake and grinned. The bridge crew had been gathered forward, where the material wouldn't reach them. The radar room and commo were already secure and the rest of the teams were on their way.

He picked up the bulky pack and secured the hose to the intake. The pack was lashed to a davit. Then he keyed the gas and backed away. He had a gas mask on, but why take chances?

Fast onset and thirty minutes until it wore off. Plenty of time.

"When can we get out of our quarters?" Djelel moaned.

"When the captain calls," Khader said, stacking a domino and picking up the set. The purser was just as bored, but orders were orders. And he wasn't going to anger the fedayeen that had taken over the boat.

"What did you say?" Djelel replied. "You are a goat fucker!" He suddenly lunged across the table, grabbing the purser and slamming him back into his seat.

Khader gasped as the other man started to choke him. His face had turned to one of the djinn, a nightmare face, and the deck was opening up into the fires of hell. He was in *hell*. . . .

Pavel slid down the fast-rope and headed for the hatch nearest to the engine compartment. The two Keldara behind him carried cutting bars, high-temperature cutting devices. If the room was locked, they could get in.

He slid down the ladder, hands on either baluster as he had in the yacht many times, and turned right. There was one more deck to go down before he reached the door to the engine room.

The entire team was wearing gas masks. The Kildar had told them they must although there was none of the VX onboard. He said there would be something else to contend with.

The ship lurched and slowed to a stop as he ran. They must have already been alerted.

He hit the next stairway and paused as a crewman started to climb up it. The man was sobbing and screaming something in Arabic. His eyes had been clawed out and from the stain on his fingers it had been by his own hand.

Pavel looked at the man and triggered a suppressed burst into his back. It just seemed a mercy.

Then he continued the mission.

▲   ▲   ▲

"Pavel has the engine room," Oleg said. "He says there is steam being released in it. He did not do it."

"Yeah," Mike said. The crew had gone nuts. He hadn't realized the stuff was going to be that potent. The Keldara had secured all of the crew members although there had been a few deaths. That was okay, nobody was leaving the boat alive.

Souhi watched, ashen, as the crew was laid out on the deck. Many of them were dead and others were screaming in madness, trussed up with duct tape.

"So," the man who appeared to be the leader said, walking over to him. "I have a few questions."

"Go fuck a goat," Souhi said, spitting at him. "What are you going to do? Send me to Guantanamo? I sleep, I eat, I wait for your Amnesty International and ACLU to free me so I can kill you like the goat dick sucker you are."

"No, I'm not going to send you to Guantanamo. Those poor boys and girls have enough dickheads to deal with including, yes, the ICRC, AI and ACLU. Are you the diver or the assistant driver?" he asked, turning to Kahf.

"You are a man who licks the cocks of camels," Kahf said.

"Oh, wrong answer," the man said, drawing his sidearm and putting a bullet through the diver's brain. "Oleg, got your first customer."

A winch was lowered down and Kahf's feet secured to the winch. Then the diver was lifted up and lowered over the side.

As that was happening, the dead crew were being lifted up, their feet secured to ropes and being dropped over the side to rest in the water. A spotlight was turned on and two large men lifted Souhi up so he was forced to look at the water.

"The sharks around here are *notorious*," the man said, smiling. "Let's see how long it takes one to turn up."

It was about fifteen minutes before the first fin swept in. To Mike it looked like a Mako. That made sense; the pelagic hunters cruised the blue water constantly, looking for the fast deep-water fish that were their primary prey. But they weren't averse to eating a human, either, as this one proved by sweeping in and attacking the head of the man he'd shot.

"Lower him a bit more," Mike said as the driver started retching. "Let's see how fast they eat him. And bring me the other guy from the boat. Time to feed the sharks."

In another ten minutes the water was teeming. The crew, most of them trying to struggle as they saw what was going to happen, were shot, one by one, and tossed over to chum up the sharks. All the while, the driver was held in place, forced to watch.

"Okay," Mike said, smiling that faint, friendly smile. "Even having seen all this, I won't kill you. You may not believe me, but I'm a man of my word. So you wanna give me the coordinates of the container?"

"You cannot do this!" the driver said. "You are *American*!"

"And that means we're the good guys, right?" Mike asked, pulling the man back by his hair. "Wrong. We're junkyard dogs that get kept on a leash. Because if we had *our* way this is what we'd do to *all* you motherfuck-ers. You think you have the market on brutality? Ask the Indians how brutal we can be. Ask the Japanese. Ask the Germans. You're finally getting a taste of your own medicine and now you're going to FUCKING TELL ME or I'm going to feed you to the sharks, one bit at a fucking time. LOOK AT THEM!" Mike screamed, holding the man's head down so he was looking right at the red churned water. The bodies were still being torn apart; even that many sharks, and there were *a lot* of sharks, couldn't finish off the crew of a freighter fast. "I'M GOING TO FEED YOU TO THEM FEET *DOWN* UNLESS YOU TELL ME THE *FUCKING* COORDINATES!"

"Fuck you, you goat sucking . . ." The man was crying now.

Mike gestured for the winch and hooked up a sling under the man's bound arms.

"Wanna talk?" he asked mildly. "Let me tell you something, you Islamic fuck. A woman I dearly loved was killed by your kind about two months ago. I can't really be said to be over that. Now, I dearly want to add you to the frenzy, just push you over the fucking side and be done with it. But, as I said, I won't kill you. *If* you tell me the coordinates. If you tell me now, you can leave this ship with all your limbs intact. But when I tell them to lift you up, you *are* going into the water. So you want to tell me? Come on, it's just a few numbers. You can do it. A few numbers. I know you know them. You've got them memorized. You punch them in and erase the track after you've done the pickup."

"No," the driver said, whimpering.

"God, you people are sooo stupid." He straightened up and gestured.

"Please!" the driver said as he was lifted into the air. "You cannot do this to me!"

"Did I listen to any of the rest of them?" Mike asked as the diver was lowered over the side. "Do you listen to the pleas of your victims? To the men whose throats you cut? To the little girls that get raped for the sins of their brothers? Do you care for those you're starving to death in the Sudan? Did you listen to the pleas of the pilots you dragged through the streets of Mogadishu? Did you jump for joy when the Towers fell? Did you, YOU CAMEL-SUCKING FUCK?"

The driver probably wasn't hearing him. He was screaming as he was lowered, slowly, towards the water. His legs were drawn up to his waist, but that just left his balls the most exposed. He must have realized that because as the first shark came out of the water after him he bent upwards, straining to keep his crotch out of the water.

"Hold it there," Mike said, lifting a hand. "Let's see how good of shape he's in. In fact, bring it up a little. I don't want them getting a bite until *I* say."

The winch was jerked up so that the driver was dangling about three feet over the water. The sharks, having finished off most of the crew, were circling underneath hungrily.

"One little set of coordinates," Mike yelled. "I've got all night. Really. We brought packed lunches."

The driver couldn't hold the pike position and he straightened out after a minute or two, his legs quivering as he tried to hold them up. Finally, they too began to straighten. The left went first, dropping straight down as his strength gave way and he screamed as his foot disappeared into the maw of a tiger shark that had turned up for the feast.

"Up," Mike gestured as the severed limb started squirting blood.

The driver was rapidly lifted and a tourniquet was on before he hit the deck, eliciting another scream as his stump hit the steel deck.

"I can do this *all* night," Mike said. "One. Piece. At. A. Time. We've got whole blood with us. If you lose too much we can give you more."

"They will kill my family," the Yemeni gasped. "I have a mother, a sister, in Yemen. They will kill them."

"We'll take care of them," Mike said. "I will make sure of it. They will be taken to a safe place. Now tell me the coordinates."

The driver gasped out some coordinates.

"Okay, now say it backwards," Mike said.

"What?"

"SAY IT BACKWARDS YOU SON OF A DIS-EASED CAMEL!" Mike screamed. "FAST!"

The driver stuttered coordinates again.

"Close enough," Mike said. "But I'm holding you to that. If it's not there . . ." He gestured over his shoulder with his thumb. "Okay, now I have a few more little questions to ask. . . ."

CHAPTER
TWENTY-ONE

"I have a probable location on the mother lode," Mike said as the Hind headed back to base. He gave the admiral the coordinates. "And you can suspend monitoring operation on the freighter."

"Will do," Ryan said. "I'll send a team to those coordinates immediately."

The radar tech's face was frozen when the CIC officer approached.

"PO, you can suspend monitoring the suspect vessel," the officer said, then paused. "Are you okay?"

"Yes, sir," the tech said, shifting the zoom on her screen.

The officer wasn't sure what was wrong. He'd gotten good at ignoring things on screens he wasn't supposed to see but he had to admit he'd sneaked a peek at this one. And there wasn't much there. Just a few boats moving south and an aerial track right at the edge of detection.

In the center of the screen there was just . . . nothing.

Come to think of it, wasn't there *supposed* to be a ship there?

It wasn't their usual job but they could *do* it. The Seahawk helo was nominally an antisubmarine warfare bird. But over time it had done Search and Rescue, flown the mail and everything else that was possible to do in a helo capable of carrying 8000 pounds over 380 nautical miles.

Now it was looking for a magnetic anomaly at a given set of coordinates. Suited up in the back were two SEALS with the mission to check out the contact, if any.

The Seahawk swept southward and slowed as it approached the coordinates.

"We got anything?" the pilot asked over the intercom.

"Negative so far," the sonar tech watching the Magnetic Anomaly Detector said. "Wait. MAD, MAD, MAD. Right on the coordinates."

The co hit the release for a smoke and fire buoy, then the Seahawk banked back around. The pilot came in low over the buoy, hovering, as the sonar tech lowered the sonar sensor on a cable.

"Yankee search," the pilot reminded him. "It's going to be a passive."

"Yes, sir," the sonar tech said, grimacing. He wasn't sure what they were after, but he had been in the briefing, too.

The SEALs, though, clearly knew what they were hunting. They'd hauled SEALs around before; he'd even hung out with a few. And these guys, under the bravado, were *not* happy campers. Whatever they were supposed to check out it wasn't a good thing. Since SEALs were generally entirely without fear if it was something they could punch, shoot or fuck, it meant whatever they were looking for fell into none of those categories. And everybody knew the entire damned CVBG was looking for VX nerve gas. Ergo . . . He was happy to stay in the bird.

He hit the control for active search as soon as the collective was in the water and got an immediate return.

"Yeah, we got something," he said, then turned and nodded to the two SEALs.

The first went over the side like a rescue diver, one hand on his mask the other on his regulator, hitting the water ten feet below with a splash. Unusually for SEALs, he was using a powerful flashlight. So it didn't pay to be tactical, apparently. Not part of the tech's area of interest, so he started lifting the sonar ball.

The second SEAL hit the water and stopped about ten feet down as the first continued deeper. But even that light turned and started to come up after just a minute or less. He popped to the top and held a thumb up, indicating it was time to winch them up.

The SEALs had brought their own commo and the first SEAL got on it as soon as he was back in the helo. Whatever he was saying was muffled by the rotors.

"We're supposed to circle the area until the frigate gets here," the pilot said over the intercom about five minutes later. The SEALs, with obvious relief, were stripping off their wet suits. If they had anything to say, they weren't talking.

▲   ▲   ▲

"Kildar, Admiral Ryan," Greznya said as Mike walked in the door of the house.

"Great," Mike replied wearily. "I've got some info that needs to be passed to Jay. We get anything from him?"

"Not recently," Greznya said. "He sent a message, though, that he thinks he has the contact in Nassau."

"We've got that," Mike said. "I need to find the guy who's giving the *orders*."

"Two of the boats taken down in two nights," Gonzales snarled. "*And* my first shipment gets caught. You are bringing down too much heat on me."

"Relax," Ritter said, rubbing his broken nose. "Everything will be fine. We have another shipment on the way, just as good, to replace that one. And more. We are going to need more boats, though."

"If they haven't found your stash," Gonzales replied.

"They . . . will not talk," Ritter said, smiling lazily. "They are very tough. And we know where their family is. Their sisters and mothers. If you violate the honor of their sisters and mothers, you violate theirs. They will not talk."

"This Kildar bastard is the problem," Juan said. "We need to do something about him."

"I am," Kurt Schwenke, AKA "Michael Ritter," replied. "I will need to use some of your people, however."

"Fine, use as many as you need," Gonzales said, standing up and walking out of the office. "I need to go fuck someone."

"It was there," Ryan said. "We're sending a recovery team down to do an inventory."

"Good," Mike said. "That was what I was waiting to hear. I'm going to be sending you the names of some people in Yemen. Somebody's going to need to secure them. Fast. Put 'em in the Witness Protection program. Treat 'em right. Okay?"

"Will do," the admiral said.

"They will kill my family," Souhi said, miserably. "All of them."

Souhi had been led to a concrete room just about filled with plastic sheeting. And a lab facility for some reason. Then he remembered the maddened crew and gulped.

"They will be taken care of," Oleg promised, standing behind him. "We have word that you told the truth so we will keep ours. And we can get you a new foot. See? I have a new leg," the team leader said, lifting up his trousers to show the mujahideen. "I had it blown off by Chechens. And now I have a better one. I need their names, though. So we can make sure they are well."

"Very well," Souhi said, picking up a pen. He scratched out a series of names of his family in Yemen. "Where will—"

The hammer smashed into his upper spine, severing the cervical vertebra and yanking down on the medulla oblongata, killing him instantly.

"The Kildar said that *he* would not kill you," Oleg said as the man voided in the chair. "He didn't say anything about *me*."

Katya was sitting on the back deck of the yacht, a pair of sunglasses on her face and suntan oil spread on liberally, when Ritter walked out and sat down next to her.

"Having a good time, Katya?" Ritter asked.

"Great, Kurt," the agent replied. "You?"

"Win some, lose some," Ritter said.

"Father of All . . ." Julia whispered. "It's Kurt Schwenke."

"And Katya knows," Lilia replied. "I wonder for how long?"

"How well did you wire the boat?"

"Pretty thoroughly, Kurt," Katya admitted. "Full sound and video. In fact, this is going out in streaming video. So is this where we go for round two?" She had met the former East German Stasi member on a previous mission. Both had tried, with minimal success, to kill the other.

"*Nein*," Kurt replied. "It's a nice day. Why ruin it? Besides, with what the Kildar probably has on standby I wouldn't live to appreciate the moment."

"There's that," Katya said. "In fact . . ."

"In fact, I think I'll take a little trip out of town," Schwenke said. "Since I suspect this boat is going to become less welcoming soon."

"Might be a good idea," Katya replied. "Just between friends, you wouldn't care to tell me where?"

"Just between friends, you wouldn't care to tell me where the Kildar is?"

"Probably drinking a beer."

Mike sipped at a bottle of Mother Lenka's best as he watched the TV.

The Prime Minister of the Bahamas, sweating profusely and grinning just as much, was standing on the deck of a U.S. Navy salvage vessel currently holding station just north of Grand Isle.

"I am extending the personal thanks of the President of the United States and all Americans to the nation of the Bahamas for their support in finding this cache . . ." an admiral was saying. "Without their help and support this mission would have been impossible."

"And I thank the United States government," the president said, still grinning, "for their ongoing support in the war on drugs and terror. Without their aid it would be impossible for our small country to police all the islands . . ."

The two black SUVs slammed to a halt at the edge of the Straw Market and the DEA teams unassed, fast.

Before the Pakistani shopkeeper could begin to react another team came in the back of his kiosk and slammed him to the floor. Fast-ties went on his hands and feet as rigger-tape secured his mouth. A black hood covered his head and he was gone in thirty seconds. All his merchandise was gone in about sixty.

Although some of the tourists stopped and stared, the merchants continued as if nothing had happened. Just another day in paradise.

"Hey, I got an interesting rumor."

Jason Cox had been working Washington for ten years and he'd built up a few pretty good contacts. Not like that bastard Woodward, but pretty good. And the latest thing that had been dropped in his ear was a fucking bombshell.

"Go," his producer said, spinning around in his chair.

"That black ops team that took down the terrorists in the Keys?" he said. "My source said they're those Mountain Tiger guys from Georgia that had that pitched battle with the Chechens last month."

"Two months," the producer said, frowning. "Not Delta or CIA black ops?"

"Nope," the reporter said, grinning. "They're called the Kildarra or something. He wasn't sure on the name. But, get this, their commander is an American."

"Yeah, that was what AP said from that battle," the producer replied, thinking. "You get a confirmation?"

"I'm going to work on one," the reporter said. "I'm meeting a source for lunch. I thought you might shake a few trees, too."

"I can do that," the producer admitted. He had his contacts, too. The two might overlap, but not by much. "We need to keep it low, though. If you're wrong . . ."

"I'll find out at lunch."

"Nice steak," the congressional staffer said. "Which means you want something."

The reporter had covered the congressman's run back when he was just a comer. And he'd cultivated the staffer, each man hoping to end up with the "big boys" but not really believing they'd be doing the Watergate thing over a power lunch. But here they were.

"I heard a credible report on something," the reporter said, waiting for the guy to take a sip of his Diet Coke. "Just wondering, you know . . . The Kildarra were the team that took down the VX, right?"

The staffer managed to not blow the Coke across the table. But it took a manly effort to prevent it.

"Who did you hear that from?" he asked sharply, trying to keep his voice down at the same time.

"You know about—"

"Let me explain something," the staffer said, leaning across the table and looking the reporter in the eye. "I don't know who you got it from but they must be *totally* out of the fucking loop. Because if they knew *shit* they would be telling you what I'm going to tell you. Forget that name. Forget anything you heard. Don't go playing super sleuth."

"Or I die?" the reporter said, chuckling. "Yeah. Right."

"No," the staffer said. "Your career does. You *breathe* that word and you have *no* more sources. Nobody will talk to you. Nobody will touch you with a ten-foot pole. You will be untouchable, unclean. I'm a pretty good source, right? You say the word Keldara on network TV, put them together with that op or any other op, and your career is toast. Trust me on this. You do *not* want to fuck with that guy."

"Guy?" the reporter said, pouncing.

"I'm serious, Jason," the staffer said, standing up and tossing down his napkin. "Do not do this."

"Well, I had an interesting lunch," the reporter said, walking in the producer's office.

"I didn't have any," the producer said. "I made one phone call and then got five more, including from the head of the network. I think we can take it that you're confirmed and it doesn't matter . . ."

"Kill the story," the reporter said, nodding. "I was going to talk to you about that."

"It is deader than a doornail," the producer replied. "That what you got?"

"Oh, yeah," the reporter said, shaking his head. "What happened to journalistic ethics?"

"I think they're pretty much moot," the producer admitted. "Especially when the head of the network said that he got calls from two *prime ministers* explaining how much difficulty the network would find in getting visas to enter countries, or anything else, if we breathed a *word* about these guys. Oh, and you don't even *want* to hear what a certain senator had to say. But I will mention things like FCC license renewal. And then he got *nasty*."

"What was the take?" Mike asked.

"There were only twenty-eight containers," the admiral said with a sigh.

"We're getting there," Mike said, cursing under his breath. "Twelve missing. Four we got. Two the Commercial guys found. I don't suppose anybody went to the pick-up points?"

"No," the admiral said. "Not so far. FDLE has them under stakeout with blue barrels sitting there. But they're probably not going to go for it."

"Probably not," Mike admitted. "Not after we got blown sky-high. Six barrels in play. They're inside, too."

"Agreed," the admiral said. "The question is . . . where?"

"Targets," Mike said. "Lots of possible targets. We're coming inside."

"Where?" the admiral said. "When you got dumped on me I was pissed as hell. Now I know what the

President meant about your nose. Where are you going?"

"Now that we've saved the Bahamas we're going to *Disney World*."

"Hi, my name's Jack. What's yours?"

John R. "Jack" Garcia wasn't sure about the latest up. The guy was wearing a Hawaiian shirt, flip-flops and cargo shorts that had seen better days. And he was looking at the GT they had on display. But, hell, everybody did. GTs were rare as hell but a customer had traded this one on a stocked-out Expedition when he had a change of life. A change from wife and mistress to ex, new wife and a new baby.

The Ford GT was one of the top performance cars in the world. With a body closely based on a 1960s Ford Can-Am racer, the car still looked futuristic. Low-slung, wide, sleek and powerful, it was a car-lover's wet dream. Bright red with double racing stripes down the middle, it was also spectacular as hell.

"Mike," the guy said. "That's a pretty car."

"Yes it is," Jack said. "Hardly used at all. And only three thousand made. Very rare. A real collector's item."

"Yeah," the guy, "Mike," said. "Hell of a sticker, though."

"Like I said, rare and very fine machinery," Jack said, mentally sighing. All the customers looked, none of them ever bought.

"Gimme a discount for a large additional order?"

"How large?" Jack asked. "And I don't think we can take much off the GT. It's pretty much at invoice as it is."

"Can't move it, huh?" the guy said, taking off his

sunglasses and turning. Jack froze at his expression. Then the guy held out an American Titanium card. Technically referred to as a Senior Corporate Agent's Card, it was called the "Titanium" because whereas a gold card wasn't made out of gold nor a platinum from platinum, well . . . The SCC was a thin stamped sheet of black titanium with, literally, no limit. "I need ten Expeditions. Black. *And* the GT. Make me your best offer."

"Holy fuck, who's that, James Bond?"

Lieutenant Bob Dunn, Orange County sheriff's department, was a twelve-year veteran of the force. He'd spent his time in traffic then SWAT then detective and finally made lieutenant. He knew the capability of his department and the groups surrounding and interacting. But this Miami Vice character . . . Fuck.

"You might want to keep your voice down," Captain Spencer Street said. The Florida National Guardsman had had a call from an old friend that told him a group was coming up to work the Orlando area and to not only treat them with kid gloves but with respect. That was all, but the tone was enough. He wasn't sure who the guy was, but he was willing to give him the benefit of the doubt. Besides, the fellow captain, a team leader with 20th Group, had sounded . . . shaken. Anybody who could shake up Tom was worth listening to.

"Fuck him," Dunn said. "Anybody that turns up at a JTF meeting in a fucking GT with some blonde on his arm is a poser."

The guy had parked in a "distinguished visitor" parking space, right by the door in other words. So he caught the end of Dunn's words as he approached, literally with a blonde on his arm.

"I see Orange County's finest are on the case," the man said. "Killed any good hostages lately?"

"Fuck you," Dunn snapped. OC had had a bad run a few years back. In four separate hostage negotiations the hostage had been killed either by the holder or, in one case, by fire from the police surrounding the house. Given that all of them had started off as domestic disputes it was, in Dunn's eyes, a tragedy and not something to be joked about. "This is a restricted area."

"Michael Jenkins," the guy said, sticking out his hand to the Guardsman. "Pleasure to meet you. Now will you ask your trained monkey to move out of the way of the door?"

"You're expected, Mr. Jenkins," Street said. "But your . . . companion . . ."

"Lieutenant Britney Harder," the girl said, pulling an ID out from under her shirt. "SOCOM."

"Oh," the captain said, starting to straighten then realizing that he outranked her. "Yes, you're on the list, too."

"They got a captain doing guard duty?" Jenkins asked, honestly curious.

"Just catching a smoke," Street said. "The actual guards are through the door. I'll escort you. We're going to be starting soon."

"So what's a nice girl like you doing with an asshole like him?" the sheriff's deputy asked as the Kildar and the Guardie headed to the security desk.

"Fucking up terrorists and killing people," Britney

said, pulling off her own glasses and giving him her best thousand mile stare. "What have you been doing today?"

"Right," Dunn said, frowning.

"Right," Britney stated. "So far *we've* stopped thirty-two barrels. And all of those on *purpose*. What's FDLE's record? Two on a routine traffic stop? You want to go beat your dick, go beat it somewhere else. I got nothing for you."

Mike tried not to sleep through the meeting. He felt like it was important to attend at least one. This one had a National Guard colonel chairing it. And the guy was . . . Mike could feel a fuck-up coming on big-time. He wasn't one of the NG battalion commanders; he was a guy sent down from Tallahassee to "manage" the situation. From Mike's perspective, the situation was completely beyond "managing." If he'd had his way, every damned vehicle heading north from Miami would be stopped and strip searched. Not that it probably mattered. Most of the barrels were on their way to the destination or there already.

"In conclusion," the colonel said as Mike tried not to yawn, "the commander's intent is to action the enemy's action plan by insertion into the decision-making cycle and loop closure. By joint tasking and transformational processes, this situation can be deconflicted in a rapid and decisive manner. I have the positions and taskers of all the associated agencies prepared, however, there is one issue on taskers. Mr. Jenkins," he concluded, turning to Mike. "What is your task in all of this?"

"I've been detailed to put my people into Disney," Mike said, lying.

"Who gave you that tasker?" the colonel asked pointedly. "The action plan for defense in the Reedy Creek AO is fully tasked."

"I think there's a need-to-know issue there," Mike replied, shrugging. "Why don't I just make myself useful? We'll mingle as tourists. Plenty of foreigners in Disney. We'll need to have Disney security aware of it, though, and I'll be making some suggestions in that regard. Actually, I'm going to be making demands. And if they're not followed, the park will be shut down."

"Excuse me?" Lieutenant Dunn asked, leaning forward. "How, exactly, are you going to get Disney to do that?"

"By presidential order under the War Powers Act," Mike said, not bothering to look around. "There are, from my perspective, five probable targets in the Orlando area. Disney, specifically the Magic Kingdom, Wet and Wild, Universal, Sea World and *possibly* EPCOT or Studio Center. The top three I listed are the most probable targets. I put Magic Kingdom as top. I've discussed this at the highest level. Disney security is good. There's going to be National Guard. Your department, Lieutenant, will be in place. And so will the Keldara. And we will be looking for very specific attacks and prepared to engage them with lethal force."

"You want to carry weapons into Disney World?" the colonel said. "Out of the *question*."

"Colonel, I can have you relieved, stripped of rank and stripped of retirement by picking up a phone," Mike said, turning his head like a turret. "You don't even *begin* to tell me what is 'out of the question.'

You don't begin to tell me what I can or cannot do to accomplish my mission. Stopping these terrorists with zero loss of life is going to be 'out of the question.' But that is our mission and I'm going to do that mission. And your job, Colonel, is to do what the fuck I tell you to do. Is that clear?"

"So you're assuming command?" the colonel snarled. "Over my dead body."

Mike shoved back his chair, walked down the conference room and jerked the chickenshit idiot out of his chair.

"You want to tell me it's over your dead body?" Mike hissed. "I'll cap you right here and nobody will say boo. Not a fucking person. Now you get this straight, jackass. Terrorists are coming to *kill* American civilians. And I will do *whatever* it takes to stop that. And if that includes killing you or everyone in this fucking *room* then everyone in this room will *die*. Been there, done that. Do I make myself clear?"

"Clear," the colonel said, gagging.

"Let go of him," Dunn said, standing up. "I swear to God—"

"Don't," Street said, holding up his hand. "What you don't realize is that he's serious. I don't particularly feel like dying. So . . . don't."

Mike shoved the colonel back in the chair and straightened up.

"*My* meeting is adjourned. We just had it. If you have any useable intel, make sure I get it. *All* of it. I'll take it from there."

CHAPTER
TWENTY-TWO

Charles Fisher, head of security for Walt Disney World, wasn't sure what he was dealing with.

He normally interacted with Orange County sheriff's department. The entire area around Disney, an area about the size of downtown Los Angeles, was privately owned. Technically, it could have its own police force. But there were problems, legal and image-wise, with corporations having cops. So Orange County handled the police work. But they were careful with Disney; it was the tail that wagged the dog.

Sometimes he worked with National Guard when there was a "credible terrorist threat." FLARNG was planning on sending a company of infantry with "support units," meaning, probably antiaircraft teams, to assist. They'd promised to stay low-profile. Disney had had heightened alerts several times and there were places they'd learned they could put the Guardsmen, even including the Slammer trucks, where they didn't alarm the guests. Disney had a surprising number of out-of-the-way spots.

But this guy was something different. The blonde with him was SOCOM but what *he* was wasn't quite clear. CIA? They weren't supposed to work in-country, but with it being terrorism, who knew?

The guy had pulled into the VIP parking at the Guest Arrival area in a GT. So either he really *was* rich as fuck or that was a cover. And he hadn't said much, just shaken hands and said he wanted to see the Magic Kingdom.

Fisher had bypassed the lines at the monorail and gotten him a front compartment. The guy didn't seem to care much about the view from there even though it was spectacular. The lieutenant with him hadn't been so reserved; she'd been glued to the window.

The monorail had a great view of the guest arrival area and then the sweeping panorama of the pine trees and palmettos that still covered most of the Disney area. It swept through the Contemporary Hotel which, given some of the resorts out in Vegas, was sort of outdated but still very cool. The guy still didn't seem to care.

When they got to the park entrance, though, he started looking around. He paused at the back of the crowd, then walked to one of the shorter lines. The gate buzzed when he walked through but Fisher waved to the gate checker; he figured the guy was carrying at least one piece. She was going to let Jenkins through without checking his bag but he handed it over voluntarily.

The checker—obviously feeling this was some sort of test given that the head of security was here—pawed through it carefully. But there wasn't anything wrong with the contents.

The guy took his bag back with a nod of thanks, then walked through the entrance area to Main Street.

Fisher was getting tired of the silence so he touched him on the arm.

"I can answer any questions you'd like to ask," he said.

"I'm forming them," the guy said but then turned. "I'd like to go behind the façade to somewhere nobody is going to wander through."

"Okay," Fisher said, leading him to one of the small gates behind Main Street with "Official Cast Only!" on it and a big Mickey waving a finger no for the kids too young, or stupid, to read.

There was a scrubby lot and the guy looked around, walking to a corner at the very back. Finally he seemed to find what he was looking for.

"Could you come here, Mr. Fisher?" the man asked politely. "I have something to show you."

"It's a grasshopper," Fisher said as the guy reached in his bag.

"Yes," he said. "You might want to back up about ten feet." He had a can of OFF in his hand.

"Okay," Fisher said, backing away.

The guy extended his arm as far forward as possible and sprayed the insect. Instead of the normal spray it came out as a stream. The insect barely gave a hop, just dropping to the ground.

"You might want to tape off this area," the guy said, carefully placing the bug in a Ziploc. "What you just saw was a demonstration of Sarin nerve gas. It will dissipate and degrade in about four hours. Until then, anyone touching it will die."

"Motherfucker!" Fisher snarled. "I can't believe you—"

"I just brought enough Sarin through your security

to kill several hundred people" the guy said, turning and taking off his glasses. "What does that tell you, Mr. Fisher?"

Charles paused, then shook his head.

"I'm not stupid," he said. "It tells me that you just smuggled Sarin into the park. Despite a very careful check. Anything else?"

"Oh, some plastique," the guy continued, pulling out a soap container. "Detonator," he continued, pulling out a multicolor pen, opening it and sliding out what was clearly a detonator. "A timer . . ." A Mickey Mouse watch. He pulled out two bottles of what looked like soda in two different colors. The labels weren't a brand Fisher recognized, but they looked legit. Something European. "Binary explosives."

"Okay, you got me," Fisher said, nodding.

"If the terrorists get you, you're fucked," Mr. Jenkins said. "Containers like this . . . Well, I've seen them before. And this is a very technically sophisticated attack. I can think of several methods of attacking the park. I would actually put this as a secondary or even tertiary attack. If you have an attack, you're going to move a lot of people into the tunnels, right?"

"How do you . . . ?" The entire Magic Kingdom was built on top of a massive tunnel that was more or less circular. It was a loop that looked something like a "male" sign, with the arm going up under Adventureland. The base of the loop was the only major entrance, a cavernous opening on the employee parking lot. The tunnels were why you rarely saw anyone in "costume" moving around the park unless they were crowd management or characters. All of the concessions and rides had back entrances to the tunnels, permitting supplies and personnel to move without disturbing the guests. Their secondary purpose, however, had a more sinister side.

Disney World was constructed at the height of the Cold War. Given the imminent threat of nuclear war that seemed to *always* be in the air, Walt Disney, personally, insisted that the entire facility be capable of keeping the guests and cast alive in the event that nearby McCoy Air Force Base was struck by the Soviets. The gates on the main tunnel entrance were heavy-duty blast doors as strong as those at Cheyenne Mountain, the concrete walls were nearly eight feet thick, the pumps to keep the facility dry were connected to interior generators, the entire facility could be sealed or vented by central controls and each of the surface accesses could function as an air lock.

The tunnels, while not a secret, were little known. Their design and original function was even less well known, including by current senior management.

"I did my homework," Jenkins said. "So, you have an attack. Doesn't matter what type. And you start evacuating people through the tunnels. Then some 'martyrs' start spraying VX or set off suicide bombs. Pleasant scenario, Mr. Fisher? All the blast doors in the world won't help in that situation, will they?"

"No," Fisher admitted.

"So the idea is to stop them before they come in the park, Mr. Fisher," Jenkins said. "Here's how you do that. You have anyone wearing a jacket," he said, opening his own and revealing tubes that could have been explosives as well as the pistol that had set of the metal detector, "open their jacket. These things are normally triggered chemically; a metal detector will not pick them up. Everyone has to take a sip of every drink. Every container of spray has to be sprayed on the person. You set up a method to keep people from approaching the turnstiles, your security area. Keep the lines back thirty feet or so. It's a massive fucking headache, I know. But those are just the baby steps. Because you're going to fucking love the rest of it. . . ."

"That's not going to be the only target," Britney said.

They were driving up I-4 towards Orlando with Mike carefully obeying the speed limit. The GT was going to be a cop magnet.

"They've got six barrels," she pointed out.

"I know," Mike said, pulling off of I-4 onto Sand Creek. "The problem is effective distribution. The cans are only going to get a few people. Sure, that's terrorizing, but they're going to want something that is going to *horrify*."

"Aerial?" Britney said. "There's a combat air patrol. Anything flying unrestrictedly will get shot down."

"Will it?" Mike said. "That's never been tested. That's why the Keldara are going to be enjoying the wonders of the Magic Kingdom while I try to figure out what the other targets are."

"Why do you have to do it all?" Britney asked as the car turned onto International Drive.

The GT, especially with Britney in the passenger seat, drew plenty of stares but Mike was ignoring them.

"Because I get lucky," Mike said, frowning. "But I don't feel fucking lucky about this op. I feel that it's fucked to the max. They're going to get through. Somewhere. We've got over three hundred *gallons* of that shit in play. Inside. Right here. Somewhere."

There was a packed line for Wet and Wild, over a hundred people in bathing suits even in this weather. One teenager, probably about fourteen, was arguing with her parents. She had the one flattest stomach Mike had ever seen. She stopped arguing and frankly stared as the GT drove by.

"They're going to get through," Mike said, thinking about that lovely little girl lying on the ground twitching like a dying cockroach.

"You are prepared?" Farzad asked the assembled fedayeen.

"Yes, Haj," Jamal said. "We are prepared to sacrifice ourselves. We will strike the infidels as they have never been struck. This will make us heroes beyond even the martyrs of the Twin Towers."

"Stay near to cover," Farzad said. "When the panic starts, mingle into the crowds. Then you know what to do. We will strike as one and the Satan will tremble."

". . . Yes, sir, I understand," Colonel Olds said, hanging up the phone and trying not to curse.

Colonel Freeman Olds had spent most of his career in staff positions. He was, in fact, very close to a perfect staff officer. He was meticulous in the extreme and could juggle multiple tasks quite effectively. He was also a workaholic, putting in eighteen to twenty hours a day pretty much consistently.

However, one of the reasons that Olds had had, in his opinion, far too few commands was hidden in his generally excellent reviews. It was not so much that negative terms were included as certain positive ones were missing. He had hardly noticed but phrases like

"capable of critical decision making under pressure"
were notably absent. That's because what many of his
reviewers had realized was that he, well, *wasn't*. He
could make recommendations and create multiple sce-
narios, but to get him to make a hard decision—one that
could negatively affect his career if he was wrong—he
had to be cornered like a rat in a trap.

He had been just as meticulous and risk avoidant
in building his career. He had carefully gotten all the
merit badges, worked the buddy system, gotten all the
right positions at all the right times. His time as a
battalion commander had, admittedly, been less than
perfect but that was understandable. The battalion
he took over had been terribly poorly managed and
undisciplined in the extreme. It could hardly be his
fault that it had failed the annual Army Readiness
and Testing Evaluation Program. He had managed
to argue that to various people who, despite the unit
being decertified for combat operations after two previous trips to the sandbox, had kept him from being
relieved and forcibly retired.

But he was well aware that this position was his last
chance to get stars. If he could manage the conditions
carefully enough, if he could avoid serious incident,
he'd pin on stars by the end of the year.

The fly in that ointment was this Kildar character.
The local FBI office, Orange County, City of Orlando,
all the other federal and state groups in the task force,
they were all on board with the plan. Maintain a low
profile. Make the public aware that there was a threat
but also ensure they knew the powers-that-be were on
the situation. Avoid serious incident. Reduce public
strain. Deconflict the situation.

This joker's idea of deconflict, though, was "kill them all and let graves registration sort them out."

Which was why he had called an old friend from the Point. The general was a couple of years ahead of him and despite being, in Olds' opinion, less than stellar in the brains department he'd managed to pin on stars almost four years ago. The general was also in a very good position, the Plans office in the Pentagon. Oh, he might complain that he wanted to get back to the sandbox, preferably with a command, but Olds knew he was just doing the Good Soldier routine. Plans and Ops *ran* the Army; commanders just followed Plans and Ops' directives.

But it also put him in an excellent position to deal with this Kildar fellow. So Olds had explained his problems, leaving out that Jenkins had threatened to kill him. The general had been pretty busy, which might have explained the bluntness of his response. It boiled down to a.) Jenkins got things done, b.) Jenkins had the support of the CJCS and the President so the general couldn't do anything if he wanted to. He'd added that the colonel might want to pay attention to actions in his AO and not spend time trying to get his support personnel changed.

Which left the colonel pondering his Rolodex. If this Jenkins character really *did* have support all the way to the CJCS—he refused to believe the idiot had presidential backing—then it would take a line of attack outside the chain of command to get him removed.

He picked up his telephone and dialed a number in Washington. There was more than one way to skin a Kildar.

▲   ▲   ▲

"Anything?" Mike asked as he walked in the suite.

There simply weren't any houses for rent big enough to take even the teams he'd brought with him. So he'd rented a floor of an off-Disney hotel. He wasn't going to be at what he considered ground zero.

"No," Greznya said. "There is nothing. Jay is trying to determine who the drops were going to but without any more drops . . . We're still getting the take from Katya but so far we haven't picked up any sign that Gonzales is directly involved."

"They had one more boat," Mike said. "But nothing to pick up and no fueling point."

"So what are they gonna do?" Britney asked.

"Strike at us," Mike replied. "They'll either try to hit the yacht or snatch somebody. Not much they can do else. The VX is in the hands of the U.S. government."

"Are you going to bring the harem over?" Britney asked.

"Hell of a choice, isn't it?" Mike asked. "But, no, I'm going to leave them at the estate with Vil and Yosif's team, what's left of it. Let 'em get a tan. If the Colombians want to tangle with those teams they're free to. Besides, the farther away from me they are the better."

"Hey, I was driving around with you all day!" Britney pointed out.

"I know," Mike said. "Which was silly, but with you around I look like some businessman with a doxie. I don't have Katya and next to her, you're the girl most likely to survive. And if you don't, well, that's why you wear a uniform."

"That's pretty fucking cold," Britney said.

"Pleased to meet you, won't you guess my name?"

▲   ▲   ▲

"Senator Grantham's office."

Steve Worrel was the Senior Defense and Intelligence Staffer for Senator Pat Grantham. He had been an Army intelligence officer, worked briefly for the Agency, then gotten out and gotten a "real" job. Shortly after hitting civvie street he'd gotten into politics as a volunteer, then worked his way up to staffer to a senator. But given that most of the senator's committees were related to domestic affairs rather than military, he wasn't by any stretch of the imagination the senator's most senior aide. Hadn't been, rather.

When someone started blackmailing the senator with videos that certainly appeared to be of the senator not only in bed with a young woman, two actually, but strangling one of them to death, he had gained some prominence. That was because he knew the people to call to, discreetly, start checking out the DVD. People who could pull it apart, electron by electron, to try to determine who had made it, where it was made. In the meantime, the senator had tap-danced. The main demand of the blackmailers had been to kill a conservative judicial nomination. The senator had instead held the nominee up in committee, arguing that to vote against him would have been too much of a reversal to stand up. And hoped like hell that Steve would pull his chestnuts out of the fire.

In the end, Steve's quiet research had turned out to be moot. Others had found out about the blackmail operation and "done something" about it. What exactly the "something" was was unclear. But there was a CNN report about a major battle between Albanian gangs in a small Albanian town known for its prostitution rings along with smaller indicators here and there: a nightclub taken down by what appeared to be a special operations team, a complaint leveled by Fiji about Americans attacking some of their troops.

And then the resignations began. Senator Traskel. Two senior career officials at State. Others in the British Foreign and Home office. A French general. The list went on and on. And none of them came back through the revolving door. It was how it worked. You got out of government service and turned right back around to work for a lobbyist or a defense firm or somebody else that wanted to swill at the government trough. It worked that way in every democracy in the developed world. But not this time, they all just disappeared. "Writing their memoirs." "Taking some family time." Not even entering academia. Just . . . left. Disappeared off the radar screen. In the case of a couple of Japanese officials, they really *had* disappeared; they went out to go SCUBA diving in Saipan and were "lost at sea." A few other officials, one Russian, two Chinese and one Italian had "died as the result of injuries." From street muggings, usually. Well, one in a fall. He'd apparently been out on his balcony taking in the night air at four AM and had managed to land fifty feet away from the building.

Following the resignations and "accidents" were the rumors. There was a man they just called "The Reaper" at first. He turned up in a private jet, met with senior government officials, usually the head of state, and then left. He carried something scary and powerful and wherever he went, careers ended. In a few cases, lives ended. In those cases he had made extra stops. He didn't require that the local government take care of "the issue." He would even do that for them. All they had to do was turn a blind eye.

Slowly another name had surfaced: Kildar. Mike Jenkins. Mercenary. Feudal warlord. He had a harem of teenage girls. He had a company of mercenary commandoes. He was a phantom; nobody knew who he was or where he'd come from. You didn't fuck with the Kildar. You needed dirty deeds done . . . well, anything but "dirt cheap" and he was the go-to guy. He was the guy that governments used when "deniable" was consideration number two right behind "has to be done, or else." He wouldn't hand you a Kleenex for less than five mil and he was worth every dime. Oh, and he made beer. Yeah, *that* beer.

And the word got around. If anybody asks about the Kildar, you know nada. Unless it's somebody trying to blow his op, in which case you warn them off, quietly, and spread the word around. You don't fuck with the Kildar. Too many people owe him, including Senator Grantham and, by extension, the entire conservative side of the Senate. And the liberal side of the Senate and House weren't going to fuck with him because . . . Well, he knew something, had something.

Nobody wanted to say what. But senators and ministers didn't resign over irregularities in campaign finance. As one governor said, it took "a live boy or a dead girl." The rumors were that it was both. And dead boys. Bottom line, you didn't fuck with the Reaper.

"Hello, Colonel," Worrel said, wincing. He wasn't a big fan of Olds, whom he considered an incompetent asshole. But that description fit a lot of people he had to deal with in D.C. He listened for a moment then blanched.

"Colonel, all I can say is that it's a good thing you called me," Worrel replied. "Have you spoken to anyone else about this? Okay, I want you to listen to me and trust me, Colonel. Do not, I repeat, do *not* try to mess with Jenkins. If something bad goes down, it will be buried and spun into victory on all fronts and you'll come out smelling like roses. *If* you do not piss off Jenkins. If you do, if you try to, pardon my language, fuck with him, you will end up sorry and sore. Nobody will know you, no favors will be big enough to cover your ass. . . . No, I can't discuss why, certainly not over an unsecure line . . . I guess that's up to you, but given that you're in charge of the task force, coming up to Washington might not look too good, especially if anything happens while you're away from your post. . . . Yes, that's what I suggest. Okay, we'll talk about it when you get back. Goodbye."

Worrel hung up the phone and considered it for a moment. Then he picked it back up.

"Maggie, Steve. I need to talk to the Boss sometime soon."

Lasko Ferani stepped through a door hidden in a mural and looked around the room.

Cinderella's Castle was built over a three-year period in the early 1970s. The base structure of the castle, the skeleton as such, was rebar and concrete. But that skeleton was remarkably small, taking up less than half of the castle's structure. The rest was Styrofoam also on a rebar skeleton. It had undergone a significant renovation for Disney's twenty-fifth birthday celebration, but that had only entailed changing the Styrofoam. It was a dirty job but somebody had done it.

The room Lasko stood in was original structure in part. The floor and back wall. The side wall, through which he'd stepped, was part of the Styrofoam structure as were the last two walls and the ceiling. The room was littered with small bits of Styrofoam that had flecked off the interior.

But there was a window, and that was what mattered. It was small and oval shaped, but it had a view straight down Main Street.

He dragged a table into the room, then a comfortable chair. He arranged them in front of the window carefully, then went back to get the rest of his gear.

Two sandbags, a mat for the top of the table, a spotting scope with thermal imagery and a bottle of water. He had a packed lunch, and Yakov was planning on coming up and relieving him, briefly, this afternoon. He very much wanted to ride the rollercoaster called "Space Mountain" but he was not sure they would have time.

He settled his arms into the straps, pushed the rifle's butt into his shoulder, settled his elbows on the mat and leaned forward. He was aware that he was going to have to stay that way most of the day but he'd done it before.

Anastasia stepped out of the Fountain and waved to Vil.

"I'll be fine," she said, shaking her head. "I'll be about an hour."

"Okay," Vil said, flexing his jaw. He wasn't sure that the harem manager should be wandering around Nassau alone, certainly not right now. But if anything happened, well, they were dialed in with the Bahamas government. It could be, as the Kildar would put it, "handled."

He turned the Fountain away from the dock and motored over to the fueling point. With the extended range tanks he had plenty of fuel, but he'd gotten in the habit.

"*Reading departure signs in some big airport . . .*" he sung quietly, perfectly on key. Vil was one of the Keldara's finest singers and the key of the songs Randy had taught them was perfect for him. Now if he could just find out a.) where "Margaritaville" was and b.) what was with "a lost shaker of salt" and why it seemed so important. . . .

Anastasia had a very specific reason she didn't want the team leader, or any of the Keldara, following her around. She was working on her agoraphobia. If she had some big strong men to hide behind, it wouldn't be the same. She needed to be on her *own*, to face the world all by herself.

She was reminded, though, of the derivation of the word when she reached the market. "Agora" was from the Greek word "to gather" and fear of the outside translated, literally, as "fear of the market." There were so many people, so many sounds, she had to pause at the entrance and gather her courage.

She'd just taken a deep breath and started to step forward when she felt arms clamp around her. Before she could even start to yell a bag was over her head. She felt a bump on her leg, one that was going to bruise, as she was tossed into a vehicle.

Then there was a strong smell and it was all she recalled for a while.

CHAPTER
TWENTY-THREE

"Kildar," Greznya said nervously.

"Go," Mike replied. He was looking at the defense plans for the Orlando area and shaking his head. Everybody was so afraid of scaring off the tourists, who were staying away anyway with the report of VX in Florida, that you couldn't really call it a sieve. It was more like a bottomless bucket. The security plans just *sucked*.

Actually, Disney, accidentally, had one of the better set-ups. Because they used a tram system to move most people from their cars to the entrance, it made getting a car bomb into a major crowd harder. The main crowd a terrorist could hit on the outside was that of the people waiting for the trams. The next major chokepoint they'd already secured with big "planters" designed to stop anything up to a semi-trailer. The areas where really big crowds gathered you could only insert individuals into. And whereas a suicide bomber could take out quite a few people in one of those packed crowds at the monorail or the boats that crossed Bay Lake, it was nothing compared to what a U-Haul packed with ammonium nitrate could do.

The monorail had him really worried though. Again, max casualties about six hundred but that would be *dead*. A suicide bomber blowing the monorail would take the entire thing down.

And none of that took into account the VX. The main threat there was crop dusters. All of the known crop dusters in the Central Florida area were registered and cops were keeping an eye on them in general. But there were a *bunch* of the damned things. Outside of Orlando and the tourist areas, Central Florida was still mostly rural and heavily farmed. With constant sunshine, lots of rain and good soil, it was a supplier of off-season vegetables and other crops on the same order as the Imperial Valley in California. But the same idyllic conditions also meant a hell of a lot of crop pests, which meant dusting.

Poison gas was, essentially, pesticide with humans being the pests; anything that could spread pesticide could spread VX. And it would kill everything else that had a nervous system just as well as humans: birds, snakes, kittens and your little dog, too.

What was really bad about VX was that it *lingered*. The molecule was very robust and didn't break down well. If any of the shit got spread around it was going to poison the area for a good long time. Unless every single surface was carefully cleaned, someone touching the underside of a door knob a year later would die. And if a couple of canisters were dumped over Disney—or EPCOT or Universal or anywhere else in the area—the shit would feed into the water system, contaminating it for *years*.

And nobody seemed to be taking the threat seriously. It was like the entire JTF was in denial. Nobody would be so vicious and cruel as to spray Disney or Sea World or Wet and Wild. Why, that would *kill* people! Yeah. And nobody would ever fly a plane into the Twin Towers.

The reports from the FBI were driving him crazy. First of all, there were reams of them. And they were . . . gobbledygook. The FBI had flooded the region with agents, most of whom were wandering around with no real clue what they were looking for or at. Agents from Seattle were trying to figure out this whole "sunshine" thing. Agents from New York were trying to "interface" with red-neck deputies in Lake County, a major crossroads area, and there had been "issues." Lake County sheriff's department had a very simple motto: Keep the FBI as far away from us as possible. Their joke was that the *first* biggest lie is "I'm from the FBI and I'm here to help." And the FBI's motto seemed to be "Ready, Fire, Aim." Flood the area and hope like hell it helped. At the very least, their ass was covered. Especially if they created *lots* of pointless reports.

On the other hand, Mike had taken one look at the DEA's reporting system and given up in complete disgust.

The FBI, though, had "determined" nine crop dusters in the Lake County area. Not "determined that there *are.*" Simply "determined." Mike couldn't even figure out what that meant. Had they secured them? Had they simply counted them? And crop dusters in Lake County didn't really matter to him; the flight time to any significant target was too far.

The FBI had also "determined" seven in Orange County. Most of them were located at the Kissimmee Airport, which *was* close enough. It was in easy striking distance of all the major attractions. But Mike couldn't see the rag-heads taking off from Kissimmee. They were going to have to load the birds. That was going to take time. They'd be in full view of airport security and, now, Orange County deputies and FBI. Even the FBI was going to be asking questions, given that very little dusting took place in winter.

It didn't even have to be a crop duster. The vortex of a plane's passage, and the vortex created by a prop, would spread the shit pretty well. Just a plane big enough to carry the two barrels would do it. Hook up a couple of big tubes, run one out either side of the plane, and you had a pretty effective distributor.

Another effective distributor could be seen every night in Orlando. Even in winter the mosquitoes in Florida could get bad. To keep them down, every county had pesticide trucks. They were converted pickup trucks that simply sprayed clouds of pesticide out the back. They only ran at night, usually in the very early morning hours. But Mike's nightmares were starting to be seeing one of those driving through a neighborhood in the middle of the night. And in the morning, the clean-up crews coming through for the bodies.

"Kildar, we have a problem," Greznya said. "Anastasia has disappeared."

"And so the other shoe drops," Mike said, looking up from the report and taking off his glasses. "Any intel?" he asked, rubbing the bridge of his nose.

"Not so far," the Keldara said. "But Gonzales' ship put out shortly before she disappeared. She asked to be taken to Nassau so she could do some shopping. And she asked to go alone. Is it possible . . . ?"

Mike looked at her and blinked in confusion, then shook his head.

"She didn't turn if that's what you mean," Mike said. "She's afraid of the outdoors. She was probably just working on that. I should have made clear that she needed an outer perimeter."

"Greznya," Olga said, walking in the room and handing the intel boss a note. "Jay."

Greznya looked at the note and nodded.

"A group of what looked like a DEA snatch team took Anastasia from the market," Greznya said. "Colonel Montcrief of the Constabulary has been informed that this was *not* one of our operations and is investigating. She won't be going out by plane, that he can confirm. Boats, helicopters?"

"Get word to Jay that we need the take from the mikes Katya planted," Mike said, nodding and looking at the reports. "And keep me updated."

"Yes, Kildar," Greznya said, frowning slightly.

"How's it going?" Britney asked, walking in and sitting down across from the Kildar. He had reports spread all over a coffee table and had put his hated glasses back on.

"I'm trying to figure out probable method of attack," Mike said, taking off his glasses. "I don't mean direct method, how they're going to spray it, but . . . There are two major attack methods if you have lots of resources. And six barrels of VX, three useable units in other words, is a lot of resources. Do you go for simultaneous attack or ripple?"

"One attack that either gathers people or emergency services, then another on the gathering?" Britney asked.

"Bang on. I'm going to make a WAG that the main attacks are going to be simultaneous or near simultaneous. The terrorists saw our response to 9/11. When the first attack hits, we're going to go to DefConOne and shut *everything* down. People are going to get distributed, fast. But they're going to concentrate in certain spots during that distribution . . ."

"What you were talking about with the tunnels," Britney said.

"Give the girl a cigar," Mike said, leaning back and looking at the ceiling. "So figure that there are three near simultaneous attacks. What are the indicators that they are about to go down?"

"If I knew that, I'd be in the intel business," Britney said. "Oh, wait . . . ! Seriously, I have not the faintest clue."

"Then use that noggin," Mike said. "What were the indicators of the 9/11 attacks?"

"Guys with box cutters in their luggage?" Britney asked. "The hijackings."

"Right," Mike said. "The terrorists don't make their own weapons; they use weapons that are already made by societies that can actually *make* stuff. Oh, sure, they use bombs and poison gas, but they're not going to make big distribution systems. One report I had the girls go over is sales of aircraft in Florida to men with Middle Eastern names. They got nine hits. I've got a standard request out there to find those nine planes. Five have been located and examined; none of them are in the process of conversion. But I also talked to

Arensky about conversion methods and he said two guys could do it in a couple of hours."

"So if a plane gets stolen . . . ?" Britney said.

"Or any other distribution method," Mike said with a sigh. "Which is why we've got all of Central Florida's dispatch system feeding back to the caravanserai. I mean, I've only got so many people here. But if anything odd comes up, they should catch it there."

"And then?"

"Well, then somebody's got to shoot down the planes."

"You heard Anastasia's been kidnapped."

"Yep."

"You don't seem concerned."

"You don't know Anastasia as well as I do."

"So, you're awake."

The hood was yanked off and Anastasia blinked at the strong light in her eyes. But she was spun away from it to look at the room she was in. There were shackles hanging from the ceiling, whips lining the far wall and a set of nasty metal tools displayed in a case. At the sight, she almost fainted, but not from fear.

"Your boyfriend has been causing me trouble," Gonzales said, walking around to stand just at the edge of her view. She was naked and strapped solidly into the chair, gagged and the gag was attached to the headrest. She could barely move a muscle.

It was wonderful.

"And you're going to tell me everything I need to know to kill him," Gonzales continued, walking across her field of view. "I know that right now, you'd *love* to tell me everything I want to know. But since I'm mad at your boyfriend, and he's not here, I'm going to take that mad out on you."

He returned holding two clips attached to cords. One he reached down and clipped to her labia and the other he clipped to her nipple. Then he held up a red plunger.

"Let us see how much I enjoy this . . ." Gonzales said, pressing the button.

As the electricity coursed through her body, Anastasia screamed in near orgasm. But it sounded enough like pain and fear.

"Anastasia was brought on board about three hours ago," Greznya said. "We got a flash of conversation in the main salon. We have a pretty good layout of Gonzales' boat from Katya's travels through it and we are pretty sure what room she's in. Katya's been informed that she is onboard. Vil's team is ready with the boats, Dragon and Valkyrie are prepared and Pad . . . Dmitri's team and Yosif's are working on an entry plan with Chief Adams."

"Uh, huh," Mike said, nodding. "Good. Great. Glad everybody's dialed in. What's this I hear about Schwenke?"

"Ritter was apparently Schwenke in disguise," Greznya said. "We don't know when Katya spotted him, or vice versa. But they had a very pleasant conversation just before he left. This was well prior to Anastasia being snatched, but it might have been . . ."

"Nah," Mike replied. "This is Gonzales. Kurt would know better."

Greznya leaned to the side, touching the earbud she had in.

"Julia says that something's happening with Katya that may have relevance," Greznya said, frowning. "We have the take in the . . ."

"Yep," Mike said, nodding. "Let's check it out."

He followed the girl to the interior room of the suite where the intel team had set up shop. It was technically a maid's bedroom, windowless and surrounded by the rest of the suite. It wasn't entirely, or even mostly, secure, but was the best they could do under the circumstances.

The intel team had changed locales so much they had it down to something of a science and the room was ringed with monitors. One of them was showing the jerky shots of Katya walking down a hallway. From the occasional harder jerk, she was apparently being shoved from time to time.

"I gotta give that girl a raise," Mike said. "She never seems to catch a break."

A door opened and Mike shook his head. Anastasia was naked and tied up, spread-eagle. Gonzales, sweating, was standing in front of her holding a whip. From the looks of it he'd been working her front and Mike shook his head when he saw the marks on her breasts.

"Never whip breasts, you idiot," he said, sighing. "When will they ever learn?"

Anastasia had a ring gag in and as Gonzales struck her again she screamed, hoarsely. Clearly they'd been at this for a while.

"Do you see this, bitch?" Gonzales said. A hand came up past the pickup and her head jerked to the side. It looked as if he was pointing her head to look at Anastasia but Katya's eyes were jerking around taking in details of the room. "This is what happens to bitches that displease me. Are you going to please me?"

"Oh, yes, please," Katya whined.

"Yes, Katya, you can have him when we're done," Mike said, pressing the transmit button on the desk mike. "Do me two favors. Wink at Anastasia and gimme a good view of the interior of the door."

The view of the wink was weird; it turned the room surreal for a moment as the processors suddenly had to shift to just one eye then back.

"I'm sorry," Katya whined, sliding down and huddling on the ground. "I won't talk, I promise!" She'd turned her head away, apparently to keep from looking at the girl, and focused on the door.

"Yeah, one bolt," Mike said, touching the transmit key again. "Good girl. Remind me when you get back I need to give you a raise or something."

Gonzales apparently didn't care for her turning her head away and dragged her over to the tortured woman. There was a brief flash of muff, then it was pretty apparent where he'd shoved her head. Greznya leaned down and put the sound on "record," then cut off the exterior speakers.

"It's late," Mike said, walking to the door of the intel room. "I'm gonna get some sleep."

"Kildar," Greznya said, exasperated. "That's *Anastasia*! You can't just leave her there!"

Mike turned back and walked to the controls, hunting around until he found the recording feature. Using one of the other monitors he backed up the recording to where Gonzales laid the whip on his harem manager and froze the playback. Then he zoomed on her face.

"See that expression?" Mike asked.

"Oh," Greznya said, biting her lip. In freeze frame it was pretty apparent that what looked like a scream of pain had been anything but.

"She's having the time of her life," Mike said, turning back to the door. "Gimme a call if it looks as if they're gonna kill her. I think Gonzales is having too much fun to do that any time soon. God knows *Stasia* is."

CHAPTER
TWENTY-FOUR

Mike stood in front of the glass doors of his room, sipping a cup of coffee and watching the sun come up. It was going to be another glorious Central Florida winter day: fleecy clouds were spotted hither and yon and the sky was otherwise clear. It was supposed to get to nearly eighty today, which was a bit much even for Orlando in winter.

He didn't turn as the door opened, just took another sip of coffee.

"You want the update on Anastasia?" Britney asked.

"I hope you weren't watching any of that," Mike said seriously.

"A bit," Britney admitted. "And, yeah, it was hard. You know the question that gets me? How many of the girls in the bunker . . . ?"

"About twelve at a guess," Mike said, still not turning around. "Sort of. If they knew it was a game, twelve would enjoy it. And, hell, probably one was ready to hit the table knowing it wasn't a game; there are some masochists who can't wait to die under the blade. But Stasia's not that far gone. On the other hand, she knows that at a certain level it's a game. She knows there's a strike team ready to go if it looks as if she's going to be killed. Intentionally, mind you. You play at that level and it's not real safe."

"Do you guys ever . . ." Britney asked, trailing off.

"Pretty close," Mike said, taking another sip. "The real bitch about it is that he's going to scar hell out of her. Bastard. No matter what you do you can't get rid of them entirely. How's she doing?"

"Oh, she's spilling all sorts of stuff," Britney said. "All total bullshit. He's a lousy interrogator. She started in on DEA and he started naming names of people he suspected were agents. She 'burned' about half of them. I checked the DEA database. None of them are agents and a bunch of them are people close to him. It's going to nuke his network if he tries to off all of them."

"She's very good," Mike admitted. "But getting her to actually break? That's tough."

"Do you . . ."

"It's her favorite game," Mike said. "She has a secret and she won't share it. I . . . encourage her to share. The last time it was a cookie recipe. Never did get it out of her."

"With whips and . . . ?"

"I told you in the bunker I'm not a nice guy," Mike said, turning around. "And you didn't believe me."

"I kinda figured that out after the freighter crew," Britney said, frowning. "You know, most of those guys were . . ."

"Innocent?" Mike asked, taking another sip. "Define innocent. Sure, they were just sailors doing their job.

In this case, supporting the mujahideen. You think the crew didn't dance when the Towers fell? You think they don't want you wearing a burkha, honey? Maybe there were one or two who weren't complete jackals. Let God sort them out. I don't have the time or the interest."

"You really are a *bastard*, aren't you?" Britney asked unhappily.

"Glad you finally got that through your pretty little head," Mike said. "Ready to go drive around in a hot car with a complete bastard?"

"Any particular reason?" Britney asked.

"It's today," Mike replied. "I can feel it in the wind, in the water. I can feel it in the depths of my bastardness. It's gonna be a hot one."

"Great security," Mike said as they cruised past Wet and Wild again. An Orange County deputy's car was parked on the concrete expanse in front of the attraction. The deputy was chatting with two striking brunettes in bikinis.

As he turned onto Universal Boulevard Mike looked over at the tourists. Despite the increasing temperatures, the water was clearly freezing. But the northerners were playing in it for all they were worth.

"Americanus Arcticus," Mike muttered.

"Say again?" Britney asked.

"Americanus Arcticus," Mike said, pointing at one little girl who was climbing out of the pool and shivering nearly to death. "Pseudo-human beings from north of the Mason-Dixon line. They're evolutionarily adjusted to arctic temperatures. The young are more poorly adjusted but by the time they reach adulthood they are impervious to cold." He pointed to an immensely hirsute man with a gigantic beer belly and beard wearing only a Speedo. The sasquatchoid was jumping off a diving board in a "cannonball" position and when he hit the water the spray reached nearly as high as the rides. "It's the layers of subdural adipose tissue. Year by year, layer by layer, they build up their resistance even as the rings of trees. As the walrus developed whiskers to find clams in the Stygian depths, and tusks with which to dig them, even thus doth the Yankee evolve blubber."

Britney was giggling so hard she nearly didn't notice her cell phone was going off. She pulled it out of her back pocket and listened for a moment.

"Mike, Orange County Services is missing a spray truck," she said, sobering instantly.

"It's going down."

Gabrel Amani had been an employee of Orange County Services for four years. He had started cutting lawns with Mexicans but had managed, over time, to work his way into the sprayer trucks. The hours were bad but the pay was much better and it was sitting-down work.

Gabrel could not be called a sleeper agent because he had not entered the U.S. with the intent of performing acts of terrorism, sabotage or espionage. On the other hand, he *had* entered the U.S. as a good Muslim who supported the Great Jihad. It was the will of Allah that all the earth be in submission to Allah and the duty of every Muslim to support that goal. If that meant that infidels must die, then infidels would die. If they would simply realize that it was their destiny to be in submission to Allah, they would not have to die. It was their own fault that they had to be killed. The will of Allah was paramount.

Frankly, though, while he didn't want to kill infidels per se—some of them were quite nice if misguided people—this mission gave him no qualms. The actions of the people in the area they were going to hit, especially the way that women dressed, were simply sinful. There was no other way to describe it. Wiping these sluts from the face of the earth would be a glorious sacrifice unto God. And if he was lucky, he wouldn't die himself.

He backed the truck up to the loading dock of the Circuit City on Universal Boulevard and parked it. Two fedayeen were already rolling blue barrels up the slope of the dock. It should take no more than ten minutes to load the truck. And then he could go kill infidels and show them that Allah was too magnificent to be defeated. . . .

"Dunn."

Bob Dunn was having a bad week. Among a billion other things, convincing the FBI to act like adults, making sure that the Guardsmen didn't go power-mad and "coordinating transportation" for a group of congressmen, and their families, who had decided that they needed to "check out the nature of the threat" at Disney, he'd had to explain to his bosses that there was a group of heavily armed mercenaries running around Central Florida and that, no, they could not be arrested.

So the one fucking person he did *not* want to talk to was the fucking Kildar.

"Jenkins. You heard about the spray truck?"

"I heard," Dunn said, sighing. "What about it?"

"It's, like, missing? And it's one of the best distribution systems they could use."

"It was being transferred by its driver to the maintenance facility," Dunn said. "It's just overdue. The maintenance manager panicked; they'd gotten the word, too. But it was driven by its regular driver. It's probably just broken down somewhere. It's only been missing thirty minutes."

"Tell me you don't really believe that? We're talking about a Pakistani who is a known worshipper at one of the most fundamentalist mosques in your area. He goes missing with a spray truck when we've got VX in play and you're . . . what? You're *sitting* on it?"

"We put out a general call," Dunn said. "What the fuck else do you want us to do?"

"I saw the call. It was a véry low priority, no possible terrorism code, no threat code at all, in fact. It's fucking nuts! One of your deputies pulls the thing over and he's fucking dead, you know that?"

"You telling me my job?" Dunn asked, snarling. "Okay, no, I don't believe that. Yeah, I think that we have a serious situation here. My *boss* doesn't. The fucking No-Go colonel we got saddled with couldn't lift his nose out of day before yesterday's reports to even notice. Why? Because it's just the regular driver. The fact that the guy is from Pakistan doesn't fucking matter, okay? That is not part of the decision-making process, okay? Nor is his house of worship, okay?"

"God, sucks to be you, doesn't it?"

The guy actually sounded sympathetic and Dunn sighed again.

"Yeah, sometimes it does," Dunn said. "But my point

is that we can't use profiling to upgrade the status. It's the normal driver taking the thing over for maintenance and currently it's simply 'missing.' If we see it, a deputy will check it out. Until something else happens . . ."

"The first warning you're going to get is screaming."

"Hey, you're not supposed to be back here," Justin Stockton said.

Justin was twenty-three years old and recently had come to wonder if sales was his career. He had dropped out of University of Central Florida in his sophomore year and lived with three friends in a small apartment on Silver Star Road. The foursome existed on chips and cheese with an occasional "healthy" meal of McDonald's or Domino's pizza. When they weren't working their various nearly minimum wage jobs they played video games. While they sometimes had trouble making the rent or their car payments, they never missed a bill from their ISP.

Justin was also, unfortunately for him, a smoker. And since it was unlawful to smoke inside of a public building in Florida, he had stepped outside. Specifically he had stepped out the back door to the loading docks. His Marlboro was in one hand and lighter in the other when he saw the four men in gas suits loading a spray truck off the dock.

"That shit's got to be bad for you," Justin continued, maneuvering to stay upwind and reconsidering the cigarette; it might also be flammable.

"We are having trouble with truck," one of the men said in a thick accent. "We are needing to refuel it." He had stepped away from the other four and now approached Justin, his hand out. "I am Gabrel."

"Justin," Justin said, sliding on his salesman grin and holding out his own. "But that's not fuel . . ." The stuff was weird and oily but definitely not gas or diesel. He'd gotten some on his hand when they'd shaken.

"Yes it is," the man insisted, lifting the hand and thrusting it at Justin's nose. "Smell . . ."

It smelled like . . .

Gabrel grinned as the man twitched on the ground. It worked.

"We are finished, Gabrel," Mahmoud said, rolling the last of the barrels away.

"God is Great."

Petra Smith was nineteen and had a bit of a crush on Justin Stockton. She'd only been working the computer section of the store for a few weeks, possibly the reason she still found Justin attractive. But she saw potential under that slacker façade. Justin was smart, he knew everything there was to know about configuring computer hardware to get the max performance for a video game—and if he'd just apply himself he could be really successful, maybe even a store manager.

So Petra had followed Justin outside "on break." Just to talk. Sure, he smoked and kissing a guy who smoked was like licking a dirty ash-tray but . . .

When she saw him lying on the ground, though, she screamed and ran over, not even noticing the two barrels dripping clear liquid onto the dock.

"Justin?" she screamed, trying to roll him over. He was twisted up in a really strange position, like he'd cramped up or something. She couldn't move him so she darted back into the store, feeling dizzy. It was probably shock. "Help! Somebody help!" she screamed, stumbling through the stock room. She caromed off one of the shelves and realized she could barely see through the tears. It was getting so black . . .

"Kildar," Greznya said. "Report of a Hazardous Materials incident at the Circuit City on Universal Boulevard."

"That's about three blocks from here," Mike said, accelerating. The traffic on Sand Lake, as always, was solid tourists. And it was moving *slow*. He seriously reconsidered his decision to turn onto it.

He cut in front of a minivan from Michigan then back past an SUV from New York. But it was bumper to bumper in front of him. And going *really* slow.

"Fuck this," he said. A driveway on the right led to the Popeye's and that he knew from reconning the area wouldn't get him anywhere. But there weren't any cars on the sidewalk.

He turned into the driveway and then onto the sidewalk, hitting his horn in a solid blast as he drove sedately down the concrete walk, tourists scattering in front of him.

Up ahead, at the head of the line of cars, he could see a spray truck in the right-hand lane. What was stopping traffic on the left he had no idea.

Mabel Zermenfuster Wassenester was seventy-nine. She had been born and raised on a farm near the small town of Blue Earth, Minnesota. Her first driving experience had been subsequent to her marriage, the lesson administered by her mother who had originally learned to drive a horse-drawn wagon. Mabel always remembered her mother's various admonitions. Never turn so fast that a bottle of pop on the floor will fall over. Brakes are only for emergencies. And if, God forbid, you find yourself on a multilane road, the *left*-hand lane is the safest and it's there that you should drive. You stay in the left-hand lane until it's time to turn right, change lanes, then turn. Slowly.

Mabel's problem was that there was a line of cars, and a spray truck, in the right-hand lane when it came time for her to turn onto International Drive. She'd never seen a spray truck out during the day and only occasionally when she couldn't sleep at night and one of the loud, smelly trucks drove by. She was heading over to her friend Margaret's house. Margaret lived in an apartment on Kirkman Road and the only way Mabel knew to get there was down International Drive. She sorely hated the road—there were simply too many fast drivers on it—but it was the only route she knew. She had never noticed that she actually *passed* Kirkman to take I-Drive. This was the route she'd learned the first time and she stuck to it.

When she reached the intersection, the light had turned green and she took a great dare. The spray truck *should* stay in the right-hand lane as it turned. She had seen that it had its blinker on and now the yellow lights were going. It was clearly going to spray down International Drive. Maybe *that* would slow some of those young tarts in their tank-tops and skimpy little bikinis down!

So she decided that the only choice was to turn with the truck.

▲   ▲   ▲

"Fuck, would you look at that?" Mike snarled. There was an old lady in a powered wheelchair in front of him, going along at a fixed rate of one mile per hour. He fucking *knew* what was in that truck and what it was about to do. He had a binary solution set . . .

"Wait!" Britney yelled, getting out of the car and running to the chair. She grabbed the controls, turned the chair and drove it off the sidewalk. "Go!" she yelled as Mike pulled past.

"Yeah, you stay here," Mike said, dropping the car into second.

"What?" Britney screamed. "Wait! No!"

"Young lady!" the old woman shouted, her wheelchair mired in a holly bush. "Just what do you think—"

He sped up, horn blaring and reached the intersection just as the two cars, side by side, completed a perfect turn. He could hear sirens behind and in front of him but none of the cops would reach the truck in time to stop anything, even if they had a shoot order.

"Let us get just a bit down the road," Gabrel said. "Then we will begin."

"Yes," Mahmoud replied. "The spray will drift behind us, though, and strike all of the cars."

"Yes," Gabrel said, speeding the truck up slightly. "Allah is with us."

Mike skidded through the turn of the sidewalk and jumped the curb just in front of the truck. He punched the accelerator and, as the car jumped forward under full torque, hit the brakes at the same time and turned the wheel to the side. The car did a one-eighty in a cloud of blue smoke from the rear tires. As soon as he was pointed at the truck he released the accelerator and popped open his door.

"Prophet's Ghost," Gabrel snarled. "Now! Hit the release now!"

"STOP!" Britney screamed, running into the intersection and holding up her hands. A rental Lincoln Navigator driven by a Brazilian driven nearly to fury by the two idiots in front of him ignored her and she jumped to the side. But the two cars behind him both stopped.

"What the fuck is going—" the driver of the right-hand minivan, a perfect male specimen of Americanus Arcticus started to say.

"POISON GAS!"

The passenger had ducked down but Mike put four rounds into the windshield on the driver's side, splattering the driver all over the interior. The truck continued to roll forward, though, a smoky haze spewing out of the rear. Mike considered that for a moment. He really didn't want to die from VX and if he just ran into a cloud of it he wasn't going to do anyone any good.

But the wind was from the north. It was spreading the cloud backwards. Of course, that was right into a major intersection, but if he could get it cut off . . .

He ran forward just as a blue sedan, the driver a white-haired old woman, cruised sedately to the north. She gave him a look of absolute exasperation, clearly placing him with the car in the way.

Mike could give a shit about her opinion. The truck,

now out of control but only doing about five miles per hour, was drifting towards the left-hand lane. He darted to the side and yanked open the door.

Two shots went past him just about at head height and he responded by pumping six into the passenger. There was a lever there that wasn't one Mike recognized and while hitting the brakes he pushed it up. The hissing from the rear stopped.

Putting the truck in park he bailed out and ran for his car, which the truck had just about hit. If that truck had hit his GT he was going to be sorely pissed.

There was a lot of screaming from up towards the intersection, but there was only one person he was worried about up there.

Britney glanced over her shoulder and blanched as the rear of the truck started to spew vapor. And, worse, the wind was carrying it right for the intersection.

She didn't have much time to decide but she also wasn't interested in dying today. And standing here was going to mean dying.

"Get back in your cars and go *that* way!" she shouted, pointing west down Sand Lake. "Get *out* of here!"

She ran down the sidewalk, paused to extricate the old lady, then took control of the wheelchair and started driving it east down the sidewalk, screaming at people to turn back.

"What is going . . ."

"Oh shut *up* you old bat!" Britney screamed, hitting the woman on the head. "There's poison gas back there! Keep going east," she added, jumping off the wheelchair and pointing down the road. "Don't stop until you reach a cop!"

She ran out into the traffic again and stood in the road, arms spread. Cars maneuvered around her until a minivan filled with a family stopped.

"What the hell is going on?" the man asked. "I'm a police officer."

"HAZMAT!" Britney screamed. "Now park it and HELP!"

Behind her she heard a crash and turned to look: the cars that had entered the intersection were now completely out of control. Probably everyone in them was dead. The cloud was now invisible but that just made it worse.

"Fuck," the policeman from Chicago said. "Honey," he said to his wife, "get the kids and start walking east . . ."

"But . . ." the woman protested. Then she saw the out of control cars ahead of her. Every car that had been in front of them was now scattering randomly across the intersection and even into oncoming traffic. As she watched an SUV that had formerly held a family from Ohio met a late model Honda head on, killing a female college student on her way to her job at Hooters. The policeman's-wife side immediately took over. She stopped protesting and just started unstrapping and grabbing kids.

Britney managed to get the left-hand lane stopped— the cop's minivan effectively blocked the right—and after getting through to the lead driver that he'd *die* if he drove forward, started getting people out of the cars and headed down the road.

The crashes in the intersection had traffic pretty effectively stopped in all directions but she wasn't sure how far the cloud had spread. So she went from car to car as fast as she could, just saying "POISON GAS! GET OUT!"

After the fifth car she saw a police car coming west down the mostly empty eastbound lanes and decided she'd done all an intel specialist should do. She was standing about three hundred yards from the intersection, head down and breathing hard because she'd been trying really hard to hold her breath as much as possible, when she heard a distinctive horn.

"Figured you were a goner," Mike said, grinning at her. "But we've got other fish to fry."

"We going to Disney now?" Britney yelled as the GT made another bootlegger's turn.

"Disney's that way," Mike said, gesturing over his shoulder. "So, no. We're going to Wet and Wild."

"Why?" Britney asked. "Besides girls in bikinis."

"What do people do when they think there's poison gas in the air?" Mike asked, making a screaming turn onto Universal and jerking into the oncoming lane to avoid a rolling roadblock. An oncoming SUV jerked to the side, broadsiding another and before you could say "Suburban" there was a beached pod of the things.

"Run for shelter," Britney said, bracing herself as Mike slid through a three-lane sweep between four cars, missing them all by a whisker.

"And if you're at Wet and Wild?" Mike asked. "There's not much shelter."

"Ripple attack," she said, blanching. "First hit I-Drive with the gas, then they get in the water. They try to get under and hold their breath as long as possible . . ."

CHAPTER
TWENTY-FIVE

Heather Parker was blue-eyed, 5'4" tall, with her hair colored blonde and brown in layers. Her favorite song in the world was "Breakaway" by Kelly Clarkson. She had just turned fourteen two weeks before and, as her grandmother put it, she was "blossoming." The bathing suit that she'd bought just six months ago that fit fine up top then was, well, way too small. But while certain parts hurt, she generally didn't mind the stares. In fact the day before, her mother had dressed her down right solid for, as Mama put it, "preening." What Heather was paying attention to through most of the dressing down, though, was a red and white Ford GT. She wasn't sure what exactly she'd give up to take a ride in that GT, but it was a lot.

Heather's family was down on midwinter break from Soddy Daisy, a small town outside of Chattanooga, Tennessee. She, her parents and her two brothers had driven down all of Friday, fighting the traffic, and yesterday was the first day they'd had in Orlando.

The parents had decided that they wanted to go to Wet and Wild so was it *her* fault if the only bathing suit she had didn't fit?

Heather enjoyed the stares but she enjoyed swimming just as much. She wanted to be an Olympic swimmer when she grew up but since the only pool she ever had access to was the county pool in Redbank, there wasn't much chance of that. But she loved to swim, which was why she did it every chance she got.

She'd done all the rides at this point and was just enjoying the wave pool. The water got pulled in through grates, then pumped back out, making the wave action. It caused a huge splash up against the wall, but you could dive down, get pushed out and back and just generally *enjoy* the water there.

It was also the main source of processed water for the entire park.

Massoud Faroud also could not be called a sleeper agent. In fact, jihadist was pushing it. "Dupe" would probably be the best word. While he, too, stood with his fellows at the end of services and shouted "Death to the Infidel," deep down he wasn't sure about this whole jihad thing. Yes, the Prophet had declared the will of Allah, that the whole world must submit to the shariah.

But Massoud had *lived* under shariah law in Afghanistan. And, given the choice, he much preferred working as a maintenance man at Wet and Wild. Yes, the Prophet had decreed that women should be decently covered but . . . The Prophet, blessings be upon him, had never been to Wet and Wild. If he had, he'd probably have written something like "women should always wear bikinis. Preferably ones one or two sizes too small on top."

But Massoud was a maintenance "engineer" at Wet and Wild. And he had lived under the Taliban. So when the imam cornered him and introduced him to some rather unpleasant gentlemen, one of whom spoke Pashtun as his native tongue, he had known he was, as his American boss would have put it, screwed. It was "Death to the Infidel" or "Death to Massoud." Looked at that way, well . . .

On the other hand, they'd also promised that it wasn't, in fact, "Death" to the infidel. The material was supposedly a caustic agent. All it was supposed to do was sting and possibly hurt the eyes, thus showing that the Movement could strike anywhere and any time. Prophet's Beard, peace be upon it, they put that in the water all the time. In fact, Massoud had tried to point out that even high molar acid in the quantities they were inserting wouldn't do much more than make people pissed. The unpleasant gentlemen had told him to mind his own business.

But he'd gotten the two blue barrels into the injection facility easily enough; it was part of his job after all. And, using all appropriate hazardous material handling techniques, he had gotten the two barrels, which had to be mixed in transfer, set up to inject. All sorts of stuff got added to the water all the time. Chlorine, of course, but also bases, stabilizers, softeners, hardeners for when the softeners were too soft and even materials to make the water more "slippery." One or two more blue barrels in the large room was nothing to notice.

"You're sure about this?" Massoud asked, taking the

lock off of the lock-out/tag-out switch. "It's not going to do much. It might not even be noticed. If it's a base, I'd need to reduce the chlorine input—"

"Just turn it on," the man snarled in Pashtun.

"Right," Massoud said, flipping the switch up. The material started dumping but it wasn't going at full flow. The suction from the injector was pulling some up, but just a trickle was getting into the water which for *sure* wouldn't be noticed. He'd have to start the pump to get it all dumped. And he suddenly realized that the Pathan asshole *probably* didn't know that. He might not notice the material was barely draining out for a while. Possibly never if he left soon enough.

There was no such thing as soon enough to Massoud.

Mike pulled the GT to a screaming stop on the same concrete pad the Orange County deputy occupied. The deputy was keying his shoulder-mounted radio with one hand and had his pistol drawn with the other. When Mike came screaming up, the radio was ignored for a two-point stance.

"Freeze!" the cop shouted. "Identify yourself!"

"Your boss is my bitch?" Mike asked. "And so are you if you don't put down the piece?"

"Lieutenant Britney Harder," Britney said, standing up with her ID out and her hands up. "Special Operations Command. U.S. Army SOCOM, that is," she added since every dinkwater town had their own "Special Operations Command" these days.

The cop duck-walked forward, weapon still extended, then did a very credible weapons control maneuver to retrieve the ID. His jaw flexed, then he looked over at Mike.

"You?"

"Oh, Mike Jenkins," Mike said, holding up his Georgian driver's license.

When the cop walked over and took it from him, Mike waited until his eyes flickered to the license in confusion then, somewhat politely, removed the pistol from the police officer's hand.

"Okay," Mike said, laying the weapon between the officer's eyes. "Here's how it's going to go. I don't have time to fuck around with you. Call dispatch, tell them that we have a WMD terrorism incident at Wet and Wild and we need more response. Clear?"

"Clear," the cop said, shaking his hand. The snatch had been lightning and his finger was nearly ripped off.

"Who I am is none of your fucking business," Mike said, dropping the magazine, then disassembling the Sig Sauer one-handed. He held the pieces out to the stunned officer. "And there are people about to die."

"Who?" the cop shouted as Mike started running for the entrance.

"Anyone who gets between me and where I'm going."

"The level is not going down very fast," the Pathan said, looking over at Massoud. "It is not going down as fast as it is supposed to. Why?"

"Hmmm . . ." Massoud said, frowning at the set-up through his mask. "I don't understand it. We're all hooked up. Injectors are open . . ."

"This is a pump, yes?" the Pathan said, drawing a pistol out from under his HazMat suit. "You will engage the pump, yes?"

"I *knew* I forgot something," Massoud said. "Damn. The *pump*!"

"You will stop stalling," the Pathan said, cocking the pistol and pointing it at his head. "You will start the pump. Now."

VX is an organophosphate chemical and, as noted, rather stable. However, one of the things that will convert it to a nontoxic chemical is chlorine. Except at very high temperatures it doesn't do so *well*, but it does do so. Thus the small quantities of VX that had been picked up had, thus far, had little or no effect. Most of the molecules were converted to an inert state, virtually harmless to anyone but a California Environmental Scientist, who would probably get cancer from them.

However, one hundred and ten gallons, dumped rapidly, was more than enough to kill anyone in the water. Especially anyone near the outlets.

Heather popped up for a breath and hocked some water out of her ear at the sound of sirens. There was a fire truck going down the side road like a bat out of hell and more sirens all around. In fact, traffic was stopped all over the place; there must have been a big wreck or something.

That was all good. Her parents weren't going to want to leave for a while with all that traffic.

She briefly considered going for a walk, but, truth be told, the stares were getting to be a bit much. So she ducked back under the water, kept riding the waves and imagined that she was somewhere down in the Caribbean, riding around with a guy that had a red and white GT and looked *just* like Brad Pitt.

▲   ▲   ▲

Mike leapt the entry stall one-handed and drew his pistol as the unarmed security guard ran towards him.

"Mike . . . crap what day is it?" he shouted. "CIA. You're under terrorist attack. Where's the place where they've got all the pumps!"

"Lieutenant Britney Harder," Britney said, holding out her badge. "SOCOM Intelligence. Answer the question!"

The befuddled security guard just stared at the badge in one hand and the gun in the other.

"You're *who*?" he asked.

"Oh, fuck," Mike said, looking around for any signs of intelligence. There was one girl in uniform who was pretty wide-eyed but didn't seem *completely* shut down. "You," he said, pointing his finger at her. "Pumps?"

"This way," she said, gesturing. "How fast should we be going?"

"Faster than this," Mike said, trotting past her. "How fast can you run?"

"I'm one of the lifeguards here," the girl said, speeding up.

"Good," Mike said. "Think Baywatch fast."

The VX traveled into a main supply pipe and most of the way through the park towards the outlets at the wave pool. From the wave pool, water was pulled in, pumped to other attractions and then, eventually, reprocessed.

It would take two minutes for the first of the load to reach the wave pool. . . .

▲   ▲   ▲

Massoud hooked up the last circuit and the pump began throbbing.

"Now it is going down," he said, pointing to the barrel. "And I'd really prefer not to be a martyr, thank you."

"You have grown soft," the Pathan said. "You have let the infidel women infect you."

"Seriously, dude," Massoud said, dropping his hands in resignation. "You need to get over yourself. Have you *seen* those bitches? Wait, don't shoot. We just walk up to the top of the pump station and you can see for yourself. Holy Allah, *seventy-two* virgins? There's about a *thousand* of them out there in these little yellow bikinis that are *sooo* tight. . . ."

"You make me sick," the Pathan said, lifting his pistol.

Mike was barely panting when he reached the door of the pump room. The lifeguard had gasped directions to him halfway across the park and he could hear she was still back there somewhere. Britney, the dear, was right on his ass. She was also unarmed.

"Back," Mike said, cursing himself for not getting God-dammed *MOPP* gear. Again. He took three breaths to steady himself and snatched open the door.

Massoud ducked and covered as gunshots rang out. He felt his body, gingerly, wondering where the bullet had gone, then looked up. A man with a smoking pistol was standing by the Pathan's body.

"If you don't shut this shit down, right now, I'm going to feed it to you," the man said.

Massoud scrambled to his feet and pulled the

connections for the pump in a spiral of sparks, then dropped the input to the injectors.

"I don't know how much got in," he shouted. "I am not jihadist! I spit in all jihadist's faces! This is not the religion I was born in!"

Mike looked at the barrels, then at the big pump room. He had no fucking clue how to run any of this shit.

"We need to stop it," Mike said. "And suck back any that got out."

"Back-feed," the man said, nodding. "I can do that."

He turned to a big control console and began hitting switches. Mike backed up, just in case any of the VX was in the air. But the barrels were well sealed. This had been a professional operation, probably because of the guy at the console.

"What happens when you back-feed?" Mike asked.

"It is a way to wash the filter system," the man shouted through his mask. "It will pull water in through the main outlets and flush it back through the system then into the sewer system. What is this, really?"

"VX gas," Mike said. "What did they tell you?"

"A caustic agent," the man said, shrugging. "I wasn't going to try to fuck with Taliban."

"You're Afghan," Mike said.

"I'm an American citizen. Have been for three years. This really *wasn't* what I was planning on doing today."

"We keep anybody from dying and I'll see what I can do," Mike said. "Wait, you're going to suck water back in from the outlets?"

"Yeah," the man said. "Anybody by them better

watch out. It's really gonna . . . suck. I'll add some agents to neutralize the poison, too."

"Shit," Mike said, running out of the room and brushing past Britney. The panting female lifeguard had just reached the entrance to the pump room when he leapt down the steps.

"Main outlets for the water?" Mike said. "Where?"

"Wa . . . Wave po . . . "

"Wave pool," Mike said, running past her. "Get on the horn. Everybody out of the pool."

Heather frowned and popped up again as the wave action stopped. There was some sort of oily slick over to her left and she instinctively avoided it. But she was the only one up by the outlets so nobody else was near it.

She considered, again, getting out, but the waves were probably going to start up again any time now. She leaned back and floated on the surface for a bit. That had gotten easier lately and she wasn't sure why.

Then she felt the water shifting around her and went vertical again, holding herself up by fanning her hands. The wave generator sucked in and then pushed back out and she felt the suction, riding it down to the grates. But it wasn't blowing back . . .

"Heather!" the woman screamed.

"Ma'am, you need to get back," the lifeguard said. They were all getting people out of the pool and driving them as far back as they could. The news had been all over the VX story with lurid details of what it did and when they got the news and saw the oil slick on the surface . . . Well, they didn't get paid enough to die.

"My daughter is in there!" the woman shouted. "She was down by the wave thing!"

The guard looked over his shoulder and could see where whirlpools had formed as the massive pumps reversed. The pressure would be enormous; if there was anyone down there they weren't coming out.

"Ma'am, I'm sure she's not down there," he started to say as the crowd surged forward and parted.

A heavy-set guy was head down, pushing through the crowd and panting hard as if he'd been running. As he passed the guard he looked at the woman.

"Where?" the guy panted.

"On the right, I think," the woman said.

"On it," the man said, diving into the water.

"Hey!" the guard shouted. "No diving!"

Mike knew he was fucked. Those were *big* fucking pumps, designed to drive masses of water like son of a bitch. Then there was the VX, which was probably in the water somewhere.

But he also could see a figure pinned against the grates. The figure's arms were up but the person couldn't reach the surface. They were caught like a spider in a web, only a few feet from air.

But inches from air could kill you.

He could feel the suction of the inlets, now, drawing him in. He rode the current, his feet forward, and slammed with both feet onto the grate. The grating was small specifically to keep people from being sucked in by the waves. It wasn't actually hard to stay "upright" sideways.

He crouched and walked, carefully, to where the figure, a girl naturally, was pinned in a rather charming spread-eagle. But at that point he was sort of stuck. He couldn't figure out how to get her unglued.

Up was the only rational choice but it was going to hurt like hell. Especially since the only thing he could get ahold of was one arm and her hair.

He grabbed both, crouched and yanked her upwards. He gained a few inches, stepped forward and tried it again. So far so good. Now if she just wouldn't die on him.

He kept yanking until he felt the flow was pulling him down instead of sideways. He could see a slight shelf just above water level. He lunged for it, got one hand on the ledge, then pulled the girl upwards against the lighter flow.

Heather had been sure she was dead. When she felt the water irresistibly pulling her under she'd taken a big breath of air. Surely they would stop the flow as soon as they realized what happened. And there were all these lifeguards and stuff around. She wasn't going to *drown*!

But as time went on, as she felt that screaming craving to breathe, pinned against the intake, all she could think was that it was a lousy way to die. She was too damned *young* to die such a lousy way. It made her want to curse. It was just so *unfair*. She'd never seen *anything*. She'd never . . . *done* anything!

She hadn't had much time so she'd prayed. She hadn't cried, though, cause she couldn't afford the air. She just hung on, fighting the will to breathe, letting out a bit of air from time to time, a trick she'd picked up in swimming class. She could feel her vision getting darker when somebody grabbed her by the arm and the *hair*! Oh. My. God! That hurt! But she hung on. Then she started being dragged across the concrete and *that* hurt. But she was being dragged up. That was good.

She was half unconscious when her mouth cleared the water but she let out what air she had left and took a big glorious drink.

"Oh," she said, taking another breath.

"Air's great when you haven't had any in a while, ain't it?" the man holding her hair said. He let go of the hair and pulled her up into a little ledge were water usually flowed out. "You okay?"

"I am now," Heather said, breathing deeply.

"Not too much," the man said. "Calm it down. Or you'll hyperventilate. And, uh . . ."

Heather looked down and realized that her bikini had . . . Well, it was hanging around her neck and covering her top about as well as a necklace.

"Oh," Heather said, blushing and tying it back up. "Thank you. For both."

"You're welcome," the man said. "I'd ask for favors, but you're much too young. And you shouldn't argue with your mother; she really loves you, you know?"

"How do you . . . ?" she asked then she ducked her head. "You're the guy in the GT, right?"

"Right," the man said. "And you're the girl with the belly."

"What?" Heather asked, looking down. "I *don't* have a fat belly!"

"I didn't say 'fat,'" the man said, chuckling. "Wave for your mom to tell her you're okay."

Heather dutifully waved, then looked at the crowd.

Everybody was out of the water and they were staying *way* back.

"What's happening?" she asked. She felt weird. She'd nearly died and now she was chatting with some stranger while perched up on an outlet in full view of a big crowd.

"Somebody dumped poison in the water," the man said.

"That's why they were sucking it all out," Heather said.

"Correct," the guy said, looking over at her. The look gave her butterflies in her belly.

"Wha . . . who . . . why . . . Did somebody stop them or what?"

"Yeah," the man said, standing up. The whirlpools were gone. "Somebody stopped them. Time to take a swim."

"Okay," Heather said, jumping into the water. She must have cut up her back because it *really* hurt. "Ouch!" she said as she surfaced.

"Pain is weakness leaving the body," the man said, then followed her in.

"What*ever*," Heather said, frowning. "Hey, can I ask you a question?"

"Sure," the man said, breast-stroking towards the side of the pool.

"Can I get a ride in your GT?"

"Not today, I'm a little busy," the man said. "But I'll find you tomorrow and you can then. If your mother says it's okay."

"What *is* it with adults?"

CHAPTER
TWENTY-SIX

"You're wet," Britney said as Mike collapsed into the seat of the GT.

"Yeah," he said. "And my cell's trashed. Could you get me the rig out of the back?"

Britney picked up the case in the back and opened it as Mike pulled out. A state trooper car pulled in front of him, trying to block the GT, and he slid around it dexterously. Punching the accelerator he began weaving through the remaining traffic on I-Drive and blew through the red light at Kirkman, narrowly missing an SUV.

The case contained a tactical communicator but one of the smallest ones Britney had seen. There was an ear bud, a throat mike that wasn't much more than a patch and a small device that looked like a PDA in a belt rig.

As Mike swept through the turn onto I-4 she attached the belt rig and the throat patch, then handed him the earbud.

Mike slid in the ear bud, weaving through traffic, then keyed on the communicator.

"Who's there?"

"Lydia, Kildar, do you want an update?"

"Two major attacks? I-Drive and Wet and Wild?"

"Yes, Kildar," Lydia said.

"Switch me to Dunn," Mike said, sliding into the left-hand emergency lane to get around a rolling roadblock. He was doing over a hundred and the suspension did *not* like the rougher surface.

"This Jenkins?" Dunn snarled a moment later.

"You could start with 'thank you for doing my job for me,'" Mike replied.

"You realize you're on national TV at the moment?" Dunn asked. "I'm trying to convince everyone that the guy flying down I-4 in a GT is *not* a terrorist and doesn't go around shooting people for the fun of it. But since I'm not sure *myself . . .*"

Mike glanced in his rearview and finally spotted the line of police cars trying to catch up to him.

"Good, at least *they're* heading the right way," Mike said.

"I'm watching you on TV," Dunn said. "I can't believe you're able to talk. The only people I know that can do that are cops. Don't ask me about eating lunch during a high-speed chase and I won't tell you the story."

"I'm good at multitasking," Mike said, slipping through a gap between two semis at about twice their speed. The cop cars in the rearview either braked or tried to slip into the emergency lanes. He was just passing the onramp from the Beeline and saw three black Mercedes stacked up entering the interstate at high speed. "Okay, now is when it gets fun. I wondered when this would start . . ."

Mark Este, chief helicopter pilot and owner of World Helicopter Rides, Inc., wasn't too sure about the latest charter. The man who had set it up said that they were photographers looking for some stock shots of the Orlando area. And the group had big bags, but they didn't look like camera bags.

But, what the hell, a charter was a charter.

"Where do you want to go?" he asked as he took off.

"Down I-4 towards Disney," the leader said as the helo gained altitude. "I am a pilot as well. Would you mind if I rode up front?"

"Sorry, FAA reg against it," Mark said. He felt a cold circle on the back of his neck as the man slid into the co-pilot's seat.

"You'll forgive me if we ignore that," the man said, strapping in and putting on the spare headphones. "My bird."

The three Mercedes had obviously been souped up since they were, marginally, keeping up with the GT. The problem was the traffic. Mike was having to find the gaps and the Mercedes were following him through them. They were outdistancing the cop cars for that matter.

He didn't flinch as the first rounds struck the GT but he did snarl.

"Those motherfuckers just shot my car," Mike said. "They are *so* going to pay for that."

"Okay," Dunn said. "I've convinced them that

you're one of the good guys. Bad guys shooting at you helped. What are we going to do about the guys trying to kill you?"

"That's handled," Mike said. "Lydia, you there, dear?"

"Yes, Kildar," Lydia said.

"Tell Dragon it's time."

"Dragon, Dragon, Keldara Base. Kildar is southbound on I-4 south of 535. Three black Mercedes in pursuit. He requests having his back scratched, over."

"Got it," Kacey said. "ETA three minutes."

The Hind had been loitering southwest of Bayhill in an area that was still undeveloped. She'd mostly been hovering over palmetto scrub and scaring the hell out of the armadillos and feral hogs that made a home of the inhospitable scrub.

Now she powered up and headed east. Time for the Dragon to eat.

The body of the former pilot tumbled into the triangle of grass at the intersection of the Beeline and I-4 as the helicopter dropped down and accelerated.

"We cannot get up to this car," the leader of the hit team said over the radio. "You might have to take him out."

"We are on our way," the Colombian pilot said. "It will take about a minute to catch up."

"You just missed the exit for Disney," Britney pointed out as Mike blew past U.S. 192.

"I know," he said, sliding into the emergency lane again and staying there. The suspension *really* didn't like it. "I'd rather keep on track. We've got friends headed in."

"Dragon?" Britney asked. "You know we're on national TV, right?"

"Life sucks sometimes," Mike said.

"Kildar, Keldara Base."

"Go."

"Be aware that police now report a stolen helicopter headed towards your position."

"Life *really* sucks sometimes."

Once past the exit for Celebration and World Drive the traffic opened up a bit. Mike poured on the gas, weaving through the tourists headed for Tampa, the three Mercedes falling farther and farther behind. But Britney had rolled down her window and now, fighting the airstream, looked behind them.

"Bell Ranger, low on the right, coming up fast," she said, sticking her head back in and tightening her seatbelts. "What are you going to do?"

"Drive," Mike said then braked. "Dragon, Dragon, heading north," he said, skidding sideways into an emergency crossing.

As he accelerated into the northbound lane, one of the Mercedes tried to cross the median and rolled over. Another got stuck. The third followed him through the emergency crossing but, with lower acceleration, fell farther behind. Not a lot. They were definitely souped to the max. However, Mike could see the Bell Jet Ranger now and it simply pivoted. The doors were open and he could see the machine guns carried by the passengers. Tracers flew past the GT as he ripped through the gears and back up to full speed, twisting through the traffic.

A line of bullet holes appeared in a CCC truck ahead of him as he drove under the fire.

"Dragon?" Mike asked.

"I see them," Dragon replied. "Look up and left."

Mike glanced that way and grinned. The Hind was dropping down like a peregrine on a dove. On the other hand, it wasn't real close.

"You know there are two birds following you, right?" Dragon said. "I think one of them's a TV crew."

"Shoot the one that's shooting at *me*. I'm not sure I could get all deniable about shooting a TV crew. Again."

Rounds cracked through the roof and into the back-seat as Mike slid into the shadow of another tractor trailer and braked, hard. He rolled along there for a second, but that let the Mercedes catch up and one of the passengers leaned out the window holding an automatic carbine. Rounds started to slam into the rear of the car. Which was where the engine sat, so that was *bad*.

"Dragon, these motherfuckers are shooting my *GT*," Mike pointed out. "This is not happy making."

"Almost there, Kildar."

He accelerated out of the cover of the truck as the Mercedes tried to drive alongside, rounds bouncing into the interior of the GT. Again, he was able to accelerate away much faster than the Mercedes could manage but the Ranger just dipped its nose and kept up. It had swung over to the right and rounds cracked through the hood. But they were going to find the range sooner or later and either take out the engine or Mike and Britney.

Another set of rounds cracked right past Mike's

head, one tracer flying by his nose and burying itself in the driver's door, then there was a tremendous explosion off to his right. Glancing that way, he saw the flaming wreckage of a Jet Ranger crashing into the fields surrounding the Kissimmee River.

The Mercedes, finally noticing that Mike had top cover, cut across the lanes and into the median. As it bounced into the grass four laserlike lines of fire tracked across it and the Mercedes burst into fire, rolling into the oncoming lane. Cars dodged it successfully. Let the local sheriff's department handle that.

"Okay, Dragon, thanks," Mike said. "Move to secondary loiter point."

"You're welcome, Kildar," Dragon replied. "Dragon Flight, out."

"Jesus Christ," Fisher said as the smoking GT pulled into one of the VIP slots in the employee parking lot. "You really fucked up your car, Mr. Jenkins."

"*Other* people fucked up my car," Mike said, sourly. "Of course, most of them are dead, now. I'd call it even but I *really* like this car."

"Yeah, I saw," Fisher said. "Was that a *Hind* on the TV?"

"Shit," Mike said with a sigh. "It *was* a news bird, huh? I hope they didn't follow me here."

"They *tried* to follow the Hind," Fisher said. "But they lost it. That's one fucking *fast* Hind."

"It should be for what I paid for it," Mike said, pulling a large backpack out of the front boot. There were some bullet holes in it so he checked the contents but they were all fine. He pulled out the body armor and slid off his shirt, then slid the armor on. The extra bulk was hardly noticeable under the Hawaiian shirt, the pattern of flowers breaking up the outline. He did have to button it up one button, though. A Desert Eagle .50 slid into the waistband of his shorts. It was, also, well concealed by the long shirt. Heavy but the stopping power was nice.

"What do you want me to do?" Britney asked.

"Stay out of the way," Mike replied, then held up a hand to forestall a reply. "I know, I've been dragging you around into nasty incidents all day. Why stop now? Because my teams have this covered and I don't want you to get hurt. It stopped being a game back there on I-4. So . . . Head back to the hotel. Please."

"Okay," Britney said.

"Just that?" Mike asked. " 'Okay?' "

"How about, 'I'm really tired of being shot at and being around poison gas,' " Britney replied with a grin. "I'm fine with sitting this one out. I'll go catch a ride." With that she headed for the employee entrance.

"Smart girl," Fisher said.

"Smarter than me," Mike admitted. "Say, I don't suppose Disney has a fantastic car rebuilding shop?"

"The studio guys do," Fisher replied. "Want me to talk to them?"

"Please. And ask them if they could redo it in black and silver. Maybe with a tiger face on the hood?"

". . . asking that everyone keep an especial lookout for any unusual activity," the sheriff for Orange County said to the room full of reporters. "I would now like to introduce Lieutenant Bob Dunn, head of the Orange County Anti-Terrorism Task Force. Lieutenant Dunn?"

"Thank you, sir," Dunn said, stepping up to the podium and blinking at the bright lights. "I've got a short statement about the events that have just occurred. Two major weapons of mass destruction attacks occurred in the Orlando–Orange County area. The first was by use of a stolen spray truck. The intent appeared to be to drive down the north end of International Drive. There was a short release near Sand Lake that, unfortunately, caused several deaths. That area is now closed off and we don't have a full casualty list as yet. Due to the nature of the attack, we are having to approach the area cautiously. When we do, and next-of-kin have been informed, we will release the casualty list. Currently there are only five confirmed casualties but, unfortunately, we are certain that there will be more. Two terrorists are among the confirmed dead.

"A second attack was attempted at Wet and Wild. That attack was prevented, fortunately without loss of life."

He took a breath and, knowing that it would be bad politics to snarl, tried to put a good face on the rest.

"Both of the attacks were stopped with the assistance of a special operations team working through the U.S. Army Special Operations Command. As you are all aware, the federal government has been providing support during this crisis under the War Powers Act. Federal agents from the FBI as well as military personnel are involved in this investigation. With their support, both attacks were stopped. I will now take questions."

"Lieutenant Dunn," the first reporter said. "There's a rumor that the special operations team was, in fact, the Georgian commando group called the Mountain Tigers. Could you comment?"

"No," Dunn said, trying not to snarl but his jaw worked. "I cannot comment on the nature of the special operations team."

"Lieutenant," the next reporter said. "About the car chase on I-4. The helicopter that took out the stolen chopper and the Mercedes was a black Hind, just like the one that was seen in the Keys. The U.S. military does not use that type of helicopter. Was it the same helicopter?"

"I honestly don't know," Dunn replied. "I am not privy to everything that is going on on the federal side. You might want to ask them."

"Lieutenant, was the car involved in the chase a Ford GT? Because only one of those has been sold recently in the Orlando area. It was sold to a corporation called Mountain Tiger Beer, Inc. on Friday according to open records. Was that the same GT?"

"I am not able to comment on that," Dunn said, angrily. "I don't know when or where the damned car was bought. For all I know the idiot—"

The sheriff stepped forward and nudged Dunn to the side with a nod of thanks.

"All the attractions in the Orlando area, with the exception of Wet and Wild and those in the immediate area of the attacks, remain open. We are not going to let terrorists stop people from having fun. We are going to *stop* them from doing that. We're just asking that people keep a sharp eye out for potential threats. Report anything suspicious through the normal 911 center or to a local security person. Thank you for attending, no more questions."

CHAPTER
TWENTY-SEVEN

Will Carter sighed when he exited the monorail. The lines to get into the Magic Kingdom were *insane*.

Will and his wife Dafney had brought their three children, Lindsey 11, Jason 9, and Allison 6, to Disney several times before. It was an annual pilgrimage from their home in Radcliff, Kentucky. Dafney's mother and father lived in a retirement community near Clermont, a town just west of Orlando. They came down on winter break because, normally, the lines were a bit better than at Christmas.

But not this time. Even though there was a terrorism threat in the Florida area, it seemed as if everyone in the *world* had descended on Disney.

The press of bodies on the monorail ramp slowly moved forward and he could see why it was so packed: Disney was obviously taking the terrorist threat seriously. Each of the entry points had a security guard on it and they weren't just checking bags but wanding each person. And "Mouse-trail" lines had been set up stopping about fifty feet back from the actual entry point. It was going to take *forever* to get through them but he was sort of glad to see that Disney was taking the steps; he didn't want his kids dying at Disney.

"It doesn't look bad once we get into the park," Dafney said, laying a hand on his arm. She knew that her husband got frustrated waiting in line.

"I can see," Will said. From the top of the monorail ramp you could just see into Main Street and it was apparent there weren't all that many people on the street. But *getting* there was going to be a nightmare. "I'll try to keep my cool."

Some of the characters were out working the line. Maybe that would keep the kids from getting out of hand. . . .

Mike walked along the line of security booths, watching the bag checkers. Most of them were following Fisher's orders, carefully checking not only the obvious contents but things that could be disguised. He saw one of the checkers pull out a can of OFF, identical to the one that he'd demonstrated to Fisher, and hand it to the person being checked. Of course, Mike wouldn't have bothered, given that it was a blonde teenager. But the girl, after a moment's confusion, sprayed some on her arm.

Mike paused as another person came to a booth near the far right. The man was Middle Eastern in appearance, carrying a new backpack.

"Konstantin," he said. The communicator was voice activated, so he didn't even have to press a throat mike. "Booth Four."

▲   ▲   ▲

Konstantin Shaynav was already on the target. The man appeared nervous, but a lot of the targets had. He kept the crosshairs on the man's head, though, dialed back far enough that he could watch general actions.

"Bag's being checked," Dzintars, his spotter, said. "Can of spray . . . Shit."

Mike watched as the checker on Booth Four, an elderly woman who had a vaguely Jewish look, lifted a green spray can out of the bag then set it back in as she pawed through the contents. She had an expression that told him she was clearly pissed at the stupidity of the intense search.

"Fisher," Mike said, gesturing with his chin.

"What?" the man said. He'd been examining the lines and trying to figure out how to move the people through faster. There were two reasons it was on his mind. One was simple customer service. People had come to Disney to have fun, not stand in line waiting to get in. There were going to be massive complaints. The second was security related; he wasn't happy with that many people packed in together.

"Booth Four. Spray can. Didn't get checked."

The man had completed his check and nodded at the checker with a smile as he started to walk away.

"Booth Four," Fisher said into his radio. "Stop him."

Mike and Fisher walked forward as the security guard backing up the checker put his hand on the man's arm.

"Excuse me, sir," the guard said. "We'd like your cooperation . . ."

"You are stop me because I am Arab!" the man said, raising his voice. "This is prejudice against Arabs! I insist that you treat me as human! You kill Arabs in Iraq and you don't care . . ."

"Sir, if you'll just calm down," Fisher said, stepping over to the irate customer.

"Sir, if you'll just look at your chest," Mike said, much more quietly.

"What?" the Arab said angrily. Or at least he *appeared* angry on the surface. But his eyes weren't.

"Look down," Mike said in Arabic. "And stay still."

The man looked down and his dark face went gray at the sight of a spot of red light wavering over his heart.

"Now," Mike said, still in Arabic, "if you'll just accompany us I'm sure that this can all be resolved quite quickly. And if you continue to present a problem to me, innocent or not, I'm going to splatter you all over the ground. Do you understand?"

"Yes," the man said, his jaw working.

"Slowly hand the bag to the security guard," Mike said. "Then step towards that door, slowly," he continued, pointing to a door marked "Cast Only." Two of the Keldara, wearing much the same clothes as Mike, including the extra bulkiness, were walking over. They flanked the man as, followed by the security guard, he was marched over to the door.

Fisher had gotten a new security guard for Booth Four and went over to the checker.

"Mrs. Meier," Fisher said as the entry supervisor hurried over. "You didn't check a spray can."

"I'm sorry, Mr. Fisher," the woman said angrily. "But this is all so stupid! Nobody is going to put anything in a can of OFF."

"Let the security guard do the checking on this one," Mike said. "I think that Mrs. Meier could do with a little demonstration."

"Okay," Fisher said. "Mrs. Meier, if you could accompany us?"

The threesome walked over to the door and went through. On the other side was a section sealed off with plastic sheeting. Inside the plastic sheeting, two of the Keldara were fitted with poison gas gear.

The Middle Easterner was standing by nervously as the security guard, gingerly, removed the spray can. The two large Keldara still flanked the potential terrorist. The security guard put the can on a tray and slid it into the sealed area through an air lock.

"Sir, if you would step in there," Mike said, politely. "And demonstrate that that is normal OFF in the can, I'd be very grateful."

"I will not!" the man shouted. "You are picking on me because I am Arab! You will stop this now! I will protest to CAIR!"

"Fine," Mike said with a sigh. He drew the Desert Eagle and pointed it at the man's head. "Once upon a time the .44 Magnum was the largest and most powerful handgun in the world. It was subsequently replaced by this one, the Desert Eagle .50 caliber, which can kill an elephant at short range. Admittedly, subsequent to that other more powerful handguns such as the Casull .454 have been developed but that is not entirely germane to our discussion since I am not currently pointing one of those at your head. I will, however, add that I'm having a very bad day. I've gotten shot at, gassed and done a rather nasty swim. My harem manager has been kidnapped and is being tortured at the moment. I'm tired and cranky and I haven't gotten laid recently. So. You can demonstrate that there is *not* VX in that can or you can be shot by a gun normally used to kill elephants. Your choice. I'm good either way."

"You wouldn't shoot me," the man said, shaking his head. "Not in cold blood. Not with everyone watching."

"Bets?" Mike asked, cocking the pistol. "This is a hollow point round. When it hits your head this entire room will be covered in blood and brains, but I've got spare clothes and I've been covered in blood and brains before."

"I will not spray that on myself," the man said, shaking his head. He was clearly terrified, but it could have just been the massive gun sitting on his occipital bone. "No."

"Georgi," Mike said, raising his voice. "Try it on one of the gerbils."

The Keldara reached into a cage and removed a gerbil, then placed it in a different cage. First he sealed the cage, then inserted the can and his hand through a rubber seal. He shook the can and sprayed a very small quantity into the cage. The gerbil began spasming immediately.

The Middle Easterner tried to run but the two Keldara wrestled him easily to the floor and slid cuffs on his hands and feet and a hood over his head.

"Now, Mrs. Meier," Mike said, decocking the weapon and putting it away. "You just let VX gas into the

Magic Kingdom and that really pisses me off. How many *other* cans did you fail to check?"

"I . . . I don't know," the woman said, her eyes wide and fixed on the dead gerbil that could be seen through the clear plastic. "A . . . a few."

"Any carried by men of Middle Eastern extraction?" Mike asked.

"I try not to *look*," the woman said, angrily. "That's *profiling*. I *refuse* to treat people differently just because of the color of their skin. If you were from *my* people you would understand that."

"This asshole wants to wipe every Jew off the face of the earth," Mike said, kicking the terrorist in the side. "Jews are, after all, descendants of apes and pigs. So I don't find you noble or honest or good or anything. I find you to be a fucking idiot. The sort of fucking idiot that thought that Hitler couldn't possibly be '*serious*.' But, congratulations, you've probably killed quite a few people today, no matter *what* I fucking do. Because we can't weed them all out, now. Congratu-fucking-lations. I hope you enjoy your moral superiority."

He stalked out of the room and looked up at the sky, shaking his head.

"Teams," he said, turning the communicator back on. "We have a live one. There may have been leakers. And some of them might have noticed this. So be on your toes. Who has the crowd?"

"Braon," Braon said. "I'm scanning but there's a *bunch* of people. Manos has over twenty potentials."

"Where's Lasko?" Mike asked.

"Cinderella's Castle," Oleg replied. "Main Street position."

"Get him up here," Mike said, looking over at Fisher. "I need a sniper transferred from Cinderella to here, fast."

"I'm on it," Fisher said. "What about the crowd out front?"

"That's why I need the sniper."

Will had Allison up on his shoulders since the six-year-old had nearly been trampled by the crowds. They were finally down to the mouse-maze but it was apparent that, for whatever reason, the checkers were really taking their time. The lines were moving slower than for any ride he'd ever been on.

"It'll be okay," Dafney said, rubbing his arm. "We're almost to the front."

"Yeah," Will said, shifting the six-year-old around. "I'm good."

He'd have been better if the guy behind him hadn't smelled like a goat. The guy, Middle Eastern or Hispanic, Will wasn't sure, clearly had never heard of a shower.

"Target Nine," Lasko said. "Middle Eastern male. Backpack. He's watching the security and he's really unhappy."

"If he dips in the backpack and comes up with *anything*, take him down," the Kildar replied.

Lasko flexed his jaw and touched his communicator.

"Target is blocked. Girl on her father's shoulder. Line Fourteen."

Mike looked past the booths, where the checkers were taking *much* more care, and spotted the target. Sure enough, some guy had his kid up on his shoulder. Cute little kid, too. Five or six with dark brown hair and clearly looking forward to a day at the Magic Kingdom.

"Take two shots."

"Honey, you're getting to be too big of a girl! I got to set you down," Will said, bending forward and sliding Allison to the ground. As he did the guy behind him turned and bumped into him, spilling both of them to the ground.

"God damnit!" Will cursed, turning and starting to stand up just as the man, who had a can of bug spray in his hand, stumbled backwards. There was a red hole in his chest and blood exploded upwards from his mouth. The can hit the ground and rolled into the crowd.

Dafney had turned to look when he stumbled and she was the first to scream. . . .

"EVERYONE DOWN!" Fisher screamed over the announcement system. "EVERYONE HIT THE GROUND, *NOW*! THERE ARE TERRORISTS IN THE CROWD! DOWN, DOWN, DOWN . . ."

"Target," Braon said as Target Seven pulled his bag around to the front. Some people were running but most were following orders and dropping to the ground. Gunfire helped with that. The suspect pulled out a can and flew backwards as blood and brains covered the crowd around him.

"Left," Manos said. "Target Fifteen. On the ground, fumbling in his backpack."

"Target," Braon said as the man slumped.

"Right . . ."

"You know," Mike said, as paramedics with stretchers moved into the still-crouched crowd, "this is actually a great way to filter for terrorists. When you tell civilians to get down, especially when bullets are flying, they generally do. The terrorists keep trying to do their mission and turn themselves into targets. The Israelis use it sometimes. I'm just glad none of them were wearing explosive vests."

"One hell of a PR nightmare," Fisher said, watching the dead bodies being loaded.

"Why?" Mike asked. "I mean, assuming all the tangos were for real. You just stopped, pretty much butt-cold, a terrorist attack. There's nine dead terrorists and, as far as I can see, zero dead guests. You should come out smelling like a rose. That is, assuming no more got into the park. You shutting down?"

"That's my next call," Fisher said. "I want to. God I want to shut down. But that's up to park operations. What's your call?"

"This was a back-up attack," Mike said. "The main attack is still to come. I'm actually of two minds. One says that to save lives, you shut down. The other says that we want to find the other VX. If they're aiming for Disney, and I'm pretty sure they are, now, then if you shut down they just lay low and either hit another day or hit another target."

"So you're saying you want sixty thousand people to act as *bait*?" Fisher asked. "Jesus Christ. That's *cold*."

"I keep repeating myself and nobody listens," Mike replied. "I am *not* a nice guy. Want a suggestion?"

"Right now my brain's sort of shut down," Fisher admitted. "So, sure."

"Ask them," Mike said.

"Thank you for your cooperation," Fisher said over the announcement system. "I'll explain what just happened. Disney was informed that there might be an attack using disguised poison gas. But we weren't sure that would occur until just a moment ago, when the first can was discovered. When that happened, terrorists in the crowd attempted to use their cans to attack, well, you people."

He paused as the crowd, which was back on its feet, sorted through that.

"By checking the contents of their bags, we can now definitely state that *all* the men just shot by snipers were terrorists. And that should be most of them. But I cannot, and Disney cannot, guarantee that another attack will not take place. I have spoken to the head of park operations and we are trying to decide whether or not to shut down. If we do, all of you will be given a voucher for another day at the park. But I also know that some of you are here on tight schedules and this may be the only day you have this trip. So I have been authorized to ask *you* what you think Disney should do. I'd like a show of hands of everyone who is still willing to risk going to Disney today."

At first none of the multicolored throng reacted, then a little girl down front raised her hand. After a brief discussion, her brother, sister and then parents raised theirs.

Before long just about everyone in the slightly

diminished crowd had their hands up. The few that didn't were headed for the exits anyway.

"Okay, folks, we're still running the security check, but . . . Welcome to Disney World."

When Will and his family reached the security station, the checker waved them through.

"You're not going to check our bags?" Will asked, holding out his backpack.

"If you're terrorists, I'm a Nazi," the old woman who looked vaguely Jewish said, holding out a sheaf of tickets. "Everybody gets a three-day pass, by the way. They're useable any time in the future. Please stay alert, though. We really *are* expecting another attack. The terrorists had the gas in those orange OFF cans. So if you have one, I'd suggest getting rid of it to prevent getting mistaken for terrorists by the men with guns. Other than that, have a good time."

CHAPTER
TWENTY-EIGHT

Mike was not having a good time. Honestly, picking out people who were of "Middle Eastern" extraction was more art than science. For various historical reasons, many Hispanics had similar facial features. And there were huge numbers of groups in the Middle East that didn't support Islamic terrorism, Lebanese Christians being the first that came to mind and descending through a list that included Druze and actual "moderate" Islamics. The guy at Wet and Wild had been one of those, pretty obviously. Mike made a mental note to ensure he wasn't thrown in jail; he'd acted damned decently, all things considered.

But there were various cultural clues. Mostly they were the way that a person walked and body language. Most terrorists had not been in Western societies enough to have those clues completely erased. The 9/11 attackers had been smart in that they *had* worked, very hard, to eliminate all trace of such cultural clues. Mohammed Atta had been one smart SOB.

So far, however, every one of the tangos they'd taken down had been pretty clearly right off the boat. They still had the Islamic Shuffle that came from always using slippers or pushing down the backs of their shoes. It just made sense when you were taking them off five times a day to pray. It was one of the things that Mike was looking for, pushed-down shoes. Such a person was not, definitively, a terrorist. It just meant they were ardent Islamics and the second did not *equal* the first. But it was more than worthwhile to watch any such person.

He was looking for other things, though. He was certain the third attack was going to be airborne. It was the best way to kill the most people with VX. So while *he* wasn't watching the sky, he was looking for people who *were*. People in Disney didn't spend a lot of time looking up; they were looking at the rides, at the shops, at maps. Anybody who was occasionally glancing at the sky was a potential terrorist. And if he found a guy with a canister in his backpack who had been looking at the sky, well . . .

So far, though, no joy. He'd walked down Main Street, turned through Future Land and headed back on the loop through Fantasyland and up through Adventureland. In all that walking he hadn't seen anyone who really twigged his jitter meter. There were a fair number of Muslim-looking people, including women in *dhimmie* scarves and men with the shuffle. But all of them were accompanied by kids. While it was conceivable that a terrorist would use kids for cover, so far none of the ones they'd taken down had been so accompanied.

Pity that Orange County had collected the one

terrorist they'd found. *He* could have gotten everything they needed out of the guy. So far, Orange County was getting nada. But he was pretty sure there was at least one that had gotten through. And he was going to find him.

Jamal sipped a cup of Coke in the Main Street Café, trying to look inconspicuous. He'd picked up enough of the conversation around him to know that most of the rest of the team had been taken down at security.

He glanced at his watch, knowing that it made him slightly conspicuous, and wished the time would go faster. Another forty minutes.

Farzad checked the connections again then nodded at the two fedayeen at the pumps. They turned on the pumps and started filling the converted Piper Cub.

Farzad had chosen the plane because it was ground transportable. It had been purchased in North Florida and driven to the industrial building near Eva where it had been parked for the last week. The doors of the building were large enough that the wings would clear when they were rolled up and there was a straight stretch of little used road in the industrial park. As soon as the plane was filled he could take off. But he was going to wait just a little longer. Everything wasn't in place, yet.

Joe Pallozzi had been a security guard at the Clearwater Air Park for about three months.

A former deputy sheriff from New York, he had come down to Florida hoping to get a job with either the State Patrol or one of the local departments. But a lot of cops got tired of the winters up north and the waiting list for slots was pretty long. While waiting for something to open up, he pulled down various security gigs working an average of sixty hours a week to keep ahead of the bills. He'd thought that upstate New York had a pretty bad cost of living until he'd moved to Florida. All sorts of people drifted to the Sunshine State expecting every day to be the beach. And a lot of them were young people willing to work for peanuts if they didn't have to go back to Bumfuck, Missouri. So wages were low unless you had a serious degree, while the cost of living was *awful*.

So Joe hung out, hoping to get a sheriff's slot or something, and humping his tail off in security in the meantime.

Despite only being at the airport gig for a few months, he'd come to know the regulars, and their planes, pretty well. He occasionally scagged rides and was half thinking about getting a pilot's license. A couple of the regulars had even let him take the controls for small bits.

One of them was a judge, a former corporate lawyer, who lived up in Dunnellon. So when Joe saw a crew working around Mr. Morris' plane he got a little suspicious. He knew it wasn't up for maintenance any time soon. And sure as hell it wasn't supposed to be going anywhere. So when the guys pulled the chocks he started trotting towards it.

One of the guys, both of whom were wearing blue coveralls, pulled out a device and opened the door. But it wasn't keys to the plane, it was a pick gun, a device used by locksmiths and car thieves. The fuckers were stealing Bob's plane!

"Hey," he shouted, drawing the lousy .38 he was forced to carry. "Stop!"

The guy still on the ground reached down to the big toolbox they'd carried over and pulled out a Czech Skorpion submachine gun.

Joe realized he was totally fucked as he dropped to one knee. There wasn't a bit of fucking cover anywhere. He triggered two rounds from the crappy little revolver and was glad to see them hit.

On the other hand, the fucker with the Skorpion had fired at the same time. The last thing Joe Pallozzi saw was the flash from the suppressor.

"Kildar."

"Go," Mike said, looking around Adventureland. Families with kids. Teenage girls. Teenage boys watching the teenage girls. Fucking nada. Disney security was starting to clear the road for the afternoon parade and moving through the crowd was getting harder.

"A plane has just been stolen from the Clearwater Air Park in Clearwater, Florida. That is just across the bay from MacDill Air Force Base. The plane is being tracked on radar and is heading for MacDill. SOCOM believes that this is the next attack."

"Fuck," Mike snarled, drawing a look from a passing tourist. "What about the CAP?"

"The current combat air patrol is four F-16s, operating out of MacDill. Two were over the Tampa Bay area but are east of the contact and are turning west. The other two were south of Orlando, covering the Orlando area. They are actually closer to the contact, so they have been vectored to intercept."

Mike had heard the sonic booms in the distance

a minute or so ago and filtered them out. Now he wanted to curse again.

"It's a feint," Mike said. "Call SOCOM and get the damned CAP turned around. You can't rig a regular plane in a few minutes to drop this shit. It's a damned deception plan. Is there an AWACS up?"

"Yes," Greznya said. "And we're getting the take from their local screens."

"Keep an eye out for a liftoff soon," Mike said. "And make sure that Dragon is aware of the situation. Put all the teams on high alert; we're going to get hit soon."

He looked around and blanched. The rides were emptying out as people gathered to pack along the street in anticipation of the parade.

"Oh. My. God."

"Kildar, what?" Greznya said.

"The *parade*," Mike said, stepping under one of the barriers and starting to trot down the road towards Fantasyland. "Call Fisher. Tell him the target is the parade."

Farzad started the engine of the Piper as soon as the three-man ground crew pushed him clear of the big doors and turned onto the empty stretch of pavement. He had gotten the word that Gibron had gotten into the air. He would soon be a martyr. But they were all martyrs, now. He did not expect to survive the flight.

The Piper nearly didn't make it into the air but it managed to claw upwards at the end of the road and over the low pines surrounding the industrial park.

The flight time to the Magic Kingdom was only four minutes. It was a good time to pray.

▲   ▲   ▲

"Kildar," Greznya said. "A contact has just appeared that is not a cleared aircraft. It took off from just off Florida Highway 33 and is headed for Disney."

"Dragon?" Mike asked. He was at the square behind Cinderella's Castle and now sped up.

"Already lifting off," Greznya said. "But she is out of position to intercept. She estimates she will reach the Magic Kingdom about the same time as the aircraft, but from the east instead of west. We anticipated that the attack would come from the Kissimmee area."

"Tell her to hammer it," Mike said, slowing down. The aircraft was going to be coming in from the northwest. It might hit Fantasyland, first, but he was just as sure that the target was the parade, which came down from Adventureland, turned at the square, then went south to Main Street. He pulled the communicator off his belt and keyed on the take from Greznya. Sure enough, the bird was coming from the northwest and already over Disney property. Dragon was up and hammering for the park but she was *way* out of position. "Greznya, gimme all teams," Mike said. "All teams. Go hot at this time. Target coming in from the northwest. Converge near . . ." He looked around and shrugged. "Converge near Haunted Mansion. Grez, give me Colonel Olds . . ." he said, putting the communicator back on his belt and dumping his backpack.

"Colonel, it's that Kildar guy," the RTO said, holding out a telephone.

"What?" Olds snapped, taking the phone.

"We have an inbound at Disney. What is your intent?"

"As far as we can determine, it is a civilian aircraft that is off-course," the colonel replied. "I don't have a shoot order from higher."

"You're *authorized* to fire at your discretion," Mike said, incredulously. "That's why they gave you Slammers. Now are you going to take it out?"

"I . . . I do not have a shoot order," the colonel stammered.

"FUCK SHOOT ORDERS," the man screamed. "TAKE OUT THE DAMNED PLANE!"

"Colonel," the RTO said. "One of the Slammers has eyeballs on the target and is requesting shoot authorization . . ."

"I will have to call you back," the colonel said, handing the phone back to the RTO. "Get me Tallahassee. I need authorization to shoot . . ."

Sergeant Ray Thompson had been an Air Defense Artillery gunner since he'd first joined the Florida National Guard. However, in Iraq there wasn't much need for ADA so his unit had been "converted" to infantry then back to ADA when they redeployed to the states.

In Iraq he'd pulled more than his share of guard duty on roadblocks, quite a few convoys and various other spots where mujahideen tried to add him to the growing list of dead and injured. And in the process he'd occasionally seen "The Look." "The Look," that is, of a guy who is bent on martyrdom. Not many guys who saw "The Look" lived to tell about it and it wasn't precisely describable. It wasn't wide-eyed it was more like a thousand mile stare crossed with, of all things, joy.

He was using a pair of 60x binoculars to ID the incoming craft. Piper Cub, steady approach, the bird was locked by the Slammer and it was headed straight for the Magic Kingdom. And he could see right in the cockpit, see the pilot's eyes. And he had The Look.

"Tell higher that this is a *definite* bad-guy," Ray said. "And we need a Go order."

Mike zipped open the large backpack and started drawing out the parts of the M-60E4, assembling them as quickly as he could. He'd assembled one as a demonstration one time in under thirty seconds. He was trying to beat that record.

"Hey, buddy," a man said, ducking under the barricade and running over to him. "What in the fuck are you doing?"

"Getting ready to shoot down an airplane," Mike said without turning around. "I'm with SOCOM. Now I'd suggest getting under shelter, sir."

The man paused and looked over his shoulder.

"Dafney! Where are the kids?"

"Allison's here," the woman yelled back. "Jason and Lindsey are up at the Haunted Mansion, I think."

"Get under cover," the man said, picking up the overlarge box of ammo and drawing out the linked 7.62 rounds. "I used to be a gunner in the National Guard."

"You got ammo bearer," Mike said, pulling the linked ammo over and slapping it into place. He dropped the feed tray down and cocked the weapon. "Greznya, where is this thing?"

"Just west of the employee parking lot," Greznya said. "It should enter the park just west of Haunted Mansion."

More people were watching what was going on, and shouting, as Mike lifted the machine gun to his shoulder. The crowd surged back, obviously fearing he was going to open fire on *them*, but then paused as it was apparent he was pointed at the sky. He could *hear* the plane now, a slow drone and low.

"Anybody else got this?" Mike asked.

"Oleg," Oleg called. "I'm . . . Fuck, Kildar, I don't know where I am. East of that big castle thing."

"Nikolai. I am in Cinderella's Castle. I have partial eyeballs on the target. I do not have enough to engage."

"Kildar, Kildar, Dragon. I am crossing Bay Lake at this time, heading for Main Street. I have eyeballs on the bird but will not arrive before it enters the park."

"Keep an eye out for secondaries," Mike said, pointing the weapon over the trees to the west. "I think this one's all mine."

Farzad had seen the Slammers tracking him and was surprised they did not open fire. That would, of course, have ruined his mission. But he still would have been a martyr. As it was, he would simply have to send many infidels to hell.

He crested the trees that surrounded this end of the park and smiled. The infidels had gathered in huge numbers to see their parade. This would be a good killing, perhaps even better than that of the martyrs of 9/11. Many of the Americans would die and that was always a good thing.

He flinched, though, as tracers flew past the nose of the aircraft and looked down. A man was standing in the roadway holding a machine gun to his shoulder and firing up at the plane.

Well, there was only one thing to do. Farzad hit the release and began to spew VX out of the back of the converted Piper.

Mike cursed as vapor began to bellow out of the back of the bird. Most of the Keldara had MOPP gear in their bags, but he wasn't wearing his and neither were any of the civilians. So he kept his finger clamped on the trigger as the plane droned across the lake, laying down a cloud of deadly gas behind it.

He'd led it by too much at first, probably just right if it had been a shot from the side but the plane was heading, more or less, just at him from right to left. As he corrected it banked towards Cinderella's castle and another stream of tracers headed towards it, falling low. Nikolai finally had a shot.

Mike kept his finger on the trigger, mentally blessing the designers of the new generation of M-60 and kept his elation down as the stream of fire finally hit the engine cowling. The engine began to smoke and as he followed the line back into the bird it banked to the side, out of control, and began plummeting downwards.

However, the thing was still filled with VX and it was headed down towards the crowd gathered for the parade. Most of the crowd had scattered, screaming, as he opened fire and it became obvious what was happening. One girl, though, was just standing there, paralyzed.

The plane shuddered again, the vapor cutting off for some reason, and staggered through the air, headed for the Haunted Mansion. Mike wasn't really paying attention, though. He'd dropped the machine gun and was sprinting across the open area towards the frozen girl.

He heard the guy behind him shout something, but he wasn't paying attention to that, either. He figured he had about a one in four chance of reaching the girl before the plane smacked into the small hill the Haunted Mansion was on and covered the whole area in toxin.

Will had kept ahold of the ammo box, watching the stream of fire from the guy in civvies and saw the plane get hit. He'd even seen the burst of blood inside the cockpit that indicated the pilot had taken a good solid hit. As the plane fell he kept his eyes on it then realized the guy was *gone*. The '60 was on the ground, smoking, and the guy was sprinting across the suddenly deserted road.

Mostly deserted. Lindsey, the idiot, was just *standing* there. Jason wasn't in sight and hopefully Dafney had grabbed Allison and made it to cover.

But Lindsey was going to be *right* under where the damned plane was going to hit.

The guy in civvies, though, either didn't realize that or didn't care. He snatched Lindsey up without slowing down, the girl's body cracking into a U as his arm hit her side, and vaulted the low iron railing around the lake with one foot on the top.

The two bodies hit the water just a moment before the plane hit the ground and the entire area was engulfed in flame. For the life of him, Will couldn't figure out if his oldest daughter was alive or not.

"Oh, fuck . . ." he said, dropping to his knees. The flames were producing a towering pillar of what could only be poisonous smoke, but it was drifting to the west, away from the park. The only deadly spot was right where the guy, and his daughter, had disappeared.

Mike hit the water almost simultaneously with a wash of flame. He'd made sure the girl was down, his hand clamped over her nose and mouth, so the flame got *his* back not hers or her hair.

The girl was struggling in his arms but he ignored it, keeping his hand clamped over her mouth and nose as he swam through the murky water towards the boats he'd seen parked by some sort of big tree. The surface of the water was on fire and some of that fuel had to be mixed with either VX or precursors, neither of which were going to be destroyed by that temperature of fire. But, somewhere, there would be clear air. The VX wouldn't have spread far, yet.

He got under the boats and found a pocket that looked clear. Popping up, he sniffed the air. Sure, VX didn't have a smell, but *smoke* did. He might survive one whiff.

He didn't die so he pulled the girl above the surface and let go of her mouth.

"I'm not trying to kidnap you or kill you," Mike said, holding her up by both arms as she got a breath. "That plane back there has poison gas. Now I'm going to do another swim. You've got to hold your breath. And *now*, because the cloud could be coming this way."

"Okay," the girl said, wide-eyed.

"Take a deep breath," Mike said, then clamped his hand over her nose and mouth again.

He swam out from under the boats, heading south. At least he thought it was south; it was away from the fire anyway.

He swam until he hit a concrete wall, bruising the knuckles of his hand, then followed it as it curved. When he'd gotten about as far from the crash as he was going to get he surfaced again and looked back.

The hill that Haunted Mansion perched on was seriously engulfed. But the smoke was mostly going straight up or to the west. That was good; most of it wasn't headed for the park.

The problem was he couldn't get out here. The edge of the concrete wall was a good six feet up.

There was, however, a landing just south of him. He started side-stroking that way, the girl still held with his right arm.

"Hey, buddy," a voice called above him.

Mike looked up and vaguely recognized the guy who had played assistant gunner. He was even carrying the M-60.

"Daddy?" the girl said. "Daddy!"

"You wouldn't happen to have a rope or anything *useful* would you?" Mike asked.

"No, but I was just going to say thanks for saving my kid," the man replied. "They're evacuating the park."

"Good to hear it," Mike said, reaching the landing. He pushed the girl up and she ran to her father who picked her up, big girl though she was. Mike followed her, getting up onto the landing then taking a knee as he just *breathed*. It had been a long damned day. And what was it with *girls and swimming* on this op?

"Seriously, man, thanks," the guy said, taking a knee next to him.

"Seriously, you're welcome," Mike said, looking at the two of them. His jaw flexed when he really looked at the girl's face. Blonde hair, blue eyes, even the cheekbones and, yeah, the lips were right. She looked one *hell* of a lot like Gretchen would have looked at the same age.

"Thank you," the girl said. She'd looked over his shoulder and could see where she'd been standing. The area was covered in flames.

"You're welcome as well," Mike said, pulling the communicator pad off his belt. He shook it and was unsurprised to see that it was still functioning. That was why he'd paid an arm and a leg for the system. "Kildar here."

"Kildar!" Greznya said. "Armenak saw you run into the fire! We thought you were dead!"

"Not yet," Mike said, standing up and holding his hand out for the machine gun. "Tell Dragon I need pickup," he continued, walking up the steps of the landing. "And put me through to Pierson. We've got some loose ends to clean up."

He paused at the top of the stairs and watched as the man, with his daughter still piggyback, walked up.

"Lass, what's your name?" Mike asked, shouldering the M-60.

"Lindsey," the girl said.

"Lindsey, I need you to do me two favors," Mike said. "You planning on getting married and having kids?"

"Yes," she replied, blushing. "*Some*day."

"Someday is good," Mike said as the black Hind hovered above and then began to drop into the open space behind him. "I want you to do me two favors in that regard. The first is you pick a good husband. Pick somebody smart and strong, somebody who doesn't beat you or shout at you and plans on *being* somebody. A guy who has it on the ball. Pick good genes, girl, that's the first favor. The second favor you owe me for this, Lindsey, is you got to name your first daughter Gretchen."

Cell phone connections had been overloaded, but Will had managed to get the whole family collected before they entered the tunnels. Will was amazed by the tunnels under the park; they were *big*. But even as large as they were, they were crowded.

Will had ahold of Lindsey's hand while Dafney led Jason and Allison. The crowd, fortunately, was moving pretty smoothly and nobody was panicking. Just shuffling forward to some unknown destination.

"The exit is not far, folks," a Disney security guard said, waving the group on. "Remain calm and keep walking. There will be busses waiting when you exit . . ."

"You okay?" Dafney asked.

"Fine," Will said, rubbing Lindsey's still-wet hair as they exited a side tunnel into a much larger area. It was still packed, though. Apparently, the whole park dumped into it. He looked back at her and grinned, then blanched. A guy who looked pretty damned Middle Eastern to Will's eyes had just pulled out a can of OFF. Since there weren't many mosquitoes in the tunnel, he probably wasn't worried about bites. And he had a weird look in his eye. It was that, as much as anything, that had Will suddenly moving, pushing his youngest daughter aside and swinging . . .

He hadn't gotten in a fight since he was in the Army but the roundhouse was muscle memory, even if diffused, and it connected perfectly. What he'd forgotten was how much hitting somebody's chin with your fist *hurt*.

"Fuck," he said, cradling his hand as the man crashed to the ground, the can of OFF rolling away unsprayed. "SECURITY!"

CHAPTER
TWENTY-NINE

Anastasia was just about worn out; this was just too much of a good thing.

Gonzales had been torturing her practically non-stop, getting every scrap of information she was willing to give. Katya had been there for most of it, and had caught more than a piece, as he brought in guards to rape and whip them both when he got worn out.

Currently she was tied belly down to a saddle with one man raping her in the ass and another taking her in the mouth. Gonzales was back to whipping, his arm having given out twice so far. He didn't even really seem to be interrogating her anymore, just punishing Mike through her.

As the man came in her mouth and backed away, she looked over at Katya, who was chained up in a corner, and rolled her eyes. The girl snorted through her gag in laughter. Hopefully, the group would take it as some sort of stifled plea.

"What does he want?" Gonzales said, pulling her head back by her hair. "What is he after?"

"The gas," Anastasia whimpered. "And . . . and . . ."

"He's after my money, isn't he?"

"Yes!" she admitted, bursting into tears. "Yes. I heard him speak of it. A great deal of money. He wishes to steal it from you. It was to be transferred by . . . b . . . p . . ."

"He knows about the boat," Gonzales said, straightening up. "Gomez must have talked. Tell Suarez to send a message, right away, to move the shipment."

"Yes, *jefe*," the guard by the door said, darting out.

"Does he know where it is?" Gonzales asked, pulling her head up again. "Tell me, bitch!" he added, striking her on the back with the whip.

"In the Keys," Anastasia said, taking a guess. "Something Key."

"Fuck, he even knows it's in Marathon?"

Katya rolled onto her side, trying to turn the gales of laughter into something else. She'd been tortured by experts over the years and while she didn't enjoy it, she knew what "expert" meant. And Gonzales was an *idiot*. If he was the quality of individual that ran major segments of a cocaine smuggling ring, well, *anybody* could do it.

Come to think of it . . .

She managed to stop laughing by turning it into a whine as if from terror.

"Katya," Julia said over the radio link. "That whine is not only extremely annoying, we're having a hard time hearing what is being said. Did he just say a boat with money on it is in Marathon?"

"Uh, huh," Katya said through her gag. "Uhhhh . . ."

"Get that bitch over here," Gonzales said, gesturing to Katya. "You wanted to make out with this one. Well, make out with her. Do it all with her. I want to watch . . ."

"Katya," Julia said. "Be advised that if you can extend the time with your hands undone, it might be advisable. We're going to need a distraction in a few minutes."

"There's the boat," John Hardesty shouted over the wind, pointing to the water below.

Mike's regular pilot had eventually turned up and upon Mike's arrival at the island had had a bit of a tiff with his boss. Tom Chatham, on being informed *why* Mike needed something along the lines of a Beaver, had insisted on driving. But John pointed out that not only did he have more time with Beavers, he was Mike's regular driver. The two had worked it out as gentlemen after Chatham pointed out who was the boss. So Chatham was driving the blacked-out Beaver while Hardesty worked the door.

Mike gave him a thumbs-up and considered the angle. Given the reported winds aloft, it was close enough. So he grabbed the edges of the doorframe and hurled himself out.

Since they were only at fourteen thousand feet, the jump didn't technically qualify as a HALO. HALO only counted if you were using oxygen. But Mike was glad enough to be able to dispense with the bulky bail-out bottle. In fact, all he was carrying was a set of battle armor, a heavy load of rounds for the Whisper .45 caliber sub-gun, a pair of silenced pistols and a few flash-bangs. Jeseph and Ivan, who followed him out the door at fifteen second intervals, were just about as lightly loaded.

He delta tracked in on the anchored yacht, then popped his canopy at 1500 feet, banking around to approach from the stern. There were two guards on the rear deck, armed guards, watching the water for boats or swimmers. Well, couldn't have that . . .

He lined up on the open deck, then drew a silenced pistol in either hand. The shots were almost simultaneous, in very rapid sequence. Both of the guards dropped without ever noticing the black parachute dropping out of the night sky like some elder god.

Mike hit the release on his harness while still five feet in the air and dropped soundlessly to the deck. The parachute sailed backwards on the light wind and vanished into the water. With no one in sight he holstered the pistols and lifted the Whisper sub-gun, moving silently forward towards the superstructure.

There was another guard posted to port. Two rounds to the head sent him overside to splash into the water. A guard came from the bow, wondering about the sound. He found out what had caused it, but it didn't do him much good as two more of the hollow point rounds blasted his brains all over the side of the vessel.

A quick check to starboard showed a fifth guard there. He, too, went over the side, just as Jeseph thumped onto the deck.

Mike looked back to make sure the Keldara had gotten free of his parachute, and that it was out of Ivan's way, then gestured to the superstructure. The topside guards were down but that wasn't the whole mission.

As the Kildar ghosted forward, as silent as a

murderous shadow, Jeseph followed as quietly as he could. There were souls to gather this night.

Yosif was still having some control problems with his nerves and on one level he knew he shouldn't be doing the op. But he had scores to settle. These bastards had helped bring in the shit that had probably permanently fucked him and he intended to send at least a few to the Cold Lands.

But he let Vugar lift the ladder to catch on the side of the yacht. He wasn't sure he had the dexterity for it anymore.

He did have the dexterity, though, to be the first swarming up the ladder. When he got on deck he dropped the rebreather and pulled his MP-5 into a high ready position, then ghosted down the port side of the superstructure.

Below were the guard staterooms. They were his team's job to "secure."

He intended to make them *very* secure.

Suarez flipped through the security screens, then backed up. The guard at the starboard security position was missing. Flipping to port, at first he didn't see anything. But checking the forward looking camera he could see a body down on the deck.

As he leaned forward to hit the alarm there was a thump outside his door. Several. Two quiet thumps then a louder one, like something hitting the deck.

He hit the alarm switch and turned to call for a guard when the door opened.

A man in black was pointing a silenced submachine gun at his head and Enrico slowly raised his hands.

"*Hola,*" the man said in a friendly tone. "Enrico, isn't it? Tell you what, back away from the computers and nobody gets hurt."

"Find out what it is," Gonzales said, picking up a knife and advancing on the two women on the bed. "It is probably your boss, come to pick up his little whore," he said, reaching across the bed to grasp Anastasia's hair. "Well, let him find a dead body instead."

Stasia lifted an arm to block but she needn't have bothered. A blow from Katya on a nerve juncture opened Juan's hand and sent the knife spinning across the room.

Katya continued the strike into an arm-bar and rolled the man backwards onto Stasia.

"Hold onto this prick," Katya said, her accent back. "I've got things to do."

One of the many enhancements that the Americans had given her was a combat drug that enhanced speed, strength and reactions. Katya sent the mental command to start the drug as she performed the complicated finger twist necessary to get the poison sack in her palm opened.

As the first, nearly naked, guard charged her, she stooped and swept her fingernails upwards, ripping the man in the crotch and lower belly. As he continued forward she knelt and used his momentum to toss him over her head in the general direction of the bed. Of course, it was only the general direction so what he really hit was the side of the bed. With the back of his neck. The modified cobra poison became moot at that point.

That only left four more to take out.
No problem.

Yosif blew open the first door and entered the room as the guards started to react to the alarm. The shots weren't his usual precise three-round bursts. On the other hand, in those close quarters just spraying and holding the barrel down worked. Messy, but it worked. He tried hard, though, to get all the rounds into the bodies. The Kildar had been strangely insistent that the boat not get too shot up . . .

Kacey brought the Hind into a hover over the back deck and waited as Pavel's team slid down the fast-ropes, then she drifted sideways and checked the bridge of the yacht. The Hind had been in a hover just beyond the nearest island, waiting for the go word. It had only taken thirty seconds for her to fly to the yacht and begin dropping Pavel's team.

There were men moving on the bridge, obviously trying to get the yacht into motion. That wasn't part of the plan so she turned, slightly, bringing the doors around . . .

Lasko targeted the moving figures on the bridge and fired three rounds, nearly as fast as a machine gun would have fired. All three of the figures dropped, red splotches on the windows behind them.

"Bridge secure," Lasko said.

Stella swarmed up the side of the ship and headed for the computer center. She passed two small firefights on the way but didn't slow down until she skidded through the door of the room.

The Mexican intel manager was wrapped into a chair with about a mile of rigger tape and his mouth covered by it as well. But his eyes bugged out eloquently when the girl sat down at the computer and typed in his password.

"Let's see," Stella muttered. "Boat, Marathon, dollars . . . Ah, here it is . . . Keldara base," she continued, keying her throat mike. "I've got a lock on Gonzales' money transfer. The boat is docked at Ocean View Marina in Marathon with sixty-two million dollars onboard. It isn't shown as having left, yet. Does the Kildar want us to pass on the information, or keep the money for ourselves?"

Mike knocked politely, then opened the door to the "dungeon."

Katya was standing in the middle of the room, stark naked and covered in blood. Most of it had come, apparently, from one of the guards who was more or less hacked to death. Three others were twisted in positions that indicated she'd used the modified cobra venom in her fingernails on them. The stuff was a very close cousin to VX and had much the same effect. A fifth appeared to have broken his neck in a fall.

Anastasia was on the room's sole bed, holding Gonzales immobile in a full-Nelson. From the looks of it, one of his arms had been dislocated.

"Hello, Juan," Mike said, stepping into the room. "I'd like you to meet Katya Ivanova. And I'd like to formally thank her for not only wiring your boat to a fare-thee-well with electronic devices but also for giving us a full layout. It made taking it down so much easier."

"You're going to die for this, you pig," Gonzales said, struggling to break free. The dislocated shoulder made that rather hard, though.

"Yes, well, others have said that," Mike replied. "And here I am. I'm not much of a gloater but I'm going to tell you something and then I'm going to write it down and return it to your bosses, attached to your dead body. It's like this. You want to run drugs, you want to fuck around with your own government, you want to blow up Colombian civilians, that's your business. People like me most of the time just won't care. But you start helping terrorists get shit like VX into the U.S.? You help kill *American* civilians. Then we care. That's pretty much it. Oh, except for one thing. The lady who's holding you? My harem manager? Major league masochist. Comments, Stasia?"

"He can't whip as hard as *you*, Kildar," Anastasia purred. "And his dick is *tiny*."

"Another county heard from," Mike said. "And I promised a lady something. Katya?"

"Thank you, Kildar," Katya said, walking over to the drug smuggler. "I've been beaten and raped by the worst pimps on earth; you're a piker compared to them. But you like to get off beating on women, women who *don't* enjoy it. Just like the bastards that raped me so many times over the years. You like to watch? Watch this."

She drew back her hand and struck with middle and index fingers, straight into the man's eyes.

"Oops," she said as the screaming man began thrashing and Anastasia rolled him to the floor, "I did it again . . ."

EPILOGUE

"When I said 'can I go for a ride in your GT,' I sort of meant around Orlando," Heather said as Mike pulled into the parking area by the beach.

"What, you don't *like* the Bahamas?" Mike asked, turning off the car.

The estate had a small road that ran around the perimeter and up to the airstrip. Mike had used the latter for a *brief* demonstration of the GT's acceleration, but it obviously wasn't the ride the girl had hoped for.

"This car is hot," Heather replied.

"I know," Mike said. "It's unfortunate that where I live, there's not many places worth driving it."

"No, I mean it's *hot*," Heather said, opening the door. "Like, why'd you go and paint it black?"

"I like black," Mike said.

Heather's family, along with Lindsey's, had been surprised by the invitation to come visit a private island in the Caribbean. However, given that many of Orlando's attractions were closed for "renovation," they weren't going to look the horse too closely in the teeth region. Especially with a ride in a private jet thrown in. The man who'd invited them might have been . . . eccentric, but he was a fine host. And, what the heck, they all owed him their lives.

"Maybe I can drive you around Orlando some other time," Mike continued. "And I'll run the air conditioner."

"Okay," Heather said, heading for the beach. "Later."

"Later," Mike replied, chuckling.

He walked over to the beach chair by Will and flopped down.

"Thanks for inviting us down here, Mr. Jenkins," Will said uncomfortably. His hand, in a cast, was propped on the arm of the beach chair.

"You're welcome," Mike replied, looking out at the scene. The entire harem, most of the intel girls and about half the Keldara shooters were playing in the water while Vil and his team were offshore giving rides and racing each other. Even Dr. Arensky was down there, wandering in knee-deep water. Although, he seemed to be collecting specimens. . . . Vanner wasn't exactly disporting, just sitting in the water, holding Greznya's hand and talking with Master Chief Adams. But he was alive at least. "And it's just Mike, okay?"

"Okay . . . Mike," Will said. "It's right nice of you, though."

"I had my reasons," Mike said. "They're strange reasons, but very real. I sort of had an epiphany around the time that I dragged Lindsey out of the water. I think in a way that Lindsey saved me as much as the other way around. This is sort of a . . . resolution of that."

"Well, Lindsey's sure getting along with your daughter," the man said, waving to where Lindsey and Martya were splashing each other and giggling fit to die.

"Oh. Uhm . . ." Mike paused then shrugged. "Martya's not exactly my *daughter*. She's one of my . . . wards. I'm her guardian."

"Oh," Will said. "I'd wondered about you having so many kids. What about that one?" he asked, pointing at Tinata.

"Ward," Mike said.

"Those three?"

"Wards."

"That one?"

"Oh, one of my . . . employees . . ."

"She looks . . . a little young . . ."

"Look, Will, just go with the flow," Mike said, accepting a beer from Britney as she walked by. The lieutenant was looking better as well. "Changes in latitude and all that."

"Yeah," Will said, obviously just a tad confused. "Nice boat, too. You doing renovations?"

Mike looked over at the yacht. The former *White Line* was undergoing an extensive paint job and some cosmetic work to its superstructure.

"Mostly cleanup," Mike said. "I live over by the Black Sea. I figure I'll drive her over there, use her to cruise around, you know? Maybe I won't have to *rent* a yacht. Next time."

He was wondering if he could manage to hang onto *all* the boats or if the U.S. government would insist on getting them back, when he drifted off to sleep in the sun.

To sleep, perchance to dream. . . .

▶ END ◀

THE LAST CENTURION

JOHN RINGO

Available from Baen Books
August 2008
hardcover

— CHAPTER ONE —

Days of Wine and Song

Call me Bandit.

Okay, hopefully that's, like, the last time I'm going to make a literary reference. But you never know. Beware . . . bewaaare . . .

There's a bunch of these stories out there now that people are getting back on the Net. I figured, what the hell? I've got one, too. Sure, we all do. But, you know, what the hell?

People started calling it the Hell Times after some pundit was spouting about it on TV. I mean, The Great Depression was taken and they didn't have the Plague or the Freeze thrown on top. I know, it wasn't a plague and all you nitnoids are going to point out that it was some fucking flu virus and plague is bacterial infection and . . . Yeah. I know. Thank you. We ALL fucking know, alright? Christ, there are times you wished it had been targeted at nitnoids. Everybody calls it the Plague, okay? Get over yourself.

Anyway, people call it the Hell Times. I dunno, maybe I've got a better personal fix on hell than they do or maybe I don't. Personally, having been in combat and blown up and shot and seen people I care about blown up and shot and even people I *didn't* particularly care about blown up and shot and having visited a volcano once and thought about what it would be like to spend the rest of fucking *forever* in one, I don't call it the Hell Times. Bad as it was, seems to be an exaggeration. Me? I call it the Time of Suckage.

This is my sucky story about the time of suckage.

So there I was in Iran again, this is no shit . . . It was my fourth trip to the sandbox in my short years as a soldier. And it was a maximally fucked up tour even before the Time of Suckage. Look, you spend any time as a soldier and you get good chains of command and bad chains of command. Good jobs and bad jobs. You deal. It didn't help that the Prez was a whiny bitch who really wanted us out of there but couldn't figure out how to get reelected *and* stab us in the back. Equipment was short, training was crap, the muj knew all they had to do was hold their ground and we were eventually going to leave.

And boy did we. Not that it helped *them* much, huh? Heh, heh.

Seriously, I met some Iranians (and Iraqis and Afghans) that were pretty decent people. And I'm sorry as hell for what happened to the good people, most of them, that inhabited those countries. But . . . Ah, hell. I'm getting ahead of myself.

Way ahead.

Maybe I should talk about myself for a bit to give a little context. I was one of the very few remaining farm boys in the Army at the time. Seriously. I mean, most of my troops were from rural areas but that's not, exactly, the same thing as being a farm boy. I grew up on a family farm. Well, I grew up on one of the family farms owned by the Bandit Family Farm Corporation, LLC.

Wait? Corporation? Family Farm? How do those two go together?

Like bacon and eggs, my friends, like bacon and eggs. Forget everything you've seen in a bad movie about family farms. If you're going to survive in *this* economy, you'd better know what the hell you're doing. And I'm not talking some hobby farm where the 'farmer' is a construction contractor and has a couple of cows or a chicken house or twain that are some added income. (Or more often a tax write-off.) I'm talking about making *all* your income from farming.

And it's pretty good money if you do it right. Farmers are the richest single income group in the US. Were before the Time, during the Time and after. Sure, some of them lost their farms during the Time but damned few. (Except for the Big Grab but I'll get to that.) Smart farmers weren't saddled with killer debt when the Times hit. And, hell, people always got to eat. Sure, there were less mouths to feed but the government was always buying.

Anyway. Grew up on a farm in southern Minnesota near Blue Earth. It was one of nine the family owned in six counties in southern Minnesota. That one was right on two thousand acres, most of it tilled in time. Pretty much the standard rural upbringing. Went to school. (Yes, I *was* captain of the football team.) Played with my friends. Dated girls. (I'm straight for all you pining fags out there.) And did some chores. Yes, I've tossed haybails. But not all that many. Baling is time and labor intensive and thus unprofitable. Better to roll. Takes one guy with a tractor the same time to clear a field of rolls as it takes fifteen guys with bales. Do. The. Math.

Did I ever get up before dawn and milk cows using a bucket and a stool? No. The family owned two cow farms. Both were run by managers. At o dark thirty the cows would walk to the barn and into their stalls. Why? Because they had full udders. Full udders hurt. The cows learned quick that if they walked to the stall the hurt went away. Cows are very dumb (if not as dumb as sheep) but they *can* be trained.

A team of people (usually four) would then hook them up to the milking machines. They'd drink coffee while the cows were getting their udder dump, unhook them and the cows and crew would then have their breakfast. After breakfast the cows got turned out and most of the crew went off to day jobs. The milk was stored in a steel vat until the truck came by to pick it up and take it to the processing plant. Manager, who was full time, handled that. In the evening, repeat.

Again. Do. The. Math. Forty cows (smaller farm.) I milked one cow, once, by hand when my dad made me 'familiarize' with it. It took me a good fifteen minutes. Figure an expert can do it in maybe five. Four guys, thirty minutes. Or one guy doing it all damned day. Sure, the equipment's a tad expensive (like a half a million dollars.) It's amortized.

Then there's the whole . . . sepsis issue. Look, milking by hand you put *milk* into an *open bucket* in *stall* that's occupied by a *cow*. Bessy is not, take it from this farm boy, a clean creature. Bessy's tail hangs down the same spot her poop (which is mostly liquid) comes out. Bessy walks in her poop. Flies surround Bessy like politicians at an all-you-can-steal lobbyist give-away.

Milk is also a prime food for just about *anything*. Including bacteria.

We had no interest in being in the news as the evil farm corporation that killed x thousand customers from salmonella or some shit.

Doing it by hand spells 'Going Out Of Business.' We

liked our farm(s). We wanted to keep being farmers. We did it the smart way.

That extended to everything. Look, combine harvesters are very expensive. The flip side is, the bigger they are the more expensive they get *but* the more economic they are. So bigger, in general, is better.

However, some of our fields were too small for the really big combines. And a combine only makes its money a couple of weeks out of the year. Harvesting is about it.

There are companies that do that shit. Since harvests, for really obvious reasons, don't happen everywhere all at once, they move around harvesting and planting. Most of the guys doing the actual work were from South Africa or Eastern Europe. (Mexicans never got in on that racket. Not sure why.)

We had a couple of small combines (price tag right at a quarter mil a pop) to do some of the smaller fields and clean-up. For the main harvesting, Dad would arrange, like a *year* in advance, to get the combine company to come in.

Farmers are planners. The Big Chill and the Big Grab really fucked with us but it was fucking with *everybody* so I'll get to that later. Adapt, react and overcome ain't just a Marine motto. Of course, the Time of Suckage proved that it just might be an exclusively *American* motto and at the time confined to a relatively small fraction. Insert sigh here.

So. Grew up on a farm. Maximum suckage once a year picking rocks. (Another essay.) Went to college (UM, Farmington) on a football scholarship. Got cut sophmore year.

Dad had a college fund for me but . . . Well, if I dipped into it for, you know, tuition and books it really cut into my discretionary income. The insurance for a

20 year-old on a Mustang GT-175 is *not* cheap. And buying the ladies *nice* dinners tends to get you laid more than McDonalds. I did *not* want my discretionary income tapped.

ROTC was just sitting there. Most of my family had been Navy. (Don't laugh. I think most of the Navy is crewed by MidWesterners.) But there wasn't a Navy ROTC program. So I went Army.

Okay, yes, there was a war on. But, again, I did the math. Death rates in that war were pretty much on a par with death rates during previous peacetimes. Don't believe me? Check the figures yourself, I'm not going to hold your hand. But it's true. And death rates among combat forces were not significantly higher than in the *Navy*. Being at sea is an inherently dangerous process. Lots of people die from accidents. Most of the people dying in the *Army* were from accidents.

And . . . Oh, hell. Yes, okay. I did have a 'desire to serve in combat.' Call me stupid. My life, my choice. I wanted to go over and fight. Look, I was twelve when those bastards hit the Twin Towers. I watched those clips over and over just like the rest of you. I knew I didn't want to cruise around on a ship. I wanted to fight. Insert appropriate lines from Alice's Restaurant here.

So I went ROTC. Got my degree and my brown bars the same day. Went off to Infantry Officer Basic Course. Which *sucked*. At the time it was my definition of suckage.

Got sent to the 3rd ID in Savannah. Which wasn't a bad place to be for a junior officer with a decent stipend from my shares in the corporation. All I had to do was put up with the bullshit aspects of the Army for six years, go get my Masters in Agronomy and I'd be Manager on one of the satellite farms until Dad retired. I was shooting for the mixed crop farms near

Hanska. The walleye fishing on Lake Hanska was great and we owned a couple of cottages over there. And since the Hanska Manager was in charge of ensuring the upkeep of the cottages . . .

And then we did our first deployment. And, oh, hell, I enjoyed it. Yes, I lost two troops to sniper fire, James Adamson and Litel Compson. They were good guys, both of them. Damned fine troops. I could talk about both of them all day.

But we were doing a tough job in a tough environment. Even with the support of the Iranian government, there were lots of people who really wanted the mullahs back in power. Not going to do an essay on that, this is about the Time of Suckage. We did our job and as a guy in charge of making sure that everything went right, well, for a first deployment I didn't do too bad. Farmers are planners; the CO and my platoon sergeant (Sergeant First Class Clovalle (pronounced 'Clo-Vail') Freeman) didn't have to tell me about planning to prevent piss poor performance. And, hell, I always got along with people. I liked my troops and vice versa. Mostly. There's always a few assholes.

But for a first time deployment as a cherry LT I didn't do too bad. And my OER more or less said the same thing. (Actually, it sounded like I was fucking Napoleon but the decent ones always do. That got explained to me in detail.)

I was doing good work and doing it well. Frankly, that first deployment made me rethink the whole Hanska Plan.

Back we went to Savannah. I got promoted to 1LT and went off to Advanced Course. It sucked but not as bad as IOBC. Then I went to Ranger School and got a new appreciation for maximal suckage. (Edit by wife: The author of this is too humble to admit he got Distinguished

Honor Graduate in Infantry Officer's Advanced Course and Honor Graduate in Ranger's School. He's an idiot but I love him.) Oh, sure, I like a challenge as much as the next over-testosteroned young idiot. But Ranger School wasn't a challenge in any way except staying awake. It was just suckage, day in and day out.

Oh, yeah, and I went to Jump School right after IOAC. Forgot about that until I remembered the maximally suck jumps in Ranger's School. Jump School, these days, just *tries* to suck.

When I got back we were getting ready for another deployment. I was too senior for a line platoon, it wasn't time to rotate the Mortar Platoon leader and I was too junior for XO. So I got stuck in battalion in the S-3 (Operations) shop.

There are jokes about Fobbits. Those are the guys who stay in the Forward Operations Base. Dude, all I'll say is that I'd much rather be out doing patrols than stuck in the fucking FOB. FOB duty is boring *and* stressful. There are more PTSD cases among Fobbits than line troops.

(Of course, most Fobbits are REMFs who wanted to avoid being shot at so they got a job that didn't involve shooting. There was one MI guy who had a nervous breakdown about once a week and had to go get 'counseled' in a rear area. Smart guy, seemed to really want to do the job, just *did not* have the constitution for it. Can't even call him a coward, just . . . didn't have the constitution.)

Not being out where you could actually *do* something was the worst part. No, the worst part was constantly having to work with Fobbits. No, the worst part was the S-3 who was a dick and incompetent to boot. No, the worst part . . . Damn, there are *so* many worst parts. The tour was maximum suck. Hanska here I come.

Back at Savannah we're doing all the shit that soldiers do when they're not fighting. I'm still in the 3 shop (new S-3 thank God and Major Clark was a real mentor during this period, wish we'd had him in Afghanistan) and we're in charge of making sure everybody gets trained back up to standard. Look, sure, combat experience is important and there are things you learn in combat you can't learn anywhere else. But . . . There are things you forget in combat, too. Things that you could have used. But guys build up a small skill-set that works to carry them through. Getting them to learn a couple *more* skills on top of that skill-set is a *good* thing.

Okay, and we had to fill in all the fucking check boxes of some Pentagon weenie who'd sort of heard there was a war on but needed to justify his existence by creating check boxes for us to fill. Yes, that's a lot of it.

And we had a big part in making sure all the equipment that had gotten fucked up on deployment got unfucked. That was mostly my stuff and Jesus there was a lot of stuff to unfuck. And find. And then admit had disappear and do reams of paperwork explaining *why* it had disappeared. I'd say 'in triplicate' but most of it was electronic. We had to *file* in triplicate, though. Thank *God* I had a clerk for that. Rusty was a fine guy for a Fobbit.

I'd done extra staff time. Either because of that or because the Battalion Commander liked my winsome good looks I got the Battalion Scout platoon. Honestly, with the way that we worked it wasn't much different from having a line platoon. But the battalion had started to use the Scouts as sort of an integral special operations unit. When there was a high value operation to perform (like capturing a particularly bad boy) and the fucking SEALs or Rangers or Delta or SF were otherwise busy sharpening their knives or taking pictures of themselves doing push-ups we got to kick the door.

It was a very hoowah fucking time for me. We went back to the Sandbox, this time to Iraq which was still having trouble over by Syria, and we got to kick a lot of doors. The 'real' spec-ops guys were busy in Iran and Afghanistan. They didn't care that various Sunni countries (cough! Cough! Saudi Arabia! Cough! Cough! Syria!) were still funneling weapons, money and personnel into Iraq. The news cameras were all in Iran so naturally that's where SOCOM went.

They didn't, per se, end up on the news. But I took a little tour of the Delta Compound one time, (Okay, okay, I was being recruited, I'll admit it) and there were some very interesting news articles pinned up in cases with small comments underneath like 'Detachment One, Alpha Squadron.'

Now, don't get me wrong. The SOCOM guys are good folk who do a hard job. But, come on, it's like anything else. When they're looking for a guy to promote or give a special (ie interesting) job, they're going to remember the guys who did their job very quietly but also did it well enough that they ended up, unmentioned, in the news. Take the capture of Mullah Rafaki. Sure, supposedly it was Fourth ID that got him. Nope. It was really a team of SEALs. And those guys are still unable to pay for their bar tab, not to mention the Platoon Leader is getting fast-tracked to Lt. Commander.

The point being, CNN and company were in Iran. Iran was the happenin' spot. We were in a backwater in Iraq which was, to most of the world, a done deal.

The downside? Nobody knew we were still fighting in Iraq and you had to explain it over and over and over again. The upside? Dude, I was the *Scout Platoon Leader*. Platoon Leaders are supposed to sit back and direct. I did that. Sure. Absolutely. That's where I got these damned scars from a door charge I (very stupidly) got too close to. But we still did the house and pulled the bad-guys. Who? Me do a door? No, Colonel, of *course* I didn't do the door.

Very hoowah time. Rule One (no drinking, 'fraternization' or pornography) was still in effect. Nobody paid a damned bit of attention to it. I was still an officer. I practically fucking *lived* with my grunts. We ran together, fought together, drank together and ... Okay, there was a degree of fraternization on that one trip up to Kirbil. With girls. Hookers. Let me make it clear that we were *not* fraternizing with each other.

Good days, good days.

And back to Savannah. And I made captain on the 'short list' and I got a company. Bravo called 'The Bandits.' Six is the military designation for 'commander.' Ergo, I became Bandit Six and have used it as a handle any time I can get away with it since.

Now, taking over a company when you've never been an XO is a bit of an adjustment. I got my first 'does not quite walk on water but can negotiate the top of mud' evaluation during my first eval period as CO. Deserved it. I was not succeeding in my primary tasks. Some personal issues but I was not succeeding.

I begged forgiveness and, even more, begged help. I'm not good at asking for advice. I'd gotten used to asking NCOs what they thought and then using it or not. But going to the Battalion Commander (Lt. Colonel Nick Richards, good guy) and admitting I was getting a bit lost in the swamps as a CO was hard.

He didn't kick my ass for it, though. He just gave suggestions. And they were very good suggestions. I got better very fast. (Getting over the personal issues helped. Okay, yeah, they involved a girl and no she did not get pregnant but thank God we also did not get married is all I'll say.)

The company considered me a bit rocky when we deployed but we sort of mutually got over that in the Rockpile. My performance was coming up even before deployment and, hell, I *like* deployments. I'd finally gotten over my tendency to (badly) micromanage the company. Just in time, too, because I was not going to be a Fobbit on deployment if I could help it. I did help it.

God forgive me for what I put my driver through, though. You see, I'd have at any time two or three things going on at once out in the boonies. In different areas. Most of the unit would travel fairly heavy, at least a platoon. I wanted to see all of it and especially when the shit was hitting the fan. So myself, my driver and two RTOs (actually, Bobby and Buddy were my bodyguards) would go raring off across a fairly questionable to hostile Kandahar Province countryside, mostly by ourselves. Occasionally this involved stopping and paying a visit to one of the local 'friendlies.' I put the quotes on it because you never knew until you pulled up (and sometimes not even then) if they were friendlies *today*.

Occasionally it involved attempts by unfriendlies to stop *us*.

Lord love my boys. They never seemed to tire of baling the CO out of a firefight. Probably because they were trying to catch up. And they never seemed to tire, either, of being in the middle of a firefight and 'Bandit Six' suddenly roaring in to jump in the fight. Days of wine and song.

(Wife's Edit: Sigh. "Attention to Orders. *Bandit Six* is hereby awarded the Distinguished Service Cross for conduct above and beyond the call of duty in actions in Kandahar Province, Afghanistan, on March 15th, 2017.

"While travelling to meet with local friendly tribal leaders, *Bandit Six* was informed that a small group of Special Operations personnel had been ambushed and were pinned down by local Taliban related forces. Without any regard to personal safety, *Bandit Six* immediately ventured to the area of combat and closed with the Taliban forces. His personal vehicle damaged by concentrated rocket propelled grenade fire which injured both his radio telephone operator and himself, *Bandit Six* exited the vehicle and engaged the enemy with his personal weapon. With the support of continued machine-gun fire from his damaged vehicle, directed by hand and arm signals, *Bandit Six* advanced upon the enemy ambush location and using concentrated fire, the expenditure of all of his personal store of grenades and person-to-person combat skills, *Bandit Six* turned the flank of the enemy position. During the process of the advance *Bandit Six* was wounded three times but continued to move forward expeditiously against the numerically superior Taliban forces until they retreated from their positions. Upon analysis of the combat the relieved special operations unit commander credited *Bandit Six* with over twenty (20) personal kills including more than six (6) due to knife and bayonet.

"Entered service in the Armed Forces from Minnesota." End Wife Edit. I swear, he drives me nuts sometimes.)

—end excerpt—

from *The Last Centurion*
available in hardcover,
August 2008, from Baen Books